Praise for the work of William Fredrick Cooper

For the *Essence* magazine/Black Expressions Book Club
bestselling novel *There's Always a Reason*

"*There's Always A Reason* is a good read for anyone looking into
the psyche of the sensitive African-American male."
—*Ebony* MAGAZINE

"William McCall's unapologetic emotional vulnerability formed
the book's refreshing heart and through him, Cooper conveys
both an understanding of and a frustration with the games men
and women play."
—*Publishers Weekly*

"Bringing out so many deep rooted feelings as I was reading it,
I was so overwhelmed with emotion that I could barely see…"
—ZANE, *New York Times* BESTSELLING AUTHOR OF *The Hot Box*,
Love Is Never Painless, Afterburn, Addicted, Skyscraper AND *Nervous*

"William Fredrick Cooper strokes his paper with heat and passion!
Heartfelt and intense! Seldom does a male writer dive so deeply
into the well of human emotion."
—TRACY PRICE-THOMPSON, 2005 WINNER OF THE ZORA NEALE
HURSTON/RICHARD WRIGHT AWARD FOR CONTEMPORARY FICTION

"Declaring that William Fredrick Cooper is a master griot of the pain and joy pumping through a man's heart is like saying Shaq is tall. It's a given, and here, Cooper unfurls the trials and redemption of William McCall, and how the love of a damn good woman can bring you back from the brink."
—CHRISTOPHER CHAMBERS, AUTHOR OF *Sympathy for the Devil* AND *Yella Patsy's Boys*

UNBREAKABLE

A LOVE BALLAD

Dear Reader:

William Fredrick Cooper stunned readers with his *Essence* bestselling *There's Always a Reason*. In the second installment of his William McCall journey, we were introduced to his love interest, Linda Woodson, who passes away. Now seven years later on Valentine's Day, William continues to grieve over Linda's death while sitting at a New York bar. He meets schoolteacher Keisha Gray, who is involved in a long-time affair with a married attorney, and his life will not be the same.

The author's description of *Unbreakable* as a love ballad is fitting for this powerful story that is memorable to the last page. With strong character development and an amazing plot with twists, it showcases endurance and the intensity of love.

A true Michael Jackson fan, William highlights his mania with the musical legend and the novel doubles as a tribute. Mixed in are poetic contributions from other writers, original lyrics to Jackson songs, even a list of the author's favorite titles. It is a creatively written and entertaining piece.

I first met William at a writer's conference where I found him to be honest about life and with a passion for writing. With *Unbreakable*, it all shines through.

As always, thanks for supporting the authors of Strebor Books. We try our best to bring you the future in great literature today. We appreciate the love. You can find me on Facebook @AuthorZane and on Twitter @planetzane. Or you can email me at zane@eroticanoir.com.

Blessings,

Zane

Publisher
Strebor Books
www.simonandschuster.com

UNBREAKABLE

A LOVE BALLAD

WILLIAM FREDRICK COOPER

SBI
STREBOR BOOKS
NEW YORK LONDON TORONTO SYDNEY

Strebor Books
P.O. Box 6505
Largo, MD 20792
http://www.streborbooks.com

This book is a work of fiction. Names, characters, places and incidents are products of the author's imagination or are used fictitiously. Any resemblance to actual events or locales or persons, living or dead, is entirely coincidental.

ISBN 978-1-59309-487-4
ISBN 978-1-4767-0396-1 (ebook)
LCCN 2013950686

First Strebor Books trade paperback edition March 2014

Cover design: www.mariondesigns.com
Cover photograph: © Keith Saunders/Marion Designs

10 9 8 7 6 5 4 3 2 1

Manufactured in the United States of America

For information regarding special discounts for bulk purchases, please contact Simon & Schuster Special Sales at 1-866-506-1949 or business@simonandschuster.com

The Simon & Schuster Speakers Bureau can bring authors to your live event. For more information or to book an event, contact the Simon & Schuster Speakers Bureau at 1-866-248-3049 or visit our website at www.simonspeakers.com.

UNBREAKABLE

THE FIRST SINGLE...

UNSHAKEABLE FAITH...

(Inspired by the song "Unbreakable" by Michael Jackson...)

In 2001, Michael Jackson and Sony Records disagreed over the first commercial single released from the album Invincible. *The King of Pop wanted the song "Unbreakable" to be heard initially; instead, Sony chose to drop "You Rock My World." Because of contractual disputes, which killed the promotional push on the album, the dynamic standout was never released as a single. Well, it never got released, but... Delivering a high-voltage jolt to my soul, I am starting my new book with a statement of transparency with the hopes that it helps someone handle life a little better than I have. Please follow me on this one...*

Picture this: We're in Miami, Florida, and the Hit Factory recording studio has rocked a Michael Jackson track produced by hit maker Rodney "Darkchild" Jerkins. Reeling you in, the ferociously funky hook and R&B-meets-gospel sound thumped.

Stomping out negativity and placing perseverance into your soul, the message in the music was blunt: Don't let anything or anyone steal your joy.

The jam, "Unbreakable," (featuring The Notorious B.I.G. with background vocals by Brandy), was an effective groove that had everyone in the studio dancing.

Everyone, that is, except author William Fredrick Cooper.

Somber from news he had received hours earlier—a disturbing

bulletin that likened him to a used car salesman—the melody was muted by tears in his eyes.

After everything that's happened in his life, he was baffled.

Should he allow cemetery dirt to be thrown on him by way of insulting opinions, or would he finally respond after years of quiet?

Letting his creativity wander, he imagined the Gloved One and Biggie Smalls on the other side of the sound room and thought of the advice they would've offered.

"Say something, but do it with L-O-V-E," the King of Pop stated.

Christopher Wallace agreed, sneering, "Let your haters motivate you. Spit something at those fools."

Taking a hand towel from his back pocket, the writer blew his nose.

"I made mistakes in life like anyone else, but people piled on and took advantage of my honesty while trying to keep me down. Others not used to my deep emotions think I'm a pity-seeking martyr, which is totally off-base." He sighed. "All of that's my fault, because I always sought validation from others instead of relying on my inner strength."

Biggie answered, "Tell them where to go, how to get there and make em' kiss your ass."

Battling laughter, MJ would reiterate his insight.

"That's not you, William. You have a beautiful heart no one understands. Again, if you say anything, do it with love, man."

Sighing, the perplexed writer said, "I gotta toughen up and remember that they talked about Jesus..."

Suddenly, the light bulb that comes with a breakthrough came on.

Feeling a surge of energy, the novelist identified with what LeBron James might have felt on June 7, 2012. With his Miami Heat on the brink of elimination—they were down 3 games to 2 in the Eastern Conference Finals—media pundits all around the globe ready to bury him forever, the organization ready to break up his team and everything he worked for hanging in the balance, he realized this was the defining moment in his life, his last chance to man up.

Then with a fearless stare he torched the Celtics and Boston Garden for 45 (points) 15 (rebounds) and 5 (assists).

He's a two-time NBA Champion now, but that was the night LeBron James became who God created him to be, a King.

"Can I borrow your gift for a tick, MJ? I won't moonwalk away with it, man," William persuaded.

Beaming, Michael Jackson knew what was about to happen.

Holding his hand for a tick, he said, "Make it funky!"

The beleaguered author wasn't done.

"Biggie, I'm gonna need yours, too."

Clearly perturbed, Hip-Hop's greatest storyteller on wax had an announcement.

"You better bring it, or there's gonna be a lot of..."

"Neck wringin' and fist swingin', if my words aren't particularly stingin'... Chill, brother, I got this," William said.

Begrudgingly, the charcoal-skinned wordsmith stepped to the scribe. Removing his screw-face, he, too, tapped the three-time author and warned, "C-4 to your door, Coop."

"Biggie... I get it."

Stepping to the mike in the live room, he knew he had reached the moment of truth in his life, and the determined glare in his eyes spoke words his mouth didn't say.

Heavenly Father, I know this is my last shot. I'll do my best and leave the end result in Your hands.

Shouting to the mastermind to so many jams for Mary Mary,

Toni Braxton, the late Whitney Houston and others, "Rodney," he screamed.

From the control room he heard a simple response.

"What up, Coop?"

"Can you play the 'Unbreakable' instrumental? In my own words I want to let something fly."

"You got it!"

"And could you play it loud?"

"Punishing loud, Coop?"

"No, *pulverizing* loud. I want the message to be clear."

"No doubt."

Darkchild, I hope they're ready for this…

Blowing out the speakers, bluntness with a bangin' beat returned to the room.

Accompanying the deep rhythm was a man with an edge. Entering a zone that comes with a renewing of mind, perhaps all the gobbledygook—being told he's "an author in title only" that "cries too much," the "My Space Wag Attack" that nearly shattered his spirit; being called "phony," "pretentious" and worse names when perceiving his passion for love, life and the empowerment of black literature as arrogance; all the mistakes trusting people with selfish agendas; the "weak" and "gay" labels by those unfamiliar with Black Male sensitivity; the outlandish investigations and job dismissals because of his writing aspirations, losing all he owned not once but *twice;* the failed attempts at love in all the wrong places while letting the right ones get away; cleaning all those toilets while fighting to keep his dreams alive; all those nights sleeping on office floors and in a prostitute/drug-infested rooming house after a devastating breakup; the four life-threatening situations with a knife-wielding man battling demons…

Perhaps all the gobbledygook in that crazy bowl of life led to this.

Rising from the ashes, he had a powerful word for all those who counted him out: the runaway train was on new tracks, coming through the station hard. Perfectly fitting this fresh swag, someone turned the flame up on the stove and the silence simmering so long in stainless steel stillness finally boiled over.

Bobbing his head, years of restraint was the detonation, and in staccato rhythm, he set off an explosion that left everyone in the studio wide-eyed.

UNSHAKEABLE FAITH
by William Fredrick Cooper

(Hear MJ's voice, and follow the original lyrics below)

FIRST VERSE
Been called so many things
I can't even blink
Ya'll tried to bury me
With everything

Now God has strengthened me
From my toes to my crown
And with things that I've endured
I'll stand my ground

Kindness for weakness you mistake
Crazy comments you'll create
All the love in my heart you'll get from me

In valleys I've learned
It's the Lord's Wisdom I will yearn
When God fights my battles, see He's too much for y'all

CHORUS
You can't perceive it
Better receive it
Cruel tricks can't change me
This heart's unchangeable

And I know you'll hate me
Try to frustrate me
Your words won't shake me
My Faith's unshakeable

AD-LIB
Duh do-duh...uh
ahn...now...

SECOND VERSE
Titles and Labels?
Try humility
Mistakes are in the past
God's worked on thee

But haters still must learn
That when in the Good Lord's game
You bring up people's flaws
You'll stay in pain

Judgments, insults you'll always make
Condescending shots you'll take
All the love in my heart you'll get from me

In valleys I've learned
That it's God's judgment I will yearn
When He fights my battles, see He's too much for ya'll

CHORUS
You can't perceive it
Better receive it
Cruel tricks can't change me
This heart's unchangeable

And I know you'll hate me
Try to frustrate me
Your words won't shake me
My Faith's unshakeable

SECOND CHORUS
(With background ad-libs from Michael Jackson—see italics)

You can't perceive it
(God's reshaped him, y'all)
You can't deceive it
Those slurs won't touch me
(You can't hurt him, why ya'll wanna try it, baby)
It's unmistakable

And I know you'll hate me

(Get on down...)
And still berate me
(Yeah...)
Don't think you'll shake me
Father molds our faith to be unshakeable

BRIDGE
You can try and mess with me, motivation it will be
No matter what you say, God's still gonna love me
Through all the nonsense and the names
My Faith will always stay the same, it's unshakeable!

Rap done in the voice of THE NOTORIOUS B.I.G. (Biggie was born on May 21, 1972. My birthday is May 21, 1966. Think about it.)

Uh, uh, yeah, uh, a mouse to a giant, my Lord's not buying, the silly games that you play when you injure the heart of His kid, buddy what planet are you from, watch God's entourage drive haters into garages, twisting all the facts, why am I attacked?, are you people serious?, y'all must be delirious, through God I'm driven, to say Forgive them, any style I pen it, I gets Love there, how can critics say that I'm not real like them HELLO?!, The flow's a gift from God, just a source fellows, Write books for the heart, mind and your soul, killin' the words of any genre I'm in, tongues waggin' I'm sick of hearing how my character's laggin', I've had knives to my neck and I pushed a cleaning wagon, I'll be me until I die, so what if I cry, God has me on His mantle, something you can't handle...WHAT!

THIRD CHORUS (REPEAT 2x)
(With background ad-libs from Michael Jackson)

You can't perceive it
Better receive it
Cruel tricks can't change me
This heart's unchangeable

And I know you'll hate me
Try to frustrate me
But you'll never shake me *(why?)*
My Faith's unshakeable

FINAL CHORUS
*(By William Fredrick Cooper, with ad-libs by Michael Jackson
and background vocals by Brandy)*

You can't perceive it
('hoos' by Michael; harmonized 'oohs' from Brandy)
Better receive it
Your words won't shake me
(Yeah)
My Faith's unshakeable

And I know you'll hate me
(You shouldn't do it)
And still berate me
(You really shouldn't do it; more "hoos" and "oohs")
You'll never break me
Lord's remade me

He's reshaped me
GOD HAS BUILT MY FAITH
TO BE UNBREAKABLE!!!!

OWW! GO ON!

As forty seconds of music closed the song, the author sat down.

The room remained silent as he rocked to the rest of the groove from the chair; his spirit still blazing from the out-of-body experience.

The microphone in flames spoke for everyone.

Forgive yourself and those who trespass against you, allow the Lord to transform adversity into artistry, continue to love thy neighbor with all your heart, and tell those who don't understand your walk with The Almighty three words…

God Bless You.

And do so with LOVE, which is the God in you.

And now, an *UNBREAKABLE* love ballad begins…

"If you enter this world knowing you are loved and you leave this world knowing the same, then everything that happens in between can be dealt with."

—MICHAEL JOSEPH JACKSON
(AUGUST 29, 1958–JUNE 25, 2009)

THE INTRO...

I wish I hadn't found the damn letter.

If his present state of mind had been as light as the snow glazing the city sidewalks, he would have been okay.

But it was Valentine's Day, Day One of the pity-party.

As couples held hands at tables and dinner booths, a middle-aged male nearly slipped out of his bar chair.

While he avoided a place on *Life's Most Embarrassing Moments*, a jukebox angel named Whitney serenaded the place with "You Give Good Love," sharing what everyone felt when eternity met that special person and great energy captured them both.

Carefully adjusting himself, he would not disrupt the romantic tenor of the midtown Friday's, but the man in love with his liquor was a trespasser on the property tonight even though he was a regular patron.

On most days, the bald-headed gent would put ten dollars into the jukebox, find his customary seat in front of the largest flat screen in the place, have his usual Chicken Alfredo dish and converse about sports and everyday life, all while nursing a Long Island Iced Tea and tequila shot.

February 14th of each year, however, was *never* most days to him.

On a day when an entire nation celebrated love and life, he celebrated an anniversary where the anguish continued its lonely talking.

Slurring, the customer motioned to the bartender.

"Donald, let me have… anutha wifha shot…"

He nearly slipped a second time but recovered before suspicious eyes caught him.

However, one set of pupils, those of a stylishly dressed woman two stools away, didn't miss the trick.

Nursing her white wine, she looked to her left worried.

She quizzed, "Are you okay?"

Before he could state his case, the bartender intervened.

Fixing the Yankees cap on his head slightly, he whispered, "He's fine."

"But he's…"

"Not yet, believe it or not."

"Are you…?"

"I know. He'll be okay. Every Valentine's Day he does this. After I close up, I make sure he gets a cab home."

"Something happened to him, huh?"

"Yeah. He's missing somebody."

The mature sister, one any man would kill to see the morning sun with, looked surprised.

"I don't understand. He's a good-looking guy."

"Ma'am, he'll be okay."

Cueing in on their discussion, the smashed brother intervened.

He tapped the left lapel of his black suit jacket and slurred, "She's right here, man…right…here…"

Reaching into the inside pocket, the man battling heartbreak produced a red envelope and placed it gently on the counter.

"My…baby left…dis, for me…I found it aftaa…"

Lowering his head to regain his composure, he then looked upward. To those monitoring the discussion from their tables, he gave the impression of peering at the ceiling overhead.

A single tear trickling down his right cheek, however, uttered words he could not say.

Even though she was gone, Linda cared for him intensely.

Even though she was gone, Linda still loved him deeply.

Impacting his life like an explosion from a supernova, the comet that had been Linda Woodson went away just as quickly; and just like that William McCall was alone in a cold world feeling even more brick on his favorite holiday.

Extending her condolences, the toffee-colored woman said, "I'm so sorry... How long has it been?"

"Seven years. Tomorrow," he blurted.

The shapely beauty wanted to offer words of encouragement, but her emotions muzzled her for a New York minute.

She moved one stool closer. "You must have loved her deeply."

"Once you had the best...screw all da rest..." Pointing to the letter, he added, "She always had to know that I was okay...I am, you knoww..."

Curiosity filled the woman. Reaching for the letter, she looked at him with a cautious, intrusive expression.

William quickly deciphered it.

"It's okay...you can read it."

Though she had been gone seven years, Linda Woodson left a remnant of her presence behind, something done with good intentions to aid William's loss. Instead, the words of love rolled around in his head, creating a whirlpool in his mind.

Whitney, deciding to stay in the place a little while longer, really went in as the jukebox swooned "Didn't We Almost Have it All?" and "Saving All My Love For You" in succession.

The irony of the songs left William mute, buried in deep thought.

For an incredible moment in time, God had loaned the world two angels, each providing a unique brand of love.

One, an astonishing instrument of sound, sight and song, had filled the world with more love than it had ever seen, felt or heard.

The other, a creation straight from His heart and placed on a Hoboken bench years ago, was all William McCall had ever wanted and needed.

But like a flower held briefly, gently and ever so lovingly, Linda Woodson was gone.

Because she gave so much to others on earth, The Creator took her to a Higher, Holy Place, one where a rose garden awaited her. She had suffered enough with terminal cancer and God wanted His angel Linda to take rest in His embrace.

For three hundred sixty-three days, William could live with that. While he felt comfort in sweet memories, there were forty-eight hours when fiery-red *why did you have to take her* emotions were released.

Seven years earlier, the Most High asked a tremendous sacrifice of him.

In obedience, William stated, *none are too high, my Father.*

Then He showed him what it was; the one thing he desperately wanted: a connection with a love all his.

Pleading with guttural moans, the ones that meant giving all you had inside, the words *Not her, God, you know how much she means to me. She's all I got... Being with her gives me joy... Just as I relearn the most precious secret of love—not holding anything back— You want to take my baby away? Hell, take anything else from me but Linda; place me in an insane asylum as long as her face is the first I see when I regain my sanity...*

Those words never left him.

But eight more did.

Two days. Please give me two days, Father.

Reluctantly, a warrior of love was granted two days of every year to lower his shield and let the battle scars bleed.

Shaking his head, William wished his mark were a mere wound; his fragile spirit had been harpooned in the heart. In some weird way, Cupid had pierced him with his greatest arrow, and for reasons only known to him, decided to take it back.

Instead he left a movie theater with a single red velvet seat and a soda fountain pumping tremendous heartache. On the screen were not Nolte and Murphy; it was the last forty-eight hours he was Lucky, the last two days love, life and Linda lived as one in his soul.

The two days he requested were for his pity-party. Always going alone on his date with the bottle, he was a hostage in a lonely place, grasping at the burnt straws of what was once his. Feeling unlucky, that he lost her did not sit well with him; it was even worse than ever knowing their precious love.

He desperately wanted Linda to stay in his embrace, but when he released his hug, all William McCall saw was a letter.

Reading it a million times, his soul mate Linda always returned to him.

Seeing her gorgeous smile and flowing locks, her existence resonated strongly in every word. He could hear her tenderness on the pages, each inflection nurturing him like no woman before or since.

Her heartfelt expressions still remained the blessing of his life.

Linda Woodson made it clear that William McCall had touched her heart in a way like no other. After years of pretenders, nothing felt sweeter than the timbre of her knight saying her name and nothing meant the world to her until that "helluva man" treasured her; even as the cancer crumbled their Camelot.

In their brief coupling William and Linda proved that real love conquered all…

Everything that is, except for the Grim Reaper.

Before she spread her wings, flew eagle free through timeless galaxies and returned to heaven, Linda wanted William to know that he received the God in her; that she was truly *Lucky* like her nickname.

Though pain had sapped all of her strength, it never robbed her joy. She beamed proudly at him, even when she was bedridden, fatigued and a gaunt, skeletal shell of herself. Even as long, fleshy digits became bent, even while battling heart palpitations, occasional disorientation and slipping in and out of consciousness, even when a tube from her nose expelled dry blood and gastric juices, she smiled joyfully when she opened her eyes.

Her caretaker was there, in every way imaginable.

In a whisper, Linda said, "I'll always love you, William. Even from heaven, you'll always be my Prince."

"I know, baby," he always replied.

Responding with heartfelt sincerity, he didn't realize how serious she had been. As passionate as Lucky was about her favorite football team—she was buried in a black and gold Pittsburgh Steelers jacket—her love was intensified a thousand times over for her man.

And two years after her death, William received a jolting reminder of this while removing some linen from a hallway closet.

A small box with his name written on masking tape fell from the top shelf and hit the hardwood floor, and pictures flew everywhere.

Standing out among their smiles was a red envelope.

Sitting on the corner of his bed with intrigue, the reflections began.

Red had always been her favorite color, William meditated. Noticing the lipstick kiss on the back, the memories of them being silly, serious and snuggling had him feeling ten feet tall.

That sentiment paled in comparison to what he would experience once he opened that envelope.

Hey Baby, the neatly typed letter started, *I guess you finally found it. And knowing you, you're wondering how I found time to do this. William, what I learned long ago is that when God controls your heart, you can do anything, even type letters through the pain of cancer. Now, if you'll excuse me, I need to take some morphine. I'm kidding. Or am I?*

William chuckled while shaking his head.

"The bravest woman I ever met in my life," he muttered.

Suddenly the empty bedroom felt warm and alive.

Linda was there again; speaking, soothing and securing his spirit.

He continued reading.

I know it's going to be difficult for you to accept how God gave us something beautiful, yet brief in its duration. But know this, sugar... WE HAD THE POWER OF HOODOO!!!

(Ha-ha! Bet you thought I was going to say something sweet there, didn't you?)

Seriously William, it's not every day that you encounter someone that makes you forget about all your problems, all your fears and issues, someone that is worth more than millions and makes you shout to the world joy and happiness. Like a river flowing in many directions searching for the sea, I looked in some crazy places for the affection I deserved, and did some crazy things.

(Don't ask, I'm not telling; a woman's heart has an ocean of secrets.)

God showed me all it took was a little patience and a summer after-noon in Hoboken and He would fulfill His greatest promise to us all, Love. From the moment I pulled those earphones out of my ears and heard the sound of my perfect stranger, I melted.

Then that tiny little whisper told me, "It's Him."

At that moment the sun smiled on me, illuminating my senses with an energy I never knew before. Knowing that you would fill my world with love, while my insides bubbled with excitement, one deep look into your eyes told me your soul needed soothing. You needed me just as much as He showed us later that I would need you.

In our unique covenant exchange, I pray I gave you everything you imagined.

Again, William spoke aloud. "Lucky, you did that, and then some."

Baby, God will be calling me home soon. And when the moment comes when I close my eyes forever and travel to His embrace, know that I'll be carrying your heart with me every step of the way. I wish I could take that instrument between those sexy thighs of yours and those amazing hips that made love to me so freaking well, but I don't think God would like that too much.

What I do know however, is that He gave us so many memories, moments that we'll cherish forever... Spencer Tracy and Katharine Hepburn movies while spooning... Watching the Steelers and Cowboys every Sunday at the local sports bar in our team jackets... Kicking your butt in Scrabble like I always did—wink... The many times we laughed without reason... The night we partied at the club until I remembered that I was sick... Our one and only snowball fight... The many times you pulled me close and talked about life... The way we held each other in the dimness of the living room while Luther told us everything would be okay... There's so much sweetness I'll own forever.

William, no one has ever loved me the way you do.

My Delta sisters and I used to sit around and talk about how real love from a good man is one of the greatest feelings a woman on earth could know; that no matter where you go, you are never without it. Validating one of the most important functions of living, it is the root of the root, the bud of the bud and the sky of the sky; the thing that makes hearts soar higher than sparrows fly. Personally, it's the thing that made my spirit create a safe haven for you. William, the love I display is a gift exclusively for your heart; fearless, devoid of issues and filled with spirit and truth.

Baby, that type of love was so hard to find in a man.

But I found it all in you, and for that I am eternally grateful.

A lump formed in William's throat. He lowered his head, bit his lip and started trembling.

The other night while sitting outside, I saw a shooting star. As I watched it fall from the sky, I knew it was confirmation that the end of our time together is near. As sad as facing the reality of it is, through my tears I prayed to God to allow me to live until your favorite holiday, Valentine's Day. (I want my chocolate heart, DAMMIT!!!) I know how much that would mean to you, so I'm going to fight this disease with all the love I have for you and hope I live to cross that finish line.

Rocking his body, William tried to keep his left leg from bouncing, but lost the battle. Hoping to feel a touch and the caress of a tender kiss on his forehead, he sobbed, "You did, Lucky...And I'm so proud of you, baby."

William, I also prayed that God not only give you strength to go on, but to bring you an incredible woman, one that will make you feel alive again. But I'm telling you, babe: she better hold your hand, have a goofy grin every now and then, snuggle with you on rainy days while watching Turner Classic Movies, be an incredible cook and... I hate to say this... but she better encompass everything that being that classy lady in public and a whore between the sheets embodies. Honey, I slept with you, so I know you need a bad girl in bed, and in those precious few times when my health allowed tender lovemaking, the many joys of sex and us screwing each other's brains out (giggle), Lord knows I tried to please my stallion with my own brand of naughtiness. We blended our bodies beautifully.

Immediately, silent sorrow waged war with an intruder, a raging fire down below.

William remembered the many times they exploded in orgasmic unison and how her deep stare penetrated his soul.

He felt chills as a moan escaped half-parted lips.

"You sure made me feel lucky."

Lust and sadness formed an uneasy truce as he took a deep breath, wiped his eyes and continued.

In short, she had better be a real woman. I prayed that God give you discernment; the ability to recognize her when HE shows up through a queen. Initially you were gun-shy with me and we almost missed out on a blessing from above. I listened to your stories concerning your dealings with the opposite sex. You own so much love in your heart, but you kept giving it to the wrong people. And once you get hurt, you unconsciously hurt others by doing stupid things to protect it. Baby, I implore you to break the cycle. That pattern drains your spirit, and it's an incredible waste of time.

You're in your forties now and it's too late in the game of life for you to hide behind a fear of a commitment. More than any one person I have ever met in my life, you deserve a great wife, and you won't find it jumping from bed-to-bed. Again, your past experiences told me that you're not a player.

"She's right," William admitted. "A player's a player because he's scared to feel."

Every time I look into your eyes, I see God's light shining on you. You're one of His special angels and He has great things in store for you. I feel so grateful that you're my man, even for this brief period of time. In spite of this cancer, nothing will darken the bright light of affection that shines in my heart, for being able to love, you made life on Earth a living paradise. And when I reach those pearly gates and see God, I will drop to my knees and thank Him for one of His greatest creations, William McCall. I'll thank Him for the way you bit your lip when holding your tongue, the way your eyes narrowed like a beam of light when you concentrated real hard, and the love you showed me in our fleeting moment in time. I'll also thank Him for giving me eternal memories to share with you.

Don't cry for me, sweetie, because I don't fear death. The painful days of chemo, radiation and vomiting will be over soon, as God has a special place where there is no suffering, sickness or sorrow, a place where there is no proxy between Him and His love for me. The cancer has robbed me of many things, but it won't take my fighting spirit, or my mind.

Just the other day, I told the disease that my heart was already taken— smile.

Evoking another series of memories: how Linda told the doctors she wanted to die at home, how she never screamed though she was in intense pain, how sharp and lucid she remained until that fateful morning arrived and God whispered, "It's time." William watched her bravery and had been a model of strength himself. Even at the funeral he remained composed while delivering a stirring eulogy about the love of his life.

Reading this letter two years later finally broke him.

More importantly, I refuse to let my sickness, or even death, prevent me from loving you forever. I will carry your heart with me always, for it has a special place in my soul.

I love you, baby. And God, you make me feel lucky.

Just like my nickname.

Linda

P.S. William, because you always overanalyze everything, I hope that you find this after I'm gone. If you approach me with this, I might cry because I know that I'll miss you so much. While I try to remain strong, sometimes this power of hoodoo wears off. Please check on my parents from time to time. They really love you. I'll miss you, my hero.

William placed the folded bulk of paper by his side and looked upward at God. From the pit of his stomach came a woeful moan. Weeping inconsolably, the salty raindrops that clouded his vision made the air stale in sadness.

It was the coldest day of his life.

The pain of reality cut through his skin and reached an already grieving heart, making the agony so unbearable that he vowed to never again visit Spartanburg's Memorial Park, her physical resting place.

In spirit he vowed to remain Lucky, so much so that he barricaded his heart.

Seven years after she went to heaven and five years after finding her goodbye love letter, William McCall still found difficulty in moving forward.

The woman placed the missive back on the bar counter and wiped her eyes.

I wish someone all my own would love me like that, she thought.

She was contrite, saying, "The love you shared was beautiful."

"Thank you," William said softly. Gulping down another shot, then chasing it with five-liquor dynamite, he asked, "What... What is yourr name?"

"Keisha... Keisha Gray. Donald," she said, motioning him over. "Could you please get him a cup of coffee? And make it black. He's gonna walk out of here tonight."

A minute later, the beverage arrived.

"Here, try this."

She fed him three sips.

Taking the cup from her, William said, "Thanks, but I got...this," and gulped down the drink, then another cup. The caffeine took hold after twenty minutes, causing him to straighten up. He was still groggy, but he could articulate without slurring.

"Ms. Gray, I didn't mean to embarrass you. I wish we would have met under better circumstances."

"It's okay. After reading that letter, I definitely feel your pain. Do you work tomorrow?"

"I started a three-week vacation today. It might be a little longer if I feel like it."

"What's with the apathy?"

"Two weeks ago I found out the firm I work for is going under."

"I'm sorry to hear that."

"It's cool. I'm at peace with it."

"So what are you doing with all your free time?

"Well, tomorrow I'm going south to check up on Linda's parents. They've adopted me as their son and I visit them every year."

"I see." Evaluating his emotional state in a millisecond, Keisha asked, "Are you going to visit her gravesite?"

"I'm not sure. I doubt it, though."

"It might help you..."

"Might help me do what?" William snapped, the pressure mounting in his tone.

Keisha quickly changed topics.

"Now about your job: you said they were closing its doors…"

"Yeah. The younger partners at the law firm I work for became frustrated with the lead counsel. Cliques and factions were formed and day-to-day operations spun out of control."

"That's messed up."

"Tell me about it. An outside consultant came in to settle the disputes, but failed. He evaluated the day-to-day operations for three months and decided the company was too fractured to continue. All the partners agreed, saying that the problems were because of personality rifts as opposed to financial situations. Or so they say."

"Sounds like greed kills."

"It's pretty messed-up stuff for a two-hundred-member support staff."

"Considering these economic times, I would think so."

"Given the nature of the economy, very few attorneys are taking their secretaries with them to other firms and the rest of us will search for jobs that aren't available." Shaking his head in disgust, William continued. "Those same rich cats are the first to complain that Obama screwed up the country when they've added to the unemployment rate."

"I know that's right."

"Shit."

"How's your head?"

"It hurts, but I'll be okay."

"You've had a lot to drink."

"Normally I can handle a lot more."

"You have nothing to prove tonight, so that won't be necessary. Maybe I should get you more coffee."

"Then the liquid courage will wear off and I'll stop talking to you," William joked. "Liquor and coffee makes me hyper."

"And blunt."

"Actually, my outspokenness is hereditary. My grandmother always called a spade a spade."

"I bet that mouth of yours gets you in a whole lot of trouble."

"Sometimes."

"Back to your job: what do you do there?"

"I'm a Law Clerk. I oversee the firm's trial prep work and adjourn conferences and motions in state and federal jurisdictions, as well as keep an eye on pending legal matters through a computer database that we call... Am I boring you with my legalese?"

She shook her head no.

"That's good." He looked at his watch and noted the time: Eight-thirty. "Keisha, it's my turn to depose you."

"Shoot."

"How old are you?"

"Now you know you're not supposed to ask a woman that."

"Okay, what's your profession?"

"I'm a schoolteacher."

"Which grade?"

"I work with special needs kids from kindergarten through fifth grade."

"I bet that must be hard, given the ever-changing school system. From hiring corporate heads with no experience in the educational system as superintendents to all these charter schools, I wonder what's up. Couple that with the fact..."

"Oh, William, I'm sorry. I'm not from New York. I'm from Michigan."

"Nice of me to assume you were from my neck of the woods, huh?"

"You do know what happens when you assume, right?"

"Don't remind me. Are you from the Motor City?"

"I live in the suburbs, but I work there. And trust me, everything you said about the plight of the educational system here, well, intensify things a thousand times over and you have the Detroit Public School System. The classrooms are overcrowded, some of the curriculums are unorganized and we struggle to get textbooks for the children. And don't get me started on our pay."

"Let me guess, overworked and underpaid."

"It's worse than that. The city is in financial trouble and they're slashing our salary every year. Pretty soon, we'll be making less than those Indonesians in those Nike factories overseas."

"Isn't that always the case in black cities? The state fails to equip them with what's needed to compete yet claim they're doing all they can do. Or they let us drown, like…"

"New Orleans and Hurricane Katrina. Let's get our Kanye on and tell it like it is," Keisha said, sipping her wine.

Tightening his lips in frustration, William agreed.

"Keisha, we're still behind in the race for equality, won't get caught up for another three generations and we can't make excuses because a black man resides at 1600 Pennsylvania Avenue."

"Maybe if we got the parents to care a little more…"

"How can they care when they're struggling to keep a roof over their heads by working crazy hours just to make ends meet? And suddenly companies use the economy as an excuse to put a cap on overtime. What's Mayor Bing saying about all of that?"

"You know, for a person that doesn't live in Detroit, you sure know a lot about the city."

"I read the papers, Keisha. Let's see what I know about Dave Bing: Seven-time All-Star for the Detroit Pistons, one of the 50

Greatest Players in NBA history, and founder of Bing Steel, one of the largest steel companies in the country."

"He bit off more than he can chew trying to run Detroit. Then they brought an Emergency Financial Manager, which reduced him to being a transient official."

"The city declared bankruptcy, didn't it?"

Keisha nodded yes and gave him a blatant once-over.

"Yeah, I could get used to the Big Apple," she said flirtatiously.

William blushed like a teenager.

"Keisha, there's something's wrong with a picture I'm looking at."

"Where?"

"Right in front of me. What are you doing alone in a different state on Valentine's Day?"

"I'm in New York to take care of something."

"Would you care to elaborate?"

Instantly, the mood in her feline-shaped eyes darkened. She tilted her head slightly, her movement simple yet sexy in its authority.

"I'd prefer not to at this moment."

"I hope I didn't offend you."

"None taken. Actually, we're even."

"How so?"

"You don't talk about why you won't visit Linda's gravesite, and I won't discuss why I'm here, deal?"

Keisha had offered a détente by way of a handshake, and the man on the other end of the pact said, "Deal."

"But William…"

"Hold up. What's with the late stipulation?"

"I hope you don't mind me being nosy, but I'm concerned."

"Oh, so I moved up in your world with the quickness. Now you're *concerned* about me."

"Look, I was concerned when I saw you falling out your chair like Ned the Wino," she growled.

William sat back, mouth agape at her feistiness.

"So I guess you done told me, huh?"

"Now if you let me finish, I was going to ask what your plans were once your company dissolves."

"I'm a survivor, Keisha."

"That's not answering my question. How do you plan on surviving? You know companies are hiring fresh faces out of school for less money than they'll pay you. It might be hard to find something right away."

"I have some money saved, so I'll be okay. I've been in rough waters before."

"How'd you make it then?"

William tapped the letter on the counter.

"She saved my life in more ways than you can imagine."

"But Linda's dea…"

With a look demanding that she stay in her lane, a man protecting his lonely heart cut her off.

"I don't need any reminders," he said brusquely.

An uncomfortable pause ensued. Keisha thought she stopped a blunt reality from leaving her oral faucet, but a drop escaped, causing William to gulp down the rest of his now-diluted drink.

Then he faced her with a cold stare straight from a *Dirty Harry* movie.

"Thanks, but I'll be paying for my own coffee. I hope you enjoy the rest of your evening."

He stood up and tried to put his coat and skull-cap on, but the alcohol in his system cornered him and landed punches to his head. His equilibrium was still unbalanced, so he sat back down.

Calmly reapplying her lipstick, Keisha asked, "Not going anywhere for a while?"

"As soon as I gather my bearings, I'm out."

"Well, I hope the rest of your Valentine's Day brings you peace."

At that instant, Donald intervened once more.

"Well, I see you lovebirds are having a nice time together," he joked.

In return, the bartender received two awkward stares, then ten seconds of silence.

Breaching the pause, William said, "Donald, could you give me another shot, then both checks?"

"Sure thing, bruh."

Tongue-tied, Keisha looked over at him, simultaneously surprised and speechless.

"What are you doing, William?"

"Keisha, today is Valentine's Day, my favorite holiday. In spite of our obvious differences, I owe you this much. You saved me from public embarrassment, and I appreciate that."

"I appreciate you paying the bill."

"No problem," William said, gulping down the last of his mood changer. "So what are your plans for the remainder of the night? Where are you staying?"

"I'm staying… Wait, didn't we agree on keeping our intelligence classified?"

"Look, after tonight, you'll never see me again, so at the very least, can I hail a cab for you?"

Keisha tensed up. Her words didn't come right away, but she had a look in her eyes like a deer seeing oncoming headlights.

Tersely, she stated, "I'm not leaving yet."

"Oh. I see." Rising, William moved past her and toward the exit.

"Well, I hope wherever you're staying has a heart-shaped box of chocolates under your pillow. You deserve the best, especially on my favorite holiday."

"Wait, you're forgetting something."

It was too late.

A man missing the love of his life had staggered into the thin, whipping snow. And after placing his red letter in her purse, a woman about to meet the love of her life at a nearby Marriott needed a Long Island Iced Tea and Patrón shot of her own.

She needed her own mood altered.

TWO

The stiff drink didn't work; neither was the erection moving inside of her.

Thinking what they usually shared would be enough: the way his lips aggressively captured hers, then nibbled on her breasts, the way he pressed his brim against her wetness and allowed his tongue to search the walls of her honey, the way his hardness seductively stirred and pleasurably disturbed her sex, the way he whispered nice-then-nasty in her ear and moaned like she had baby-you're-the-best-never-had-better kind of love, the way he released warm ecstasy as his body stiffened and relaxed...

On this night, the intensity wasn't there.

With her lover steady pumping away, his eyes closed in concentration, Keisha looked at the white ceiling and wished for a fan to blow away her empty feeling. Realizing one wasn't there, she moved just enough to give a better illusion than Penn and Teller did with their magic tricks; a figment of the imagination women often gave that stroked many a male ego.

Keisha was disconnected, buried in many thoughts. There would be no joyous tremors capturing her, no love by way of oxytocin leaving her, for she was moist like a woman in need, not a woman totally immersed.

Oblivious to her disgust, her lover groaned, "Ooh, yeah... This feels so good." Growling her name loudly as the movement of his midsection became manic, the swelling of his bulb told her he was close to nirvana; *his*, not her heavenly feeling.

Feeling him plunge deeper into her intimate playpen, Keisha's thick frame took stiff, rhythm-less strokes, one last thrust, then watched his masculinity spasm when grabbed the sheets from above.

A warm gush of liquid coated her garden with milky rain, the satisfaction he thought she needed.

Light-headed and breathless, his body jerked violently like a passenger in the front seat of a car hit from the back. After post-orgasm pumps, he stopped her hip motion when his body smothered hers.

Then he tumbled to her left.

Soon, his drowsiness turned into a great sex slumber.

Keisha lay there staring at the hotel suite walls unsatisfied, fighting desperation and agitated at the woman in the mirror when her eyes made it there.

This has got to stop. I'm too old for this.

But could she stop something she initially wanted; something free from obligation or demands, something that made her feel safe from her fear of commitment?

She rose from the bed, moved to the bathroom and looked in the mirror. Taking a deep breath, Keisha allowed silent tears to blur her vision.

As soundless as the tears forming her unhappiness was a disturbing memory. For years, Keisha Gray asked herself if she deserved to witness something so tragic that it fostered a dread of giving her soul to another.

Battling bitterness, as much as she wanted the kind of love that continued to grow after decades of heaven on earth together, as much as she craved the little pleasures that come when two became one, and as much as her soul required an energy that turned flickers of hope into eternal flames...

Something caused her to shut down.

That *something* was a terrible occurrence, one that left her definition of love in total disarray.

SMACK!

"I better not catch you slow-pokin' around, you stupid bitch! Now why isn't my dinner ready?"

His right-handed special connected with Ramona Gray's left cheek; the impact of the blow sent her sprawling to the kitchen floor.

With courage, the beautiful woman picked herself up, pulled herself together and walked by her husband as if nothing had happened.

But the resentment in her scowl spoke volumes.

The look was met with disdain by her tormentor.

"If you're going to get your panties in a bunch, that's on you. You need to keep going to therapy."

With that, Alfonso Gray stormed into the living room of their two-story townhouse.

That slap embodied the pain in Ramona's deep brown eyes. Never mind the fact she had a job to tend to—she was a dentist's assistant near the Indian Village area of Michigan—her husband, Alfonso, had to have dinner on the table every night by seven-thirty; even if it were an hour after she arrived home.

If it were a second late...

Then heaven help Ramona Gray.

Watching the daily abuse was a seventeen-year-old teenager named Keisha, the sole offspring from their marriage. Resentful of any cold-cocked fist in her mother's direction, she pleaded for her to run from the rage.

"Mommy, you have to do something. Why don't you have him arrested?" she begged, running an ice-cold rag across her mother's swollen face.

Ramona's weary voice wallowed in resignation, as if her fighting spirit were splintered into a thousand pieces and hurled into the Clinton River.

Sighing, she responded, "Who would believe me?"

There was truth behind her statement: At a time when the middle-class shadow of Detroit was thriving with auto plants and hard-working ethnicities, Pontiac, Michigan was rich in affluent role models.

None, however, loomed quite as large as the Grays. Upwardly mobile, well respected and loved by all within the community, many residents looked upon Alfonso and Ramona as a loving, God-fearing couple. A graduate of the Detroit Metropolitan Police Academy and a survivor of a tour of duty in Vietnam, Alfonso joined the force in June 1967, one month before the 12th Street Riot and four years after he was blessed with a beautiful daughter. Receiving high praise for his efforts in quelling the unrest, he became a local hero when he stopped racist members of the predominantly white police force and Michigan National Guard from shooting his brothers and sisters down like dogs.

To the public eye, they were an ideal family. Tall at six-feet-three, dark, with muscular arms, brown eyes, a small waist and wide shoulders, Alfonso was built like a chocolate Adonis. And his lovely wife, Ramona, was a stunning creation as well. Sexy thick and a well-developed five-feet-eight, her flawless coffee tone was a collection of curves and contours that flowed in wonderful harmony. And their pout-lipped teenage daughter, Keisha, a younger vision of her mother's perfection, was a straight-A student at Pontiac Central High School.

On the outside, things seemed to be cool, like the other side of a pillow.

Yet the weight of living up to the Cosby image long before the Huxtables dominated the Nielsen ratings slowly suffocated Alfonso.

Sighing with frustration while driving through the rough streets of Cass Corridor, Officer Gray shared his views.

"In the fifties the neighborhood was so different. A lot of the guys came home from the war and the GI bill gave them the opportunity to get an education or provide homes for their families," he told Sgt. John Roman one day. "Now it looks like Skid Row, and I bet this crap started when Nixon got reelected."

Smirking, his white partner suggested, "They need to blow the area up."

Fury kidnapped Alfonso's eyes. Enraged by his colleague's insensitivity, he chose his words carefully. "What we should be doing is asking city officials why they've let pockets of the community rot," he argued. "For instance, take a look at Jumbo Road. The area is wasting away and they're herding people together like cattle without offering hope. No one cares."

"Should we care about those who don't care about themselves?"

"It's up to the City of Detroit to show them better, and then maybe they'll do better. Let's convert some of those old buildings into homeless shelters and crack down on the run-down hotels and pawn shops. And let's get the social agencies involved so they can help us. You do that, and I bet the crime rate drops."

With racism in his eyes, his partner shook his head.

"Come on, Gray, are you running for office? The last time I checked, Coleman Young, the mayor of this fair city, is one of yours. He's not doing his job."

"Even the mayor needs help, John."

"He shouldn't have eliminated the STRESS unit. That unit kept those animals in line."

Recoiling in horror, Alfonso couldn't believe what he was hearing. His thoughts were piranhas in a pool of anger, swimming in circles while accelerating anxiety and agitation. That he maintained control of the wheel was a miracle.

The STRESS (Stop the Robberies and Enjoy Safe Streets) unit was killing our people like roaches, but that's besides the point. Not only is this guy a racist, but does he have to be politically incorrect and ignorant, too?

"He didn't eliminate STRESS; Former Mayor Gribbs did," he said, calling out the previous administration.

"Maybe the politicians want all the winos, prostitutes and drug addicts in one place rather than having niggers scattered throughout the city."

Perilously close to putting a hollow point in his partner's eye, Officer Gray lost it.

Fittingly, a red light stopped their movement.

"Look," he said, the rage in his voice measured yet evident, "I don't care if you've been on the force longer than me, or that you're my superior. If I ever hear that word leave your mouth again while you're in this car, I'll fucking bury you!"

Not only did Alfonso have to deal with bigoted officers battling integration, he felt boxed in, trapped in a hopeless world where environmental and psychological trauma surrounded him. Shackled in silence to a crime world he never wanted to be a part of—in 1976 he was transferred into the Narcotics Division; a move he vehemently protested—for five years he overworked himself on the beat, all the while struggling to keep from unraveling.

But the things Alfonso Gray saw.

Refusing to bring gruesome details of the job into his Pontiac home, how could he share stories of corpses found in condemned structures, many of them meeting their Maker with syringes attached to lifeless veins? How could he tell his wife that city officials contributed to the madness he patrolled by turning it into a dumping ground for those who hit rock bottom?

Slowly undergoing a metamorphosis, he became dependent on vices.

First, the cigarettes controlled him.

Then, it was alcohol.

His flesh weak from smoking two packs of Kools a day, the consumption of Martell Cognac VS and Black Label Beer also frayed his senses.

So did cocaine. He needed something to heighten his alertness to danger, so he used the nose candy as a stimulant. Snorting himself numb, he surveyed dilapidated buildings and run-down tenements, sifting through the heroin junkies and hookers to collar Detroit's major dope peddlers.

The drug, another roadblock to his soul, had his overstrained nerves ready to pop like a rubber band stretched too far. How could he talk to his wife about the many shootouts while doing narcotics work, the death of seven colleagues in a hailstorm of bullets, or the newborn baby he found cooked in a microwave during a drug deal gone south?

He found the supply that night: thirty kilos of heroin, twelve kilos of coke and 500 pounds of marijuana; and when no one was looking, he made sure he took some of the snow for himself.

While cocaine sharpened his street sense, it made him abusive to his wife.

Alfonso's domestic cruelty was brutal. Calling her a "stupid cow" because of a weight gain and the way she kept their condo, nothing seemed good enough anymore; she was the target of all his frustration as he slapped her face with ridicule.

The spirit-damaging venom of his words cut deep, leaving her perplexed. Panicking because she was puzzled, Ramona Gray was so desperate to fix things that she reached out to a therapist for self-improvement.

Washed away by a tsunami of fear, gone was the energy-producing sounds of marital love.

Sinking into a tormented quicksand, the cocaine had demons of turbulence roaming Alfonso Gray's mind. The doting, affectionate husband had been dismissed, and taking his place was a monster straight from Detroit's Cass Corridor.

Soon, a family would find out how monsters define freedom.

Delusional and paranoid, for years Alfonso thought his wife of almost two decades was having an affair.

One night, Ramona had taken an hour at a local grocery store, and upon entering the condo, a husband hovering on the edge greeted her in the kitchen.

With bulging eyes, he demanded, "Where the fuck were you?"

"At the st..."

Before she could complete her answer, he clocked her with a coffee pot so hard that it shattered into tiny pieces.

Scared to death, Ramona fell to the floor amidst dangerous slithers of glass, crying, hyperventilating and trying to ward him off with all her strength.

Alfonso pounced on her, and the coffee pot was now a deadly weapon. Assaulting her with it, blood spurted everywhere.

"You're having an affair with your therapist, aren't you?" he yelled. "You're a fucking whore!"

When she saw crimson on the floor, the wooden cabinets and the bottom of the refrigerator, Ramona screamed. "You're hurting me!"

In her room Keisha heard the loud commotion, then felt the walls vibrate in anger. Coming downstairs, what she saw paralyzed her for a split second. She fought her own anxiety attack before letting loose a loud scream.

"Daddy, stop it!!! Stop it, now!!!!"

On the outskirts of danger, she fell to the carpeted floor, sobbing uncontrollably.

Alfonso had his fists clenched, ready to resume the pounding. Looking back at his daughter in an altered state, his bizarre gaze indicated he was on the verge of blowing like a whistling teakettle. He rose from atop his spouse, turned calmly, opened the blood-splattered refrigerator door, reached for a twelve-ounce can of Black Label Lager, and moved to the adjoining living room as if nothing had happened.

Frantically, Keisha rushed to her mother with dishtowel in hand. Wanting to curse her father for his violence, resentment filled her young soul. Soon, the two rushed to the hospital, where Ramona received stitches for deep cuts and bruises, then was released.

Driving home in their navy blue Buick Electra, the wife of a growing monster talked to her daughter, saying, "Baby, years of abuse can wear down the strongest person and make them question their self-worth."

"Mommy, you don't have to put up with this," Keisha argued. "You could leave him."

"And he'd hunt me down and…"

Ramona pulled the Deuce-and-a-quarter over, then addressed her daughter in a calm voice.

"Keisha, I love you with all my heart and soul. Please, whatever you do, don't ever let this happen to you. Never let a man control your life. And don't let anyone hurt your heart the way your father has hurt mine."

"So why don't you leave him, Mommy? You can do better."

Defiant, Ramona Gray shook her head no.

"He wasn't always like this, and I know this is a bad time for him. I love him too much to leave him. He'll die without me. I have to help him with whatever he's going through."

"But…"

"Keisha, I won't leave him."

After a few more beatings, Ramona Gray was singing a decidedly different tune. With franticness rooted in fear, she tried going to the local police to report the disturbing nature of their relationship, but her husband was connected to the Blue Wall; her charges were dismissed as minor disturbances. Pleading with the church for assistance, she was told that her stories of domestic violence were interfering with their ministry.

Incredibly, Ramona Gray's voice went mute in the ears of a deaf community.

But a chilling prophecy went straight to the soul of the one person she sought to save.

"If I die, it will be at your father's hands," she told her daughter one winter morning in December 1981.

"Mommy, please leave him," Keisha begged.

"Tomorrow, I'll speak to a cousin in Lansing, one your father doesn't know. We'll stay until the end of month."

Exhaling like a baboon was lifted off her young back, a teenager nodded in agreement.

"The debate team is having a meeting after school, so I'll be home late."

"I know. Keisha, none of what we just discussed comes home, okay?"

"What discussion?"

"I love you, baby."

"I love you too, Mommy."

Young Keisha kissed her mother goodbye.

Arriving home early that afternoon, Ramona dutifully prepared her husband's favorite dish, tuna casserole with asparagus stems. Getting a six-pack of Black Label Lager, she decided to try one, along with a cigarette.

Anything to ease the pain, and the recollection of a bad dream.

That morning she awoke in a pool of sweat after an unsettling nightmare. The dream began with her out late at night searching the streets for serenity and support she couldn't find at home. Walking in the darkness, she found the only block with streetlights and stumbled upon an abandoned home. The house looked horrible, like it had been damaged by a hurricane. Chipped paint on the outside, broken windows, the front door dangling like a loose tooth, shingles missing from the roof and grass so high that one might have thought it was a jungle.

Ironically, there was a row of thorny plants where, almost defiantly, roses of all colors bloomed.

Ignoring the decrepit state of the house, the arrangement out front reached a warm spot in her soul, touching her deeply.

I bet with a little work, this place could be fixed right up into something beautiful, she thought.

She entered the house carefully and received the shock of her life. Bloody bodies were everywhere, death illustrated in every way conceivable. Corpses were beheaded, impaled with knives, victims of shootings, lynching and additional forms of torture.

Almost immediately, she ran from the building.

Dismissing the vision as her mind battled with turmoil, Ramona took two long pulls from the narrow tube of tobacco and coughed.

How do people smoke these every day?

She was putting the cigarette out in an ashtray when she heard the lock turn.

A wired Alfonso came into the kitchen, looking pensive.

"We gotta talk," he announced rather stoically.

"Okay," his wife complied. "Would you like to get something to eat first?"

"Sure."

Maybe it's not that bad, Ramona thought, watching him wolf a plate down, then another helping.

She was right; it wasn't that bad; it was worse.

Somewhere in the middle of that second helping, he bridged the silence by dropping a bomb that wasn't used in Nam.

In a-matter-of-fact tone he said, "We're having a baby."

"But I'm not pregnant."

"I know, but someone else is."

Ramona's mouth dropped slightly, and her beautiful eyes widened. Desperately trying to process his emotionless tone, the words were a punch to her gut, and the loving expression filling her face with hope for better days was replaced with the color of an ominous shade. Feeling her passion wane, anger and disbelief bulldozed her spirit.

Calmly, she asked, "Who is she?"

"Karen. The young woman from the trustees board at…"

"I know who she is," Ramona growled. "You had an affair with a woman at our place of worship? Don't you realize how humiliating that is for me?"

"We were discreet."

"BUT GOD KNEW!"

They stared at each other.

Then Alfonso cleared his throat.

Continuing his bad news, he said the early pregnancy test came back with a blue plus sign last week. He had taken yesterday off to confirm the results through a blood test, then argued through another day about abortion.

Ramona asked, "What is she going to do?"

"She's keeping it. She told me that it's her body and she could do whatever she wanted. Now she wants to be religious, *after* committing adultery," he said sarcastically before adding, "Well, I guess she found her golden parachute."

His wife barely made it through the bulletin. Still as stone, too devastated to bellow out in pain, she focused on the lips spitting out this awful truth as her body shook from jangled nerves. Shaking her head in an effort to shrug off the missile that blew open her heart, her soul was irreparably damaged.

Finally succumbing to the reality, Ramona's lips quivered and the tears fell.

Her cry, while excruciating, wasn't a cry that needed comfort, nor was it one begging for self-pity by way of undeserved pain. It was a silent cry of strength that waved the white flag of surrender while uttering the words of all people, Popeye the Sailor.

Ramona Gray had all that she could stand from her husband, and she couldn't stand no more.

After hearing him out, she calmly wiped her red eyes, rose from the dinner table and moved toward the staircase.

Her husband, puzzled by her unreadable silence, followed her upstairs.

"Don't you have anything to say?" he asked.

Now in their spacious bedroom, Ramona spoke slowly. Like a surgeon using a scalpel, her words were cutting, drawing blood in the form of truth serum; a nasty medicine her husband had to swallow.

"Alfonso, the news of a child outside our marriage shattered my world. Tonight, I sat at the table and watched your arrogance on full display. There you were, sitting there like a CEO telling me that our company is bankrupt. I'm supposed to accept that? I'm supposed to accept the bullshit you put me through without a word when you destroyed everything we created, all that we invested in? I tolerated your verbal and physical abuse, and now this? Having a bastard child goes too far. I love you, Alfonso Gray, but this won't go away. But I am. I'm leaving you tonight and I'm taking Keisha with me."

Halted in his tracks with shock, a soldier's pride had been destroyed. The hollow-point bullets penetrated the emotion-proof vest, piercing his heart.

Wounded, he refused to let her leave the room. As she neared the doorway, his desperation caused sensory overload, and the dam holding memories of murder both here and abroad, all those shootouts, the junkies, the homeless and mentally ill, the perverts living in boarded-up buildings, the newborn child in the microwave overcooked like a burnt pot pie, the booze and cocaine…

The dam broke.

He grabbed her neck and tried to choke the life out of her.

"Bitch, you aren't going anywhere!"

Struggling while being strangled, somehow Ramona managed to bite his lip so hard that blood spurted over both of them.

Seeing his own red enraged Alfonso further. Using a deranged, perverted strength, he flung her down the staircase so violently that she slammed into a hard wall, distorting her facial features into an unimaginable shape.

Ramona felt the broken bones in her face as she crawled toward the kitchen. She was in terrible pain and could barely see, but if she could make it to the door, pry it open and let out a scream...

She never made it.

Reaching her quickly, her husband put the accent on her facial damage by kicking her further.

His wife gasped for air as he stomped her ribcage with his size fifteen shoes, breaking more bones in the process.

Then there was an eerie silence, then footsteps as Alfonso went back upstairs.

Ramona heard a closet door open and close, then the thud of death coming back down. With each step, she knew that her life had seconds remaining.

That dream, she now realized, was a premonition straight from Hell.

In the millisecond before he arrived, she prayed for God to forgive her husband.

Through blurry vision, she saw her knight in shining armor with a sawed-off shotgun, a Remington 870. Pumping slugs into the barrel, Alfonso aimed the weapon at her face, ready to close the book on their fairy tale.

Ramona gasped for breath through the left side of her mouth.

"Please think of Keisha," she begged.

The love of her life showed no remorse.

"I am thinking of her," he responded coldly.

After a single slow blink of his eyes, he fired, reloaded, and fired again.

Climbing the stairs once more and returning to the bedroom, there was one more thing Alfonso Gray needed to do before he felt truly free. Getting fully dressed in an old police uniform, he sat on the edge of his king-sized bed and calmly placed a 9 mm handgun to his temple. Closing his eyes, he prepared for a high-velocity splatter as well as the afterlife.

Then...*BANG!!!*

Minutes later, Keisha Gray arrived home...

And screamed!

At her feet, she found her mother lying in a pool of lifeless crimson, surrounded by blood-stained walls. Perpendicular to the firearm, her face was unrecognizable; it had been partially blown off. Her left knee bent and her right leg underneath, near her torso and covering a single gunshot wound to the chest.

Keisha ran past her corpse in horror, ignoring the lingering scent of gun smoke in the air.

"Daaaddyyyy," she hysterically shouted, sprinting upstairs.

What she saw next...

"NOOOOOOOOOOOOO!!!!!!!!!!"

Part two of the savage reality lay on the bedroom floor; his brain fragments decorating the room.

In complete shock, she stumbled back downstairs, screaming frantically.

As she reached for the kitchen phone, she slipped and fell into an expanding red lake.

The memory of her mother was all over her as she struggled to rise. Shaking uncontrollably, barely able to hold the receiver, Keisha called for help.

"Nine-one-one. What's your emergency?"

Her body rocking in numbness, she screeched, "I need help, please come quickly," into the phone. "My mother and father... My mother and fatherrrrrr... They're gonnnneeeee..."

"Ma'am, I need you to calm down. What is your address, ma'am?"

For some strange reason, the call disconnected.

Totally frantic, Keisha called back.

"Nine-one-one. What's your emergency?"

More grief-stricken wails traveled through the cable wires.

"Theyyyyy'rrre goonneeeee!!!!!... Please hurryyyy... Pleeassss-seeeeeee!!!!!" she screamed.

The operator again tried to still the nerves of the terrified voice.

"Ma'am, I need you to leave the premises immediately. Do not touch anything and wait for the officers to arrive."

"Theyyyyyre goooonnneeeee... Theyyyyyrrreee goooonnne!!!"

In the elegant bathroom of the Marriott hotel suite, her sleep-deprived eyes still cried.

They're gone, Keisha sobbed, more than three decades later.

Since the dawn of the new century, more than a billion dollars had been poured into midtown Detroit, including many buildings owned by Wayne State University on the outskirts of the Cass Corridor.

Unfortunately the hub of the neighborhood still struggled with a Sodom and Gomorrah image. With efforts to re-create the area reduced to mixed results, the neighborhood didn't own all the madness of its wild, reckless past, but many pervasive vices remained. Still ensuring the needs of those lost in the struggle were drug dealers feeding habits with crack cocaine, weed and heroin; and while not as brazen as those Red Light District days, prostitutes solicited their services and panhandlers searched the South End for better days. Further emphasizing the conflict of growth and pain were abandoned redevelopment projects by way of usable-yet-empty apartments and the conversion of decomposed buildings into affordable housing.

Thirty years later, the reconstruction struggle was in full tilt.

One thing that couldn't be reconstructed, however, was the spirit of Keisha Gray. Three decades later, after countless sessions of post-traumatic therapy, many years of sharing her story as a testimony in courage; after many years of being a portrait of resiliency when moving forward to complete a Master's program at the University of Detroit—she received a full ride from the state—after many years making a difference in the Detroit Public Schools system working with the Special Education Department of many troubled schools, every time she tried to wrap her mind around her gruesome memory, tears poured from her eyes.

The foundation of her life was robbed and a special part of her was left for dead in that lifeless lake of blood, right next to her mother.

Peeling fragments of pain and misery off the bedroom wall, she was unresponsive and icy toward commitment. Letting the dark shadows of her past shape her present, Keisha formed an impenetrable wall. No one had access to her core; this in spite of her ability to make men fall head over heels in love with her.

Living the lie, as if she looked up the definition of *nice* and fell in love with the Latin derivative *nescius*—meaning ignorant; not knowing; a fool—she used a brash attitude as a defense mechanism to keep her heart at bay.

She vented her frustrations anytime she pleased. At twenty-four there was the caramel-skinned brother from the Bahamas she met at a mixer at the Paradise Atlantis. Articulate and affluent, Devon Mason was part owner of a jewelry store on Cable Beach and wanted to share his world with Keisha. There was free airline travel, dancing at the Zoo nightclub and steamy nights where he must have thought his love was safe and secure in her hands.

Devon had given her all of him and hoped for eternal devotion.

Instead, Keisha went away, leaving him alone in a world as cold as hers.

Her pattern now established, selfishness became her calling card as she dated men for a short time, dropping them the minute they got too close. Listening to that voice in her head, one that sounded like DeNiro in the movie *Heat* when it said, *Don't let yourself get attached to anything you're unwilling to walk out on in five seconds if real love knocks on the door of your heart*, her actions were untamed, ruthless and calculating. Even detaching her emotions from sex, any mistake a male suitor made stirred up visions of her father, Alfonso, pulling the trigger of that Remington 870.

They didn't have to go home, but they had to get the hell out of her life immediately.

That's what she had told Brian Clark, the Defense Attorney from Chicago. Loving the raucous scene at the United Center when Jordan, Pippen and Rodman were in their Last Dance, she was flattered when he proposed to her via scoreboard at Game Five of the 1998 NBA Finals.

Jordan, flashing his thousand-watt smile, recognized him and gave him a thumbs-up sign.

Unfortunately the Bulls lost that night.

And a few months later, so did Brian.

The reason for his demise?

Do you watch Hanna-Barbera cartoons?

Think a dysfunctional "Quick Draw, McGraw," and you get the picture.

After a quick release, his Clark Bar stayed melted and El Kabong didn't swing to the rescue.

Neither did Viagra or "Baba Looey."

Keisha especially loved married men, because in her words, *they could always go back home to their wives.* More than capable of keeping things simple, she never confused the trysts for what they were, nights of physical and temporary companionship where her morals were as masculine as the men she let move inside of her. Lavished with gifts from these unavailable men while taking care of her needs, the emotionless engines of her RMS *Freedom* were put astern. Cruising at twenty-four knots, its maximum speed, the captain of the vessel couldn't imagine any condition that would cause her ship to sink into the seas of love.

The guy sleeping peacefully in bed changed that.

THREE

It was midnight, and William McCall wanted the night to stay forever.

In seven hours, dawn would come, but for now, all he thought of was goodbye.

How Linda looked at him with love, even though her vision was gone.

How she sent him to the store for ice cream, so he wouldn't see her go to heaven.

How a bad feeling jolted him and rushed him home, and sadly, how he held her lifeless hand at her bedside.

Placing a mixed-selection CD into his stereo, he moved into the kitchen for a bottle of champagne. Popping the cork while returning to his living room, he said, "Well, babe, seven years ago today, you left me for your Rose Garden. I wish I had you cremated, because I'd be sleeping with the urn tonight. I'll always love you, Linda."

He slumped to his leather couch and reached in his suit pocket for the letter.

Not there.

Panicking, a worm of sweat ran down his temples, and he frantically searched his pants, briefcase and his coat pockets.

"SHIT!"

Normally when he lost things, he resigned himself to a sigh, for in time he knew he could replace them.

Not this time, however.

Someone pounded his head with a mallet and his vision became blurred. He wanted to go into the bedroom, the one he and Linda shared, but he couldn't get his feet to move. Sprawling on the couch like he lost his best friend, even Luther's comforting *It's alright, it's alright* in "Superstar" couldn't ease the pain that usurped his soul.

No, everything was not alright.

Gone was his last physical piece of Linda, and to say he felt terrible was understating his devastation.

"You fool!" he screamed. He fell into a zombie-like trance and warred with the dreadful reaction that comes when you feel like you've lost your mind. Making their annual visit, sadness and madness unpacked their bags, got some champagne and vodka, dimmed all the lights in the Jersey City flat and decided to break night by throwing a party in William's room at the Heartbreak Hotel. Moving from the couch to the floor with his back against a wall, an unwilling hostage to this emotional takeover sat in a daze by his stereo system.

And the music played all night long.

With each jam, history was revisited.

Barry White reminded him of how it all began, how a chance meeting with a woman on a park bench turned his whole world upside down in a fantastic way. Linda repositioned the chairs of his heart, redecorating them with her tender loving care. In making a tailor-made suit exclusively for her, the real love she displayed put pep in his step while bringing a masculine dynamic from him even he didn't recognize.

Falling head over heels, William McCall thought his search for love was finally over.

Sadly, cancer brought back the blue.

On cue, the Mighty O'Jays reminded him of the night when a visit to the doctor's office marked the beginning of the end. They stared at the high bedroom ceiling with their eyes wide open, silently wondering how many days God would allow their sun to shine together. Holding each other tight, letting the tears trickle down their cheeks, they knew many types of pain awaited them: The pain of her chemo, the pain of her helpless king not being able to do anything accept hold her hand, the pain of watching the effects of radiation, the brave smiles of faith from Lucky that failed to disguise deterioration, distress and despair, and sadly, the pain of the inevitable...

But a cruel reality started when they cried together after Linda found out she was dying.

Suddenly, he heard her snippiness.

There she was, flashing a beautiful smile.

Linda's spirit invaded the darkness.

C'mon baby, man up. You know I'm always with you, she said.

William asked, "Linda, why did you leave? Why'd you have to go and die on me? I gave you my soul, and all I needed was your love. For the first time in my life, everything felt so right. Why did you leave me?"

Did you want me to stay here and suffer?

"No. I wished it was me with the cancer. I hated to see you in pain."

You sure put up a brave front. But that's what I loved about you. As sensitive as you are, the bigger the problem, the stronger you get. You channeled your emotions and became the man I always knew you were.

The guy I met on that Hoboken bench was a fighter and didn't even know it.

"You brought that out of me. But now I feel so empty inside. I need your love, Linda."

Sweetie, you know you'll always have that.

"It's not the same, you being up there. Women down here aren't like you. Instead of letting an inner strength glow, everyone's defined by a dysfunction they don't even understand. Some of them actually enjoy being unavailable, like…They're like…"

Go on, William. Say it, honey.

"They're like emotionally crippled men, Lucky. Anger and disappointment are confusing gender roles, and periodicals, books and movies that tell one sex to think like the other distorts everything further. Love ain't a damn game; it's turned into a power struggle, and you know what that power struggle is?"

No, but I'm sure you're gonna tell me.

"It's FEAR, Linda. Fear of being yourself while tossing your hat in the ring. Fear of surrendering and submitting to one another and sacrificing for love. People searching for love today are paradoxical."

What makes you say that?

"No one wants to lose control, yet you can't fall in love when you're compartmentalizing pieces of your heart. The freedom that comes with that energy makes weak men strong and women soft with compassion. Being in love means total transparency without fear of being hurt."

Well, nobody likes pain, sugar. You were afraid of me when we first met, remember?

"Yes, but you showed me that fear and faith don't live together. How can you fall in love when you're so afraid of pain that you become selfish? Linda, the pain I feel right now is because I gave everything I had inside with no regrets. And in this pain is the beauty of love, because I knew energy secure in its oneness; one that transcended time, space, sight, senses and sound. Ours was a love taken from me for no reason whatsoever, yet I have peace in this pain because I loved you fearlessly and lost you through no fault of my own."

Then why won't you let go completely, William?

"Because you knew what love was all about, Linda."

Baby, sometimes you must be willing to learn while taking the lead.

"Lead who? Nobody wants to listen to anything a brother has to say about love except when he's in a position of financial, political or religious power, like that's supposed to matter."

The liquor clearly took over, as evidenced by William's impersonation.

"Linda, Forrest Gump wasn't a smart man, but even he knew what love was all about."

That was good, baby. Maybe you should take acting lessons.

"Seriously, it's like we're blinded by unrealistic images when it comes to love. An ordinary guy sweeping streets might actually know the deal. Hell, a dishwasher might, too."

What if they worked in Mickey D's, like you did when I met you?

"You still got jokes, huh?"

No, baby, that wasn't a joke. The fabric of your heart busted through that uniform and showed me a love I thought never existed. I'm so glad God used you to bring me joy.

"He used you, too, Lucky. Thank you for saving my life."

On a scale of one to ten, William, how much do you still love me?

"An eleven, Linda."

C'mon, baby, get your drunk ass up and dance with me.

Atlantic Starr's "Am I Dreaming" filled the room and their seductive vocals fueled the fantasy. Joining hands in this flight of imagination, they were together again slow dancing in their tiny world of two. Holding her close in his mind, William felt lucky again.

Playfully, she wiggled to the floor while rubbing her firm, wide backside against him, then returned face-to-face. Linda tried to go through him; she wanted to be closer than close.

Again taking what was always hers, she felt empowered when his primal urges aggressively took hold of her locks and kissed the nape of her neck.

Mmm, sugar, you know I like things a little rough.

His erection coming alive, her building orgasm intensifying in his mind, oh how William yearned to touch, kiss and be with the blazing inferno that was, even in remembrance, the love of his life.

Oh how he wished this dream was real, so the echoes of her moans would awaken the city across the river that was strangely asleep. Oh how he missed sending shockwaves through her nervous system with a tireless tongue taste-testing that triangle between her thighs; the flavor of her treasure always enticed him; it was so sweet, William recalled. And oh how he wished Linda were there, so they could do something so out of this world one would have thought God had given them permission to create it.

Maxwell entered their private affair, locked the couple into a neo-soul room complete with red lights and stopped the cops from knocking and interrupting the moment. Returning to the floor, William sipped from his vodka and allowed his fancy to fly above the clouds. Linda lovingly licked her lips and stroked his thing before placing it in her wetness. Cruising at an altitude of forty thousand feet, shivering sensations scaled his senses as he imagined hitting the right spot in her moist tunnel over and over again.

"Can you feel me swirling in it? Can you feel how much I've missed you?" he asked.

Damn, baby… You really have missed me… Please give me more…

"I told you, honey." Thinking about up and down, fast and slow, hard and soft, envisioning the precious times his embellishment flowed within her blessing, the more he thought of loving her in their special way made him temporarily insane.

But he couldn't let go of the make-believe, not yet.

His dream was now flowing; the passion kept growing.

Sexually serving his sweet lady with his mind, knowing and holding every inch of her body, William wanted Linda to be jonesing for him as she sang with the angels. Pumping with precision, passionately pleasing her pleasure point with a powerful pillar of purpose, the joy of making her feel good made him slow the movement of his midsection.

Get those corners, babe, Linda cooed tenderly, her deep Southern accent nurturing yet naughty. *Be a good boy and hit every spot… That's it…get it for your baby now.*

"Oh, I'm gonna get it for you, Linda, no worries," he announced.

Going deeper into her well of ecstasy, William felt her contract the muscles of her walls around his sword with all the love she owned for him.

To that point he had been tender while understanding her need to be pleased. Now his strong stokes demanded she shudder, shake, then sing the song of climactic delight for his ears only. He increased the tempo of his thrusts and wasn't letting go of her until she was overpowered by his strength here on Earth.

Absorbing her energy, he knew she was close when he saw her

eyes become glassy. He knew she was closer when those glassy eyes rolled to the back of her head and pretty purrs evolved into a symphony of animalistic moans.

He could hear her panting and his soul connected with spiritual nerve endings, causing an electrical current he felt from temple to toes.

Linda's excitement reached its apex, and a familiar twang came from that subterranean place; a beautiful melody made by harps in heaven.

Letting her man know that he still made her speak in sexually satisfied tongue, *yes, baby, yes, yes, yes*, she shrieked to the ceiling in total surrender.

Linda begged for more and like Usain Bolt sprinting through the finish line, William ignored her crescendo and kept going.

Yes, William, yes, baby, yes, yes, yes, yes, I'm yours forever...

Descending on wings of satisfaction, Linda's heart fluttered into the arms of a man who truly loved her.

Breathless, she purred, *"On a scale of one to ten, baby..."*

"A million, Linda."

The next song brought reality back, for an angel named Whitney prevented him from blissfully holding her close.

Time's up, she said to Linda.

"No," William screamed.

His fantasy world had been doused with the cold waters of reality.

Unwilling to relinquish his vision, he begged, "Please don't take her."

You'll see her the same time next year, Whitney said, pulling his soul mate away.

Engaging in an emotional tug-of-war, William wailed, "She's all I got, Whitney, and she's all that I need. Please leave her be. I love her and I don't want her to go. Please..."

William, she's right, Linda said. *I must leave you now. But you know where I'll always be, right in your heart. You said so yourself... Oh baby, please don't cry, you're stronger than this... Baby, please don't cry. I'll be back next year... Happy Valentine's Day, my dear... I'll love you always...*

Again taking Whitney's hand, Linda Woodson was about to leave for an eternal wonderland when she heard a faint sound...

"Wait."

Fighting through sniffles, a simple request came.

"May I have one last dance before you go?"

Rising off the floor, Whitney's "I'll Always Love You" brought more reality to the dark living room. Clinging to her spirit with all his might, William's stomach still did flips over the woman who held his heart.

Yet on this night he was unable to hold her; seven years to the day that Linda returned to God.

And left all alone in a dark living room dancing with air was a drunk still in a wilderness of pain.

FOUR

Daylight smiled.

Emerging from its forty winks, it rushed through the windows of the Marriott hotel room.

Yet Keisha had been awake for hours.

She watched her lover continue his peaceful sleep, revering him even in her confusion. After all these years, she was still lost in him.

His intelligence made her think she was with a superior being.

His wisdom made her feel regal; a queen in the presence of a king.

His kindness made her senses smile.

His compassion gave her comfort.

Those things together made him an extremely seductive man, one that meshed natural attraction by day with dirty thoughts after dark.

And boy, did Keisha act on those dirty thoughts.

His touch always sped her pulse up, and when their bodies moved together, they were live firecrackers on the Fourth of July. Making her dizzy with delight, the insatiable moans leaving her whenever his hard urgency met her wet hunger were ones that craved more than simple intercourse; their physical joining was not piecemeal.

It was romance, affection, passion and lust transformed.

The four-letter energy Keisha avoided abruptly ended her "it's all about me" stage. Blindsiding her senses, a foreign emotion invaded her heart, shined its light, then walked, talked and quacked the forbidden word in her vocabulary louder than *AFLAC*.

What went through her mind every time she saw this man? What did she feel when he repeatedly told her she was beautiful?

Love.

Why didn't she feed him crumbs like she did others while maintaining her independence?

Love.

What was in her eyes when he sent her spiraling into a vortex of ecstasy when their bodies collided?

Love.

The *RMS Freedom* had not seen the iceberg in time, and after its collision, five watertight compartments became flooded with an emotional connection of mind, heart, body and spirit. The bitterness of Alfonso pulling the trigger sank to the bottom of an ocean of resentment, while Keisha's diamond-shaped heart stayed afloat, enjoying the electric sensations exploring her soul.

And for a long time, it had.

But she had to let go once and for all, she decided.

Against her cardinal set of rules, one that screamed "RUN" as loud as one would foolishly shout "FIRE" in a crowded movie theater, she didn't scatter or scamper from the madness she enjoyed.

But Keisha had to flee so that hostility and heartbreak wouldn't have her acting brand-new with a different kind of resentment; one filled with anger, sleepless nights alone and unleashed possessive vulgarities when you were caught up.

Carlton Austin noticed early on that Keisha had an irresistible way with men, even though she was an orphaned teenager needing legal guidance from his father regarding matters beyond her years. Around the time Billy Sims and Isaiah Thomas enlivened the Pontiac Silverdome and America tied yellow ribbons around trees because Jimmy Carter had rescued American hostages from Iran, he was twenty-four, engaged to a beautiful woman and being groomed to run the family business, a major Detroit law firm.

He had remained focused on the matter at hand: making money. He'd always been that way.

Growing up, Carl channeled his inner energies. Articulate, witty and polite, he was more interested in worldly success than he was in women, save his wife-to-be, Amanda, for whom he made the seven-hour trip from the Motor City to Syracuse, New York whenever the chance arose. A dead ringer for his father at six-two, two hundred twenty pounds, he was a sable-shaded prince: young, ambitious, the proud owner of a strong family name and going places.

In an inner-city torn between affluence and poverty, one where people of color actually had a chance in politics, that would have been enough for any woman dying to exhale.

But he and his wife relocated to The Big Apple.

Securing a Harlem brownstone for his family, he opened a private litigation firm on Adam Clayton Powell Jr. Boulevard, right around the corner from Abysinnian Baptist Church. With his father's political tentacles stretching five hundred miles, Motown's major power brokers networked with the Big Apple's black bureaucrats, thus guaranteeing financial prosperity for Wallace Austin's only child.

By the late-nineties, Carl's practice was so successful that he merged with Finley, Rogers, and Gumble, one of the city's biggest law firms.

He had the world as his personal oyster long before retirement age. Everything was smooth sailing in his life; even his titanic temper born from the tragic loss of his mother had been suppressed by accomplishment.

Yet every time he came home, he always asked about the young lady whose face was filled with intrigue and curiosity decades earlier. Remembering her fluid movements, because she was seven years his junior when their paths crossed, he had not make a pass.

Years later, he still thought of her.

"I can't get her out of my mind," he told his father at a Pistons game in 2002.

From their season tickets, the distinguished man of wisdom stared at the championship banners hanging from the ceiling in the Palace at Auburn Hills.

"Son, you have it all: a beautiful wife who looks half her age, a loving family and a truckload of money that will secure young Carl's future. Let it go."

"Yeah, I guess you're right."

That thought stayed with him for a quick second; that is, until his eyes scanned the crowd.

In Section 100 was a stunning set of cat eyes glued to his. Not only was her brown skin glowing wondrously, her lips were fixed in a radiant smile.

Noticing the wave of excitement wiping out his son, signals that told the person gazing appreciatively from afar "I'm available," Wallace Austin took a deep breath and shook his head.

In an admonishing tone, he said, "Carl, don't ever mess with anyone who doesn't stand to lose as much as you do if things get crazy."

"Duly noted, Pop," his son replied, winking.

Before he came to his senses, adrenaline enveloped him and his heart dictated his course of action. He rose from his seat and was on his way.

Keisha acted coy, ignoring the fact he was making a beeline toward her. But from the corner of her eyes, she battled impure visions in her mind. His thin waist, bushy eyebrows and well-groomed goatee shining under the Palace lights ignited sparks. Owning a long Denzel-type stride and a presence devoid of fear and insecurity, his broad shoulders moved easily, like he was trying to minimize his power.

The closer he got, the more she hoped he wouldn't notice her lust, but as fate would have it, there were empty seats on both sides of her.

In a sexy baritone voice, Carl asked, "So are you enjoying the game?"

"I wish the Pistons were playing better."

"Well, they won fifty games last year, and I think the acquisitions of Chauncey Billups, Rip Hamilton, and Ben Wallace, GM Joe Dumars has them going places."

"I sure hope so. Dumars was playing the last time they won."

Watching her take a sip from her soda, Carl smiled at her.

"You don't remember me, do you?"

"No. I don't. I'm sorry. But I do know the man you're seated with. He did some work for me a long time ago."

"I know."

"How do you…"

"It doesn't matter how I know. So, can you tell me why you're here alone?"

"I love basketball and my girlfriends canceled on me. Better for me. Maybe I can pick up one of those millionaires."

"You're joking, right?"

"What do you think?"

"You really want to know what I think?"

"I wouldn't have asked if I didn't want to know."

"What I think is that you're too gorgeous to be sitting up here. Come with me."

The heat from Carl's hand traveled through Keisha when he helped her from the seat, filling the air around them with instant passion.

"Where are we going?"

"You said you want to pick up a millionaire, right?"

"Uh, yeah."

"Then let's go find you one."

"You're joking, right?"

"Follow me and we'll find out."

Together they moved to the first row of the black courtside seats, drawing looks from fans thinking they were graced with the presence of Halle and Denzel on that historic Oscar night.

They returned to the VIP section near the Piston Bench where his father sat.

"I'm sure that you remember my father, Wallace," Carl said with a smile. "From what I understand, Miss Gray, he handled some legal matters for you. And I know it's rather late for me to say this, but I'm sorry about what happened."

Keisha swallowed hard. "Thank you."

Extending his hand once more, "I'm his son, Carlton, Carl for short, and you're Keisha," he said, helping her into an elite club chair. While checking out the outfit that clung to her vivacious frame—sexy tight blue jeans, a peach-colored sweater and navy blue shoe boots—her ample, upright breasts seduced his eyes, not to mention wine-colored lips and white teeth; all of which high-lighted her creamy, cappuccino complexion.

Again feeling the heat of attraction, Keisha's face felt flushed when she searched him with her eyes. Needing to find some flaw or defect in this good-looking brother, all she saw was the diamond wedding band on his finger.

She asked, "Married, huh?"

"Yeah." Carl smirked, pointing to the team benches. "But that's irrelevant. You're looking for a millionaire, right? There's some to the left and right of you, and there, shakin' and bakin' on the hardwood. Go get em', Tigress."

Wallace saw his own swagger in his offspring and laughed a naughty laugh.

He asked, "Son, don't you think she's a little too sophisticated to be chasing those young boys?"

With her lungs breathing in passion and hope, Keisha sat there.

Carl smiled a secure smile, as if he knew what she thought and felt, then eased back in his chair and watched Mr. Big Shot drain a cold-blooded three as the shot clock ran down.

He's right. Maybe the Pistons are going places, Keisha thought.

Shortly after her assessment, the halftime buzzer sounded.

"Would you like to get something to eat?" Carl asked.

"What makes you think I don't want to get my millionaire?"

"I already know one that's crazy about you."

"And who might that be?"

He extended his hand once more to hers, this time hoping their objectives were mutual. "You'll find out soon enough. Pop, you'll be okay?"

Although Wallace's face was an auxiliary scoreboard flashing a warning sign, the words escaping his lips were paternally diplomatic.

"Sure, son, go enjoy tonight. It was good seeing you again, Ms. Gray."

Keisha arched one of her pencil-thin eyebrows and was about to say something when Carl intercepted her muse.

"I live in New York, but I stay with my father when I'm here."

"I was wondering why I'd never seen you before."

Leaving the Palace, Carl asked his date to follow him in her gold Lexus to his father's house on Dow Ridge Road in nearby Orchard Lake, where they parked her vehicle in his three-car garage.

Though cool on the exterior, Keisha's insides were bumper-to-bumper with the urge to scream, *take me now, baby.*

Carl whipped out his cell and placed a call.

"Can I speak to the manager? Thanks… How are you, Ms. G? It's been a long time. I know it's late, but if I get there in time, could you keep the place open for me? I need a table for two. Thanks… I'll be there as soon as I can."

"What was that all about?" Keisha asked.

"You'll see."

"How did you know that I love surprises?"

Entering his black Hummer, he turned on the sound system. Revealing his inner visions was Stevie Wonder, telling the couple the crazy game they were about to play with love would be strange and secretive, their future unclear as the satisfaction they hoped to find in each other's lives.

Carl and Keisha would have to figure out whether love would be fair to them or not.

Not at that moment, however.

Both wanted fun.

Both wanted pleasure.

Yet at the beginning of their trip, both were soundless, strangely quiet.

As they ventured up I-696 East, Keisha initiated a remedy to the restlessness.

She said, "Carlton Austin," the admiration in her tone evident.

"That's my name," he responded.

"It sounds regal."

"I wish it were."

"You look like you're doing okay."

"That was my father's house. But I do okay, if you want to know the truth."

Ripping out page four of the Gold Digger's manual where the questions about employment, financial status and image appeared highlighted and in bold letters, Keisha felt this man's power and played it cool.

"Numerically, Carlton Austin is a very good name," she announced.

"Why do you say that?"

"There are thirteen letters in your name. That means you're a lucky guy."

"Well, to be completely honest with you, I feel lucky that you took my hand in the Palace."

Again, Carl had put himself out there, yet there was apprehension behind his boldness. While women flirted with him—especially in the city, which always seemed alive with temptation—for the most part, he curbed his libido. As handsome as Carl was, he was as straight-laced as Tim Tebow, which only magnified his charisma and allure.

Although many found him desirable, the ladies seemed to know that he was a faithful man.

"Women know who does what. *They always know*," his father said repeatedly.

Besides, five hundred miles away was a tall, beautiful woman with a powerful love that was all his. Amanda Austin had a dazzling smile, wide hazel eyes, smooth brown skin and a life of her own as a drug counselor in Harlem Hospital.

Carl loved his wife, yet he was in a trance, smitten by Keisha's aura for more than two decades. Her beauty, charisma and attraction caused his ticker to overrule his head. Making statements he normally wouldn't make and taking risks way beyond his normal standards, the overwhelming feeling of wanting to know what she looked like when sleeping and what she looked like at sunrise had planted seeds of adventure in his soul.

Cruising along, moving from I-696 to I-94 East while passing billboards promoting the lions, tigers, and casinos, they approached Exit 237, the one toward Mt. Clemens.

Carl asked, "What time is it?"

"Nine-fifteen."

"Just in time."

"For what?"

"You'll see."

Exiting the interstate, he turned left, onto North River Road. Keisha's eyes widened when she saw the magnificence of Lake St. Clair at night. The stars meshing beautifully with the nighttime sky, luxurious condominiums graced the shoreline as well as numerous yachts docked.

In a word, the waterfront setting was spectacular.

Even more breathtaking was Harrison Township's Harbor Grille Bistro. Upon entry, the couple was greeted by the scent of fresh seafood that accentuated the nautical experience.

"In the summertime I take the long drive up for the weekend to sit on the deck of the poolside café," Carl shared.

"All the way from New York?"

"You'd be surprised what a couple of Coronas and the stillness of water can do for peace of mind."

At the top of the stairs, the general manager awaited them with a warm smile.

"Hello, Mr. Austin. Nice of you to return," she said after a heartfelt embrace. "Taking another break from the hustle-and-bustle, I see."

Carl nodded.

"And you know I had to come to my favorite place."

He paused.

"Oh, this is Keisha, my father's former client."

Until that moment, the younger Austin made sure nothing else mattered in the world but Keisha. However, the words "former client" made her speeding emotions crash into a brick wall, knocking the wind from her excitement. The reality of the label stood out like a "Last Exit" sign on an expressway before crossing a bridge leading to emotional confusion. On the other side of the overpass was a place where women sneaked around corners, pretended they were insignificant and hoped the gifts lavished upon them would assuage the lonely feeling being the other woman offered.

Searching the red carpet for consolation, Keisha hid her disappointment with grace.

Accurately decoding her spirit, Carl absolved her complex by holding her hand, and once again a smile appeared on his date's face.

Keisha surveyed the establishment and loved the boat-shaped chandeliers that graced the ceiling along with the gorgeous piano area. Hunched over the ivory keys in a posture radiating love was a white man tickling the atmosphere with a dreamy melody. Large glass windows showed the lake in all its glory, and the dining area, complete with strong oak tables and aqua-blue cushioned booths, gave the impression they were on a vessel at sea.

The casual-yet-elegant ambiance was regal, an ideal setting for two people on a first date.

In the restaurant area, Carl pointed to a booth where red napkins and menus were placed.

"Is this one okay?"

"It's fine."

Instead of sitting across from him, his date moved next to him.

While flipping through the menu and forgoing the preliminaries, her line of questioning was direct.

"So Carl, are you happy?"

The brightness in his face dimmed.

"To be honest, I really don't know," he confessed. "I have an amazing woman at home and a son that never caused me a sleepless night. He's at Morehouse, and I think he'll become a Pastor. God has definitely touched him."

"Morehouse College produces men of God like USC produced tailbacks back in the day."

"What do you know about the Trojan backfield?"

"I used to watch the games with my father on his good days," Keisha said.

"So you remember Mike Garrett, O.J. Simpson, Sam Cunningham, Ricky Bell, Charles White and Marcus Allen."

"You forgot one."

"Who?"

"The one that scored six touchdowns against Notre Dame in 1972, as well as four more against the Irish two years later in a 55-24 blowout."

"That's right! How could I forget Anthony Davis? You really know your football."

"I sure do." Keisha beamed proudly. "I almost went there, but the University of Detroit offered me a full ride." Pausing, she continued, "Your son, what's his name?"

"Carl, Jr."

"A chip off the old block?"

"Not really. Keisha, do you have any kids?"

She shook her head no. "Don't want any, either."

"Have you ever wanted a family?"

"I have forty kids seven hours a day for ten months. I can live with that." Keisha paused. "Besides, I had my tubes tied years ago after two miscarriages."

Carl did a double-take.

"Wait. Isn't it illegal to do the procedure on a childless woman? Isn't there a mandate of two kids, at the very least? From what I understand, doctors will fight with women who've had just one."

"You're right, Carl. Unless it's a medical issue, doctors encourage a woman to have at least one child. I was an exception."

"It's like a man having a vasectomy."

"Almost."

"So, no kids. Next question: why aren't you married?"

"I don't trust men," she said bluntly.

"I understand totally."

She felt her blood pressure rise as the image of her father and the sawed-off firearm resurfaced. In her pregnant pause, she sighed, took a deep breath and fought the memory that persecuted her.

Emerging victorious, sadness caused a tear to roll down her face.

Carl, sensing the need to make their moment sweet again, dabbed at her pain with his napkin.

"Your strength is something I've admired for years. You're a very brave woman to overcome that tragedy. You kept it moving."

"That's what my mother taught me to do."

"She was a very smart woman."

"The best mother a girl could have," she said proudly.

"I lost my mother tragically as well, in a car accident when I was seven. My father never remarried and wouldn't allow himself to grow close to anyone else. He was scared he might lose them."

"He must have been lonely."

"Quite the contrary, Keisha, he's had his share of women. But my mother was his Ava Gardner."

Keisha nodded. "She was the love of his life, like Gardner was to Sinatra: sexy, sassy and a femme fatale image."

"You got it."

"Do you know what you want to eat, sweetheart?"

A term of endearment had slipped out, one that revealed dream-like feelings she wasn't supposed to own, and instantly Keisha wished she could take it back.

"It's been a long time since I heard that," Carl replied, his smile as wide as the mass of water surrounding the moment.

He opened up further as their hunger was sated with a fresh blend of seafood, pasta and crunchy vegetables, emptying his soul as if he were confessing to a priest. Admitting that a dreary same-ness had held his life, a dull, dreadful flatness, he tired of the monotony. The toll of being everything to everybody every day—being supportive of his wife's ambitions, the long hours at his Harlem office, answering every client letter and phone call, always being reliable and reachable, the indefatigable assistance he gave others when saddled with their personal, financial and health-related issues—wore his spirits down to a nub.

Keisha asked, "What does the wife have to say about all of this?"

"As long as our lifestyle doesn't change, she's okay with every-thing."

"Have you ever cheated on her?"

"I almost did once, with a judge who invited me to her house. She was an attractive woman in a beautiful home and many ideas ran around in my head. John Keats stopped me."

"Let me guess, 'Ode on a Grecian Urn.'"

"I see you're familiar with nineteenth-century poetry as well."

"I'm a schoolteacher, Carl."

"I wanted us to be like the figures on that vase Keats described, our hands almost but not quite touching."

"Bold lover," Keisha quoted, "Never, never cast thou kiss."

"You get it."

"So what happened next?"

"I told her our destiny was to go through eternity without touching and we needed to roll with that."

"How do you feel about Keats now?" she purred seductively.

"Don't ask me that."

"Why not?"

"This is a different scenario."

"How so?"

An amorous smile capturing his countenance, Carl Austin shared a deeper admission, one showing that he found that place that released him. Surrendering to something greater than desire, he listened to his heart and spoke.

"I've been crazy for you since you walked in my father's office. When I saw you, I couldn't breathe, and my fantasies grew more breathtaking over the years. This reality, you being here, kidnapped my entire thought process and returned it along with a feeling that makes me want to caress your heart forever, Keisha."

His utterance wasn't that of a man merely satisfying a tremendous lust rushing from an even bigger rush of testosterone. Sailing in deep waters to a world of mystery on a ship called *Enchantment*, Carl fell deep.

For now Keisha stared at him deeply, the emotional look in her eyes ignoring his wedding band. Seeing truth and power in his pupils, her heart fell under a spell that produced inner joy, a feeling far more fervent than a fusion of limbs, lust, the taste of anatomical juices and orgasmic release brought on by temporary madness.

By the time the wine had stopped pouring, both knew that their evening would not end staring at Lake St. Clair.

By the onset of a new day, Carl and Keisha shared a secret devotion that rained balloons and confetti on their hearts; an energetic emotion much deeper than the average soul could see.

Two people sharing something so sweet;

Two people feeling something so right;

Two people sharing something meant for more than one night.

But it would start with one night.

That night.

Carl Austin was spot on about two things. By 2003, the Detroit Pistons had constructed a nucleus that won an NBA Championship a year later while making six straight Eastern Conference Finals appearances.

And like the basketball franchise that brought them together, those two were going places.

The lovemaking that night, Keisha remembered, was intense. She inhaled his Perry Ellis cologne when he wrapped his arms around her and her heart skipped a beat. Looking into his eyes, seeing a sparkle that told her everything was okay, all those years of being frigid, all those years of playing stupid mind games to protect her heart, all those memories of her mother literally loving a man to death…

She finally succumbed to it all.

"It's okay," she recalled Carl saying. "It's okay to cry."

She buried herself within his wide shoulders and a waterfall of emotions left her.

After a while, the tears stopped, and the joy of feeling something deep had her alit with anticipation and needing to express an overwhelmed emotion.

"Let's go to bed," she said.

Entering the bedroom of the suite they rented, Carl gave her his tongue immediately. Keisha met his passion head-on and their unhurried tango was like molten lava slowly moving down the side of a volcano.

Soon, their shared kiss evolved into sensuous pecks.

Before completely losing herself, she asked, "Are you sure you want to do this?"

Studying her for a moment, as if he wanted to mingle with her mouth until she was breathless, Carl's wife, Amanda, was now an afterthought.

"I want to know all of you tonight," he said.

The low-rumble confirmation moved past all the locks that hid her heart. Smiling with that cat-intoxicated-with-a-romantic-kind-of-catnip smile, Keisha seductively licked her lips in a way that would make LL fall back.

Next was a look of desire, a purposeful gaze.

Keisha intended to give as much as she would receive.

Feeling emboldened, she took his hand and led him to the king-sized bed where they melded magnificently.

French-kissing affectionately, their tongues found each other's hearts. Somehow the clothes came off and they pressed their hungry bodies together.

Keisha admired the animation of his oral creature.

"Damn, baby, I bet you can…"

"You'll see," Carl whispered, forcing her back to the soft cotton sheets. Then he began exploring her frame, kissing her lips once more…nibbling on her neckline…licking her pearly whites…sucking her full, merlot-stained lips…placing pliant pecks up and down her beautiful canvass…gently kneading her delicious double-D mangos while the brush at his brim aroused her nipples…then moving downtown, where feminine treasures were uncovered…

Like the backbeat rhythm of a song, throbs of heat rushed through Keisha, the lyrics leaving her by way of melodious moans and generous groans. Her body set aflame, Carl added kerosene to an already out-of-control blaze when he teased her treasure by lasciviously licking her labia. Feeling her body shimmer in expectation, he tongue-stroked the tingling flesh between her thighs ever so gently.

Simmering sensations touched her when he fluttered that talented tongue against the outsides of her soaking grin. Then he turned the grin into a drenched smile by easing in two fingers while strumming her pearl like an erotic harp.

Keisha closed her eyes. Rotating her hips while flexing, the pool between pink walls began to boil as pieces of an orgasm assembled at her core.

Sensing her explosion, soaking up all of her affection, Carl's face became bosom buddies with her hips and inner thighs. Searching and sucking her sex zone, he used his creative critter to draw dew from her paradise.

Keisha's orgasm was now on a journey of freedom from its epi-center. "That's it," she moaned, each ragged breath releasing rumbling mini-explosions at her core. Wrapping her legs tightly around his head, she sang his praises through a series of heavenly contortions, uncontrolled convulsions and breathtaking spasms.

Then she screamed, "Baby, I want to drown you."

Losing it completely, her back arched violently, almost forming the letter "U" with her body while she flooded she sheets.

"Get it all, baby," she screamed as she shook.

As per her request, Carl quenched his thirst; but not before letting her drench his face.

At that moment, the letter "U" stood for his unbelievable oral skills.

His urgency fully unleashed, Carl returned to her face, and in a low, sexy voice, he commanded, "Lick my face. Taste yourself."

Hungrily, Keisha complied.

Slipping his tongue in her mouth once more, the energy of Carl's kiss screamed another orgasm in her mouth. When he sucked her bottom lip, he reawakened every nerve ending at her core.

Wanting his hard urgency to stroke the hell out of her wet emergency, Keisha shifted her legs slightly so that the soaking wetness of her needy ache meshed with the swollen tip of his heat. Aligning it with her puffy exterior, Carl's aroused vein swelled even larger while a wave of insistence had him reaching the point of no return.

He had to get it.

Keisha needed him to get it.

Spreading her legs, between choppy breaths, she shuddered, "Please, Carl…"

Placing her lovely stems on his shoulders, kissing and sucking her firm calves while doing so, a man in love with a woman that wasn't his went to work. Starting with the tip, then the root, his tempo flowed within her watery walls. Slipping and sliding, dipping and diving, Carl released a fusillade of movements. From tiny circles to figure eight strokes, he found himself fighting the energetic sensation that comes from what feels so good, all the while holding her like she was all he had in this world.

"Damn, baby," he moaned, the onset of an overwhelming rush swallowing him.

There was this look in his eyes, Keisha recalled, *something that told me he was vulnerable, starving for the affection we shared*. While power and energy remained in his body, *this look* she saw in his eyes stirred an emotional pot and soaked itself in passion, thus creating a spiritual gumbo. Saying everything that moans from mouths in heat couldn't say, *this look* she saw was the one men owned when machismo and ego were stripped away, exposing vulnerability within the fabric of their flesh.

Try as men might to avoid *this look*, that search for love within the confines of sex, *this look* she saw was a black man saying things that women begged for years to hear orally: his fears of coping with subtle and blatant racism, his fear of repeating the mistakes his father may have made, his need of maternal love from her, his anxiety over using his power the wrong way like David did with Bathsheba, his tendency to run like a little boy when you got too close to his truths, his conflict about showing you his heart through action and communicating what's on his mind as well…

Keisha saw *this look* from the giver of life with his semen, the head of households and the person supposed to lead. *This look*, she deduced, is why God originally reserved physical unions between man and woman to "I do."

That's the way He planned it, Keisha thought. *But the serpent, the apple and sins of the flesh created a gray area.*

On that night the gray area that released sins of the flesh had never felt so good.

Carl's well-defined body regained a small measure of control and started moving again, rocking back and forth, stroking in and out of that spot. With rhythmic fury, he was driven to make all her hopes, dreams and desires obsessively crave his love.

He was also determined to make something else his.

Devon couldn't do it; Keisha played mind games there.

Brian and his melted chocolate bar?

No elaboration necessary.

But Carl Austin, the Harlem attorney who had made love to her a million times in his mind before this wondrous moment, was a master of movement. Raising his body on his fists, doing push-ups in it, stirring, swimming, swirling and swerving within the squishiness of her soaking sweet sugar, loving Keisha this way made him feel bionic like his fictional brother Steve, the six million dollar…

I think you get it.

The temperature of her thermostat rising to heights unknown, a low, sultry sound escaped Keisha.

"Oh God, Carl…," she purred as he quickened the pace of his passion. Locking eyes with the man she'd fallen for, reaching for, grabbing and pulling him close, her hungry kiss sent a strong message: she wanted him to brand her well and make it his only source of nourishment. Wanting his stamp in her sauce, during coitus she craved unadulterated madness within the physical artistry, her sweaty skin slapping against his insane thrusts of lust. But when they were done, Keisha wanted to land in a place where gorgeous blue waters led you straight to bliss; that special place where a symphony of two satisfied souls composed one emotion.

Love.

Convulsing fiercely as Carl neared his crescendo, the orgasmic vibrations within an unchained animalism shook her from temple to toes.

Her shaking wouldn't stop as he moved faster and faster.

Carl also fought that inevitable, incredible sensation; his body tensed, then relaxed while his steel became rock-hard.

Keisha, feeling his climax move from root-to-base-to-tip and again responding to his motion, couldn't stop coming.

Twitching and trembling while pushing himself deep within her waters, Carl grunted and shuddered. Exploding, his world became blurred as a dizzying rush had him floating to a place where breathless orgasms dwelled.

Collapsing in her arms, drowning in the sweat of affection, in a winded voice, Carl said, "I love you, Keisha."

"I love you, too," she remembered saying with a glazed satisfaction etched on her face.

Over a decade later, *I do love him*, she thought while a combination of soap and hot shower water washed another night of sin down the drain.

I love him, but this can't go on.

FIVE

riday morning seeped through his blinds, disrupting the shadows that were snoring. Leaving his living room a mess, darkness had partied all night with its bubbly and Ciroc, finally putting a halt to the fun at nine in the morning.

Gingerly, William rose from his leather couch.

Shining like old gold, the sun mingled with winter's blue skies. Yet the heat of God's creation couldn't reach William's heart, for the anniversary of a painful moment and its bittersweet memories obstructed his peace of mind.

Shaking his head, his skull felt swollen, like someone had cracked him from behind with a two-by-four.

And another kind of rush overwhelmed his senses.

Damn, I can't believe I lost the letter.

Praying for a miracle, before his trip south, he would check Friday's to see if Donald or another bartender had recovered it.

He checked his cell phone and saw two messages.

The first was from Linda's mother.

MESSAGE: Good morning, William, Mamie Woodson said. *We're checking on you to see if you're still coming home. It's a long drive and we understand if you've changed your mind. Please give us a call to confirm. We love you, son.*

He would return the call once he got on the road, he thought.

Hearing a familiar tone to start the second message eased his headache slightly.

MESSAGE: What up, Black, the voice said, making reference to a shared seventh-grade nickname. *I know today's an anniversary you wished were different, and I'm checking on you. Holla back at your boy.*

As had been the case for three-and-a-half decades, Steve Randall called right on time. His best friend, basketball mentor, sole confidant, adviser and grief counselor all wrapped into one, over the years their bond paralleled the purpose of the Million Man March or T.D. Jakes' ManPower conferences. Fighting a stench of negativity festering in the black community between insecure men, their friendship painted a portrait of brotherly love.

Nino Brown and Gee Money, *New Jack City* street hustlers perpetuating self-hatred with drug transactions and black-on-black crime, didn't receive the memo; neither did brothers with jeans sagging off their asses.

Ride or die, Steve Randall had always been his brother's keeper.

Ride or die, William McCall always returned the love.

Raising each other with spirit and truth, together through all types of weather, their ride-or-die union fortified them with resolve when doing the hardest job in America…

Being a black man.

Touching his name on his smartphone, William smiled warmly when hearing his voice.

Steve said, "Yo."

"What up, Black? I saw that you called me."

"Yeah, man. I was checking on you. If I didn't hear from you by noon, I would have called again."

"I'm cool. Had a few drinks last night, came home, finished the job and listened to some jams. How are Anita and the kids?"

"Nita's cool, and the kids miss their Uncle Will."

"I miss them too. I'm so glad you moved back to Delaware. It wasn't a coincidence your trucking company allowed you to branch out."

"Yeah, that was a blessing. I'm closer to my parents in New Castle and they need me. Pops ain't doing too good."

"Give him my love. I might stop through on my way back from the South. I'll call if I do that."

"Enough of the small talk, Black. Are you sure you're okay?" Steve asked.

William sighed.

"It still hurts, but I deal with it."

"It's been seven years, right?"

"Yeah, Steve. Seven years since I lost her."

"Black, the number seven means completion. God created the heavens and earth in six days, and rested on the seventh. There are seven days in a week, no?"

"Where are you going with this?"

"Natural creation was completed on that seventh day and a lot of things in the Bible follow patterns of seven. Seven women, seven pillars, the seven-day feast of unleavened bread. Seven years of mourning for Israel."

"What are you trying to say, man?"

"Black, I'm gonna give it to you straight: you've been mourning Linda's death for seven years, and it's time for you to go on with your life. You've completed the grieving process. Tear down the wall, let go of the memory and have some fun."

"Steve, how can you say that? How can you tell a person how long they're supposed to mourn?"

An awkward pause ensued, one filled with tension that comes with complete transparency.

"Do you want me to go there, William?"

"You know the drill. Keep it one hundred."

"You're afraid to fall in love again."

Suddenly, William heard Roberta Flack in his ears, killing him softly with fact. Steve Randall sang a truth his boy needed to hear, and the silence that followed when masculinity is stripped to its vulnerability made him continue.

"Let me change that, Black. Your head is so far up your ass that you have Brown Collar Syndrome. Wipe the sad shit off your collar and move on."

Sarcastically, William asked, "What is this, a Pat Riley motivational ploy?"

"No, it's the truth. I know you're tired of being John McClane, and I can understand that."

"John McClane?"

"Yeah, man. For years, all kinds of devastating things happened to you, Nakatomi Plaza, airport-takeover-during-a-winter-storm-type shit. Women calling you gay when we were teenagers; the Andrea Richmond love triangle in your early twenties and the failed marriage that followed; the Anna Daniels/Markham Chandler engagement fiasco that got you wrongly terminated from a job. You going into a homeless shelter and working at McDonald's. And then once you finally find true love, the woman gets cancer and dies on you."

"I couldn't leave Linda the way she was."

"You weren't supposed to. But Lucky's been gone seven years, and she wanted you to move on. Didn't she say so in that letter she left you?"

The letter, William thought. *I can't forget to go by Friday's.*

"Yeah, Black. She said I should find a greater love."

"Then maybe you should follow her advice."

"I don't have it in me anymore, man. I'm burnt out."

"How can you be burnt out? It's been years since you gave your heart to anyone and I don't want to see you drown."

"Steve, you said that to me once before, years ago."

"That time I meant it in terms of not letting your pride get in the way of asking for help. Now I'm saying it because I don't want to see you become an old man hiding your feelings behind pussy."

"You're sick!"

"Seriously, you should start thinking about growing old with someone special."

"Can I be totally honest with you?"

"Haven't we always been that way?"

"I haven't had any since Linda died."

Another pause.

"You're kidding me, right?"

"No, I'm not."

"But you're a man."

"I know that, Black."

"Men need sex, and you're telling me that you've gone without for seven years? Have you even tried?"

"Once. It didn't go too well."

"Damn! What've you been using, Ms. Palmer and her five fingers? You might have to dust the cobwebs off the little fella. You sure you remember how to use it?"

"You're a trip, Steve."

"You know how they say that sex clouds the judgment? In your instance, maybe it'll bring clarity."

William laughed.

"Seriously, Black," Steve continued, "it's been that long?"

"Yup."

"Man, you better stop holding on to your past. Chart a new course for yourself and run with it. Don't be scared of something you want, something you deserve. Live the rest of your life with no regrets."

"Steve, you're so right. Maybe I need to let go. I'm not gonna lie, man, I'm scared." William paused. "Sometimes I wonder why this love thing comes so easy to others and so hard for me. What did I do to piss off God? Why doesn't it work for me?"

"Black, you're killing me with the self-pity. The reason why it doesn't work is because you want it too bad. Relax and let it come to you. You're like LeBron James."

William shook his head. "First, I'm John McClane, and now I'm LeBron James."

"Yeah, man, think about it. He wanted that first championship so badly that he kept trying too hard. It wasn't until he started living in the now that he got what he wanted, and then some. Start living in the now and watch God give you the thing you want most when you least expect it. It happened with Linda, and I'm sure it'll happen again."

"But I feel so numb, Steve. You know, all I want is that feeling Michael must have felt…"

"Oh boy, here we go with another MJ analogy."

"Seriously, Steve, this one makes sense."

Steve acted like he was forced to listen to a St. Olaf story from Golden Girl Rose Nylund.

"Okay, let's hear it."

"Have you ever heard 'I Can't Help It,' from the *Off the Wall* album?"

"The jam Stevie Wonder wrote for him?"

"Yup."

"And you're going *where* with this?"

"Well, at the end of the song he goes into this wordless scat, like he unlocked the key to indescribable joy. It's so mellow in its triumph."

"The *Triumph* album was one with his brothers after *Off the Wall*," Steve quipped.

"It had some great songs on it, too. 'Can You Feel It,' 'Lovely One,' 'This Place Hotel'…"

"William!"

"Okay, I'm back. Anyway, that scat is the joy I desire with a woman. That's the joy I deserve, Steve!"

"Well, like Michael and his brothers said, 'Time Waits For No One.' Thaw out and go have some fun, Black."

"Steve, I don't know how I could thank you for…"

"C'mon man, you know the drill. We ride together…"

"We die together…"

In unison, they spoke, "We're bold brothers in life!"

"Call me if you flow through. Maybe I'll take Monday off," Steve said.

"Yeah, man. Peace."

"Be easy."

Like the Green Lantern with his power ring recharged, a reinvigorating buzz swept through William. Knowing how difficult it was to rise in a supremacist society that still looked at his chocolate skin as inferior, it felt great to know he wasn't in the struggle alone.

Shutting his cell off, he gathered his travel gear for the seven hundred-mile trip. He could have traveled by plane or Amtrak, but the twelve-hour drive to South Carolina always gave him tranquility, time to think. Filled with a sense of adventure, a world without time restraints, demands or responsibility, he felt free.

The job, he decided, could wait on him.

By the time I get back, the damn place might be closed, he thought.

He looked forward to seeing the Malloys, who rolled out the red carpet upon his arrival like he was a hero returning from Afghanistan. Thinking of Mamie Woodson's outstanding cooking, his mouth watered in anticipation of her scrumptious menu: barbecue or smothered chicken, collard greens cooked with turkey flavor, her mouth-watering mac-n-cheese, grilled salmon that melted in his mouth, her famous potato salad, and lastly, his favorite dessert, Cherry-Swirled Cheesecake.

"We need to fatten you up, William," she always announced with a huge grin.

Davis Malloy, Mamie's husband and Lucky's former gynecologist now retired, would sit there smiling.

Although the couple was in their late-seventies, they remained vibrant and full of wisdom. But William knew that his presence in Spartanburg meant more to the couple than what lay on the surface.

Seeing him kept Linda alive in their spirits.

Seeing him kept Linda alive in their souls.

No matter what was going on in the Big Apple, he always returned South in mid-February.

Another place to return to was Friday's to retrieve that letter. Though fully comprehending Steve's gospel, like a man with his favorite cigar, the spirit of Linda Woodson still burned smooth and pleasant.

The memories of her unforgettable spirit would never explode in his face.

But trying to find love again might, he thought.

Venturing into a dating world where issues between mid-lifers were more pronounced could be lighting a bad leaf of tobacco; the taste of pain lingering long after a negative presence.

Before allowing the energy that brought men and women together for intimacy back into his heart, William McCall needed some wisdom from his elders, elders that were happily married seven hundred miles away.

After loading his luggage in the backseat of his tuxedo-black Taurus Limited, he eased into the leather-trimmed bucket seat. Starting the engine, the booming audio system filled the car with Drake calling an ex from a club, telling her she could do better.

He grimaced.

I love you, Drake, but I'm not interested in hearing you getting drunk to holla at a chick.

Pressing the CD button, a funky mechanical beat made his head bob.

The thumping bass and voice on the song "Xscape" expressed a desire to get away from the pressures of a system that entrapped him.

Tragically, the voice could no longer "Xscape" to a peaceful place on earth.

I miss you, man, thought a man trying to free his mind from his own problem world.

Donning his sunglasses, William looked in the visor mirror and admired his *Low Down Dirty Shame* look: dark shades, smooth bald head complementing chocolate skin and a salt-and-pepper goatee.

And an unreleased-to-the-public Michael Jackson track was his cool-ass theme music.

He opened the sunroof slightly and let the cool winter air embrace an even cooler driving look as he sped off in his whip.

Temporarily "Xscaping" was William McCall, straight chillin'.

SIX

The light that Carl brought into her life would never dim, and moments they shared in their ten-year affair burned like an eternal flame.

Keisha's body tingled in remembrance when she thought of how breathtaking the Las Vegas Strip looked while dining at the Top of the World Restaurant; she felt like a rocket shooting into the stratosphere when he kissed her 800 feet above ground. There were extravagant shopping sprees at the Ala Moana Center in Honolulu, intimate getaways like traveling to Milwaukee to see where his grandparents lived, romantic trysts like sipping champagne as a Chicago night twinkled its approval, and the revelatory moment of a Mother's Day visit to her parents' gravesite.

He never stopped showing his heart, she thought.

Neither would his surprises. As with many of their secret rendezvous, the Tuesday before Valentine's Day she received a call telling her that a plane ticket awaited her at DTW (Detroit Metro Airport).

Saddled with bills, she told Carl, "I just finished paying the tax man what I owed him from last year and I won't touch my emergency funds."

"In three hours, a stretch limo will take you to the airport," he replied calmly.

Once her Delta plane touched down at LaGuardia, she saw a man holding a sign in the luggage area.

In bold red letters, "GRAY" was the inscription.

"For Keisha Gray?" she asked.

The white driver nodded yes.

In the parking area was another black limo.

She opened the door and gasped when she saw three-dozen Fire and Ice roses, straight from Ecuador.

He's so romantic, she cooed.

Then there was Carl's intellectual brilliance and pride for his race, both of which made Keisha's eyes shine like glittering diamonds. Knowing he was of the subordinate group—a powerful black man calling his own shots—*he'd never forgotten the shoulders he'd stood on*, Keisha mused.

Whenever they talked about the plight of their race, he passionately shared his thoughts; some of which were shared over dinner after President Obama's stirring address on the fiftieth anniversary of Dr. King's March on Washington.

"Black people are dying to take care of America, yet we won't ever get our due," he stated over dinner. "I'm one of the fortunate ones, Keisha."

"You don't think things have changed in our country?" she quizzed.

"Sure, we've progressed. But when a gymnast like Gabby Douglas wins Olympic gold in London and the accomplishment is downplayed, it makes you think. Instead of calling her 'America's Sweetheart,' 'The Fierce Five' was featured on commercial ads. Do you need more proof? Take a look at some of the team pictures and you'll see that she's never front-and-center. Put her in the damn middle, like Mary Lou Retton!"

"But she appeared on Leno, Letterman and Oprah's cable network afterward, Kellogg's gave a huge Corn Flakes endorsement and she won Female Athlete of the Year honors all over the place. Stop reading into things too much," Keisha argued. "Maybe things have leveled off so much that it doesn't matter what color Gabby is."

Gritting his teeth, Carl disagreed, stating, "Cornel West was right: as much as we've accomplished, in many ways black character is still not respected." He sighed, then added, "The only time America understood fully what it was like to be 'niggerized' was on nine-eleven."

"Don't forget about those Boston Marathon bombs made of shrapnel, ball bearings and nails."

"Tell me about it. If the terrorists were one of us, the media would have held us collectively accountable."

"What about the Navy Yard killings where the murderer was black? They swept it under the rug. You sound like a racist, Carl."

"I'm not a racist. I love my people so much that I'm compelled to call it as I see it."

"Darling, don't we have a black man in the White House?"

"One they attempted to humiliate by offering millions of dollars for his birth certificate and college records? One they have called 'indecisive' because of the scenario in Syria? And don't get me started on the economy. America's been borrowing millions-a-day for years from other countries, and now that they're having trouble paying it back, it's his fault? What a bunch of crap. "

"You forgot about the Republicans and their fight against the Affordable Care Act. For crying out loud, they shut down government operations for sixteen days," Keisha added. "Do you see the lengths ignorant people will go to prove a point? It's like the GOP wanted to see America fail, so they could say, 'We handed The Magic Negro a mess and he made it worse.' Sometimes I wonder if he was merely a figurehead put in place to keep us in the dark, a neat little trick by Charlie."

"I've wondered that, too, Keisha, especially with the way he's being treated. In so many ways it parallels what Jackie Robinson endured. He absorbed so much hatred being 'The First' that he died only sixteen years after his playing days. The abuse took years from his life. Then I look at Barack and worry. I mean, have they blatantly disrespected any other President like this? It's 'keep him in his place' bullshit of the worst kind, and it doesn't matter that he came from the womb of a white woman."

"They also love to see our brightest minds disagree publicly."

Immediately, Carl knew where his lady was headed.

He said, "If Tavis Smiley had a problem with Obama's moral leadership, he should've made his criticisms in private as opposed to airing them out on *Meet the Press*. Didn't he know his actions were the personification of those Willie Lynch letters? In front of millions that Sunday morning, Tavis and Harvard Professor Charles Ogletree fell for the divide-and-conquer-banana-in-the-tailpipe gag. It was so painful to watch."

"I couldn't believe they took the bait."

"Neither could I, but it's a perfect example of how at the highest levels, the game still hasn't changed."

"I never thought of it like that."

"Keisha, are things really equal for us? Were Doctor King's efforts rewarded with total equality?"

"We have a holiday named after him, don't we?"

"That doesn't mean a thing."

"They don't have one for Malcolm X."

"Don't get me started on that. They associate his name with hatred despite the fact he also spoke of cultural empowerment.

Spike Lee had to borrow forty million dollars from celebrities to finish the movie, Denzel played the hell out of the role, and what was his reward? He received an Oscar years later for playing a rogue cop. That's an excellent illustration of how we're praised for negativity, pain, drama, grinning and shuffling, but if we use our minds to enlighten, we're considered arrogant troublemakers or uppity."

"How do you feel about Huey and Bobby?"

"The Liberation Movement was necessary, because it forced the oppressor to respect the passiveness of Dr. King."

"But it didn't stop him from getting killed."

"Do you want to know why I think King was assassinated?"

"Sure."

Carl looked around the table, under his chair.

"I gotta make sure the CIA or FBI didn't bug the place."

"That's not funny."

"Seriously, once MLK shared philosophies of other countries: free education and healthcare for everyone and employment with equitable wages, he was a marked man."

"That sounds like communism," Keisha said.

"Wanting equitable treatment for everyone is communism?"

"Didn't Bobby Kennedy monitor him?"

"That was an oxymoron." Once Keisha nodded, he continued. "He monitored him to see if he was a communist while protecting him from harm."

"Reverend King focused on civil rights, no?"

"Sure, but not so much on race in his later years. The quality of life for all Americans meant more to him."

"He also opposed the principal money-maker of the day, Vietnam."

Carl nodded. "Once the connection between militarism, materialism, poverty and racism was established and he wasn't afraid to speak on it, he became even more dangerous because he was a black Robin Hood threatening the economic construct."

In unison, they said, "Get your hands out of my pockets."

Carl continued, "It gets even deeper. Had he lived, his next speech was called 'Why America May Go to Hell,' and it would have detailed some of the political, economic and cultural problems that could possibly destroy our country, troubles that exist today. Knowing that he would have given that speech on Sunday, April 7, 1968 makes you think."

Keisha agreed. "Back then, speaking on anything was trouble. It was bad enough leaders of the movement were killed whenever someone felt the need to send a message."

"It was either that, or J. Edgar Hoover infiltrated our political groups."

"He was a cross-dressing Pontius Pilate all-too-eager to stop racial progress."

"That's deep. Keisha, who was that *someone* behind who killed King?"

"Oh, I'm not touching that one."

"I think wealthy pockets orchestrated the assassination. Personally, I think Dr. King knew his time was up. I believe God told him so the night before he was killed. Listen to that 'Mountaintop' speech carefully."

"A heartbreaking piece of genius," Keisha added.

"I agree. But did you know those close to him said he spoke about death more that night than ever before? He used a philosopher's intellect and went in, thanking God for allowing him to live in the exact time in which he did. Then he acknowledged fate by identifying with Moses and how he didn't make it to the Promised Land, yet his Father used him, and in that, he knew glory."

"He knew," Keisha said. "He knew."

"Afterwards, he was so overcome with emotion that he had to be helped to his seat. That was a sign that his assignment here on earth was complete, and he probably knew who was behind that trigger. James Earl Ray may have merely been a pawn in the chess game, much like Lee Harvey Oswald years earlier."

"Honey, do you really think it was bigger than one shooter?"

"I'm not sure, but any time a country can have a president that believed abortion was necessary to prevent interracial couples from having children together, it really makes you wonder."

"I don't believe that."

Carl said, "Go listen to Nixon's private tapes from January 23, 1973 and get back to me."

"You better watch your back," Keisha joked.

"Things are done different today, babe. They'll attack my character and spirit, then sit back and hope I self-destruct like Mr. 9-9-9 did. And to think, the GOP actually gave him the platform to implode."

"Herman Cain was like that crazy relative in your family who makes sense for two minutes, then you're handing him a SYAD Award."

"What's a SYAD Award?"

"SYAD is an acronym for Sit Yo' Ass Down."

Carl, maintaining his cool, cracked a huge smile.

"Sit Yo' Ass Down Award," he said, shaking his head. "Thank goodness Obama's squeaky clean."

Stimulated mentally by their ebb and flow, Keisha's fearless knight had her eyes beaming like the afternoon sun on a still body of water.

She took the silk of his blue tie and fondled it seductively.

"There is no one," she said, sealing her reverence with a kiss, "and I mean no one who speaks like you."

He's an incredible man, Keisha thought, leaving the memory in the bathroom along with the sin of the night before.

He's an incredible man, but this can't go any further.

Keisha knew she had to let go. Already hurting because she knew becoming Mrs. Austin was no longer a possibility, her emotions had spiraled out of control. For years Carl voiced his unhappiness about his marriage, giving her hope that one day her dream would come true.

He would leave her soon, he kept telling her.

Carl even went to the point of seeing a psychotherapist with hopes that she could free him from his marriage. After opening up to Dr. Helen Slattery, he allowed the hired gun to do two things: 1) prescribe him a pill cocktail of Paroxetine, Diazepam, and Halcion; and 2) give him an eighteen-month plan on how to leave his wife.

"That's how long the process takes," she had said.

While the pills enlivened his mood, helped him sleep and increased his sex drive to that of men half his age, they didn't sway him either way concerning a divorce. He loved his mistress, but the idea of marrying her never overshadowed the foot-dragging reluctance to leave his wife.

Seeing his confusion rise as high as her skyscraper of emotions, Keisha had finally conjured up bravery to face the inevitable. The secret affair with Carl would forever stay in memory, and she hoped the misery that came with saying goodbye wouldn't linger. But in order to receive a love all her own, she would have to deal with it.

Much to her surprise, her lover had risen from his slumber.

"Good morning, beautiful!"

Not only was she in love with his mind, his solidly built chest, biceps, forearms and legs, there was something about his baritone voice—its securing warmth and calm—that nurtured her spirit.

Before she uttered a word, Keisha sighed.

This is going to be hard.

Her heart felt heavy and she wanted to cry.

"Hey," her voice trembled.

"Can I get a hug from my Valentine?"

"Sure…"

After the embrace, Carl asked, "What's wrong, Keisha? Are you all right?"

She sat down on the corner of the bed, took a deep breath, and let words flock in her head like birds to bread. Knowing that a severe withdrawal was ahead, her mind raced through a decade of love faster than the speed of light.

Again, Carl asked, "What's wrong, Keisha?"

She patted the bed softly. "Come sit down, baby."

The hunk of a fifty-something-year-old man complied.

"What's on your mind?"

As raindrops flooded her eyes, she rose from the bed and stood in front of him.

Then she spoke; slowly, methodically, and miserably.

"Carl, I have never loved anyone the way I love you. And you've always reciprocated the feeling. You make me feel complete, like a whole woman. You gave me comfort, self-esteem and have impacted my life in more ways than you can imagine."

"I love you, too, sweetie," Carl responded.

Normally his terms of endearment that produced heaven in her heart were followed by a kiss or a hug. And deep down Keisha wanted another display of affection from this enormously compassionate man.

Yet she remained resolute.

"You've been my lover, my mentor, my guiding light and my best friend. I can't imagine what my life would be like without you."

"Keisha, what are you trying to tell me?"

She paused and gathered herself.

"Carl, we can't see each other like this anymore."

Her lover's jam clamped tight, as if he'd been bit by a rattlesnake.

"What did you say?"

"We have to end this, Carl. You're not leaving your wife and I can't keep doing this to myself." Sighing, she paused, then continued. "I'm lucky I never met Amanda face-to-face. I wouldn't be able to look at her, knowing I've slept with her husband for the past ten years."

When Carl rose from the bed, there was a look in his eyes Keisha couldn't decipher.

A tense climate grabbed the hotel suite.

Flipping his demeanor, the tone of his voice hovered between panic and anger when he snapped, "Now that's mighty selfish of you, don't you think?"

"I beg your pardon?"

"You didn't give a damn about her when you were going on all these trips, spending my money and fucking my brains out, now did you? Now it's 'fuck you, Carl,' I can't do this anymore. Is this how it ends?"

"Carl, you've been telling me that you're leaving her for a decade now. One day you're telling me we could be seen in public together, the next day you change your mind. You told me last summer that we would spend it together, then a few days later, you said that we couldn't."

"It's hard for me to leave Amanda," he admitted. "We have history, over thirty years."

"Well, I'm doing us both a favor. This isn't right for me anymore. And you know it's not right for you. I'm sorry, Carl, but it has to be this way, for both of us."

As he moved toward her, a vein on his left temple stood out and he felt a weird sensation in his brain. Looking down at his hands, then at Keisha, the sensation caused his lips to snarl, his eyes to become daggers with intent and his nostrils to flair like a bull running the streets of Pamplona.

The look still didn't register with Keisha, even as his rage grew.

Clearing her throat, she said, "Carl, I'm so sorry, but it's over. I love you, but…"

The piercing stare still didn't reach her senses, even as the sensation in him grew.

If her mother were alive, she would've immediately recognized it.

But Ramona Gray was gone, the victim of obsession and abuse.

And she couldn't scream DUCK to her only child when the strange sensation in Carl, now moving through him with rage and expediency, traveled down his arms and sent his right hand directly into Keisha's jaw. Connecting, there was a slapping sound of masculine flesh striking female flesh; the force of the masculine flesh hitting the female flesh so violently that it instantly swelled her left cheekbone.

Unable to quell his anger, the transformation was now complete.

Carl Austin was now an evil barbarian.

Smacking her again, this time he drove her into a wall.

Then the barbarian screamed, "It's *over!?!* It's *over!?!* Who the fuck do you think you are? Our relationship is over when I say it's fucking over!"

Red liquid now flowing from her left nostril, Keisha was functionless; too shocked to scream, too numb to cry out. She turned her face to lessen the impact of his fist, but it, too, landed flush.

Finally, the barbarian wrapped both of his hands around her neck. Squeezing tightly, a little life left her when he slammed her against a hard wall.

In a calm voice, he said, "If you even think about leaving me, I'll fucking kill you. Do you hear me? I'll kill you, Keisha."

Then he threw her to the floor and moved into the bathroom. With emphatic cruelness, the evil barbarian had made his point.

Morphing back into the man she knew, it was time for Carl Austin to get ready for work.

Coughing to regain her breath, Keisha finally recognized her reality. Trying to scan the room quickly, terror and disbelief disconnected her from her senses. Feeling dizzy, she leaned on the corner of the bed, the place where the irrational incident sprouted its wings of disaster.

She tried to rise and collapsed to the floor.

In this semiconscious state, Keisha Gray saw a vision of a brown fist, cocked and flying toward her at the speed of sound. Then she saw a head with patches of hair missing from its crown.

Battered and bruised, the face was so swollen that you couldn't see its black eyes.

The disfigured visage smiled through the pain of a savage beating, asking the fist, "Are you done yet?" as blood dripped from its mouth. Then the head was banged against a wall and pounded on the second step of a wooden staircase until it was dizzy.

Somehow swollen lips calmly spoke to Keisha's mind.

"Close your bedroom door, honey. Everything's going to be okay," it said in a nurturing tone.

Everything wasn't okay, however. Pummeled and punished some more, slapped and slugged unmercifully, the torture continued in the bathroom, where the figure was forced to drink urine from toilet water while crying to a porcelain god for help.

Finally, she saw her father pulling the trigger of a sawed-off shotgun.

Then she heard her mother scream, possibly the last sound of her life.

The vision jogged Keisha's senses like an ammonia capsule. Gathering herself, she would stay on the carpet for several minutes, playing possum.

Carl, emerging from the bathroom fully dressed, towered over her. After kicking her to see if she was breathing, his mental evolution continued.

In his mind, Keisha Gray had been the love of his life; the operative words being *had been*.

Now she was his whore, and whores needed to be paid for their services.

Taking a fifty-dollar bill from his wallet, Carl crumpled it into a ball and tossed it on her back, saying, "Clean up and go buy yourself a drink."

Lying there motionless, Keisha wanted to tremble, but fear paralyzed her.

It had taken years, but she finally left her fantasy island on Reality World Airlines. Unlike the first-class ticket to the friendly skies of a world of tender loving care, the return flight traveled in darkness. With each passing mile, turbulence gripped its wings and charted its destination to the unknown.

Fearing that she would see her mother at death's airport, Keisha combatted disorientation with concentration.

With freedom being the impetus, her plan of action would be in effect once she heard two things.

The first was Carl's voice.

With arrogance, "I'll see you at Fashion Forty later. And have a martini waiting for me," he ordered, referring to their designated hangout spot.

The next thing she needed to hear was a door slam, which followed seconds later.

Keisha struggled to her feet, wobbling slightly. Moving slowly, her steps were uneven; she needed support from a wall while staggering into the bathroom. Using the counter to help her balance, she looked in the mirror, and the image staring back at her made her gasp.

The right side of her face looked normal, unblemished, yet the left side wore the brunt of Carl's fury. Her cheek was red and slightly puffed, her thick bottom lip partially swollen and her left nostril dripped blood. Underneath her left eye was a small mouse masquerading as luggage.

Keisha closed her eyes and shook her head.

Although she avoided becoming twins with Batman nemesis Two-Face, humiliation took occupancy in her psyche and the scent of its psychological damage permeated her skin.

The pain that reeked from her pores was a result of past and present danger; Keisha had become Ramona Gray, and the irony was inescapable.

Her spirit finally broke, causing her to bury her head on that countertop. Weeping without noise, her soundless cry came from a place of hurt and devastation, a place still mourning her parents' tragic death and mortified by the woman in the mirror.

But a resolve in the pit of her stomach remained, and five minutes after the emotional downpour, that resolve switched on the autopilot.

Keisha was a bad check that had to bounce from that hotel room.

She hastily applied light makeup to cover his cruelty, gathered the short black skirt and red blouse she had worn the night before and threw them in her travel bag along with her toiletries. Finding a pair of fitted black jeans, she put her sculpted stems in them and threw on an oversized black sweater to cover her wide hips and round backside. Accentuating her attire were black Sam Edelman booties, dark eyeliner and cherry-colored lipstick.

The outfit seemed fitting, as last rites were administered to Carl Austin, the man formerly known as her king.

Now ready to move, she looked in her pocketbook and saw the boarding pass for the return trip to Detroit was missing; Carl had removed it when she was in a daze. To make matters worse, she couldn't remember the time of her flight.

Further assaulting her psyche was the fact that the currency he threw at her and a twenty-dollar bill in her jeans pocket was all she had. That fifty-dollar bill was like bird-dropping running down the side of a shitty sundae.

Ten years of love and Keisha Gray was reduced to Alexander Hamilton, a crumpled Ulysses S. Grant and a pimp slapping.

Surprisingly, a red envelope remained untouched.

I want to drop this off at Friday's, she thought, opening the door to her freedom.

Entering the hallway, her body may have been battered and bruised, but Keisha's injured spirit was ready to resume a life without madness. Singing like Celine Dion while it rose from the bottom of the ocean, the heart of her *RMS Freedom* would repair its engines and go on.

Or so she hoped.

SEVEN

Her rhythmic stride was still exotic even though she felt unattractive.

She wheeled her travel bag across Forty-seventh and Broadway, ignoring the sunny skies that softened the outlines of city skyscrapers. Men admired the fluid song her womanly curves hummed as she walked by, though a black cashmere coat left room for the imagination.

At fifty, she still possessed physical architecture that could halt midtown busyness. Yet masking the anger Carl had chiseled in her face were dark sunglasses and a hint of red rouge. Using the bill of a stylish denim hat to cover whatever her makeup missed, a sexy red scarf tied around her neck served as a choker.

Although an ocean of sadness threatened to drown her, Keisha's stunning looks still deceived the eyes of men.

All women are liars, she thought. *From the weaves in our hair to the heels we wear to make us taller, not only do we lie to men, but sometimes to ourselves. Men love our lies, for the shallower our waters are, the better for them to row superficial oars. It's all part of a game I've never been able to understand.*

Now on Seventh Avenue, she turned right. Continuing her stroll, she passed by Three-card Monte players running a game and stopped at Fiftieth Street for a pack of gum.

The owner of the newsstand was an elderly black woman.

"This is a surprise, seeing you here," Keisha said, handing over the fifty Carl had thrown at her.

Looking for change, the merchant smiled. In a jovial-sounding tone, she said, "Winter, spring, summer or fall, I've been here for over thirty years. The city tried to force me out, yet here I stand."

"Michelle's in the White House making a difference and sisters still fight for everything."

"The battle is never ours, my child. It's always the Lord's fight."

"Even when it pertains to our hearts?"

"In time, God reveals everything. Until then, you must remove whatever's ugly in you so He can fill you with His love. The God in you always attracts good men."

"I receive that."

After touching a hurting part of her customer, the old sage returned the large bill.

"I'm sorry, but I don't have change," she said.

Keisha started to put the breath refresher back when she felt a firm hand grip hers; a hand passing along strength in sisterhood.

"It looks like you've had a rough morning, child. This one's on me. Go treat yourself to a nice lunch with that fifty."

A single tear escaped from beneath Keisha's camouflage.

Fighting a frown, "God Bless You," she whispered in a nasal tone.

Had her voice been louder than a murmur, she would have cried.

Dabbing at her face with a tissue, she crossed the street and entered Friday's.

It was noon, the place had just opened for lunch, Skip Bayless and Stephen A. Smith were embracing debate on all flat-screens and Donald was again tending the bar, completing the back end of a grueling day-after-night shift.

"I see you returned to us," he said, smiling as Keisha pulled up a chair.

His smile turned upside down once she removed her shades and he saw the pain in her face.

"Can I have a Cosmopolitan?" she asked.

Almost immediately, a nerve calmer appeared in front of her.

"Put some music on, and this first one's on me," he said.

Breaking a shackle to her misery, she handed him the fifty, received change and immediately strolled over to the jukebox.

There, she searched for her Dr. Feelgood.

Instantly, Friday's was filled with the mid-tempo music of a phenomenon; a black kid from Gary, Indiana with a wide nose, big brown eyes and plump cheeks.

She needed him now more than ever before, and a slither of a smile emerged from the darkness when Keisha heard the first note.

"*Got to be there,*" the prodigy belted out.

Hearing his voice always produced fond memories; like the first time her parents took her to see him and his brothers.

Immediately transported back to a mid-October night in 1970, she was an innocent seven year old with cute ponytails, blue bell-bottom jeans and a bright red shirt. The whole family entered Detroit's Olympia Stadium bubbling with anticipation.

"They're young, black and amazing, like you," her father said, sharing his excitement with fifteen thousand fans.

Dressed in gold shirts, brown bell-bottoms with matching suede boots, the five afro-wearing brothers on stage didn't disappoint. Dancing with choreographed precision and playing instruments like seasoned veterans, the talented group sang about feelings they'd yet to experience.

Their performance left everyone in The Old Red Barn mesmerized.

But the one in the middle, Keisha thought, shaking her head, *the one in the middle...now he was unreal.*

Jermaine and Tito, strumming the guitars, made her smile.

Jackie and Marlon, harmonizing with love, gave her joy.

But the lead singer was a freakishly powerful kid in the middle who stole her heart.

From the funky bubble-gum songs to the bluesy ballads he sang with the agility of an old soul, young Keisha couldn't believe what she was hearing...

Or seeing; his dancing was breathtaking. Employing one-legged slides, splits, spins and a speedy foot shuffle, Keisha felt the emotion in every step he took.

Like a cartoon anvil dropping from the sky without warning, the weight of his talent was mind-blowing. Keisha gazed up at her parents and saw them tapping each other with did-you-see-what-he-just-did amazement in their eyes.

A whole family couldn't believe what they were witnessing.

Unfortunately, neither could the capacity crowd; by the middle of the concert, people were falling over themselves as they swarmed the stage.

Seated in the fifth row, it was a miracle the Gray family didn't get toppled.

While the Jackson Five couldn't finish the show—stadium security ran on the stage and got the kids off just in time—their job in leaving an unforgettable impression on Keisha was complete.

She had found her teen idols and her bedroom was never the same.

The walls were filled with posters of the group; especially of *that one in the middle*. Until her mother demanded she put them away, her carpeted floor was littered with *Right On*, *Seventeen* and

Tiger Beat magazines. Every Saturday morning she turned her television to ABC to watch the cartoon version of their show. Mimicking their dance steps, the room vibrated with energy only *that one in the middle* could fully understand.

Michael and his brothers always gave me love, Keisha thought.

He also brought calm during her parents' grinding times. When heated arguments turned violent, Keisha closed her door and hoped love through song would bring peace.

Once, Alfonso punctuated a shouting match with a punch that would have crumbled the Great Wall of China, and like a slave determined not to let "Massa" see her pain, her mother took it on the chin without flinching.

Keisha, watching the moment with tears in her eyes, ran upstairs, slammed her bedroom door and played a vinyl J-5 album on her turntable with the volume on high.

Harmonizing the chorus with his siblings, "It All Begins and Ends with Love," Jermaine sang loudly.

Togetherness and unselfish love Michael preached in another tune.

The powerful words from the mouths of babes worked; the disagreement stopped.

Unfortunately on that tragic night when Alfonso couldn't take it anymore, she didn't get home in time to play a record.

Over thirty years later, Keisha Gray sat at a bar, nursing an extra-strength Iced Tea while trying to will away another devastating experience.

Now flying solo on the jukebox, Michael Jackson went from being that child prodigy with cheeks you could pinch to an almond-eyed adult whose music healed so many hurts.

Yet in the song that played, in a beautiful voice he asked for the one thing missing in his life; the very thing he gave so freely to millions.

Michael Jackson wanted love.

Not just any love, mind you.

Yearning for something he searched the world over, his heart needed an energy not compartmentalized by words; a force unrestrained by verb, noun or adjective definition. Simultaneously sensitive and strong, longing to be rescued from his handicapped feelings and aching to be a hero all at once, his only request was that a woman meet him halfway.

"Someone put your hand out," Michael prayed.

Wanting just once to feel God's most precious gift, he yearned for the type of love that produced sun and rain to wash away lonely pain.

And so did Keisha; her watery eyes said so.

But her spirit had been demolished, much like The Old Red Barn when it faced a wrecking ball in 1987.

Donald interrupted her zone when he said, "For whatever happened to you, I'm sorry."

She took a deep breath and gave a half-hearted shrug. "It's okay. Shit happens."

"Tell me about it. You know," he continued, "There's another person I know who loves Michael Jackson as much as you do. As a matter of fact, here he comes now…"

Keisha looked right and did a double-take.

Rushing through the door was a handsome man wearing a three-quarter-length suede coat.

Removing his sunglasses, the desperation in his eyes indicated a singular purpose.

The man pleaded, "Donald, please tell me that you found the letter that I left here. Tell me you found Linda's letter."

The millisecond seemed like an eternity before Donald shook his head.

"Nah, man, I didn't see it," he said. "I'm sorry."

The man's shoulders slumped. Looking like he wanted to collapse, he swallowed a deep breath and cleared his throat like Cronkite did after that tragic confirmation in November of '63.

Seating himself, "Give me the usual," he said, further distancing himself from the world surrounding him.

Peering at him, Keisha noticed his head buried in his hands.

With empathy, she went into her purse and placed the red envelope on the bar. Gently sliding it over, she made sure he would see it when he came to.

Finally, William McCall left his stupor. Looking left, he saw the letter, then the face of the woman who found it. Noticing the scratches on her neck peeking from under her scarf and the mouse under her eye, his concern produced a heartfelt sigh.

All of a sudden Linda's note seemed irrelevant.

Delicately, he probed. "If I asked you what happened, would you tell me?"

Keisha shook her head no.

"Are you sure you don't want to talk about it?"

"No, I'd rather not."

"Okay. Thanks for holding on to my letter."

"I wanted to drop it off before I went home. Something told me that you'd be looking for it."

"That little voice was right, Keisha."

As he stared at her, *his* little voice kept screaming two words: *Help her.*

But common sense opposed that voice.

Thus, the trial of tiny voices in his head began.

In its opening argument, Common Sense brought the facts,

saying, *a woman will let you know if she's willing to talk, and she said that she's not. Besides, she's on her way back to Detroit, and you'll never see her again. Are you looking to make another movie, John McClane? You know what happens when you put your heart out there. What did Dennis Hopper say in those old Nike commercials? 'Bad things, man, bad things.' Don't take ownership of her troubles; it's obvious she has them.*

Compassion's statement, however, went like a little like this: *William, you can't be scared of the unknown. While I agree with Common Sense in terms of not getting involved, it's obvious that she needs a friend right now. She needs you to tell her she's worthy of the good things life has to offer, and you can do that as a friend with no strings attached. A friend would find out how damaged her spirit is and offer support; though I suggest that you tread lightly while doing so.*

Common Sense went ballistic. *OBJECTION! Man, the writing's on the wall; even Compassion said to tread lightly. HELLOOO??? Take a look at her lip, dude. She has a duck-billed platypus beak, and probably got popped in it for being a smart-ass! Slowly back away from the vehicle, McCall, before it runs you over with its issues.*

With those words Common Sense backed Compassion into a corner.

What would be its response?

William, Compassion said, *sometimes you must be willing to learn while taking the lead. You can do this by offering friendship. Help her, man. At the very least, you can drive her to the airport.*

Sometimes you have to be willing to learn while taking the lead.

Those words sounded eerily familiar to him, in tune with his spirit.

So was the dreamy ballad that played, one that came from the Jacksons' *Destiny* LP. Racing through the restaurant was a stylist singing away the tears and pain of being pushed away. In terrific tenor form, the young singer wished for dreams of two to become one.

Dreams of love are what Michael sang about.

Dreams of helping someone love themselves are what William thought about.

Hopefully, he wouldn't be pushed away.

"Hey," he said to Keisha, "so you're not going to tell me what happened?"

"I thought we already went through this," she snapped.

"Keisha, you don't have to chew my head off. Are you hungry?"

"William, I want to finish my drink and get to the airport."

"Which airport are you leaving from?"

No response.

"What time is your flight?"

"That's none of your damn business!"

Bitterness and anger made its journey from Keisha's heart, through her chest cavity and out of her mouth.

The snipe hit its target in the face and produced an arched eyebrow.

Remarkably, William remained poised.

"It's cool, Keisha." He nodded, his face unchanged. "I have my car in a parking lot not too far and I thought you might need a lift. Getting cabs midday can be a beast, especially on Friday. I'll let you finish your drink."

In the depths of his mind, Common Sense felt validated, saying, *I told you that chick has issues.*

Yet Compassion stepped to the forefront once more.

Getting Donald's attention, "Can you consolidate our checks? I'll pay for whatever else she wants," William requested.

Nodding, his favorite bartender smiled.

"I got her first drink already," he said.

"Then I'll have her second, and lunch if she wants it."

"You got it, Will."

From the same place her anger and bitterness lived, surprise traveled to Keisha's eyes, causing them to widen as she looked William's way.

The peace returned her way made her feel foolish.

"Tell me something," she asked. "Are you always this kind?"

"You returned my letter," William said. "And you did me another favor by playing MJ on the jukebox."

"I know. Donald told me right as you entered."

"During my lunch hours, I always listen to Michael. Something about his music energizes me."

"He made us all feel good," Keisha said.

"I miss him so much."

"So do I. He was the Greatest. He revolutionized the way we experience music."

"I'll second that." William smiled at her. "You know something? Anyone that loves Michael Jackson almost as much as I do can't be all bad."

For a nanosecond, Keisha didn't know what to do or say next.

As her eyes watered, the words came.

"William, I'm sorry I snapped at you. I had a tough morning and I'm a little sensitive," she said, dabbing at the tears messing with her makeup.

"It's cool, Keisha. I figured I may have been a little pushy."

Unraveling, her voice trembled, each syllable shattered by raw emotion. "I feel so out of it... I feel so bad... Excuse me..."

Feeling the onset of another meltdown, Keisha bolted to the bathroom, taking her napkin and pocketbook while leaving the travel bag at the bar.

William watched her scurry off, feeling helpless. No stranger to agony yet strong enough to show her that hearts can heal from all types of pain, he wanted to weld her ruptured soul together with the energy of his spirit, but knew that he couldn't. Once she reached the ladies room, she would release an agonizing wave of helplessness that soaked you in sadness while suffocating sanity with suffering.

Ordering her a glass of ice water, *if she's not back in fifteen minutes*, he decided, *I'll go see if she's okay.*

With a minute to spare, she returned, with makeup reapplied to her reddened face. Her movements, however, were jittery and a thawing-out process had disrupted her poise.

With effort, she climbed into her seat.

William said, "Are you okay, Keisha?"

"I need to chill for a moment, if that's all right with you."

Another ten minutes passed, during which Skip and Stephen A. argued about whether LeBron would leave the Heat at season's end while Michael's vocals glided with the magic of being in love. Going *Off the Wall*, in subtle rhythm he hoped that Keisha would relax her mind, groove with happy thoughts and help him rock the place.

It worked: his sensual, suggestive musical charm vibrated off the walls of Friday's and into her soul, causing her to answer questions William asked an eternity ago.

She said, "I don't know when my plane leaves. All I know is that I leave from LaGuardia Airport."

A Galaxy Smartphone slid across the bar in her direction.

"Call your airline while I go to the bathroom."

Ten minutes later, he returned to two plates of Chicken Alfredo on the bar.

William said, "I see you got hungry."

"Yes. Thanks for lunch."

"That means you're feeling a little better, and that's a good thing."

"Well, I'll turn a cartwheel when I leave New York."

"Did you find out the time of your flight?"

All of a sudden, discomfort returned, causing Keisha to pause. Looking at William awkwardly, she wanted to cry out, "I got nowhere else to go."

Fighting embarrassment, she said, "I'm not leaving until tomorrow morning."

"And you definitely can't go back to where you stayed last night."

"No way in hell I'm going back there."

William asked, "Do you have a place to stay? Do you have any relatives who live here?"

"Well, I have a cousin that lives somewhere in Brooklyn, but he's out of town."

"Do you need money for a hotel?"

"No, you've done enough for me by being so nice. My girlfriend Theresa in Detroit can wire me some."

"I hate to sound like your father, but…"

"My father's dead, William," she snarled.

An awkward pause ensued, during which the police detective in *Menace 2 Society* became William's conscience when it said, *Now you see? You done fucked up. You know you done fucked up, right?*

"I'm sorry, Keisha. What I meant to say was…"

"A woman's supposed to travel with something in case of an emergency. I didn't think…"

Again her face became red, an unsettling complexion of pain. Bowing her head in dejection, she felt something on her skin and flinched.

"Don't touch me!"

William, trying to take her hand, had reawakened memories of recent abuse.

"Look, Keisha," he said. "I'm sorry that I startled you. But I have an idea."

"You could have shared it without touching me!"

"My bad."

Now you see? You done fucked up again. You know you done fucked up, right?

They shared another stare. In that stare, facts were revealed without words.

"Keisha, you should never let a man hit you."

"So anyway, what's your idea?" she asked, dismissing her truth.

"When do you return to work?"

"Not anytime soon. The kids are on winter recess next week."

"Would you like to come with me to South Carolina?"

"William, are you out of your mind?"

"No, I'm not. I could use some company on the road, and it'll give you time to recover from this experience. Plus you'll be in the company of some really nice people, people that care. You already have clothes and toiletries in your travel bag, right?"

"What if I need something else to wear?"

"I'll get you another pair of jeans if you need it."

"Wait, aren't you going to see Linda's parents?'

"Yeah, and…"

"Don't you think that would be a little awkward, given your feelings?"

Taking a deep breath, William paused. Then, with a hint of frustration in his tone, he asked, "Look, am I asking you to sleep with me?"

"No."

"Okay, then. Last night you said that you came to New York to escape, right?"

"Yes, but…"

"And from the way it looks to me and my boy, Donald, you need an escape from your escape, am I correct?"

"Yeah, but…"

"Listen, the only thing that butts in life are goats and rams. So are you down or not?"

"But what would Linda's parents think?"

"Let's find out. Give me back my phone."

William searched his contacts, found the one in question and touched the screen.

"Hey, Mr. Malloy, how are you? Okay, Davis. After all these years I'm still not used to calling you that. …It's always good to know that you're okay, especially since that small stroke a couple of years… How's Mom? Tell her I'm looking forward to seeing her… Oh yeah, I'm still coming. I miss you guys… Yeah, I had a rough one last night, but I'm cool now…I wanted to know if… of course, I'm looking forward to the feast. Would you like for me to bring you some scotch? We can have that while watching the Lakers on Sunday… They play LeBron, D. Wade and the Heat. Listen, I wanted to know if I could bring a travel buddy with me? Yes, she's a woman… Stop that, man, she's just a friend. I thought you calmed down when you got older… Oh, your mind gets dirtier? That's a little too much information, but I do appreciate you giving me a glimpse into my future… Do you think Mom would mind? What do you mean she's glad to hear that? Okay, so you'll fill in the details when I get there… Listen, it's a long drive, so I want to get on the road as soon as possible… I may be getting there early in the morning. Thank goodness you guys gave me a key… Okay, I'll see you… Bye." The call disconnected and he looked at Keisha.

"Problem solved," William said. "They're glad I'm not coming alone."

Feeling ambushed, Keisha still had reservations.

"And how am I getting back to Michigan?"

"The navigational system in my Ford Taurus will take us there."

"You're going to be one driving soul."

"Don't worry. You'll be taking the wheel, too."

"Oh, really?"

"When I need a few winks you will."

"How do you know that I can drive?"

"Michigan. Auto industry. Car plants. Gee, you think?"

"But, what about Car... I mean, what about my plane ticket?"

"Can you get a refund on it?"

"I didn't buy it."

"Listen," William said, cautiously joking, "I'm not stepping on anyone's toes, am I? I don't want to have your boyfriend coming after me. It's been a long time since I kicked someone's ass."

"No worries," Keisha said, chuckling softly. "He's married."

William's eye sparkled with swagger.

"Oh, really? Well then, whoever he..."

"Carl. His name is Carl," Keisha blurted out.

"Is Ole' boy the dude that put his hands..."

Her answer came without words; she lowered her head.

"Well, I guess he's going to have to build a bridge and get over himself, isn't he?" he said.

"Look, William, I really appreciate all that you're doing, but I want to make sure..."

"Keisha, I have no expectations, nor do I want anything from you. Right now, you need a friend, and I'm available. I'm on vacation, I plan to enjoy myself and I thought traveling with someone might be fun. So I ask again, are you down, or what?"

Rapping on her core with an adventurous opportunity, a strange rapture gripped Keisha. A couple hours earlier, she had fled the scene of the second most horrible moment in her life, a traumatic experience that caused her worst nightmare to resurface.

And now here was a moment pregnant with possibility staring her in the face. She was in the presence of a man who looked past her physical, emotional and psychological bruises to offer his friendship.

Someone had put their hand out.

But could she trust it?

Before she could say anything, a song written by soul pioneers Kenneth Gamble and Leon Huff interrupted her thoughts. With a smooth Philadelphia sound, the message coming from the jukebox tapped her on the shoulder and said, *Go ahead and see what doing something like this would be like. You can trust him. He won't disappoint you.*

The lead singer hammered the point home with his soaring vocals. Hitting high notes during the bridge and breakdown, the song he sang was eerily fitting.

Let me show you how to overcome, Michael crooned.

The job will be hard, but trust me, we'll get it done, Michael sang.

With a little help from his brothers, Dr. Feelgood was at it again.

Keisha peered at possibility with soft, trusting eyes.

In return, what she saw was a cool smile and an extended hand.

And in a tone as cool as Billie Dee Williams, William asked, "Well, are you going to let me show you what I'm about, or do you want my hand to fall off?"

EIGHT

At five o' clock, he found an open spot at the Fashion Forty bar, and waited.

An hour later, what was once an intimate, orange-painted lounge in the heart of the Garment District had turned into an eclectic after-work hangout. Perched on a platform doing some computerized mixing was DJ Kaos while sexy smiles of all ethnicities sat at the brown dinner tables enjoying their mouth-watering appetizers. Taking advantage of the two-for-one drink specials were professionals socializing about dreams both real and imagined.

Passion of all flavors surrounded Carl Austin: different sizes, shapes and levels of sophistication. There were attractive women with the vision of snaring brothers with deep pockets and others making their own paper but hoping one-plus-one could erase the pain of their economic struggle. Different flavors of passion with drinks in their hands using what they owned—intelligence, emotion, sexual energy—to define their meaning of love. Diverse tastes of passion that, when alcohol-sparked, looked more stunning on the surface as it lured men into spending money on its gratification.

Unlike the pretenders in the place, brothers whose wallets breathed a huge sigh of relief because of the drink special, the well-dressed millionaire before them had enough green paper to make any passion he desired a reality.

Yet Carl Austin sat there, waiting for his martini from Keisha.

To his left, a brother made a joke about a wrinkled Barbara Bush looking like the Quaker Oats guy, a pun that made him smirk. Seeing people chill after a long week doing who-knows-what filled his heart with remorse over what happened hours earlier.

Though he had never put his hands on a woman before, something in him snapped when Keisha said that *it* was over. Hoping that he would be granted leniency for his actions, the thought of losing her left him depressed. While dedicated to his responsibilities as a lucrative lawyer, that special part of him was highly vulnerable.

Keisha's rejection of his heart, one he gave with real, pure love, was akin to someone digging up his mother's grave, opening the casket, slapping her corpse, laughing, then slapping her again.

Feeling like that made him blow a gasket.

Feeling like that made him want to kill.

Bringing ecstasy in his world, their decade-long affair stopped Father Time from invading his bloodstream. Possessing a youthful pep in his step, a four-day-a-week workout regimen had Carl feeling like a younger man. Carefully sculpted with detail and diligence, with his 12 percent body fat ratio, he was the envy of men half his age.

He looked even younger after eliminating his wrinkles with facial surgery.

Whenever she was away, Keisha remained at the forefront of his mind, and when she was around, he felt splendid, proud and happy, brilliantly complete. Taking comfort in her pleasant nature, he had thrown himself full-throttle into satisfying her every need.

Seeing her eyes as if she were there, they were as bright as some of the diamonds he'd brought her. Envisioning her beautiful glow, the solitary dimple on her right side when she smiled took him places emotionally that he had never been before. A beautiful mouth he never tired of kissing and the memory of her soft bosom only made things worse.

Learning her body completely, its fragrance and firmness, the way her sweetness felt when he parted the fleshy smile between her legs left him addicted as well. Confident that his steel broke skin made solely for him, the thought of Keisha kissing another man or submitting the sweet sounds of her sex to the sensational strokes of someone else.

The unconscionable vision filled his eyes with wickedness.

Staking ownership like a flag atop the pole in his slacks, *it's still mine*, Carl thought.

It was still *his*, all right.

That is, if she ever got there.

Soon, one hour would become two, and the number of martinis he consumed grew to three and a round of Cosmos for a group of ladies who sniffed out his prestige.

One of them, a bronze-colored siren in a low-cut dress with zipper-down front, planted herself in a seat next to him.

Aggressively making her play, she said, "You must be waiting for someone special."

"To be honest, yes," Carl replied.

"With all these women around and you being so handsome, I don't know why she kept you waiting this long."

Carl dismissed her chatter.

"The woman I'm waiting for is my wife," he said.

With emphasis, he showed off his diamond wedding band.

"Damn, baby, how long have you had that problem?"

"For over thirty years. Now, if you'll excuse me, I'd like to enjoy my space."

Undaunted, the sexy woman in knockout-tight attire revealed

her busty cleavage when she rose, the scent of Burberry Brit perfume invading his nostrils. Seductively placing a business card in front of him, she pressed her full red lips against his left ear.

"My name is Monica Greer. If you ever want to try something new, give me a call. I'll always be available for you."

With those words, on long, stunning legs she strolled to the ladies room, swaying her hips with the confidence of a woman unaffected by his truth.

After finishing his drink, Carl elected to return to the Marriott, with the hopes that Keisha may have decided to wait for his apology.

Twenty minutes later, that depressed feeling was eclipsed by anger when he saw an empty suite. The maids had gotten rid of his abuse by making up the bed and replacing the bathroom towels. In spite of the room's immaculate condition, the morning stench remained: Keisha hadn't left a trace of her presence.

Not knowing her whereabouts infuriated him further.

Calling her cell phone twice, all he received was her voicemail; texting her didn't produce a response either. He phoned Delta Air Lines to see if she moved up her flight, and as far as customer service knew, her travel plans hadn't changed; she was still scheduled to leave Saturday morning.

I bet she can't even remember her flight information, Carl thought. She didn't have any money, and he had her return ticket to Motown. Or at least he used to; removing it from his suit lapel, he ripped it up and threw it in the trash.

Alcohol fueling his frustration, Carl stopped thinking about his love for Keisha and pulled out a business card; he would deal with that later, he decided.

"Hello, Monica. This is Carl, the guy at the bar. Can you hear me?"

"Boy, that was quick," she said.

"I apologize about my rudeness earlier, and I'd like to make it up to you. What are you doing now?"

"I'm outside, getting ready to go to another spot with my girls."

"Do you really want to do that?"

"Why, what'd you have in mind?"

"Can you meet me at The View for dinner?"

"That's the revolving restaurant at the Marriott, right?"

"It sure is. Can you be here in twenty minutes?"

"Are you gonna have a Cosmo waiting for me?"

"That's not too much to ask."

"I'll be there in ten."

Touching the "End" button on his phone, Carl thought, *I have another night here. I might as well not waste it.*

At one time, she felt complete, as if life had granted her everything she'd ever wanted. Riding along clouds of joy, it seemed like the sun shined on her every day, as his true love made all the difference in the world.

But in the last decade something had changed, and lately she had been unable to control her hostility.

What am I doing wrong? Amanda Austin asked herself.

Feeling her frustration bloom, she cried herself to sleep many a night when Carl went away.

She put on a brave public façade, wearing a smile to cover her pain, although deep down she knew something was wrong with their marriage once the justifications for his constant traveling stopped. And on those rare nights when a full moon brought about physical hunger, sex became a tedious chore; workmanlike and unmemorable.

But what could she do to fix things?

Thirty years ago, she would have never thought the man who held her heart in his hands would ever make her feel like she was on her own.

Yet Amanda was alone again in their luxurious brownstone battling a lonely reality that couldn't be rocked away. As intelligent and alluring as she was—statuesque at five-feet-ten, her more-than-womanly bosom and radiant smile belied an intensity that enabled her to do 150 sit-ups straight after twenty-five minutes of cardio—she was no longer the primary consideration in her husband's life.

Bravely, she tried to suppress her loneliness by focusing on saving the lives of others. As a drug counselor at Harlem Hospital, her encouraging words lifted the spirits of many an addict on the road to recovery.

Yet like a social worker listening to case after case, she needed to purge her soul by talking to someone else.

For three decades the man whose heartbeat and body temperature was one with hers had provided a shoulder that even the strongest of women occasionally need. For three decades she was everything to Carl: his best friend, confidante, cook, motivation by day, sex siren by night.

But lately, Amanda Austin would look into her husband's eyes and see a vacant why-did-we-ever-get-married look.

From talking to a couple of her sorority sisters, ones who knew the gaze and experienced the painful I'm-leaving-you-for-a-younger-woman outcome that followed, she became edgy; difficult at times.

Renee Hampton, her line sister at Syracuse who was handed divorced papers thirty-five years after being "meant to be," told her the depression that engulfed her was akin to going through all of life's storms in a raft, only to have the damn thing deflate when you're almost to the other side of the river.

Unwilling to experience the charred feeling of emotional failure, she wasn't interested in becoming a middle-aged divorcee. Searching her soul, Amanda decided that her union was something she held important and she would fight to keep the flames burning.

Even if it meant that she suffered in silence on nights like this.

NINE

The winter twilight kidnapped the sunshine attempting to warm Keisha's heart. Bravely, she tried to filter her sadness, but a suitcase containing memories of Carl remained open, and while she turned off her phone to ignore the where-in-the-hell-are-you blitz she knew would come, periodically, tears that came from an emotional journey disrupted her peace.

And the guy at the wheel of his Ford Taurus gallantly tried to navigate her through the melting iciness.

That she agreed to this leap of faith was commencement of the healing process.

Faith will break her chains of doubt, William thought.

Doing whatever he could to offer comfort, as they headed south he changed his travel music to Miles Davis and hoped the mellow sounds would soothe her spirit. Then somewhere along I-95, William would enter the belly of her beast and discard layers of pain, leaving them in a pile on the highway for speeding cars to run over.

Help would come once he reached the Spartanburg exits on Interstate 85, but for now his mind was yelling *do something* before his noble effort crashed and burned.

If that happened, the snickering laugh of Common Sense would taunt him endlessly.

Drat, drat and double drat.

And for the first two hours of their trip, a tense stranglehold threatened to choke the life out of William's good intentions. Keisha made herself comfortable in the passenger seat, silently staring at the tenth-mile markers on the New Jersey Turnpike.

Nearing exits leading to the Atlantic City Expressway, William asked, "Keisha, do you gamble?"

In a prickly tone, she replied, "I've gambled away the last ten years of my life."

Now you see, that's three times. You know you done fucked up again, right?

"We're in no rush and we can stop at any time. Where would you like to have dinner?"

"You know this part of the country better than I do, so you tell me."

"They have a really nice seafood place at Baltimore Harbor. I can't think of the name of it right now, but I'll know it when I see it."

Keisha's mind went back to that first date with Carl: the seafood, the poet Keats, the flirtations and the way he savored every inch of her during their torrid lovemaking. Every memory reinforced her detachment struggle; each red carpet recollection tugged at her heart, making her wish her soul was back in the Big Apple. Despite doing the right thing when she raised anchor, memories of her *RMS Freedom* being docked at Carl's port restored things she tried to delete from her brain.

Yet there they were, torturing and teasing her from the recycle bin.

"Do you know of any other places?" she asked.

Keeping his eye on the road, William quizzed, "Goin' through it, huh?"

"Going through what?"

"All the memories."

"How did you know?"

"I've been where you're at, plenty of times."

"Well, maybe we can stop at an Applebee's or something along the way."

Like George Washington, they crossed the Delaware River; only their trip was made on a twin-suspension bridge that linked the Garden State with Blue Hens.

Keisha finally looked over at William and saw dejection in his eyes. She lowered her defenses.

"You know what? We can stop at the Harbor if you like."

"Keisha, are you sure you want to do that? I mean, I'm tripping over myself trying…"

"Stop trying, William, and just be. I'll be okay."

"I hate seeing you like this. I know you need your space, but I always want to help someone, not run away."

"Sometimes helping someone means giving them space to find their way."

William chuckled. "Yeah, that's always been a problem of mine," he said in a self-defecating tone.

"That's not a problem. You're very thoughtful. More men should be like you."

"Would you to like to hear a story?"

"Sure."

"On the morning of 9/11, I got off an express bus in front of a hotel across the street from the World Trade Center about eight thirty-five. I was about to go get a book from Borders in the concourse of One World Trade…"

"What type of books do you read?"

"Sports books normally. However, that particular morning I was looking for David Halberstam's…"

"*Summer of '49.*"

"Nope."

"*October 1964.*"

"How'd you know about that one? I'm impressed."

"I read books, William. I'm a schoolteacher."

"But I wouldn't expect you to… Anyway, can I finish the story without you interrupting me?"

"I'm still waiting for the name of the book you were thinking about getting from Borders."

"*The Best and the Brightest*, the one about the foreign policy decisions of the Kennedy and Johnson administrations and how they inflamed our involvement in Vietnam. Did you realize that initial reports suggested we deploy over a million U.S. troops to defeat the Viet Cong?"

"My father did a tour of duty over there," Keisha said solemnly.

"Wow. Again, I'm sorry about your father. Was he a casualty of the war?"

Feeling her neck hairs bristle, Keisha became fidgety as she again saw the recurring tragedy, the engine behind her present melodrama. Opening and closing her hands, she quickly regained her composure, though a residue of her pain escaped.

With abrupt coldness, she said, "He died in a different type of war, one I'd rather not talk about."

"Are you okay, Keisha?" William asked.

"Could you finish the story?"

"Okay. So anyway, instead of getting the book, something told me to get breakfast instead. I went to a Blimpie's on a strip called Park Row, about two hundred yards northeast of the towers, give or take a few. I'm sitting in the sandwich shop when this explosion shook the place. All of a sudden people started choking off the scent of smoke. I go outside and about fifteen minutes later I see the second plane hit."

"I bet you peed in your pants," Keisha said.

William shook his head no.

"Immediately I knew that it was a terrorist attack, so I went to police nearby offering my assistance. After fifteen minutes of helping them tell people to avoid the subways, I took a couple of pregnant women to the bathroom of a nearby restaurant, and even joked about finding the sixth cell in the movie..."

"*The Siege*, right?"

"Exactly."

The man trying to help Keisha finally exhaled when he saw the seed of hope he had planted hours earlier blossom.

"Anyway, Keisha, the reason why I shared that story is because my first instinct is to help. I hate when I'm on the subway with no money in my pockets and a panhandler is begging for change. Sometimes I close my eyes because I feel ashamed that I can't help. I always try to be my brother's keeper like the Bible says."

"I noticed that last night."

"You noticed that even through the liquor?"

"William, you have a generous spirit. I bet Linda really appreciated that."

To that point, he hadn't been thinking about his fateful anniversary, but when Keisha mentioned her name, the shadows returned. Yet for the first time since God called her home, the struggle in his eyes ceased to exist. Given a reprieve from the pain he always felt, the noose wrapped around his neck was loosened, causing him to speak freely.

"Yeah, she loved that about me, Keisha," he said. "She died today, seven years ago."

"You mentioned that to me last night, remember? By the way, I know it's a little late, but I'm glad you made it home safely. I was a little worried about you."

"Oh, so I moved up another notch in the world."

"You're still a smart-ass, I see."

"That's Mr. Smart-ass to you, Ms. Gray."

"Seriously, did you get enough rest?"

"Not really. What I felt last night is what I saw in your face this afternoon, sadness and pain."

Keisha nodded.

"Sounds like we both have demons we're running from," she said.

"Keisha, have you ever thought maybe that's why God brought us together, to help one another?"

"What makes you so sure?"

"I've been here before, too."

"You sound like Bruce Willis in one of those …"

"*Die Hard* movies," William said, finishing her sentence with a chuckle.

With a touch of sarcasm, Keisha said, "I guess Jedi Master Yoda knew that was coming too."

"I'm John McClane, and this is a *Die Hard* movie we're making, *not Star Wars*, so let's get it right," William cracked, feigning annoyance.

Keisha pinched his thigh.

"Ouch!"

"You deserved that!"

"Woman, you better not make me crash this car, or we'll be walkin' to South Carolina."

"Shoo, maybe we might need to do that."

"Do what?"

"Walk to South Carolina. It'll help me lose some of this freakin' weight."

"Keisha, what are you talking about? You look great."

"Right now I don't feel so great."

"Well, that's to be expected. You had a rough morning." Pausing, William knew where he wanted to go with the conversation, yet apprehension gripped him. The thoughts in his brain were rapid-fire: *Why would an attractive woman subject herself to physical abuse from a man? What did she find so irresistible about Carl that made her love him with all her might? C'mon, Keisha, help me help you.*

She must have had telepathy; suddenly, she went in, saying, "He never hit me before. But when I said that it was over…"

"How long were you and…"

"Ten years."

"That's a long time to be dealing with a married man."

She muttered softly, "He was very good to me."

"Hell, he should have been. What made you break it off all of a sudden?"

"He was never going to leave his wife, and I was bitten by the love bug."

"Ole' boy had Keisha sprung, huh?"

"Yes, I loved Carl," she huffed. "He's a good man who treated me right."

"He couldn't have been that good if he put his hands on you when you broke it off. If he truly loved you, he would have let go for the sake of your happiness and dealt with it. It sounds to me like Carl has control issues."

"He made a mistake, William. Haven't you made mistakes in your life?"

"Plenty."

Rolling her eyes, Keisha snapped, "Well, then, stop being so hard on a brother."

William giggled, his titter further frustrating his passenger.

"What's so funny?"

"Where's Tammy Wynette on disc when you need her?"

"Tammy Wynette?"

"Stand by your mannnn…" William crooned.

"What's that supposed to mean?"

"Are you sure you want me to answer that?"

"Please. And don't pull any punches."

"You're making excuses to justify ole' boy's…"

Keisha screamed, "For the last time, his name is Carl! If you don't get it right, I'll make you drive me back to New York."

"Why are you getting upset with me?"

"You're not being fair."

William firmed his stance. "No, *you're* not being fair. You asked me for a truth, and here it is. You're making excuses to justify the selfishness of a man that refused to leave his wife. Your boy was having his cake, eating it too, and you allowed it."

"I didn't allow anything. I chose to deal with it."

"You wasted a lot of time in second place. Now all of a sudden you were tired of being his backdoor woman, tired of being a well-kept secret and tired of downplaying your feelings, which spiraled out of control. *Tired, tired, tired*, like Chris Rock. And when you took his cake away, Carl got bent out of shape. You know, I bet he'd been saying that he'll leave her from hello, right?"

Silence.

His words were shocking in their candor. Most men would have honored the code and sugarcoated their bluntness, but Keisha asked for brutal honesty, and with that request she received an age-old truth.

That truth was this: Adulterous relationships usually ended with someone kicking rocks. And as much as Carl had put her heart on a pedestal, in the end Keisha wound up kicking rocks while holding an ice pack against the left side of her face.

The silence after William's words indicated that his crusade was working, so he continued saying, "Again, as much as he loved or was in love, he didn't leave his wife for you."

"Maybe he wanted to keep his family together. He's been married for over thirty years."

"Does he have children?"

"One. He's in college."

"His kid is grown. That's no excuse."

Keisha argued, "Put yourself in his position, one where you tell a wife and child something that would risk everything you hold important."

Famous last words, William thought before saying, "All those things were at risk anyway when he was dealing with you. Again, there should have been nothing stopping him, unless he's a prestigious man hell-bent on maintaining a certain image."

More silence and truth, the veracity of which filled the car with tension.

William couldn't miss the bull's-eye, or so it seemed.

"You're kidding me. Ole' boy, I mean, Carl, is a baller?"

"I told you he treated me good."

"He could have given you Buckingham Palace with all the trimmings. The man didn't leave his wife for you, Keisha, because he didn't want to part with his money or his image. There's something to be said about that. How you accept things dictates the level of respect you'll receive from a man. But I guess we all do what makes us feel comfortable and until this morning, you were comfortable with your conditions."

Keisha took a deep breath; one she hoped would quell an internal storm. Feeling persecuted by what she felt was a denouncement of her character, the frustration in her gut rose as she struggled to release a response.

Taking another intense breath, she controlled her ire.

"What makes you comfortable, William?" she asked.

"What makes *me* comfortable?"

"Yes, William. What makes you comfortable? Does mourning someone who told you to move on after she died make you feel like a superhero? Well, here's a dose of kryptonite, Superman: Before you start judging others, come down off your self-righteous pedestal, stop hiding behind the memory of a dead woman, pull your big boy pants up and take some chances with your heart."

Her effective counterpunch rocked William to his core, renewing sadness in his eyes and forcing a strained smile through his teeth.

Keisha, sensing imminent destruction, went on, the rage in her voice a controlled staccato tone when she said, "You need to live, brother. You know what? I bet you haven't even been on a date since Linda died, and I'll bet even more money Boy Scout Will hasn't even gotten laid."

Rendered mute, in a flash William recalled the only time he had tried.

Serena Murray, a forty-something chocolate-toned siren, had an alluring smile, generous hips and a body like her tennis namesake. She desired him once she had seen him move at a Rhythm Revue Party at Roseland and became flirtatious after he initiated a dance.

A special mix of "Remember the Time" blared from the speakers and William, needing someone to share the large ballroom dance floor with, approached her.

Tickling her fingertips with his, he grabbed her hand without asking.

Before a word escaped her full, sensuous lips, he said rather sheepishly, "I'm sorry, but this is Michael Jackson. I hope you don't mind."

DJ Felix Hernandez must have felt his presence, for after he remembered the King of Pop, he reunited him with his brothers and jammed "Dancing Machine."

"Can you do the old steps?" William asked.

"Are you serious?" Serena said.

"Watch."

About halfway through the song, he went in. Feeling the funky instrumental interlude, like a robot he did a mechanical shuffle, a triple spin at tornado speed, then took her hand, all on beat.

Analyzing his quicksilver moves in a millisecond, Serena took mental notes for her sexual scouting report, which read like this:

He has loose hips and live "electric" movements. Outstanding feel of rhythm, often dances within the beat. He's definitely not Jurassic, like your run-of-the-mill middle-aged man.

"Damn, you move like you're twenty-five," she exclaimed after completing the set.

Still bashful even in midlife, William blushed.

"Michael Jackson does that to me. Would you like to have a drink with me?"

Penetrating his senses with a sexy look, Serena agreed.

Soon, one drink led to light-flowing humorous conversation, heated advances, and a cab ride to her Upper West Side apartment to back up some sexual trash-talk. Once they entered her modern-deco apartment, hunger and desire took over.

Moving close to him as he stood by the door, she touched the heat between his legs and lustfully licked his ear lobe.

"Are you gonna be a good boy tonight?" Serena purred.

Damn. Linda used to say that.

He could have stopped there and called it a night, but the swelling at his groin overruled his brain. Breathing heavily and intoxicated by her aura, William was down for whatever; or at least he thought he was.

Tracing her lips with his index finger, he leaned closer.

"I'd rather be bad," he said sensually.

Starting with a seductive slow kiss, Serena's speedometer didn't stay at zero very long. Soon, her hunger for satisfaction began a hostile takeover of her fantastic frame, making its way from toes to tongue.

William matched her passion with his own erotic electricity. Buttons flew everywhere when he ripped off her silk blue blouse, matching bra and sexy black skirt.

"Ooh, you're an animal. I like that shit."

Hearing her words brought a moan from her partner in passion. Groaning while positioning them on her couch, his heart pounded loudly in his ears. He enjoyed her ample bosom and for the first time in years, a familiar excitement raced through his body. Arousal became his pulse as he explored her firm, Hershey-colored form.

Wildly sucking her pointed nipples, he could feel her approval growing by way of her sexy writhing, deep moans and involuntary wails. Tasting her navel, licking her athletically carved calves, then sucking on her toes, he reached her slick, saturated rainforest. Sliding a finger in, then two in and out of her dripping warmth, the flickers of her climax were like movie trailers; passionate previews of pleasure to come when she felt something thick moving within.

Rubbing his chin, then his nose against her sensitive spot, the lively lizard between William's lips began acting up as Serena begged for him to eat it.

Suddenly he saw Linda's face, and the hardness between his legs went soft.

Following suit, the desire to please the beauty at his mercy went out the window.

"Serena, look, we better stop. I can't do this."

"What's the matter?" she asked with evident fuckstration in her voice.

"I can't do this. I can't have sex with you."

Serena rose from her position in passion and stormed around the living room in her naked beauty.

"Why in the hell not?"

"Because…"

His head now aching with guilt, William spoke softly.

"I'm not ready," he whispered.

He explained at length his ordeal and gained a small measure of sympathy, but not enough from a fantastic-looking woman in heat.

Serena politely asked him to leave. "Anytime you want to finish this, you call me," she said, closing the door after letting him out.

While in the hallway, William overheard her rejected feeling while on the phone yelling to…whomever.

"I never heard a man say 'no' before… He's too old to be scared of a little… He claims he's strung out over some chick that died a few years back. It's okay though… Probably got no stroke in his back," she said to…whomever.

Shaking his head incredulously at her brutality, feeling like a fool for sharing his truth with a near one-night stand, he thought, *and the Academy Award for Best Actress in a pseudo-empathetic role goes to Serena Murray.*

A few years later, William McCall of the Academy of Motion Picture Arts and Sciences had given an Oscar to the woman seated beside him; one that pulled out her switchblade and cut him deep with truth.

And for the next seventy miles silence again visited the Taurus

Limited, becoming its best friend. The couple continued down I-295, bypassing Baltimore Harbor, Camden Yards and the home of the Ravens while Whitney Houston sang. In song, she told them that their heated exchange might have been two lonely worlds talking.

A solid hour passed, and not a word was said.

Without warning, William veered into the right exit lane, and suddenly I-295 became Route 50 West, via the New York Avenue exit.

Keisha asked, "Where are we going?"

"We have to eat, right?"

"I thought that…"

"Look, Keisha, I didn't ask you to come with me on this trip so we can argue about history. Your past is your past, and I shouldn't have been so harsh, so judgmental. If I hurt your feelings with what I said…"

She snapped, "We're cool, William."

"I'm sorry about…"

"I'm sorry, too. I said some pretty mean things also."

"You felt like your character was under attack, so you defended yourself. But you were right about me getting back into the dating game. My boy Steve told me the very same thing this morning."

With compassion she said, "I bet it's hard for you."

William nodded. "And to answer your question… No, I haven't had sex since Linda died."

"Really?"

"Yes really."

"I don't believe you."

"Why would I lie about it? I've abstained for seven years."

Silence.

Keisha tried to suppress her surprise, but a sly, one-sided smile in his direction gave her thoughts away.

Flirting, she said, "If you'd like, I could help you out."

While lights of surprise flickered in his brain, William's heart lurched in his chest. It was a miracle he didn't crash the car.

"Who said I needed help?"

"Well, I figured since you were kind enough to…"

"I appreciate the offer, but no thanks." Chuckling, he muttered, "Boy, that's a first."

"A first?"

"In all my forty-seven years on earth, I never met a woman bold enough to offer herself to me that way."

"In what way?"

"That way."

She asked again, "In what way, William?"

"That way!"

Pause.

Keisha said, "You can't even say it! You're shy, aren't you?"

"I have my moments."

"We're mature adults, William, and we all have urges and needs. We all need maintenance at some point. I'm an independent woman, yet I like to be spoiled, held and made soft by the touch of a man every now and then. Needs and maintenance are human nature."

"I respect everything you just said, Keisha, but at this point in my life, I hope I'm wired different in that my brain overrules the head downstairs."

Easier said than done.

There was another pause, during which the man at the wheel felt a tingling in his trousers. It'd been a long time since he'd felt the inside of a woman's wet enigma, one given to men either for consummation or during a momentary diversion. Longing for feminine marks on his back while seeing a glassy-eyed look in her eyes, the flesh at his groin missed swimming in a woman's slickness, missed the lively feeling that came with pumping, pleasing, the slapping sounds and the sweat, missed hitting spots that caused greedy gasps and out-of-control rhythm that came with making a woman feel good all over; and missed the shuddering wave that captured him while releasing.

Whether in love or lust, after seven years of celibacy, William and the flesh between his legs missed the joys of sex, but he wouldn't settle for satisfying his lustful cravings. He was a middle-aged man who'd been spoiled by a woman who bonded purpose, passion and God's most precious energy, one that created a nocturnal partnership better than any Fred and Ginger tap dance performed on the silver screen.

The reason why sex with Linda was amazing was because of love, and William wanted to be touched by love again before the lust.

Still, he was flattered by Keisha's unique thoughtfulness.

Finally he said to her, "Like I said before, I never had an attractive woman make an offer just because."

It became Keisha's turn to pause.

"I can't believe a handsome man who hasn't had any in seven years said no to me. You must be starving."

"I'm not a robot. I have my cycles of horniness. But I choose not to act on them."

"What, are you scared that you're going to have a heart attack or something?"

"My heart is definitely not a problem. I had a physical last week, and the doctors said that I have the metabolism of a middle distance runner."

Running her hand through her natural black hair, Keisha said, "You know, I really admire your self-control, especially since they say a man thinks about sex once every fifty-two seconds."

"Who said that?"

"Dr. Louann Brizendine, author of *The Female Brain*. You should read it sometime, along with…"

"Trust me, Keisha, I've read my share of how-to books. *The Hite Report*, all the books by Alexandra Penney; *How to Drive Your Woman Crazy in Bed*, *The Sensuous Man*, *The Sensuous Woman*…"

William's voice trailed off. Reestablishing boundaries with a reality check, he continued. "I am *your friend*, Keisha. Right now you need that more than penetration, and I need that more than trying to get some of what I would probably enjoy. The left side of your face told me that. We're just friends, on a little trip."

"Okay," Keisha said, her voice not quite seductive but…curious.

"Okay," William repeated.

Silence.

Silent thoughts running all over the place.

We're just friends, on a little trip, the driver thought as they entered the nation's capital.

If his eyes weren't glued to the bright lights, nightlife traffic and electricity filling the streets of Barack and R.G. III, he would have met the gaze of feline-shaped eyes and a pretty face wearing the look of a cat burglar.

A cat burglar stealing looks while admiring the candor and kindness of something unfamiliar.

TEN

His step was a little slower and the hair that remained was mixed; yet he stood sturdy, much like Ossie Davis in those twilight years. He had suffered a mild stroke a couple of years back yet remained sharp and lucid, thanks to a soul mate that challenged him with Scrabble and chess matches at his hospital bed.

Davis Malloy, the retired gynecologist, still had a lot of living to do; not only for him, but also for the lovely lady by his side.

"I'm never letting your mother go," he said to his stepdaughter years earlier. An old school lover that preferred Sam Cooke, The Delfonics and Temptations to "today's noise," his words to Linda were on the square.

And dancing behind an amorous beat after all these years was a woman that still adored his affection.

Mamie Woodson beamed proudly at her shining knight, much like Ethel Thayer did when gazing at her Norman in *On Golden Pond*. Thanking God every day for a second chance at love— her first husband, Julian, was tragically killed—a small framed, cocoa-complexioned librarian with bowed legs was humbled when, like Ruby Dee, her Heavenly Father reignited those magnetic sparks with a man who not only worshipped his queen but her daughter as well.

And on those steamy nights where time stood still, the statute her husband had at his groin still fit her to a "G."

Over thirty years later, two near-octogenarians loved each other like giggly high school kids.

However, one winter day almost rocked Mamie Woodson to her core.

For seven years, this mother had missed her daughter.

However, every February 15, this mother missed her baby.

Knowing what she had endured bringing her into the world—as Linda entered, Mamie almost left it when massive bleeding and two strokes had her in a coma for three weeks—only intensified the pain of Lucky leaving the world first. The tears came at that exact hour she closed her eyes, and memories of mother and daughter flashed through her mind: her first steps, that birds-and-bees-talk, her senior prom, the mother-woman Sunday conversations, the college and master's degree from SUNY New Paltz, the many days of comfort she provided when Linda was told she was barren, the cancer, and how she would read to her until that final day.

The memories replayed throughout the day and emotional downpours were scattered throughout. And as much bravery as Davis displayed for them both; on February 15, sometimes valor wasn't enough.

Seeing their adopted son always helped. Both parents felt the fuel of rocket love in their veins when he visited, an overwhelming, uncontainable rush of joy.

But until he arrived, they decided on a slumber party, watching a *Golden Girls* DVD on their plasma television into the wee hours. Spooning on their chocolate sofa with lounger, they chuckled through the "Thank you for being a friend" intro, and gales of laughter were more intense during the happy musical interludes.

Like the studio audience, they loved the bright, sexy, witty humor of four senior citizens in Florida.

And like the audience and millions of fans that turned to NBC every Saturday night, they weren't ready for their tearful farewell.

But seven years is a lifetime in television years, and nostalgia would endure forever in syndication, outliving Sophia, Blanche and Dorothy.

Seven years of memories also lived in the box sets.

Ironically, this night the couple decided to watch that final episode, and so many thoughts filled the air.

As the opening credits played, there sat Sophia and Rose sharing a quiet moment in character, yet in real-time feeling the conclusiveness of their journey.

"Given your job experience, I know you ran across a few Blanches in your lifetime," Mamie joked.

"So many that I married my own," Davis responded.

"What's that supposed to mean?"

"I have a hot-looking woman that still looks sexy even as she approaches—"

"Davis!"

"Aw, baby, you knew I was going to say you age like Jack Benny, forever thirty-nine."

The strong lines in Mamie's forehead playfully crinkled.

"You're really sinking yourself now, you old poop."

"How's noting that you're thirty-nine sinking myself?"

"You know damn well you always tell a woman that she looks twenty-four or younger!"

Continuing their loving charade, Davis shamefully tucked his head neatly in his wife's back.

"Well, I guess I know my punishment."

"The old poop gets none of Mama's loving until the kids leave."

Noting the time, Davis said, "They should have been here already."

A pause followed, during which all thoughts returned to South Florida and those four ladies of laughter. Dorothy Zbnornak gave love another shot with Uncle Lucas, a character played by Leslie Neilsen.

"So good that they named their sex, 'honey,'" Davis quipped.

"They sound like us."

"Dammit, Mamie, I gotta wait until Sunday for some…"

"Big Daddy, they'll be here soon."

Finally the ladies tearfully said goodbye to what was, in the eyes of Bea, Estelle, Rue and Betty, a pleasant senior moment.

"Baby, are you okay?" Davis asked, slowly sitting up on the sofa.

Mamie, knowing where he was going, wiped her eyes.

"That ending gets me every time."

"Mamie…"

"I miss her so much."

"I do, too. You've been very brave this year."

"Each year it gets a little better."

"I can't imagine what you must be going through."

"With you, Davis, I feel I can do anything, even cope with the loss of my baby. I'm not saying it's easy. You've seen the tears, heard my cries. But knowing that you're here eases the pain."

"I'll be here to love you until God returns me to dust and lifeless bones." After a tender peck, Davis changed topics with the ease of a champion ice skater. "I'm glad to hear that William's bringing someone with him. That's a hell of a drive to do alone."

"He's been doing a lot alone for years," Mamie added.

"Do you think he feels something for this woman?"

"He's bringing her here, so I guess she's important."

"I'm gonna talk to him," Davis decided.

"I'll tell you what, she better be worth his time, or I'll cuss her out from 'Amazing Grace' to how sweet the sound."

"Behave yourself, woman."

As much as they appreciated his nobility, the elderly couple hoped their adopted son would become a bold eagle and soar above the annual storm that lowered their spirits.

So at three in the morning, the elders decided to give their adopted son a push from the nest.

Then they fell asleep in each other's arms.

There were reminders everywhere: the pictures of mother and daughter during happy times and some with Davis and William for good measure.

The bedroom furnishings where she slept remained the same as well. The queen-sized bed, matching night tables with polished silver lamps, the scented candles, a beautiful rose-colored armoire and a mirrored dresser with silver handles; all of which filled the surroundings with peace. There were rose drapes banded with a pink satin cord, and a mountain of pink and lavender pillows rested on a rose comforter.

Like jazz notes clashing to create blended harmony, a big black football helmet bearing the Pittsburgh Steelers logo was on the dresser next to a football autographed by Mike Tomlin; one that Linda received when the head coach of the six-time Super Bowl Champions heard of her unlucky plight. Hanging outside of a walk-in closet was a Lynn Swann jersey, and on the floor was a team rug and matching slippers.

The only thing Lucky loved more than her Steelers was a man she'd met on a bench in Hoboken.

Keisha Gray also felt like she clashed with the environment, so much so that she lay awake as the rest of the house slept.

If Linda meant so much to him, then why would he have me in here?

Her tension headache building, unknowingly William added to her lonely world with the resting arrangement. Arriving an hour after the Malloys' tumble into wonderland, they brought in their belongings and tiptoed ever-so-quietly upstairs.

At the bedroom door he whispered, "You can crash up here. I'll sleep in the basement."

Instantly, the mirth created over dinner in the nation's capital and rest of the journey south vanished.

Before Keisha could protest, he was gone, surfing to catch a wave of sleepiness he felt as they neared Spartanburg on I-85.

She rubbed the left side of her face and felt the senses returning, yet her cheek remained as puffy as the confusion that clouded her mind. *What will Linda's parents think when they see my face? What do I say to them? I'm a foreigner in the South with a kind stranger still recovering from a tragic loss. Why in the hell am I here? I wonder what Carl's doing...*

Holding herself hostage to agony, once again she allowed tears to trickle down her cheeks.

Although they had left behind New York's winter chill, the coldest day of her life followed her seven hundred miles and Keisha had nothing to cover or comfort her, nothing to cling to. Daylight couldn't quell the terror that swallowed her peace and no one was there to tell her everything would be okay.

Bravely, her mind countered her confusion with a reality check: Carl Austin was a man creeping on his wife and one who had slapped the tar out of her when she decided the number two was no longer their lucky number.

Keisha clutched and tugged at the collar of an oversized baby blue T-shirt, hoping to redirect her heart.

A soft knock on the bedroom door temporarily ended her state of flux.

A maternal voice on the other side asked, "Are you decent?"

"You can come in."

Opening the door slightly, Mamie was concerned when she saw the mouse under Keisha's eye.

Weakly disguising an anxious grimace, she said, "You're up early, dear."

"I have a lot on my mind," Keisha responded.

"I'm Mamie Woodson, Linda's mother."

Standing, a woman in pain bravely tried to smile.

"William said so many wonderful things about you on the way here. I'm Keisha Gray," she said, extending her hand.

"Child, family doesn't do handshakes. Come give me a hug."

Keisha shuddered from her maternal touch, then collapsed into her arms.

Holding her tight, then tighter, Mamie was obedient to her motherly instincts, which caused her to say, "Baby, whatever it is, know that God brought you to the right place. We'll take care of you here. If you want to talk, we'll talk about it. And if you don't, then I understand."

Finally releasing her human lifesaver, Keisha paddled ashore to a safe land filled with the promise of better days.

"I'm so sorry to hear about your daughter," she said, returning to the bed. "I know it must be tough, even after seven years."

Mamie smiled.

"I miss my baby, but I've found peace in two things: one, she's in a place where she's not suffering; and two, God blessed me with a beautiful child, even for a brief moment in time."

"William really loved her."

"I know. Keisha, there's a lot of sunshine in that man sleeping in the basement, not to mention a strength that's contagious. He gives and gives, and when you think he has nothing left, the Good Lord gives him more to work with. He's a walking blessing that's helped both Davis and I immeasurably."

"He's trying to help me, too." On cue, Keisha put her soul on display, telling her life story, leaving little detail out while battling emotions that were suppressed way too long. Mamie choked back tears when she spoke of watching domestic abuse that culminated in brutal death and commended her for not allowing history to repeat itself.

She asked, "Does William know about your parents?"

Keisha shook her head no, then posed her own question. "Ms. Woodson, did you ever think that life was unfair?"

"Sure, baby. I lost my first husband to the bullets of drug dealers when I was pregnant with Linda, and almost died in the delivery room. And seven years ago my baby returned to God. I thought I wouldn't survive all that, but somehow I found the strength to stand, brush myself off and press forward. It's not easy, because we're flesh and blood, filled with all kinds of imperfect stuff. But you reach deep."

"After what happened to my mother, I wouldn't…"

"And your father. You need to forgive him," Mamie interrupted.

"Not to be disrespectful, Ms. Woodson, but I was right the first time I said it. For a long time I wouldn't let anyone close to me, but I still had needs," Keisha confessed.

Analyzing her words, Mother Woodson nodded to herself. "What woman doesn't have needs? Before I met my Davis, I had my share of Misters, but I was careful about the men I brought around my daughter."

"Did you take advantage of any of them? Did you hurt anybody while dealing with your hurt?"

"Never. I asked nothing from them other than time."

"I can't say the same," Keisha confessed. "I've been very selfish."

"In other words, you were masturbating."

"Masturbating?"

"I didn't stutter, child. You're so afraid to forgive your father for what he did to your mother that you made it your business to satisfy all your needs with little regard to what others felt. Instead of sharing your heart, you selfishly masturbated the love you had inside all over the place, leaving sticky situations for others to deal with. Sooner or later, that life catches up with you. It always does, because no one's heart remains impenetrable."

"Men play with our feelings all the time," Keisha argued.

"Some of them do, my child. But let me ask you something personal: Has anyone other than your father hurt you?"

As always the case, wisdom silenced the young. No words left Keisha's mouth.

But more words left Mamie, who said, "From the way it looks in my seat, for years you spoke an entitlement language. Try giving more of yourself as opposed to taking all the time. Stop masturbating and give your all to someone other than yourself."

Finally, Keisha spoke.

"I did. I fell in love with Carl."

"The married guy?"

"Yes."

"Are you sure that you loved him, or were you playing it safe by leaving yourself an escape hatch?"

"I loved him with all my heart."

"Did you really love him, or did you love the terms and conditions of your relationship, which were to your advantage?"

More silence, which meant Keisha was again being dunked in soul-searching waters. For years she was heartbroken, assuaging her pain in the gifts that Carl lavished upon her; masking deep hurt with shopping sprees, exotic trips and sexual moments.

What she failed to realize was that she was not drowning her pain; she was *drowning in it*. And if she were submerged totally, all possibilities of finding real love would float to the surface lifeless, like a piece of old wood. Sure, sexy lingerie and nights of disconnected passion would provide temporary joy; not to mention the fact that she would continue to do as she pleased. But at fifty years old selfish masturbation by way of manipulation grows stale, especially when a person grows old and the reality of being alone stares at them.

Other than self, Mamie said, everyone needs somebody to love.

Other than self, Mamie said, everyone wants unconditional love.

And in order to receive that kind of love Mamie said, you must be willing to give from your heart sans expectation.

Ever since her father pulled the trigger on that Remington 870, Keisha had allowed fear and anger to deny her a love all her own, a point emphasized by what came next from Mamie.

"You're a lioness looking at your reflection in a pond. Although you're attractive and self-sufficient, you still don't like what you see in those waters. If you did, then you wouldn't restrict yourself to dead-end love. It's time for you to stop looking in that pond and hold your head high. And remember that a lioness' pride, the family your heart has craved since your parents' death, might be staring back at you from across that pond."

Pausing, Keisha Gray took time to digest Mamie's gospel. She had spent years devaluing her worth, settling for half-empty as opposed to full, complete love. Yet in leaving Carl the shades of hope were lifted slowly, revealing a brilliant, beautiful work in progress. She had made mistakes, yes, but she was resilient. She had flaws, but she wasn't a weak woman. And yes, she was afraid of giving and receiving unconditional love.

She realized the root of the problem had been the woman in the mirror, and as a work of progress, she was willing to pick thorny issues off herself daily. Some thorns would always remain, for she was imperfect, a constant work in progress. But with Mamie Woodson's gospel, this work in progress was infused with new life and deserved unconditional love from another work in progress; one that would be a love all her own.

Keisha looked into Mamie's eyes, lustrous brown pupils that sparkled in spirit and truth.

A warm smile eclipsed the sadness hanging overhead.

"You're right," she admitted. "I've been beating myself up over things I had no control over, so much so that I wouldn't let anybody in. And when I finally cracked the door, it was for someone who wasn't available, which meant I never really opened that door."

Rising from the bed, Mamie said, "So what are you waiting for? Stop letting fear prevent you from opening that door."

"Yeah, I guess it's time."

"You know there's a guy in the basement..."

"Ms. Woodson..."

"Yes?"

"Don't even go there."

"Child, let's make breakfast for the guys."

Emphasizing the establishment of a new bond, they shared a laugh that only women sharing secrets recognize.

The Saturday was overcast, yet the buttermilk pancakes, turkey bacon, rib-eye steak, Mamie's special home fries, cheese grits and freshly squeezed orange juice made everyone's morning bright as the sunny-side-up eggs Davis loved so much.

Confirming such, he said to his wife, "Damn, baby, you really put your foot in the food."

Mamie yelled out, "I can tell. You're eating like no one's around, smacking and using your fingers like a wild animal."

"Baby, only you know the place where I'm a wild animal."

"You got that right, sugar. What do the kids say today, you're the bomb-diggity?"

"You're damn skippy!"

Leaning close, they shared a slow, patient peck.

Across the lavish kitchen table, two wounded souls looked on.

Keisha asked, "Are they always this mushy?"

Smiling, William replied, "I'm afraid so."

Davis responded immediately. "Y'all should try this."

Mamie playfully frowned. "Stop that, baby. You know they just met."

The silence that came from the other side of the table screamed embarrassment and tension.

"I don't know, Mamie. Those kids look right for each other."

Mamie sang, "Matchmaker, matchmaker, make me a match, find me a find…"

Davis announced, "They don't know anything about Zero Mostel…"

"And *Fiddler on the Roof*," William interjected, completing his sentence.

Keisha chimed in, singing in beautiful tone, "Sunrise, sunset." Her voice, while untrained, had a spiritual sound that caught everyone at the table off-guard.

Sharing a knowing smile, the Malloys exchanged a look like they knew something the pair across the table didn't. They saw a man fighting to conceal his love impulse and a woman afraid to reach out unknowingly trying to connect the dots to their hearts. Together, their pain connected like algebra, two negative dilemmas equaling a positive solution.

The senior couple knew the deal; that they were witnessing the beginning of something, and that two parties brought together by way of chance did not.

"I sang in choirs growing up in Michigan," Keisha said sheepishly.

"You didn't tell me that over dinner," William protested.

"You didn't ask."

"Don't ever make that mistake again, William," Mamie warned.

Pointing across the table, William joked, "Mr. Malloy, look at what you started this morning."

"You did that to yourself, son. The women got you so rattled that you can't even call me Davis."

"Sisterhood," William mocked. "There ought to be a law against immediate chemistry."

Together, everyone laughed. Sharing revelations and more laughter, William's adopted parents took a liking to Keisha and by meal's end, a comfortable rapport had replaced her initial anxiety. Mamie Woodson felt like she had found another daughter and Davis joked with her as if he had known her forever.

They moved to the living room where Keisha asked, "How did you know that she was the one for you, Davis?"

Puffing out his chest like a proud rooster, he looked at his wife and smiled fondly. "I knew she was a light in the sky that dimmed any rainbow's glow."

Now seated on the sofa, Keisha continued her query, asking Mamie, "And how did you know he was the man for you?"

"From the way he made sure my Linda was okay after he told her that she couldn't have children." After hearing the story of Linda's hysterectomy, Keisha's eyes watered with regret when she admitted her tubal ligation procedure.

Thinking she would hear harsh criticism once she learned the retired doctor's profession, instead, she received empathy.

"I don't know what lay on the other side of that door," Davis said, pointing to the front of their home, "but judging a person's past doesn't fly around here. Your past is your past."

William, leaning over to her position on the sofa, tapped her.

"You heard that hours ago, didn't you?"

Keisha exhaled, and then asked Mamie, "Did it bother you that your husband was a gynecologist?"

"Child, please," Mamie scoffed. "If anything, that told me that he knew his way around a woman's body."

Keisha blushed.

So did William.

But soon, William's blush turned to sadness when the conversation shifted to Linda. Memories of Lucky were bandied about between Davis and Mamie, recollections that made them smile, yet tore away at his spirit.

Once again, the memory of a lost love clobbered him over the head. For twenty minutes he stayed and listened to the chatter, but once the windows to his soul revealed pain, he stood.

"Excuse me," he said politely. He made his way through the kitchen, opened a door near the end of the back porch and ventured down some stairs. Turning on the lights to the basement, he made a beeline to the full bar, fixed himself a shot of Johnny Walker and downed it quickly. He tried to dissolve the tears flowing down his cheeks with another shot, then another.

The whiskey wasn't working.

Suddenly he heard music, by way of a surround sound system.

Aaliyah's voice filled the room, singing a Donny Hathaway classic about giving up.

"Mind if I join you?"

It was Davis, planting himself on a barstool.

Bravely, William smiled.

"A shot of Black Label, young fella." Noticing his drink, he added, "That's pretty strong stuff you're drinking."

"I need it, Davis."

Obliging to the request, a shot glass filled with Black Label came his way. Swiftly downing the shot, his elder asked for another and tossed it back as quickly.

"Good whiskey screams sophistication," Davis said.

"And bad whiskey stumbles like a drunk redneck in the mud," William added.

"You've learned your lessons well."

"Thanks for teaching me the difference."

For two minutes, there was silence.

Then Davis said, "I bet you any amount of money Donny hugged her when she walked through those pearly gates."

"I didn't know that you knew about this remake."

"What, you think because I'm old I don't appreciate good music? That youngster sang the hell out of this."

"She sure did," William agreed.

The two men sat there deep in thought as Aaliyah went away. Fittingly, Stevie Wonder's "Seems So Long" followed.

Davis asked, "Have you ever paid attention to the lyrics?"

Nodding, William listened intently, and found irony in every word. A lady love had left him in a world that, by the middle of a second decade of a new century, seemed frostier than ever. Linda had returned to her Maker, leaving him longing to feel the love from a hand craving this energy as much as he. In this crazy world of dating that seemed to glorify reality-show drama, cynicism and defense mechanisms, it had been seven years since he had trusted a woman with his heart, but it was time to search that special place, that deep place within. Once it was revealed that an ember of affection still burned, he would try again; provided he found someone to trust, to hold, and to love.

As the song ended, William looked at his elder.

Davis said, "Keisha told us that you weren't going to visit Linda's gravesite."

"No. I can't." Pulling a folded red envelope from his pants pocket, William handed it to Linda's stepfather.

After reading the note inside, Davis gave it back, paused to gather his thoughts and took a deep breath. "William, you know how much Linda meant to all of us. But even she encouraged you to move forward with your life."

"It's not that easy, Davis."

"You're not getting any younger. How old are you?"

"Forty-seven."

"Are you ready to quench your thirst, bachelor lion?"

"What's that supposed to mean?"

"An older bachelor lion should want to quench his thirst by allowing himself to fall in love."

"I did that with your stepdaughter," William contested. "And she's gone."

"Yeah, sadly, she's gone, and back into the wilderness you went with the other bachelor lions, running around looking impressive in a group, but sad and scared alone. You're not shallow like younger bachelor lions, but your edges are jagged, and your mane is beginning to deteriorate. William, you have to wander away from your fears to quench your internal thirst for love. Most men hide their fears behind machismo for years, running with packs of bachelor lions until they realize they're too stubborn to compromise, too set in their ways to change. And then the emotional alarm clock goes off, waking them up too late to share life with a woman."

William sat there, speechless, soaking in Davis' words. In less than three years, he would be fifty years of age, and Lord knows he was weary of the cautious starts and painful stops that accompanied the quest for love. Given a taste of the real thing from a strong sister from Sparkle City, a healthy morsel of hope, although Linda Woodson had returned to God, she provided a blueprint of strength; a point emphasized when Davis continued.

"Sometimes, the pond that quenches your thirst for love might be far away, and you have to leave a cluster of bachelor lions to receive what God has in store for you. But that journey can become a place of cleansing, one where issues, insecurities, pain and tragic loss are left along the road. That journey gets you ready to love again. Son, you've been on that journey for seven years. Your season of mourning is over. Go take another sip from the pond."

Dramatically making his point, the wise man rose.

"Thanks for the drink, bartender," he said, leaving his adopted son sitting behind the bar, alone in thought.

For a solid hour the troubled man analyzed Davis' words, allowing them to stir in his soul.

Then he stood up.

His eyes were focused, but his hands trembled and his heart carried a two-ton boulder. With no words, he moved upstairs, struggled with the range of feelings that caused his bottom lip to quiver, made his way through the kitchen, walked past the trio sitting in the living room—totally ignoring Keisha and Mamie's "Where are you going?" surprise quiz and Davis' "Leave him be, he's got some business to take care of" response—grabbed his suede leather coat from the closet, put on his shades, unlocked his whip with his car keys, opened the house door, and bolted out.

William had something to do.

Making his way through the entrance of the cemetery, he navigated his Ford Taurus through a series of twists and turns before stopping behind a series of cars waiting to vacate the premises.

Her parked his vehicle, took an arrangement of lilies from the backseat and made his way downhill on a concrete path. While it was a well-maintained graveyard, the architecture of the grounds seemed outdated; the overcrowded cemetery was over a hundred years old.

Soon, the paved walkway turned to soft dirt, and he continued his trek, carefully sidestepping the resting place of many ancestors. Further adding to the congestion was a sad procession of mourners who had come to bury a seventeen-year-old baby, one who made the bad decision: He tried to rob a convenience store with an unloaded gun and was shot dead by the local authorities, thus creating a major controversy.

Seeing the wide range of emotions while passing, William released a powerless sigh.

Another brother lost before he found his way. God, grant that mother Your peace.

A gentle breeze captured the sixty-two-degree weather, making the air a little chilly.

Finally, he reached a clear area where there was a single plot beneath a shady tree. The headstone simply read: "LINDA WOODSON—GOD'S MIRACLE BABY August 29, 1958– February 15, 2007."

That was the way she'd wanted it: no fuss or fanfare, just a simple resting place devoid of recognition for the extraordinary life she lived, William mused. In a unique way, Linda's humility reminded him of God's only begotten son, a man who had performed miracles yet never stuck around to admire his handiwork.

He simply kept it moving.

Seven years earlier, William's "Lucky Lady," a vehicle of love that lived with the God in her on full display for all to see, saved his life and kept it moving.

Placing the letter near her headstone, then her flowers, "Hey, Baby," William said softly as he sat in front of her grave. "I remember how much you loved lilies and brought some for you. I know it's been a minute since I've been here, but that note you left jammed me up for a while. Baby, you filled my life with so much love that it took years for me to grasp the reality that you were gone. In those precious months we shared, you were everything that I ever wanted and needed.

"So many nights I've wished you were here, smiling, laughing and making me whole again. But I know God needed a special angel to handle some special assignments, and He called on you. Lord knows, I wish He would have waited, but I try not to question His master plan for us all.

"It hasn't been easy for me. Life can be so cold, and the people living in this world even more ruthless. But one thing that I carry with me is the love we shared, and I try to show it in everything I do. When I do that, you continue to live, for you embodied all that God intended people on this earth to be.

"Your parents are doing well. I check on them from time-to-time, but during this visit they parroted the words in your letter, that I should move on. It's so hard, Linda. You were a rare diamond, one that shined with love and peace as the pressures of life got tougher. You took my heart, mind, body and soul on a pleasurable ride and I was under a spell where I fell in love anew every single day. While I'm aware of the fact that each love experience should be different, the connection we shared, one that filled me up emotionally, spiritually and physically was, and will always be unbreakable.

"But you, Steve, Davis, Mamie and Keisha—I'll tell you about her one day—are right; I must move on. The memories will come, and I'll smile, maybe shed a tear or two of unmitigated joy. Thinking of you every step of the way, I'll transfer some of the love we shared into motivation to love again, totally, with sensitivity and transparency.

"I want to love again with a bond so unbreakable that even you might be a little jealous. Then again, you'll probably smile, because you always want the best for me. That's how unselfish you were.

"Until that unbreakable love comes along, one that makes me oblivious to the selfish world I live in, I will remember you fondly, and thank you for renewing my hope that real love exists, whether it's for a minute or a lifetime. You showed me this and I thank God every day for the experience of loving you. And knowing that a woman like you loves me forever makes me feel doubly blessed. Thank you, Lucky, for loving me unconditionally for all eternity."

Wiping away a single tear as he rose, the sun broke through the clouds that followed him to this gravesite.

She's smiling, William thought as he walked away.

Although she was gone, the paradise that was Linda Woodson would always live within him.

Now it was time for William to create a new paradise here on Earth.

UNBREAKABLE

THE SECOND SINGLE...

(We'll get back to the story in a tick, but my publisher, Zane, has ordered another single, so back into the studio I go.)

PLEASE DON'T DUMP YOUR HATE ON ME...

(Inspired by "Why You Wanna Trip On Me...")

In 1991, Michael Jackson wanted a new sound. After three ground-breaking albums with Quincy Jones—OFF THE WALL, THRILLER, and BAD—his vision was to adopt a thought-provoking formula that made you dance. Enter Teddy Riley and the New Jack Swing. Fusing Hip-Hop and R&B, Riley blended street beats, soulful voices, and samples to create an aggressive musical swagger. Rappers and singers combined edgy grooves with drum machines while paying homage to Black Music's roots. Bobby Brown, Keith Sweat, Guy, Blackstreet, Heavy D and The Boyz, SWV and En Vogue all influenced this new foundation, but the New Jack Swing needed someone to seal its place in history; someone... DANGEROUS.

DANGEROUS became the sound's biggest-selling album. It's easily my favorite Michael Jackson album not only for the way Teddy's wizardry complemented MJ's musical muse, but because of the social commentary within the framework of the songs. One of which, "Why You Wanna Trip on Me," allows me to make another statement.

follow me: Ocean Way Recording Studio Complex, Holly-wood, California is where Teddy Riley and William Fredrick Cooper jammed to a Michael Jackson record. They filled the

Record One control room air with artistic personality and spoke a shared language about unity and love as Michael's layered vocals added to the scenery.

"That electronic snare gives it kick," William said. "And what's that trick you did with the background vocals?"

"Don't worry, Coop. You're singing lead on the remake, so I'll hook you up," Riley announced. A sudden firmness captured the mood when he continued. "You have to sing this song… In actuality, you need to…"

Perplexed, William asked, "What's with the urgency behind me singing it?"

Suddenly, the music stopped.

Teddy imagined what The King of Pop would say.

With profound sadness in his eyes, a musical genius behind a slick series of sharp beats and his vision of the greatest entertainer who ever lived, shared a look that said, *He doesn't know, does he?*

Still mired in darkness, William said, "What?"

Teddy Riley approached the author. Long before he was a hit-making prodigy with a signature sound, long before Michael Jackson chose him to work on a socially conscious work of art, he was a kid from the streets of Harlem who kept it real.

And this was one of those times where it called upon his roots to deliver a message. Taking the writer to the side, he explained to him what was needed; for him to go deep, for him to get personal with his issues, for him to heal with his own words and help others in the process.

Again, William asked, "What do you want me to say?"

Peering through a periscope, Riley saw his emotional vulnerability. "Do what Michael would have done: Tell the truth, brother. What drove you to the hospital in 2008? What was the reason for the suicide hotline call three years later?"

"Okay, I get it…" William snapped, the tears in his eyes threatening to spill over his lids.

"Growth is painful, Coop," Riley said, his voice barely above a whisper.

"Yep, yep."

Once the musical mastermind heard his trademark slogan, he smiled. Knowing his New York brother was about to bring energy, depth and substance to his sound, he hoped the musical statement would inspire those who battled chemical imbalances and life's hardships; all while delivering a message to those who don't understand that every human has a breaking point.

Teddy Riley knew what to say next.

"Michael Jackson spoke his mind through the music and I want you to do the same. Think of artistic family members who battled this sickness. Fill the cracks and crevices in their hearts with your words. And Coop, I want you to give me something that rattles the souls of our ancestors. In spite of Barack's accomplishment, many of our brothers are still being systematically destroyed; by drugs, self-hate and racism. And think about Trayvon Martin, the killer that took his life before it started and the hometown verdict. Now go into that sound room, get on that mike and HURT ME!"

Stepping to the microphones in the world's most respected studio complex, one that allowed Sinatra, Nat King Cole, Mick Jagger and Kanye West to create history, an author raised in the West Brighton Projects on Staten Island had his marching orders. After a killer guitar solo signaled the onset of a funky lick by Teddy, a poppin' snare and the steady thump of the "Why You Wanna Trip On Me" instrumental occupied the room.

And William Fredrick Cooper, summoning deep emotions from his core, had a job to do. In a clipped tone he would let his truth fly with purpose.

Hurt this jam, for Michael Jackson and the thing called the New Jack Swing.

Hurt this jam for all those who warred with depression, some winning, and others...

Hurt this jam for a race that in spite of accomplishment and progression, still should recognize the struggle.

Hurt this jam for a fallen son.

And more important, hurt this jam while finding closure with a painful chapter of his life.

PLEASE DON'T DUMP YOUR HATE ON ME
(Hear MJ's voice and follow original lyrics below)

FIRST VERSE
Depression's victim?
The pills were in his hand
How big were his problems
Please try to understand
He had no employment
His spirit was in need
And people 'round town
Sat there hatin' on me

Who said it'd be easy
Almost left him on the street
You had many people
Who turned their backs with glee
There were many hookers
Bangin' on his door
You had dope dealers

Who thought they were the cure
Please spare me...

CHORUS
Please don't dump your hate on me
Please don't dump your hate on me...
Quit hatin'

SECOND VERSE
He had more drama
Than his eyes could see
He popped one sleeping pill
A couple more made three
Wrote that goodbye letter
Then God intervened
He said it's not your time
He said I'm all you need

You've got a bad condition
This sickness makes you weak
You've got so much potential
My Son just lean on me
I've got words for cynics
Trying to break your spirit
Repeat this simple phrase
This will stop them

SECOND CHORUS
(With layered background vocals by Michael Jackson)
Please don't dump your hate on me

Please don't dump your hate on me
(*A very low "tell them"*)
Please don't dump your hate on me
Please don't dump your hate on me...
If you'll quit hatin'
They'll quit hatin'
Everybody please start lovin'

New Jack interlude by Teddy Riley...

THIRD CHORUS
(*LOUD—With layered background scats by Michael Jackson*)
Please don't dump your hate on me
Please don't dump your hate on me
Please don't dump your hate on me
Please don't dump your hate on me...
(*MJ pleads: Make them comprehend this...*)

FOURTH CHORUS
(*LOUDER—With layered background scats by Michael Jackson*)
Please don't dump your hate on me
Please don't dump your hate on me...
(*MJ pleads: Brother, tell them, make them comprehend this...*)

FINAL CHORUS
(*EVEN LOUDER—With background vocals/scats
by Michael Jackson*)
Please don't dump your hate on me
Please don't dump your hate on me
If you'll quit hatin'

They'll quit hatin'
Everybody please start lovin'

Start lovin'
Start lovin'
Start lovin'
Please start loving!!!

After a boom ended the song, the writer looked at the beat guru. With tears now connecting at his chin, he nodded.

A musical genius nodded back; his watery eyes spoke for Michael Jackson as well.

All three minds were one in message.

When you feel you have nothing or no one else, you have God. Lean on Him, and He'll be your forklift from the valley of pain. And once He gives you the strength to stand, seek professional help.

As you just read, I know from experience. Now let's get back to the story...

ELEVEN

our call has been forwarded to an automated voice message; (313) 555-2459 is not available... After the tone, please record your message. When you are finished, press "1" for more options...

BEEP. "You know who this is...I don't understand what's going on here. This is the fifth message I left and you haven't returned any of my calls. I want to hear your voice so I can fix things. I know I screwed up when I put my hands on you, and I know I shouldn't have done it, but... Call me, Keisha, so we can talk. Please."

The tone of his desperation drifted between displeasure and disbelief and his countenance wore an angry shade of anxiousness. Carl didn't like the downside of his Rock em'-Sock em' Robot game with his mistress, and the cranky patient inside him stubbornly refused the medicine that was the repercussions of his actions.

And like that cranky patient being force-fed, an IV injected his veins with a bitter truth.

Infuriated that he heard nary a word from Keisha since he had tossed a fifty on her back, an awful feeling tortured him.

Ten years of secret love was over, just like that.

Baffled, the questions he owned only poured salt into his open wound. Hadn't he made her feel like a sweetheart? Hadn't he compensated for the fact that he hadn't left his wife with everything he did for her; paying her bills when he could, the expensive gifts, the wonderful trips everywhere? Couldn't his love clear the mud from waters left by physical transgression?

Temporarily pacifying his frustration, Carl brought Monica Greer back to his Marriott suite where anti-depressants, alcohol, angst and one sexy-ass woman led to one thing: making her sugar walls clench his steel in bliss after a serious pounding.

Before venting in physical form, Carl cautioned, "Monica, don't fall in love with me. We're just a man and a woman in a room, fucking."

His date understood completely; she was down for whatever.

Sauntering over to him seductively, Monica fluttered her eyelids, then said, "Sweetie, when I'm finished with you, you'll be giving me that fat wallet of yours." Aggressively sliding her tongue into his mouth, Monica licked his teeth, then sucked passionately on his lips.

Carl whispered, "Damn," when he felt nomadic hands tickling his crotch.

"Mmm," she purred, unloosening his pants. "I bet you have a great deal to work with, Mr. Austin."

"You're about to find out."

Sure enough, seduction, saliva, sweat and skin were synchronized in sexual surrender, their orgasms more physical than emotional. Shaking violently several times, Monica wanted more and more of him; she couldn't get enough of his engorged heat.

Yet as much as Carl enjoyed Monica that night, his heart was elsewhere.

He didn't know where Keisha had taken it.

The morning after, his lover addressed the confusion over a Times Square brunch.

After seeing him barely touch his food, she asked, "What's troubling you?"

All Carl could muster was, "I've got things on my mind."

"Your wife stood you up last night, so I can only imagine the problems you're having."

"Monica, you don't even know the half. But," Carl added, "I had a great time with a gorgeous woman last night, one that I'll never forget."

"You make it easy. A woman could get lost in you. Shit, you fucked the kitty like you were a paroled brother getting his first piece in a minute."

"It hurt so good, huh, Monica?"

"It hurt very good, thank you very much."

"Maybe we'll do this again someday."

"Don't write any checks you can't cash, sugar."

In his heart, Carl Austin knew this was a one-shot deal. Staring into Monica's eyes, remembering their fusion of chromosomes in passion, he could no longer fix his mouth and say they should accept the stolen moment in time for what it was: a man and a woman in a room, fucking.

Their joining produced mind-numbing memories and two sexually sated souls, but Carl had to let it be, for his love for Keisha was like cocaine; addictive to his soul while jolting him with a feel-great sensation.

And wasn't he married to a beautiful woman, one who awaited his arrival home?

By the skin of his teeth, two was company, and three would definitely be a crowd in his life.

The Tribune Society Dance, normally scheduled the first week in November, had been pushed back to Black History Month so a fraternal body could pay tribute to a powerful attorney; one who had given many generous donations to their organization.

Happiness filled the air of Marina del Rey, a classy catering hall in the Throgs Neck section of the Bronx. Amongst a sea of influential African-American professionals, the wife of the honoree sat alone at a banquet table, watching her husband make the rounds during cocktail hour.

Amanda Austin was trying not to live a lie, but her spirit had been anesthetized; in part as a result of the Xanax she'd taken to steady her nerves, but for the most part because of her husband's indifference when it pertained to their rocky marriage. Remembering the loving phone calls when he was on the rise, they had stopped long ago along with the apologies for working so much. She finally summoned the courage to confront Carl once he arrived home from his "business trip" and was hit with a bland "we'll talk later; they're honoring me at a function tonight" response.

Our marriage is more important than a freakin' banquet, she thought. *Years ago, he wouldn't have been so insensitive.*

In spite of feeling rejected, she continued her support. Playing the fashion consultant, she thought the dark pinstriped suit with powder blue shirt he was wearing was perfect, but the tie—a pink color with geometric patterns—had to go.

After fitting him with something navy, she said, "Now, you look very nice."

Once more Carl showed detachment; refusing to acknowledge her help, he simply walked away.

Years ago, Carl Austin loved his wife; years ago she'd been all he needed.

Sadly, *years ago* was not this emotionally stormy night.

And Amanda felt a strange sense of abandonment. Normally at public events she was draped on her husband's arm, portraying the role of a loving wife who kept things real when other spouses discussed trivial things such as shopping, home decorating and their husbands' promotions within the New York Judicial System. Intelligent as a Rhodes Scholar and built like a brick-house—"she's quite the looker," senior clerks and judges often told Carl—humility by way of a down-to-earth spirit oozed from her pores.

But none of that mattered to Amanda, for a soul once set on fire by a man holding her heart in his hand was not at ease. While the community saw strength, she was tired of smiling to cover a growing avalanche of hurt; tired of wearing public disguises and hiding private pain.

Watching her husband hob-knob intensified her agony, for she knew once they were home, the adulation and adoration would stop and she would reenter her personal house of horrors, a house owned by a man who refused to answer her only question: Am I losing you?

Interrupting her train of thought was the sight of someone approaching the banquet dais. At six feet five inches and 250 pounds, his striking good looks should have been enough to get the crowd's attention, but he tapped his glass anyway.

"Ladies and gentlemen, could you please find your seats so that we can begin our presentation?" the articulate glass of chocolate requested.

In record time, three hundred of New York's powerful people of color complied.

Commencing the ceremony, in strong voice, the man said, "Tonight we gather to honor a man who embodies the very essence of our Tribune Society. The bedrock of our organization is to improve the administration of justice and ensure equitable treatment for those who not only work in the New York Unified Court Systems, but for those our hallowed institution proudly serves.

"Tonight we acknowledge a man who'll take his place amongst

the likes of Star Jones, Earl Graves and Paul Robeson, Jr., all the while paying homage to Johnnie L. Cochran, Jr., Gil Noble and Derrick Bell, Jr., recently departed contributors not only to our race but to the storied history of our organization.

"As you know, we have a scholarship award honoring Tribune members Alphonso B. Deal and William H. Thompson, both of whom heroically lost their lives when putting the needs of others, a community and a nation respectively, before their own. That award wasn't enough to honor these brave heroes, so tonight we unveil our first Thompson/Deal Plaque of Merit. From this day forward, the award will be given to inspirational leaders in both community and charitable services. And now it gives me great pleasure to introduce to you the first recipient of the Thompson/Deal plaque of Merit, Mr. Carlton Austin."

Calmly striding to the podium, the proud recipient of the award quickly looked down at his speech. Lifting his eyes to the crowd, he sported a dazzling smile that mesmerized everyone.

Then he addressed his constituents as if he were a Baptist preacher.

The words that left him were a powerful psalm. Humbly reminding everyone about the extraordinary lives of William Thompson and Alphonso Deal and how they ended way too soon, he transformed the negatives of each tragedy—Deal was killed trying to protect his community from robbery and Thompson perished in 9/11—into a positive by focusing on how their untimely deaths impacted him so deeply that he felt the need to give his all to the community.

Encouraging others resting on the trappings of their success to unselfishly follow suit, with emphasis, Carl exhorted, "At the end of the day, what you accomplished is not about you. Alternatively, it's about the shoulders we stand on and establishing a solid foundation for lives that come after ours. We must combat the mindset of these generations who are being raised to only think of themselves when we're called to also think of others. We must put an end to the selfish conditioning that's poisoning our young people. It's not about me. Rather, it's about *we*. We… Not me."

Upon completion of his speech, his words lingered in silence for seconds, infusing stagnant souls with hope and direction. Then the ballroom was electrified as the patrons rose to their feet and cheered him as if he'd given an inauguration address.

However, the elegant woman wearing a fitted navy blue dress and pearls remained seated at the main banquet table. Struggling to remain composed, the honoree's wife kept dabbing at her eyes with tissue.

Edging close to her, "He's such a great man," the wife of a senior official admitted. "You must be very proud of him."

Amanda gave her usual public response.

"I am," she said in a voice drowned out by applause. "I am."

The fawning over Carl continued when the ceremony moved into party mode. A few women not affiliated with either the courts or the organization seemed enthusiastic that he worked the room as if he were a bachelor. Wanting to tell all wannabes to "get a life," Amanda watched them press their bodies against his. One actually had the audacity to slip her phone numbers into his suit pocket.

Slithering next to him, she whispered, "If you were my husband, I wouldn't let you out of my sight."

It was bad enough Amanda wanted to gut that groupie like a fish, but seeing her husband's reaction—a sly smile—left her confused. *He's a man, so he's loving this*, she mused, trying to downplay their domestic situation, or lack thereof.

He's doing something, because he ain't doing shit with me.

She needed answers and hopefully after all the cheering stopped, she'd receive them.

To be honored the night before at a prestigious gala reaffirmed his power, but when it was over, the thunderstorms rained inside the head of the man who normally operated to his own rhythm and rules.

Growing more melancholy by the moment, Carl felt depressed and irritable, especially after contacting Delta and finding out that Keisha never boarded her flight.

Anxious, he placed another call to the source of his frustration.

Your call has been forwarded to an automated voice message; (313) 555-2459 is not available... After the tone, please record your message. When you are finished, press "1" for more options...

BEEP. "Keisha, this is my sixth call. That you haven't returned any of my calls has me pissed... I don't know who or what is messin' with your head, but you better not be giving my shit away; do you hear me, whore? You better not be giving my pussy away!!!"

Seconds later, he called again, this time sounding contrite...

BEEP. "Keisha, Look, I'm sorry about that last message... I'm...I'm worried about you... It's been a couple of days, and I feel bad about what happened... Keisha, please forgive me... Call me so that we can talk it out."

One day I'm the best thing that ever happened to her and she can't live without me, the very next is goodbye, he mused.

His thoughts were interrupted by an adamant tone standing in the kitchen doorway.

"WHO'S KEISHA!?!"

Busted, cannot be trusted, and disgusted.

Letting loose her alarm, his wife of thirty years stared him down.

More words needed to rise, but they couldn't. Paralyzed, her head throbbed from a combination of shock, anger and disbelief.

"ANSWER ME, DAMMIT! WHO IN THE HELL IS KEISHA??!!"

A million knives stabbed Carl's body, each blade representing a form of embarrassment. Trying to save face, he said, "She doesn't mean anything to me. Nothing. Zilch. Nada."

Opening an emotional faucet, everything flowed from Amanda. "When you were shutting me out, I kept trying, trying to save us. And all that time, you were throwing us away, you were seeing this heifer. How long, Carl? How long were you seeing this whore?"

Silence.

"TELL ME, HOW LONG HAS IT BEEN?"

In an inaudible mumble, he groaned, "Ten years."

"What did you say?"

"Ten years."

"OH GOD..."

Amanda collapsed into a kitchen chair. Bravely, she regained something that resembled composure, but her vision was blurred from everything except for a shocking revelation: Her husband had created another life, one filled with everything she tried by herself to save in theirs.

Burying her heavy head in her hands, she sobbed, "I can't believe you. Thirty fucking years...ten of them lies... lies."

This was not only a fling she was dealing with, or the alternative, some affair. This was outright betrayal.

Finally lifting her head, Amanda's eyes hardened and her skin wore the complexion of agony and sorrow.

By then, Carl tried another approach. Moving close to her, he insisted, "You've been real good to me, Amanda. If you can give me..."

Before he could finish, he felt wind and a hard backhand in the face.

Stumbling backward, he almost fell to the floor, but recovered.

"You sorry son-of-a-bitch! What am I supposed to do with the rest of my life? How could you be so damn egotistical?"

Carl dabbed at his mouth and saw red; blood trickled from his brim. Surprisingly, he didn't retaliate physically.

But the barbarian resurfaced verbally.

With cruelness, he blurted out, "You knew we had problems, but at this point it doesn't matter. I should have told you sooner, because I feel like I wasted thirty years of my life."

"What did you just say?"

"You heard me. You knew this was coming."

"Is this what you wanted to talk to me about *later?* Is she the one you were going on all those business trips with?"

"They weren't business trips."

"You were with her, weren't you?"

"C'mon, Amanda, you can't be that dumb."

"I don't believe you, Carl."

Again wilting under the oppressive heat of devastation, tears again flooded Amanda's eyes. The same phony mask her husband wore in public, one that made everyone feel like the most important person in the world, best described their thirty-year marriage.

To people lauding him, Carl Austin was a great man. But they never saw the transformation that was only reserved for his wife; to Amanda Austin, Carl was Mr. Hyde, a manipulative impostor who destroyed a considerable portion of her life.

Amanda's shoulders slumped when she asked, "What is Carl Jr. going to think?"

"It's not like I'm asking him to choose between us, so he'll be okay," he responded in a cold tone. "He's grown now."

Hearing another heartless reply had Amanda wishing for a golf club and a black Cadillac Escalade for Carl, so that she could go ballistic, break the windows out and club him with a 3-iron. Instead, shame and humiliation were at her heart's doorstep, and she had to grit her teeth and bear the pain.

Remarkably, she regained her poise, and her anger gave way to silence as she continued listening.

"In a couple of weeks, you'll hear from my attorneys," Carl said coldly, "And after I find a place..."

"For both of you?" Amanda asked.

"That's not your concern. You'll get your share of money for your services..."

For my services? Amanda thought, her facial expression now perplexed and that of a person nearing a boiling point. *For my services?*

"Please leave... Get out now... Please... Right now...," she said, her tone controlled, but vibrating with her anger. "Go...NOW." Shielding her heartache, the devastated woman stood stock-still, warding off a trembling sensation. However, in her fixed stance there was vulnerability, confusion in her gaze as well as her thoughts.

You fucking bastard. What do I do now? How am I supposed to start over?

If this had been a Parker Brothers board game, Amanda Austin would not have likened her husband to *Monopoly®*, though he had as much money as the bank.

Carl Austin was now *Sorry®*.

Sorry motherfucker, she mused. *Every mistake a man makes is with the other woman and a sexual accelerator.*

Now outside, Carl felt a sense of relief, for the cat had finally been let out of the bag. Originally he thought maybe he and Amanda would do a trial separation but concluded that would only continue his waffling. Besides, he was a pragmatist: the sooner he resolved this, the less likely he would be entangled in drama between two women, something that could tarnish his good name and possibly bring all he had accomplished crashing down on his head.

By leaving his wife, Carl felt he'd been given a clean slate. There would be no more potential-client dinner lies, no more phony conventions or conferences, no more doing whatever he could to avoid being bored in a brownstone with a woman he wasn't in love with. Tired of being dedicated in his responsibilities as a loyal family man, *Keisha never neglects my needs*, Carl thought.

It was time for him to get her back.

Only one problem; he didn't know where to find her.

TWELVE

The Shekinah Glory Ministry would have been proud of the mass choir at Spartanburg's West Baptist Church, for they magnified God's name in worship with a stirring rendition of "Praise Is What I Do." Feeling the spirit and truth of those lyrics were four people in attendance giving honor to the Most High. Davis and Mamie, zealous church members joyously consumed by fellowship and ministry, sensed that God had wisdom for William and Keisha to take with them on their journey to Michigan, something that would illustrate the beautiful portrait they immediately saw.

Obedient to his inkling, Sunday morning Davis extended an invitation to worship.

William readily agreed, but Keisha hesitated.

A lump of sadness formed in her throat. She tried to will away the raindrops staining her cheekbones, but was defeated by her emotions.

As the choir sang, she said, "I don't think God is very happy with me right now."

Ever the nurturer, Mother Woodson responded immediately, saying, "God loves you beyond measure, and His love is endless and forever forgiving. The blood of His Son on the cross covers a multitude of sins and He's already forgiven you for everything you're feeling. Let go, and let God comfort you."

God must have heard Mamie's word, for right before Reverend Tim McCann gave the congregation spiritual food, he had an announcement.

In a commanding voice, he said, "Don't measure God's love for you by how you feel or by your circumstances, because His love and mercy are steadfast and never changes. He created you, so in you resides this type of love as well. Don't let anything change or break your bond with Him and the God in all of us, which is love. The love in all of us is unbreakable."

Stunned, the woman battling pain looked at the maternal figure seated in the pew to her left, and saw a divine smile.

Softly, Mamie said, "Trust in God, child. He'll never leave or forsake you. Be still and let him erase all your doubts."

Inspired by what His Father had given him, the preacher let the Holy Spirit speak to his soul, and the words of his sermon left him in a booming voice.

"Without love, we are empty vessels. To live without this energy renders our deeds unproductive, our knowledge fragmented, our trust lacking, all we give insufficient, and all of our achievements irrelevant, immaterial, and inconsequential. To live without God's greatest gift, dwelling within is like going through life without a pulse. Better yet, let me amend that statement and say that going through life without feeling, giving or receiving love is like being dead.

"The priority of all our lives should be as the Apostle Paul eloquently defined in First Corinthians 13. Mirror the words God allowed to move through His faithful servant and let them become a reflection of Him. Let God move through you, so that the God in us, which is Love, becomes you in totality.

"Let love abide in your soul and make it the reason for your existence. Communicate it in words, deeds, actions and faith.

Never forget it in all your relationships; with your elders, your family and children, in your spiritual relationship with Christ and in fellowship with your Christian family. Let love serve as an aid of enhancement to all aspects of life, let it transform your soul into a tower of power. Eat, sleep, breathe, give and be a God-like example that shows faith's birthplace is in a heart of love.

"Your spirit should radiate the love that you share with everyone, and it will provide an atmosphere that would attract people in a compassionate way. You want your love to manifest itself in a warm hug, heartfelt handshakes and fist-bumps, a sincere smile or encouraging words. The God inside should be so overwhelming that it inspires hope in others, casts away doubt, replaces fear with strength, courage and resolve, energizes the spirits of those downtrodden and gives the hearts of wounded souls a powerful, positive transplant. And when we do this, when we attempt to live life in love, then the greatness of God meets us halfway, fills us up and has us glowing anew. Never give up on the love inside of you, for not giving up on love means you haven't given up on God and His plans for your life. Don't ever give up on God's love, and His Love will never give up on you. God is love, and once we recognize that God is in us, then we understand that we are love as well."

When William looked over at Keisha, he saw more tears, and reached for her hand. Praying quietly, he asked God to decrease her pain while increasing her peace.

A tingle moved through Keisha once she felt his fingertips. Looking in his direction, she saw him blushing as she dried eyes that projected unpleasant memories.

Her poise allowed daylight by way of a tiny smirk.

"Remember, we're just friends, on a little trip," she whispered.

"I'm only trying to help."

His good-nature made Keisha feel safe and cherished, and her heated gaze indicated such.

Slowly leaving the sanctuary together, the elderly matchmakers watched the exchange quietly and hoped the vibes between them were of mutual affection.

Mamie whispered to her husband, "The lioness stopped focusing on her reflection…"

Instinctively, Davis finished her sentence, saying, "…and looked across the pond and saw a bachelor lion trying to quench his thirst for love."

"You talked to him, huh?"

"And you did her."

Sharing a loving smile, two seniors still in love clasped hands like teenagers.

Mamie said, "Baby, when the kids leave, throw on 'Smokestack Lightning' and dance for me."

"Oh woman, you know my knees hurt."

"Well, will you at least howl for me, sugar?"

"Give me something that will make me howl."

"I always do, my love… I always do."

Later in the evening, William prepared and served dinner. His adopted stepparents were familiar with his turkey ziti, green beans marinated in butter-and-garlic sauce and potato salad, and as always they loved his cherry swirled cheesecake.

Wide-eyed in amazement, Keisha made a startling confession.

Struggling to contain a smile, she admitted, "No one's ever cooked for me before."

Blushing once more, William said, "I feel honored that I'm the first."

Then he uncorked a bottled of merlot straight from Napa Valley.

Davis intervened, instigating playful drama once more.

"He comes with a bow, too."

His wife added, "Child, you better not let him leave Michigan."

Admiring his completeness, now it was Keisha's turn to blush; her face was the color of the fermented juice she sipped.

"It tastes rich, and the flavors are balanced and harmonious. It's like pine bark mulch or moldy firewood in that the aroma is pleasant. Little to no alcohol is noticed in the smell," she purred.

Davis smiled.

"I take it you're a wine connoisseur."

Keisha beamed.

"This one came from vineyards in the Upper Valley district, in Northern California. Cakebread wines have a vibrant taste to them, probably because the 2009 vintage… It is 2009, am I correct?"

Davis nodded.

William sat there flabbergasted.

Keisha continued, saying, "The 2009 vintage was so detailed that it paid attention to the barrels they wanted their product to age in. This particular wine spent six months in French barrels, then another year after blending in those same barrels before bottling. It'll be even better a couple of years from now, so you better order a case now."

Mamie grinned.

"We have a few bottles in the basement, so we're ahead of the game."

"Good for you! I can't wait to come back and girl-talk while blaming it on the alcohol."

"Keisha, as long as God gives me breath, you're always welcome here. Be sure to bring me some Malibu Coconut rum. That's my favorite."

"Ain't nothing but a word."

Arm-in-arm, together they moved to the living room, with Davis following closely behind.

William stood in the doorway that separated the kitchen from the living room. Studying the peace in Keisha's eyes while admiring the serenity that oozed from her, he took delight in her tranquility. Gone was the misery that captured her in New York, the type of misery that produces pity-parties or, in his instance, sits in a dark room and listens to somber songs while singing sorry sonnets to the nearest bottle of liquor. Replacing that morbid state was an aura of confidence that announced that all was well in her space on this planet. Her brown cat eyes sparkled with pleasure, and the smile tilting her mouth with happiness awakened him to her natural beauty. Cappuccino-colored with ruby-red lips, her strong cheekbones emphasized the broadness of that frown turned upside down.

As she crossed her thick legs seductively, William caught himself fantasizing about their smoothness if he touched them. Always a leg man, while he acknowledged that her ample bosom lost nothing to Father Time, he could see the sculpted firmness of her calves through her jeans. And when she walked, the dark shoe boot she wore definitely enhanced the wiggle of wide, womanly hips.

Her voice was mellow, nurturing with a Midwestern flavor. She was vibrant, well educated and unpretentious, yet possessed an edge that knocked you upside the head if you didn't step to her correct.

Yes, he found Keisha to be very attractive. Although it wasn't old-fashioned lust that had his senses simmering, the involuntary chills moving through him were powerful and telling; it was like he had finally cracked the code to a long-standing riddle.

For the first time in years, he experienced one of those perfect moments within an imperfect world where everything felt right, like it was *supposed to be.*

Like it was supposed to be.

Tearing his thoughts away from the moment before him, he went to the basement once more, this time to use a computer.

He searched the Internet and there was a traveling performance he wanted to see while it was in the Big Apple yet overtime work obligations had been a roadblock to his urge. As fate would have it, the next tour stop for the show would be in Hitsville.

Smiling as he purchased two tickets for the Tuesday night performance, an executive decision had been reached. William decided that he wanted to take that *supposed to be* feeling on the road, and see where the journey would leave them.

At seven o'clock, the Tuesday morning air was a little chilly, but the South Carolina sun shined bright on the hearts of William and Keisha as they packed their things into the Taurus.

Once again, Keisha put on fitted black jeans, and her black turtleneck sweater had red hearts and white diamonds on the front.

Taking notice, William asked, "You look great, but what's with you and all this black? Are you in mourning?"

Keisha shook her head.

"I was when I got here, but any problems I had before I met those two wonderful people are in my rearview mirror."

Pointing back to the house window, William saw Davis and Mamie waving.

He looked at Keisha. "Aren't you glad we stayed the extra day?"

"I sure am. I enjoyed playing spades last night, even though they kicked our asses. I'm convinced they have secret codes."

"I don't think they want us to go, and we're not prisoners of the clock. If you'd like, we can stay a couple of more days. I'd have to rearrange something."

"William, I want you to check out Michigan. I think you'll like it. And you could stay with me, if you like."

"Wow, so I'm really moving up in the world."

Keisha paused, smiled, then responded, "You're *all right*."

William smirked.

Sometimes when a woman tells a man that he's "all right," it's a major endorsement meaning her defense mechanisms are down and she's loaning you the key to her heart, the operative word being LOAN. Dismissing failures when exploring a potentially pleasurable possibility, "all right" can be an announcement that she's feeling you and you better not screw it up. Because of many disappointments, the "all right" endorsement is a woman's way of regurgitating fear while taking a small leap of faith. That's step one. When she announces that you're "all right" in front of others, you'll know she'll work with you at the very least. One can never be completely sure these days, for the only sure thing about love is that you never know. But in this instance "all right" is good, "all right" is very good.

In a sweet voice Keisha asked, "Can I drive?"

"You don't have to. I was kidding the other day when I said…"

"No, William, I want to. You have the directions, right?"

"I have a built-in GPS system, remember?"

With authority and a smile, "Keys," Keisha demanded.

Graciously, William handed them over.

They were seven hundred and eleven miles from Motown, nearly twelve hours on the road, and the first hour of the trip was covered in silence. But there was nothing awkward about the simplicity of it, as both were in deep thought. Perhaps they were preparing for what seemed inevitable; perhaps the words of the elderly couple, blatant opinions on chemistry they saw had finally caught and held their minds.

As they zoomed along I-26 West toward Ashville, North Carolina, a sweet tone breached the quiet.

Keisha said, "Your car rides so smooth."

William smiled proudly.

"I'm glad that it does. It gets about thirty-two highway miles per gallon, one of the best in terms of fuel economy. It has 2.0 Eco-Boost engine, the power of a V6 and the efficiency of a four-cylinder engine."

"I see you know a lot about cars."

"I only know about this one, Keisha. Ever since my boy Steve had his white Taurus when he worked at the post office, I have always wanted one because his car looked so fly. That was about twenty-five years ago. Soon, it became my dream car. And a couple of years ago, I finally got it. My first car. Fully loaded, too."

"Still feels like a new toy, doesn't it?"

"Yeah, I feel blessed. By the way, I want you to meet Steve one day. He lives in Delaware."

"Oh," Keisha said with a drop of irony on her tongue, "so there's finally a sighting in the King's universe."

"Touché."

"Once my best friend, Theresa, returns from Europe, you'll meet her. She has a beautiful condo overlooking downtown Detroit."

"Cool."

"Turn off the satellite radio and play some Michael."

"Any particular album?"

"What's in the iPod rotation?"

William said, "Everything."

"Then put on the *Moving Violation* album. I bet any amount of money you don't have that."

He laughed, then spoke like a car salesman. "Not only does my Taurus offer a high-quality surround sound audio system with twelve speakers that you can hear in every seat, but…" Syncing his iPod with HD Radio, it seemed fitting that "Forever Came Today" brought electricity to the moment.

"Thank goodness for modern technology," he said.

Perhaps the song's lyrics, ones that spoke of suddenly finding an unreachable emotional place was their story leaving the troubles of their past behind and stepping into an energy that caused courageous confessions: feelings, fears, hurts, hang-ups and hopes. Maybe, just maybe, the purpose of this coupling was to produce a unique paradise. Maybe forever walked into their lives, shined its bright lights and led their hearts to an everlasting love exclusively for them.

Or, maybe these were two friends sharing a common link: their love for the greatest entertainer who had ever lived.

As the album played, with a beguiling smile William stole a glance at the woman behind the wheel.

After this thoughtful look, he said, "This is so wild."

"I know, right?"

"Are you having a nice time?"

"I sure am. I can't thank you enough for everything you're doing."

"Everyone needs a break from the drama life brings to your door, and I thank God I was available. Speaking of drama, I hate to ask this, but has Carl called you?"

Her sudden frown indicated that her soul still felt the aftershocks of a bad earthquake. Her feel-good sensation disrupted, the reality check was like a Penske car speeding into a pit stop at the Indy 500: It wasn't something you wanted to do when you were in cruise control, but it had to be done. Refueled with optimism, Keisha hoped her pit crew would change the tires of her dragster quickly, so that she could roar back onto the motor speedway with the rush of excitement she was feeling.

After sighing, she took the pit stop when she said, "He's been bombarding my answering machine."

"He's crying inside, Keisha. Ten years of memories don't suddenly fade away. Ten years of feelings aren't washed off in a hot shower."

"I know this. But he lives in New York and that alone will force me to stop thinking about him so much. Time and distance always heals the heart."

"Keisha, it's only been four days."

"Actually the disconnect had been longer. I came to New York to end things, but I got caught up one last time. Don't get me wrong, William. I still love him and want the best for him. But I can't go back there, and don't want to either. I deserve a love all my own."

"Wasn't he good to you, like you told me on the way down?"

"He was, but I wasn't good to myself. I haven't been since…"
She stopped herself.

"Since when, Keisha?"

"I won't get into it now, but I promise when the time is right, I'll share everything."

"I'm holding you to that. In the meantime, how are you gonna handle…"

"What's there to handle? He's unavailable and the last time I saw him, he put his hands on me. It's over, William. It's done, finished."

"We now return to our regularly scheduled programming."

"Yes, please, let's do that… Put on the *Dangerous* album. I want to hear 'Jam.' That song sets my mind free."

"That's your transitional song, Keisha."

"Exactly. It makes you wanna get up…"

"And rearrange things…"

"I know that's right! Those brass horns…"

"And subtle scratches…"

"Heavy D droppin' rhymes, God rest his soul…"

"And Michael's thought-provoking lyrics…"

In unison they said, "It makes you want to jam!!!"

No sooner than they finished their skit, the glass-shattering opening and rhythmic tension invaded their souls. Catching a sparkle in her eyes and a hint of a happy color return to her face, William's gaze narrowed when he examined her soul. Not seeing a phony bone in her body, an exciting awareness made him nervous.

Are you kidding me? What are the chances that I would meet someone who loves Michael almost as much as me? She's gonna love what's in store once we hit Detroit. This is… Wait, ease up and take a chill pill, Will. You're just two friends, on a…

Keisha broke his train of thought with a question.

"Can I use my lead foot to open her up?"

"Be careful for the state troopers."

This part of the interstate had sixty and sixty-five miles-per-hour speed limits, but Keisha, feeding off the liberty of her passenger and looking at an open stretch of road, took the car twenty miles faster.

A few minutes later, "She Drives Me Wild," the fourth track off the album, added to the surrealism.

The onset of the jam brought a declaration from the woman at the wheel.

"William, this song is the reason for my attire."

Bobbing her head to the experimentation of strings, sirens, slammed doors, car horns and New Jack funk, Keisha went in. The music, the moment, the man beside her and the banging beat brought about something metaphysical, and the transformation left William openmouthed, awestruck and aroused all at once.

In her altered state, Keisha was marvelously mature, yet her smoldering sensuality rivaled Rihanna, Ciara or any woman half her age. In those four minutes she became the flirtatious lyrics of the King of Pop's creativity, a voluptuous brick-house with sexy swag. There she was, wearing dark sunglasses and cherry-red lipstick, rhythmically rocking to a groove that was fire while going damn-near-ninety in William's well-polished whip. Wearing hiphugging black jeans and a sexy black sweater that had her "girls" at attention, if she decided to pull over at a rest area along the way, the song her killer walk would sing in high-heeled boots would definitely get a rise from redneck truck drivers and other patrons.

She had the look all could see but none could have, and if anyone made a false move, she had a defiant go-to-hell gaze ready to roll.

With this swag, with that look, she was driving William wild.

Once the song ended, Keisha begged, "Please play it again."

"Nope."

"Why not?"

"Because we can't."

"Why not?"

"Because we can't, that's why."

"You know what I think? I think that you're jealous of the fact that I love Michael Jackson more than you."

William's eyes widened.

"Oh, really?"

"Yes. I'm sure of it."

"Is this a challenge, Ms. Gray?"

With a cheesy grin, Keisha responded, "Let's go."

"Wait."

"Are you wimping out already, Mr. McCall?"

"No, let's establish some ground rules. Each of us asks a question about Michael Jackson. It could be anything having to do with his music; his likes and dislikes, anything. Each correct answer gets a point. First one to twenty wins."

"Make it to a hundred," Keisha mumbled. "We have plenty of time."

"Oh, so you want to get down like that?"

"William, I'm from Motown, where it all started."

"Actually, Keisha, it started at Steeltown Records, a small record label in Gary, Indiana."

"That's right. There were two singles released under the label…"

"'Big Boy' and 'We Don't Have to Be Over 21(to Fall in Love).'"

"Ooh, sugar, I'm so sorry, but you didn't let me finish the question. What were the B-Sides to those singles?"

Sitting back in his seat, for a good two minutes William looked stumped.

Keisha smiled. "The names of the songs were 'You've Changed' and 'Jam Session.'"

All the man in the passenger seat could do is smile.

"Sweetheart, when you're too bad for everyone else, you're right for me."

For the next hour or so, both listened to a remarkable legacy and allowed their bodies to feel the music, all this while peppering each other with trivia questions. Moving from I-26 and US-74 west through the Cumberland Mountain area on I-40 West, Keisha blitzed William with all kinds of information; how the Gloved One ate KFC chicken with the skin peeled off; his love for glazed doughnuts, pizza, popcorn, cookies and ice cream.

"But especially," she said proudly, "he loved his M&M's. Which color did he not eat?"

"Brown," William responded.

"What's the score now?"

"Thirty-nine to seventeen. You're winning."

"I'm killing you, William. I told you I loved him more than you."

Holding on to his calm, he responded, *"Au contraire, mon cherie.* The party's not over."

Soon as those words left his lips, a special Jackson Five album blared from his car speakers, eliciting a schoolgirl scream from the driver.

"The *Lookin' Through the Windows World Tour, Live.* Munich, Germany. November 4, 1972," he said coolly.

With that, the tide of the challenge shifted in his favor. Like a high-powered football offense out to prove that no lead was safe, from Knoxville, Tennessee into Kentucky, he impressed Keisha with his extensive knowledge of Michael's bookshelf. She was surprised to hear that a song-and-dance man read *Lincoln's Devotional* by Carl Sandburg, *My Autobiography* by Charlie Chaplin and the biography celebrating the life of Bruce Lee.

William quipped, "Greatness inspired *greatness."*

Keisha asked, "Didn't he read Edgar Allan Poe?"

"Yup."

"I wonder what he thought about that evil eye, in 'The Tell-Tale Heart.' That was a crazy story. Any time it takes a person an hour to enter a room because of an evil eye…"

"I know, right?"

They shared a raucous laugh, but only for a second; William had a startling revelation.

"For those people who thought that he wasn't aware of the Black Experience, he read the same books we read."

"One that resonates in me is *Before the Mayflower* by Lerone

Bennett. There's an excerpt I remember which described the heads of slaves being impaled by long bed nails and how the corpses were tossed to the sharks. I felt pain reading that, and I feel pain talking about it now."

"I'm sure he must have thought the same thing."

"He read it, too?"

"Yes, along with *Black in America* by Eli Reed, *In Praise of Black Women* by Simone Schwartz-Bart, as well as books about our heroes and, unfortunately, those with lynching photos. Contrary to popular belief, he never sold out."

Shifting gears, Keisha asked, "William, I'm curious. How do you feel about race relations today?"

"Are you sure you want my answer?"

"I wouldn't have asked if I didn't."

"We should stop using racism as an excuse and become responsible for our actions, but we can't act like the elephant has left the room because of two terms of Obama. Sadly, there are times where it stomps on our consciousness as a reminder that it still exists. Take Hurricane Sandy for instance, a catastrophe that should've rendered prejudiced thoughts moot. I did some relief work with some brothers and sisters on Staten Island and don't you know that one of the shelters on the South Shore refused our clothing? One place even declined food when mentors and their kids cooked for them. Can you imagine the scene? People rejecting food because of skin color, and they have no place to rest their head. Unbelievable."

"Staten Island, wasn't that place hit the hardest by Sandy?"
William nodded.

"Maybe there was an overflow in aid," Keisha countered.

"That may have been true, but that I still have thoughts like this is an indicator that there's still a problem, one that's not contrived by some angry black man. In some instances it may be worse because we have a Black POTUS."

"You can't blame him for something that's existed since slavery, William."

"I'm not. But what may happen is that Obama will be viewed in some circles as an aberration as opposed to a new standard, and a portion of that theory, whether we like it or not, is based on the color of his skin. I'm so glad the media hasn't attacked his past, like they do so many of us."

"They never let us forget our mistakes."

Her passenger agreed. "Charles Ramsey was a hero in Cleveland, and all they focused on was his abusive past. Never mind the obvious, that he courageously restored three lives that day. The media harped on his transgressions. It was like they said, 'Today, you're a good Negro, but we remember when, and sooner or later you'll show your true colors.'"

Keisha added, "Have you noticed that they're focusing more on the perpetrator these days than they are the hero?"

"Great point! They needed SYAD awards."

Blindsided with irony, Keisha almost pulled over the car.

"William, what did you just say?"

"What, that the media probably said…"

"No, the part about the awards."

"Keisha, SYAD stands for…"

"Sit Yo' Ass Down."

"You get it."

With a beautiful smile, she said, "Yes, I most certainly do."

"I'm glad that you do. So many people don't understand the fact that no matter what's said or done, a considerable portion of

America will have a barrier in understanding the Black Experience, and because a biased faction governs the media, many opinions are still slanted in ignorance."

"That's why we have to preach progress to our kids and remind them of the shoulders they stand on."

William co-signed on her statement with emphasis. "And of the struggle that still continues. We need look no further than at our male teenagers, who are more prone to juvenile incarceration and more likely to be sentenced to an adult prison because they can't afford proper legal representation."

Keisha added, "African-American teenage boys are fifteen percent of the youth population, yet almost sixty percent of them are being sent to prisons. What's even scarier is that one out of every three male teenagers born after the year 2000 will end up behind bars."

"That or they get Zimmermanned by way of assumption, like young Trayvon."

"Tell me about it. That verdict set us back fifty years."

"Keisha, it was a cover-up from the moment he died. From the medical team's botched examination to the end result of the trial, it was a ruse. Where was common sense? Can an aggressor plead 'stand your ground' as a defense when he disobeyed orders and left his vehicle with intent?"

"William, did you hear the Anderson Cooper interview with the anonymous juror? I almost lost it when she said Zimmerman wasn't racial profiling. Then she had the nerve to say that she would feel comfortable with him on her neighborhood watch provided he didn't go too far. She sounded more sympathetic to what she feared for him *after the verdict* than she did over a dead Trayvon Martin."

"That whole thing was atrocious," William said.

"It was atrocious yet predictable, if you know your history."

"Really?"

"Last summer I taught history in high schools. On the Monday after the acquittal, I taught the kids about the racist history of Sanford, Florida, and how it was named after a man who was a proponent in the belief that America should ship blacks back to Africa in the nineteenth century. He also endorsed a Belgian king's agenda in the Congo that put women and children in chains and starved them to death, all for rubber wealth. Henry Sanford was his name."

"Wow."

"There's more. Are you a sports fan?"

Glancing, Keisha saw him nod and continued. "Do you remember the scene in the movie, *42*, where they showed Jackie Robinson being accosted by an angry mob in the South? Guess what city that was?"

"Sanford, Florida."

"That's right. Only the movie didn't show the reality, that members of the KKK led the mob."

William was speechless for a full minute.

"As much as I cried that Saturday night, I wasn't surprised."

"Neither was I, Keisha. I prayed with a group of kids on the subway that night and told them that the verdict in that trial delivered a message far more powerful than any word from their parents or grandparents. Now they can see the struggle for themselves."

"It's in the classrooms, where we fight against overpopulation, unmet demands for relevant textbooks and financial support."

"Your teaching in Detroit makes a difference, more than you realize. But you can't do this alone."

She nodded. "We all have a part to do. At home, in the community, even in areas of entertainment like music and literature. We have opportunities to deliver messages, but how many are willing to do it?"

"There are too many people with political and financial power getting paid to fit in as opposed to having the courage to speak up."

"I know that's right!"

"That's why it's imperative to keep Obama's legacy from becoming a historical footnote, a brilliant yet brief sideshow in the lives of people of color."

"How do we do that, William?"

"By being better fathers to our children, holding each other accountable for hurting one another, becoming active in the church and community and promoting education, which leads me to this; it's imperative that we support these historically black institutions by steering our kids in their direction. Education is more than books, and seeing a reflection of self-reliance in terms of our culture is imperative. While knowledge is power, it's also about seeing your own people unified in progress. Black colleges demonstrate our strength in numbers."

Keisha said, "I agree, but how can we get our young to see this when all their role models barely complete or don't even go to school? How can they get the message when so many in our communities are battling addictions and are in and out of detoxes?"

"Keisha, I know a lot of them see rappers and athletes and think that they're a step away from Jay-Z or LeBron, but we must emphasize that they're the same distance from being Obama, T.D. Jakes or Don Thompson, the CEO of McDonald's."

"Don't forget Oprah and Ursula Burns, the head of Xerox for our girls. Or they can even be pilots, like the all-female crew that flies Delta."

William agreed, "Exactly."

"The remembrance of our ancestors who were raped and publicly flogged; the broken necks of others who were lynched; children who were hosed, bitten by dogs or killed for taking a stand, and others like Trayvon who died before he ever had a chance, all hinge on our growth from Barack and Michelle."

William smiled. "As much progress as we've made, we have to remember our roots in all we do. It keeps the fire burning."

"Wow," was all Keisha could say verbally, but her insides leaped for joy.

"So, how many points do I get for my answer?"

"None. In the past couple of hours, you've passed me."

"That's right. I'm beating you, fifty-nine to forty-seven." Playfully, William chanted, "Here's something that'll blow your mind; look at the score, you're behind!!"

"This Michael Jackson contest is far from over, Mister."

"By the way, aren't you tired of driving?"

"You're not getting this car back," Keisha joked.

"Seriously, Keisha, are you okay? I can take over if you like."

"Driving this car gives me peace. Besides, you'll have a long drive back to New York."

Her voice trailed off; the utterance came with a hint of sadness.

Desperate to return a warm smile to the edges of her mouth, the man in the passenger seat said, "We have plenty of time before we say good-bye."

Maybe we'll never have to say it, Keisha thought.

Maybe we'll never have to say it, William thought.

Five brothers seemed to be listening to their musings.

As fate would have it, a Jackson Five song came through the twelve-speaker system, strongly encouraging them to never say goodbye to God's greatest gift to humanity. Invading the silence of two people hiding feelings behind fear, the strange vibrations songwriter Clifton Davis wrote about had the sexy sister at the wheel healing and hoping simultaneously, and the brother by her side wishing, wanting and wondering what love would feel like after seven years on the sidelines.

THIRTEEN

It took seventy-two hours, but the hole in Carl's soul grew as large as a crater on the moon.

Clinging tenaciously to a wing-and-prayer hope that Keisha would appear in his office with something resembling peace of mind, the more hours that passed, the more a tornado-like truth swept through his life, leaving a dismal disposition in its wake.

Already overwrought from this revelation, that he finally received a call from Keisha early Tuesday morning further exacerbated his turmoil. Short and succinct, the "Mr. Austin, this call is to let you know that I'm okay. I'm on my way home," message seemed cold and distant, aloof.

There was no anger in her tone, but what he heard was much worse: indifference.

She finished her communication by asking for him to FedEx her house keys.

It's like one minute I'm all that she needed, the next she's saying goodbye, he thought. Soon, sullen thoughts evolved into popping pills like Skittles. Though Dr. Slattery had warned him about the dangers of mixing prescriptions—it could cause schizophrenic reactions, she said—he added the dietary supplement Tenuate to his drugs of choice.

Now wired, he began speeding through his morning assignments like a "D" express train motoring from 125th Street to Columbus Circle. Yet the loss of his lover seemed immeasurable, and once he was done, he closed his office door and tried calling Keisha's cell five times within an hour, refusing to leave any messages when her answering machine picked up.

No answer on her home phone either.

His lips hardened and his eyes flashed the colors of anger. The veins in his neck revealed the pain stabbing his heart and the sting of this latest rejection had him on the verge of transforming into the lunatic that caused his present state.

The only thing that stopped him was a meeting with a potential client.

She better not be giving my shit away, or I'll kill her.

All East Coast residents are familiar with the I-95.

Traveling parallel to the Atlantic Ocean, the primary highway of the region serves all the major cities in the North and the beach party areas of the South. I-95 runs like a nineteen hundred twenty-five-mile bloodstream, giving life to commuters with a vertical vein which extends from Maine to Florida. Connecting its antennas to other cities like Boston, Raleigh, and Charleston, it is the pulse of fifteen states, more than any Interstate Highway in the mainland.

Though it ranked seventh on the mileage list of national roadways, you couldn't tell William and Keisha that I-75 North wasn't as long. Speeding through Kentucky's Madison County, they entered the Richmond area, passing the Eastern Bypass, on Exit 87, then the Martin Bypass three miles later.

Keisha sighed.

William asked, "You okay?"

"Carl's blowing up my phone."

"He's worried because he doesn't know where you are."

"I left a message on his phone this morning telling him to return my house keys."

"And now he won't leave you alone, will he?"

"I feel like I made a mistake by calling him."

"You skipped town on him, and sooner or later, you had to let him know that you're okay. The true test comes when you actually speak to him."

"William, like I said earlier, I gave him more than a decade to leave his wife, and he didn't do it. So I closed that door and threw away the key. And once a man's out of my life, he's out."

"Feelings have a life of their own, Keisha. They might change if you talked to him."

"Nope. He hit me and said that he would kill me if I thought about leaving him."

"That sounds like obsession."

"I'd never seen him like that before. He became another person, a monster. I'd always known that he had a bad temper, but to choke me…"

William let the seriousness of her words marinate. He tried to visualize what had happened to her when her former lover wigged out, but couldn't. Instead he saw a woman struggling with a season of good and bad memories.

Then he said, "Keisha, when one door closes, another opens wide, showing you a better, greater love. The woman I met on Valentine's Day deserves to be happy. She deserves love. I want that for you more than myself. And from everything that you told me about Carl, he wasn't the one."

"What about *your* happiness, William? Are you ever going to revisit love and its possibilities?"

"I already have. I promised Linda that I would when I visited her gravesite."

"So you went after all."

"Yes. It wasn't as bad as I thought it would be."

"Well, that's cause for celebration. Can I buy you dinner once we get to Michigan?" Seeing his surprise, she asked, "What? Haven't you ever received a dinner offer from a woman before?"

"Yeah, sure, but…"

"But what?"

"I invited you to come on vacation with me."

"So."

"Okay, I'll make a deal with you. I'll let you take me to dinner after my surprise."

Keisha added wide eyes to her pleasant facial expression.

"What surprise?"

"You'll see."

"What surprise, William?"

"Trust me, Keisha, you're gonna love it. I promise."

"Let's get back to the contest."

"Keisha, baby, I'm killing you. What's the score?"

"It's eighty-five to fifty."

"It's a slaughter. You're gonna lose, Keisha. Give up."

"William, I haven't used my heavy artillery."

"C'mon, you're thirty-five points down. What could you possibly know about MJ that we haven't discussed? I destroyed you when it came to his production teams and songwriters, even number one hits, remixes, album chronology and his background contributions to other artists, like the Doobie Brothers, Stevie Wonder and James Ingram."

"Since you're so confident that you don't think I can catch up, then why don't you up the ante? Give me five points for every correct answer as well as the questions you don't."

"And if I answer a question correctly, I get five points, too?"

"Sure."

"That means all I need is three more answers and I win."

As she motored past the Lexington exits, Keisha's fascinating mouth formed a sly smile, and right on cue the thumping beat of MJ's "This Time Around" filled the vehicle with its bluntness.

She asked, "William, do you know the address when the Jacksons first moved to California?"

After hearing another pause, Keisha answered, "Sixteen-oh-one Queens Road, West Hollywood. I have fifty-five points now."

"I got one. For twenty points, name four of Michael's favorite movies."

"That's easy. *To Kill a Mockingbird*, *E.T.*, *Shane*, and the 1956 version of *The Red Balloon*."

"I saw *The Red Balloon* when I was in the first grade. PS 92, in Brooklyn."

"That's good to know. By the way, I have seventy-five points, William."

Just like that, a seemingly insurmountable advantage had been whittled to ten.

Keisha mockingly said, "I'm gaining."

"I'm still ahead."

"Not for long."

"Give me another question, Keisha."

"For five points, give me the name and address of Michael's favorite Indian restaurant."

In a casual tone William answered, "Chakra Cuisine, on South Doheny Drive, Beverly Hills."

"Name a food on the special menu in his honor."

"I get five more points for that, right?"

"No."

"Why not?"

"I was asking to see if you knew."

"You don't want to lose, that's all."

"I'm not going to lose, William. I hold a trump card. So we'll keep going until I decide enough is enough."

Enough is enough.

Muttering the same thing, it would seem Michael Jackson had been listening to their banter and decided it was time to take a page from the old Superman television series and clunk their heads together. Infusing a teenage presence, the song "We're Almost There" brought a companionable silence that came with deep thought.

Startled by the pleasurable intrusion, an electric sensation seized Keisha, one that spread heat throughout her gorgeous frame. Feeling flustered as a fuzzy expression filled her face, the message from her Dr. Feelgood produced conflicting emotions. A single tear trickled down her right cheek, then another. She had witnessed an unconscionable tragedy, made mistakes protecting her heart and had been beaten by what she thought was love. Internally, every instinct should have been screaming, "Oh, hell no," to this sudden adrenaline rush; yet a prodigy implored her not to give up on that dream of sharing her life completely. The one more step Michael begged her to take might have been a mere touch of the hand of the man seated next to her. Longing to feel cuddled, Keisha wanted nothing more than to reach a place where the pain of heartbreaks were no more, where rainfalls were romantic and the sun shined brighter each day, for God's greatest energy, love between man and woman, was there to share and care.

Her heart was almost there, but she couldn't reach for his hand. Lord knows, she wanted to, but she was afraid.

And so was William. Trepidation gripped him as the talented teen sang about precious emotions he had yet to realize, for beneath a benevolent façade lay an enormous heart wanting what he now felt for Keisha to finally be *It*. Turning his face to the passenger window, the mile markers, billboards, and wooded scenery became film frames of a thirty-two-year quest for *It*. He searched the debris in his soul, rubble comprised of hard times, hopeful hellos, tragic goodbyes and agonizing disappointments. He'd been labeled effeminate in his adolescence, gone head over heels while in a love triangle, made monumental mistakes trying to repair his broken heart, lost all he owned after another bad experience and had a soul mate help him get back on his feet, only to watch her die and take what he thought was *It* to her grave.

For over three decades, *It* was the one thing he coveted more than anything; he wanted *It* more than the bluegrass air he now breathed.

Returning his attention to the woman driving his car, he saw her tear and felt her nervousness.

Sometimes you must be willing to learn while taking the lead.

Sometimes, learning while leading also meant taking a step of faith with your heart; according to the gospel of Michael Jackson.

Taking another leap of faith, William would do just that.

Casting his own apprehension from his core, he took Keisha's free hand.

He asked, "Are you okay?"

Keisha responded, "I'm sorry. I miss Michael. He holds me together when the shallowness of the world tries to smother me."

"Me, too. I loved him like a family member."

"The world was a better place with him around."

"I agree, Keisha, but have you noticed that even in death, he still inspires love through a cosmic connection between all his fans? So many hearts opened up on the day he died, and they had to because it was sudden and no one knew what to do or who to turn to for comfort. We turned to each other to fill that vacuum, that hole in our souls. To this day, we share a unified love for him that only true fans can truly understand. It's as much spiritual as it is emotional."

"Tell me about it. I have a friend who broke up with her man after MJ died because he couldn't understand why she was so distraught over a man she'd never met. One guy who asked me out said that I needed to let go of my Michael Jackson stuff. 'Girl please, he's dead' were his exact words."

"Ouch. Needless to say…"

"I told him to never call me again. He had the audacity to ask why."

"It's an MJ thing, so he wouldn't understand."

They laughed a laugh reserved for fan club members.

William said, "You should see my Facebook page. Michael Jackson is all over the damn place."

"He's all over mine, too. Sometimes I feel more comfortable with my friends that love Michael than others in my daily life, and I'm okay with that."

"I can understand why; because you're identifying with people who share the same love, energy and passion for him as opposed to someone ignorant to what he created for and amongst his fans."

"He gave so much love from his heart that to this day, you can't imagine living in a world without Michael Jackson in it. I still can't believe he's gone."

Together, they sighed and said, "Gone too soon."

Keisha asked, "How do you feel about all the posthumous mud-slinging?"

William sighed. "Sure it hurts to hear all the crap flying around, but none of it has any bearing on the gifts he shared with the world. In my twenties, people threw his flaws in my face like I was his PR manager."

"Isn't it amazing how people who always focus on the mistakes of others ignore the log in their own eye?" She paused. "That AEG live trial messed me up, William. For all he did to spread love it should've ended better for him. It was like they used him up, then ran like roaches when the lights come on once questions were raised about his death."

"The verdict says they weren't enablers, but…I wished he loved himself a little more than he did."

"Me, too. He was a genius who mastered the art of loving others through words and actions but couldn't quite figure out how to receive it."

Silence.

William breached the pause when he said, "I hope I get involved with a woman who loves him as much as I do, because at the end of those long hard days, we can always turn to Michael's music…"

"To clear the clouds away and ease the pain that a cold world can throw on love."

"Exactly."

If Keisha hadn't been driving, the deep gaze of a man mesmerized by her would have hypnotized her. But the strong thump of her heart let her know that she, too, was under a spell, not to mention an unfamiliar need traveling down her spine. Every vein sparked like electrical wires and her primal urges screamed for her to find the nearest secluded spot and curb an aching sensation created by desire and potential devotion.

She wanted and needed to be loved.

She wanted and needed to be made love to.

Intuitively, she knew this man could do both.

The man in the passenger seat knew it, too.

Captivated by a potent passion, one that combined romantic heat with the swift pitter-patter of his heart, his slumbering emotions were reawakened by her aura, leaving his ticker defenseless.

William had wanted other women before, but not like this.

Never like this.

She's going to love my surprise, he thought.

The gasoline had been poured on the firewood, and a gloved wonder casually tossed a match over his shoulder. Moonwalking away from the blaze, that he left the seventh tune from his *Invincible* CD behind added more fuel to the flames. Starting seductively as a terrific tenor, the King of Pop began with a romantic rumble. Then suddenly he expanded his vocal wings in the song's second verse. Floating and fluttering in fantastic falsetto form, he captured the essence of love in the eyes of two souls craving this wondrous energy. Carefully opening their cocoons, in song he wished they would touch, caress and kiss, then make each other's dreams come true for an eternity.

Step one came when William offered his help.

Step two came when he held her hand.

Step three, the kiss, would happen soon enough, for their heartbeats hinted toward unison.

Moving closer to what was no longer unthinkable, William and Keisha were giving each other butterflies.

The Queen City.

Arriving there in six-and-a-half hours, they could have driven all the way to Motown, but seeing the beauty of downtown Cincinnati from the Brent Spence Bridge elicited freedom from the woman at the wheel.

Keisha asked, "Have you ever been here?"

William shook his head no. "I always wanted to see a Reds game. I remember watching the Big Red Machine on TV when I was a kid."

"They were the most complete team in baseball history." Before William could utter his amazement, she continued, "My father and I used to go to Riverfront Stadium all the time. He used to love the Reds, especially Joe Morgan, Johnny Bench and Pete Rose."

"Didn't ya'll root for the Tigers?"

"They weren't very good until the early eighties. By the time they won in '84…" Serenity leaving her face, she tried to still her pain by allowing silence to complete her sentence, but she couldn't hide the anguish.

The windows to her soul put the sting of a lingering nightmare on Front Street.

"Keisha, what happened to your father?"

"William, I promised I'd tell you when the time was right."

"Well, there's no time like the present."

No response.

"Keisha, whatever happened still bothers you. I can feel it. Sometimes talking about painful things is like opening a closed fist. It allows new things in our lives that might be good for us."

Another pause.

After sighing, her voice remained controlled when she said, "I guess you're right." After crossing the bridge, they traveled a half-mile to Exit 1C, Fifth Street and the Fountain Square District. A slight right and another quarter-mile later, they paid for parking on Vine Street and entered the Westin Cincinnati Hotel.

Going through a revolving door together, heat simmered at

William's groin when they brushed against each other, and slowly the hormonal craving became a sensuous tingle gliding through his athletic frame.

He joked, "This is the last time I let you lead, Keisha."

Flirting, she responded, saying, "Sugar, we're in the lobby of a hotel. Most men would love a sexy woman leading them to the brink of passion. And you have your choice of hundreds of rooms to do whatever you wish with me." Pausing, she dropped her punch line like Betty White. "Oh, I forgot, it's been a minute for you."

"You got jokes, I see."

Her wide smile lasted a millisecond, then faded. Grabbing both his hands, she looked deep into his eyes, the seriousness of her gaze a portent of what she wanted to share.

She said, "Come on. I know a place where we can talk."

They went to a quiet lounge located on the skywalk level of the hotel, quietly tucked in back of the lobby. Overlooking the street below, the overhang was several feet over the sidewalk, thus making the name of the establishment, Over Vine, literal. From blue-tinted, atrium-style windows you could see the nearby PNC and Carew Towers.

The white, modern-deco bar area is where they sat, in stylish-brown chairs. Scanning the scene, William noticed that the place was empty, save a couple of portly, pear-shaped brothers arguing about politics.

As two cosmopolitans arrived, he said, "I bet this place gets packed on Friday."

"I haven't been here since it opened a couple of years ago. I've been meaning to ask you, what cologne are you wearing?"

"*Obsession Night.* It's quickly become my favorite."

"It's becoming mine, too."

William lowered his head.

Grabbing his hand, Keisha said, "I can't believe a man near fifty still blushes. It's like you're a man-child."

A few seconds later, William complied.

"Keisha, I have to confess: It's been a long time since I've been around a woman that I truly cared about. And suddenly you appear and have me thinking about things. Given your present state, I'm not expecting anything from you in terms of...anything, actually. The only thing I'm asking of you is to promise me that you'll never settle for a halfway crook."

"A halfway crook, William?"

"A halfway crook is a man who's not available to give you his heart completely, yet wants exclusive devotion. They paint magnificent pictures with empty promises and selfishly want all of you. You deserve a man who wants what you want, and you can't be afraid to put yourself out there completely. That's the only way you'll receive the love you deserve."

Tightening her jaw, Keisha looked lost; lost in a painful memory that produced a tragic vision that had her running for years. The rancid odor of remembrance filled her with a sadness she had carried around in a heavy, hideous-looking knapsack. Also filling the backpack were mementos of misfortune, sorry souvenirs saturated by selfishness, broken-hearted body bags, shattered spirits, mind-numbing mood swings, and a violent experience when finally trying to shed her weighted nuisance.

But here, in Cincinnati, Keisha would search her heart for bravery, finally take the bag off, fling it into the Ohio River and become a queen who deserved a king.

Starting the process, she asked, "William, have you ever been scarred so deep that it had a lingering effect on everything in your life?"

"I've been through some things."

"Have you ever seen something so devastating that it jacked up your entire outlook on life; your behavior, your interactions and perspective? Have you ever been frozen in fear?"

Seeing him pause, she dabbed at her eyes with a napkin, took a sip from her drink, then said, "The reason why I got involved with Carl was because of my father. He was an abusive man to my mother...to the point of... He beat her...then... They're both... gone, William. Gone."

She couldn't complete her truth, for the tears sliding down her cheek formed a river at her chin. Soon the river was a tidal wave of pain that wiped her out. Completely unhinged, she collapsed into William's arms, crying for Ramona, herself, a shattered past, a damaged present and an unknown future.

For ten long minutes she cried barely audible sobs; six hundred seconds of emotional cleansing.

William held her every second, even when she tried to gather herself and failed, sobbing in heaves while struggling to breathe. He had encountered tremendous sorrow, but nothing quite like the unspeakable tragedy that had handcuffed Keisha's heart. Without words, he knew what had happened, the brutality thereof, and the consequences that confined her soul to misery.

Finally the grieving stopped, and through sniffles Keisha confirmed all thoughts when she said, "He used a sawed-off...to blow her head off... Then...he killed himself... I fell face-first in her blood..."

My God, William thought. Knowing there were no words that could adequately express his sympathy, he asked his Maker for something...anything.

Another five minutes passed.

Finally, he spoke.

"Keisha, those scars have made you a star, because you haven't given up. So many people have been broken over a lot less. But you kept going."

"I wasted a lot of time acting in my best interests, not giving a damn about anyone's feelings but my own."

"We've all been selfish, Keisha. But you can redeem all that pain by learning to love one step at a time, one day at a time. Do you know how much courage it took for you to leave Carl? You realized that you were no longer someone's jump off, and you bounced. When you did that, you not only began a new life, but..." He pointed skyward. "You redeemed your mother's life by not staying with an abusive man."

Keisha turned flush, crimson. The mourning that crossed her face minutes ago had been replaced with a faint smile.

William continued, "Today is the first day of the rest of your life. While you'll never forget what happened, you go forward learning from it all. It took guts to look in the mirror and realize that something was wrong, and even more *sheroism* to fix it. God will help you turn tears of sorrow into tears of joy and teach you how to love in the process. Stop getting in His way by beating yourself up."

Fully recovered from her meltdown, that glimmer of a grin on Keisha's face was gone; in its place was enough wattage to light up the Buckeye State.

Grabbing his hand, she said, "You're a beautiful man, William. Don't ever change."

"Many years ago my first love told me that."

"She knew what she was talking about."

"Then she married someone just like me."

They both laughed.

Then Keisha said, "I bet Linda did cartwheels when she met you."

"For a brief moment we were both blessed. In spite of all we went through, it was the happiest time of my life."

"How long were you two…"

"Six months."

Keisha arched an eyebrow.

"Really?"

"That's all it took. I was living in a homeless shelter after some really tough breaks. A friend of mine had died and I needed to regroup, so I took a trip to New Jersey and there she was, sitting on a park bench. She took me in when my spirit was bent, and helped me become the man you see before you today." With his voice cracking, he continued, "So Keisha, when I tell you to stay encouraged…"

He was about to drop his head when he felt a soft palm at his chin.

It was Keisha's turn to inspire, and she did this in a soft yet firm tone. "Pick your head up, William. God knew your burdens and gave you what you needed, even if for a moment. Right now He's showing you that you're never alone."

"He showed you that as well."

"…this weekend. And I'm so grateful."

Remembering something, William wiped his eyes and jumped up, as if someone startled him.

"Keisha, what time is it?"

"A little before two."

Whipping out his smartphone, a man with a surprise had to check something out.

"Excuse me."

Moving about ten feet away, he bypassed the automated response and spoke quickly. "Hello, customer service? I wanted to know if your ticket office stayed open on performance nights... Up 'til an hour after showtime? Great... Thanks so much..."

"What was that all about?"

"We have to be in Detroit by eight."

"We're about four-and-one-half hours away."

"We better go eat something and get moving."

Venturing to another lobby venue, McCormick & Schmick's Seafood & Steaks, they sat amongst professionals trying to close lunchtime business deals, people like them passing through town and waiters trying to earn generous gratuities. As utensils clanked against stoneware, scrumptious aromas of seafood, pasta, steaks and specialty meats filled the air, playing with the palates of two in a hurry.

Ordering coconut shrimp, steamed mussels, and cedar roasted Atlantic salmon and blackened chicken linguini entrees, William blessed the table, then looked across at the woman he had met only five days earlier. An hour earlier, difficult memories had faded the glow from her eyes. Now it reappeared along with a happy-yet-mysterious smile that curved her lips, a smile that sent a curious shiver down his spine.

But what he saw in those eyes, a gentle, happy gleam, made him feel good.

Finally her pupils met his, holding them with an eerie power, a sense of certainty.

Then her gaze dropped to his lips. Staring intently like she wanted to hold the air between his teeth hostage, her mind had landed in a place where carnal cravings met real emotions to create something spiritually special; a place where tongues joined, moans made magical melodies and bodies gelled to create ecstasy.

William was already there but he had restraint. There was a surprise to enjoy, then something very special to ask of her.

On Valentine's Day, Keisha was a stranger helping him with a cup of coffee.

In five days, she had become so much more.

And in a few hours she would find out just how much.

FOURTEEN

Keisha had finally arrived home.

The frosty Motown air told her so and the fact that the home of the Red Wings sat on the banks of the Detroit River made the twenty-degree weather seem colder.

Eager to leave his footprints in a new city, William took over the wheel of the car, and the Ohio cities connected to I-75 breezed by: Arlington Heights, Lockland, Miamisburg, Dayton, Bowling Green, Rossford, Northwood and finally, twelve miles of Toledo.

The closer they got to the Wolverine State, the more excited Keisha got. Fidgeting like a little girl, a burst of nervousness made her heart dance to a peculiar, pleasurable beat.

The schoolteacher emerged when she said, "Did you know that the name Michigan is a French derivative for the Indian word *Mishigamaa*, which means *large water?*"

William asked, "Aren't you surrounded by five lakes?"

"Four: Superior, Huron, Michigan and Erie. The fifth one, Lake Ontario, borders Canada and us. It's so beautiful in the summer, William, seeing all the boats come in."

"I can imagine."

"I hope you can come up and see for yourself."

The comment stood in the air for a few seconds, seconds that seemed like an eternity for a woman putting the depths of her core out there.

Humbly, William said, "That would be cool."

"It would mean a lot to me."

"Keisha, don't we have to get your car from the airport?"

"No. I left it in my driveway."

Finally, they arrived in downtown Detroit. Beautiful violet sky-rays added majesty to early evening skies and the Riverfront Plaza basked in its stateliness. Standing tall were skyscrapers and office complexes, and the landmark's promenade areas were coated with enough snow to allow tourists to stroll in a mid-winter wonderland.

Passing by Hart Plaza, William saw a large bronze fist.

He asked, "Joe Louis?"

"Yes. Not only did he represent the power of his punch in the ring, but it represented the power of our city."

"Nice."

"William, did you know that Detroit made the middle-class bracket?" Hearing silence, Keisha continued. "Henry Ford wanted his workers to be able to afford his cars, so he paid them well."

"People forget that your city was the main freedom point of the Underground Railroad before the Fugitive Slave Act of 1850 was passed."

"I'm impressed."

When William sought confirmation about Detroit being one of America's deadliest cities, Keisha bristled. Sure, the Motor City had its rough patches, unsafe areas like Brightmoor, Joy Road, Mack and Bewick, Grand River and the North End, as illustrated when she bluntly stated, "New Yorkers do a bunch of talking and arguing. Here, after a few words, we shoot. They have concealed carry gun laws up here."

"Wow."

"In some places, it's like rolling the dice. But the strong survive."

"Did your parents live here?"

"We lived in Pontiac, about forty minutes away. I live in Roseville off 13 Mile Road, in Macomb County."

"I see."

Soon, they parked in a garage on West Jefferson Avenue. Walking through a tunnel, Keisha clutched his arm. Sensuous and ladylike all at once, her killer walk and warm facial expression threatened to undo the poise of onlookers nearby.

Knowing her power, she joked, "Ebony man needs a hot babe, doesn't he?"

William muttered, "I guess."

"I know we're going to Joe Louis Arena. What's going on there?"

"Keisha, consider this a belated Valentine's Day present."

"Or, my early Sweetest Day present." Hearing a pause, she continued, "Sweetest Day is like a second Valentine's Day celebrated on the third Saturday in October."

"Valentine's Day is my favorite holiday."

"Imagine if you have two to celebrate? You could remember Linda on one and me on the other."

"You know what?"

"What?"

"I'm beginning to like Michigan a whole lot."

Casting a spell with his words, Keisha's heart thumped madly in her chest and her smile was enchanting.

And when it couldn't get any brighter, as they entered the arena, William handed her an orange souvenir program.

"Let's pick up our tickets."

Keisha grinned when she saw the capitalized inscription and felt like she'd won a trip to heaven.

Someone created a concert experience in honor of her Dr. Feel-good, a theatrical production that fused fantasy with circus-like imagination, aerial artistry, street entertainment, visual illusions and the soulful essence of the King of Pop.

"William, you're incredible!!! I don't know what..."

Her gratitude was interrupted by a simple request.

"Keisha, let's make tonight special."

Finding their seats in section 103, they were among a legion of fans refusing to relinquish their love for a man who transcended generations. With Michael Jackson's spirit hovering over them, William and Keisha were transported to a romantic Neverland, a place where unguarded hearts and smiles were warm in compassion. Arriving at the gates, they were hugged and handed a champagne glass filled with a special potion; a concoction made by a genius with his greatest energy.

Love.

Throughout this two-and-a-half-hour extravaganza, it wasn't the incredible imagery, spectacular special effects, sensational stage lighting or acrobatic ability that made them remember a ridiculously riveting time. Nor was it the finely tuned choreography, the powerful pyrotechnics, extraordinary ensemble of talent, or the videos of a magical man in motion that moved them in many directions.

It was Michael's love.

And it was the music.

Magnificently mixed to tell a story about a man on a journey, the couple went along for the ride, following Michael through the years like happy mice following a Pied Piper. Rediscovering their "childhood" along with the mimes on stage, William and Keisha started something when they became dancing machines that shook their bodies down to the concrete floor; blaming their uncontrolled joy on their boogie.

Moving together, they thoroughly enjoyed the gangster melody. "This Place Hotel," an insecurity-based song of confusion, was stripped of its music and sounded even more sinister. Watching an exotic pole dancer do a sexy tango, the couple became smooth criminals, simulating dance moves together in their seats as the moment's magic became another part of them.

Completely absorbed, Michael made them feel dangerous, and when they saw their synchronicity in movement they looked at each other with wide-eyed amazement, shrugged their shoulders and laughed.

Temporarily intruding their space was an elderly couple sitting one row above them.

Pointing to the stage, the husband said, "You two should be up there."

His wife immediately stepped in, saying, "Leave them alone, honey. Can't you see they're in love?"

Right at that moment, the stage lights went out and black-suited aerialists with circular lights attached to them meshed with il-luminated airborne rings and a black backdrop. Their bodies, contorting and connecting, looked like stars in a galaxy forming a colorful constellation.

It was breathtaking.

Keisha, totally immersed, allowed the song "Human Nature" into her spirit. When Michael sang about a city's heartbeat, she leaned over and allowed her lips to brush ever so lightly against his.

Was it scary to William? Did it threaten once dormant emotions?

Quite the opposite; William was overjoyed, but he had to keep his cool until later.

On cue, "Thriller" and Vincent Price injected more youth into the hearts of the middle-aged couple; they replicated the famous video steps.

They were not alone in their world: Michael Jackson was pulling out all the stops with the hopes that both wouldn't stop loving each other; that is, if they ever admitted it.

The second half of the production touched them. When "Scream" lit up the darkened arena, Keisha said, "I'll be Janet, you be Michael."

Grinning, her date agreed, and together they sang a duet better than Sonny and Cher ever had.

Emotions changed quickly when the mime dancer performed "Gone Too Soon." There wasn't a dry eye in the house. When William saw Keisha's eyes, he gently wiped away a tear that escaped red rims.

"You are so precious," she whispered.

Mechanical robots felt The Holy Ghost during a stirring rendition of "They Don't Care About Us." Moving to a spiritual chant-and-call in the middle of the segment, they took people of all creeds and colors to church, denouncing racism with images of the KKK and children orphaned by war appearing on the large screens.

Recalling a conversation in their travels, Keisha tapped her suitor. William nodded.

Without words, they knew.

Yet one question went unanswered; could two people who had known each other for five days truly heal one another? If the glowing red hearts brought out during "Will You Be There" weren't indicative of them pushing aside fears, doubts, frustrations for unmitigated joy as opposed to enduring sorrow, then what followed…

As a video montage showing an eleven-year-old prodigy singing about making pacts and faith played on all the jumbo screens, Keisha reached for William's hand and lip-synced, "I'll be there for you."

William's heart pounded at a frantic pace and he took a few seconds before responding.

"That's good to know."

About fifteen minutes later, after dancers moved through an incredible "Can You Feel It/Don't Stop 'Til You Get Enough/ Billie Jean/Black or White" megamix, the couple's trip to Neverland reached its emotional conclusion when a prince of peace encouraged all in attendance to improve the world with internal change.

Look at that man in the mirror, Michael said, and do so with love; God's love.

The house lights came up, and Keisha wouldn't move.

Neither could her date; he, too, hadn't finished remembering a time when a force of nature with super-human grace, quicksilver motion and the God in him made millions around the globe feel good.

She wiped away a joyful rainfall.

"I miss him so much."

William smiled, his brown eyes twinkling with affection.

"I miss him, too."

The couple shared a deep stare, both of them lost in an intimate sea of irises.

Her spacious living room had champagne-tinted vertical blinds, perfectly positioned so when daytime streamed in, leafy plants received much needed sunlight. Transforming the area into a den of serenity was a truffle-colored furniture set complete with sofa, loveseat and a low-legged recliner. Plush cushioned and skillfully matched, the Old World fixtures were beautifully sophisticated. Freshly polished end tables supported by bronze-colored metal and a large bookcase filled with black literature enhanced the elegance.

A connoisseur of black art, several WAK prints hung on her walls, getting William's attention immediately.

"I see you're a fan of Kevin Williams. His work captures the essence of our people," he said, referring to the paintings.

Keisha replied, "I love his work."

Two pictures stood out prominently. The latter portrait showed a man on one knee, palms raised paying homage to his queen.

The other illustration, one showing the most natural demonstration of love God created, had William grappling with his past, a beautiful present that went into her bedroom to get comfortable, and three decades of emotions at his core.

He was frightened, but he was in love again.

Seeing her contented sighs and starting to feel them in his mind, he wanted her body close so he could protect her heart with all the compassion, kindness and affection he could muster. Desperately craving the connection of magical moans and intense groans, before the bubble bath with peppermint oil, before the joining of two in passion, before their tongues taught one another what heaven felt like, before the consummation of climaxes in never-ending sexual satiation, he had to ask one question under the glow of low-lit lights.

Would she be *It*?

Would she be the woman he had always wanted, one who could love him 'til his dying day, through good and not-so-good, forever and a day? Would she put all her trust in him, as he would her, caring for each other's souls while sharing God's greatest energy? Would she, could she do him the honor of being by his side, no matter where the crazy roads of life took them?

Would she be *It?*

Would she be that lady?

After three decades on an emotional rollercoaster, William was about to find out.

Keisha reappeared before him, looking stunning in a black maxi-dress that clung to every curve of her voluptuous frame. Radiating beauty and class, her splendor consumed him; there was little air left in his lungs, she looked that breathtaking.

Seeing her had him feeling some kind of way, but before his arms enveloped her in his embrace, he had to ask himself again; would she be *It?*

Bringing him a glass of merlot, she sat next to him on the sofa. "You're scared, William. I can tell."

"You're just as afraid as I am. That means our feelings are real."

"So what do we do now? Do I let you go back to New York and accept our journey for what it was?"

"No."

"Then what? What do we do?"

"Let's just be."

He told her this, but the little voice in his mind was screaming at a high decibel.

Sometimes you must be willing to learn while taking the lead, it said.

"Keisha, can I play something for you?"

"Sure."

Docking up to her music system, he pressed a button on his iPod and returned to his seat.

Tears of complete vulnerability escaped him, an avalanche of emotions that erased every ounce of fear within.

Delicately taking her hands, he said, "Listen to this."

The first notes of an expressive ballad swirled around them, an extended version of the ninth song on the biggest-selling album of all time. The song's first verse found a sound filling the room with a love, which illuminated the darkness that hurt and fear bring to a heart, provided the lovers had the courage to trust once more.

Touching her with his entire soul, Keisha's hopeful mate wanted to warm her with the fires of his heart; it would feel right if you walked with him into paradise.

William wanted no money or applause, the second verse stated; he would trade all his earthly possessions for real love and a day where he would hold a woman so close their bodies would become one. But her feelings had to be in accordance with his, no charade, no waffling, no mystery. Weary from planting hopes in painful lands of make-believe, he prayed Keisha would be the one he cherished until the sunset of his golden years.

At the most important moment of his life, William McCall and Michael Jackson were one, singing with every molecule what his humble dust desperately wanted; a lady in his life. Poignantly relaying his truth, praying she would be by his side through trials, tribulations and triumphs, he wanted to bring his lady euphoria along with an endless paradise, one that took forever on an unforgettable ride with God's greatest form of love, that between man and woman.

With an audacity of hope, William wanted Keisha to stay with him until the end of time as the lady in his life.

Sounding spectacular through the verses and chorus, there was another part of William that Michael revealed in the song's closing minute and a half, one that turned his sensitivity into sheet-scorching sensuality. The lady in his life would feel his passion full-blast and its heat would radiate all over...all over...all over... all over... He would love her mind, her spirit, her soul; and when they deliciously devoured one another, his swollen sexuality would give her soaking sweetness love in a special way, with so much passion and force that it would dominate her completely; physically, mentally, spiritually, sensitively, simultaneously. Orgasms would set them free in a world where magnificent moans were mandatory and lovemaking became marvelously majestic as a million lights burned through the night.

Wanting to hold her body tight, praying for the opportunity to treat her right, he loved Keisha and she wasn't going anywhere. Her heart could finally exhale, and she would run no more from what's in store.

Tearful eyes of truth knew that.

At song's end, he took a deep breath. A single word escaped his quivering lips; a heartfelt word expressing humility, power and everything he owned inside.

"Please?"

What he saw looking back at him was a woman who had waited all her life for two things: to feel soft, safe, and secure in her submission, and to satisfy an entitlement for exclusive love, a love all her own.

Glowing like a lamp, the smile that curved Keisha's lips was a silent dare for him to fulfill both of their desires.

Moving closer, a man in love with the lady in his life answered the dare with his heart. The tip of his tongue teased her lips until he parted her brim completely with soft, sensuous pecks. Politely, their tongues caressed within the framework of a fantastic kiss that lasted a good fifteen minutes.

Moaning softly as his mouth temporarily said farewell to hers, erratic breaths of pleasure left Keisha as his lips danced with her forehead, her earlobes and her neckline. Simmering with anticipation, her legs turned to jelly as the desire between her stems showed itself in liquid form, but William didn't know that yet.

And he didn't want to; his head found her sweet-smelling bosom, and there is where his famished mouth went to work. Licking both left and right, claiming both continents of fleshy mass, he focused his attentiveness on the tip of her breasts by dampening her beautifully distended nipples. Feeding on them as if he were born again with a feeling so right, he wanted to hear shallow breaths of anticipation from the woman he loved.

Looking up at his queen, he saw her sensuously simmering where love marinated her soul in its spicy sauces. Eyes glazed, smoldering with expectation, Keisha moved her hips to every suck and bite on her perky mounds.

Gasping, letting erotic tickles consume her, "That's it...get it for your lady," she purred.

Hearing her vocals increased William's urgency. As he continued massaging her cleavage with his mouth, he felt her tongue licking his bald head.

"Are you trying to tell me something?" he asked.

"Yes I am, baby. My man has been clogged up for too long."

Rising, Keisha took his hand, but not before purposely tickling the stiffness at his groin.

Her bedroom was an opulent brown color, lending to a sensuous atmosphere. Accompanying the four decorative columns on her poster bed was a box cornice design which took the Old World tradition to another level. The matching mirrored dresser, nightstand, leopard print area rug and chest added grand style to Keisha's superb sense of detail.

William, immediately noticing the rug, smiled.

He said, "I should have known by your cat eyes."

"You should have known what?"

"I love tiger and leopard print. It brings out the animal in me."

"Well, tonight you're on a safari, exploring a whole new world."

"You're my type of woman."

In a low tone, the lady in his life said, "Made especially for you."

They stood in the middle of the room merging their hearts. With their long kiss, they became arsonists setting their painful memories afire, burning them beyond recognition in a red-orange blaze. Replacing them was a hearted-shaped blue flame, one that floated in zero gravity and was weightless in its burdens.

Spiraling into a special place where they were so aroused by each other, they could barely take the pleasure, shivers and sounds that awaited them; shivers that indicated what they were about to experience would be life-changing, and heavenly sounds that accompanied the spiritual release of their great energy.

Lying on the queen-size mattress, Keisha raised a forefinger.

"Come here," she said softly, her open mouth requesting that he again taste her tongue.

William obliged. The heated hook rising at his groin, he wanted to make her addicted to his thrust and retreat, but not yet. Tenderly titillating and tantalizingly thorough, he again traced the protruding points of her peaks, then sucked with seven years of famine.

Stimulated by his hunger, Keisha cupped his head in a nurturing, naughty way.

"That's right… Get it, baby."

Wanting to enjoy the taste of both nipples simultaneously, he continued sucking while pressing her mounds together.

"Damn, baby, don't you want some?"

Hell yeah, William wanted some, but he had made himself a promise; the next time he shared his spirit with a woman he loved, he would be thorough.

Emotional consummation meant her gratification before his starvation.

Her gratification before his starvation meant taking his time; savoring every curve and contour of the woman he loved, cherishing every crevice of her gorgeous frame. Her gratification before his starvation meant drinking her essence with slow kisses, kisses that electrified her soul as it levitated into a love that required total immersion. Her gratification before his starvation meant making her body ache beautifully as his tongue ran across all intimate intersections, ultimately taking her fountain of love powerfully with his mouth, his heat and his heart. Her gratification before his starvation meant before carnal cravings connected, he needed her eyes glassy, her tongue cold from breathless pants and her body quivering from a pleasure so intense that in her exhilaration, she would fail to realize that she had yet to be penetrated.

By tasting the place that released her emotions, simply translated, her gratification before his starvation meant ladies first.

After removing her dress and his clothes, he kissed down her frame and teased the peripheries of her pleasure, pecking and licking her inner thighs and her thick calves.

Squirming, magnificent mini-eruptions sent feelings of bliss all through the lady in his life.

"Damn, baby," Keisha moaned. "You gotta…"

"Shhh… I got this."

Determined to make her feel his fire, William finally reached her special place, that heaven between the outstretched wings of sculpted stems. Prying open the puffy lips of her center, glimpses of his famine finally escaped him. With an unleashed animalism, his face became fast friends with her hips as he dove in orally.

"William…what…damn, baby…okay…okay…okay…"

Feeling her rosebud swell as it rose against the tip of his nose, he decided to rub his bald pate in it, then his chin. Trying to extract every erotic nerve ending she owned, he was on a seek-and-satisfy mission to find every responsive place her soaking triangle possessed. Determined to be the key to the light in her eyes, William wanted Keisha to remember this moment, how and what he did to her, during good days and bad, happy moments and sad, when skies bled a happy blue, rained an emotional gray and snowed white.

Needing the lady in his life to have his name on her tongue forever, his seductive smacks sent sensuous sensations shooting through her, causing her heart to stutter.

Feeling her buttocks tense, Keisha moaned, "What are you… What are you doing to me?"

"I'm loving you with all my heart."

Twitching, losing a battle to the pleasure that boomeranged between the crown of her head and the soles of her feet, the orgasms that once screamed internally began to surface as she moaned beautifully.

"Oh, God… Oh, God, yes…"

Continuing his exploration, William's oral flute composed a score for the ages. Tickling her tunnel with a tireless tongue, his lips lapped her delicious pit with loving licks.

"Please, baby, make it cum," Keisha demanded.

The mind-blowing motion of his mouth sent her to the brink of an ecstatic meltdown complete with quivers and quakes.

Sensing she was near, William sucked her sensitive folds, gently nibbled on her pearl, then munched inside on thick pink walls in an effort to make her cat eyes slit-like.

He would find out soon enough. Keisha, pushing him in, wrapped her legs around his head tightly. Shuddering and arching her back, her pelvis was off the bed when she shivered and screamed.

"Yes, baby… That's it… That's it… Oh, God… Oh, God…"

A deluge of exclusive love filled her man's mouth, a torrential overflow that could have drowned ten men.

Gulping furiously, William drank as much of the waterfall as humanly possible. He gave up halfway and let the rain cover him, smearing his face in it.

Soon, the quivers subsided, transforming into wonderful *ah's* as Keisha curled her voluptuous frame in a fetal position.

William met her face with a tender kiss. "Baby, you taste so good."

"Let me taste." Like a sated lioness, she licked his neck, chin and cheeks.

The air in the room was already blanketed with the aroma of two in love, but the fragrance needed something greater.

And the lady in his life reminded him of such. Sliding her hands down his body, she arrived at his groin. Gripping his length, Keisha slowly stroked it from base to tip.

"It hooks," she purred.

Swelling, hardening, throbbing in her hand, William groaned as an intense array of feelings became impossible to ignore. Pulling her into another passionate kiss, with a voice raw in emotion he whispered, "I need you right now."

Keisha's hips quivered as her body readied itself for what was no longer unthinkable.

Slowly, William teased the outer lips of paradise with the head of his covered sex.

"Are you sure you want to do this?"

"Please," she begged, her hands resting on his strong forearms.

Reflexively loose-limbed, Keisha didn't wait for him to thrust down and in; she placed it in.

William's eyes watered, as did Keisha's.

Emotions mingling with ecstatic pleasure, there was no going back now.

"It's okay if you're excited," she said, breathing through that initial, overwhelming feeling. "I know it's been a minute."

Her man heard this and smiled.

The lady in his life hadn't read the memo.

Her gratification before his starvation meant wearing it out.

With a powerful, easy grind, William eased himself in and out of her with exquisite slowness, not only for their mutual pleasure, but to acclimate himself with her heaven, a heaven already soaked and talking to him.

"You hear that, baby? She likes you already," Keisha moaned. Meeting his movements with small waves, her thoughts began to scatter across a land of bliss. She made soft, sweet sounds while contracting her muscles around him, and a fantastic feeling connected with something deep inside her stomach. The hip rolls and pelvic tilts she learned in dance class years ago made his eyes twinkly bright.

Kissing her kissable-mouth with emotions that transcended sex, William increased the tempo. Romantically rhythmic, with amazing intensity he went from zero to sixty. He wanted his woman to fly a wet flag of devotion on his staff, one that screamed to the world colors of ecstasy. Spreading her legs wide, he grabbed the soles of her feet. Using them as support, he made round-the-world circle strokes with his hips, plunging all of him deep, then retreating.

Meeting his thrusts with hers, Keisha wrapped a hand around the back of his head, pulling him close. Mouth to mouth, pelvis meeting pelvis, she gripped his hard steel with her love muscles while their tongues again moved in each other's mouth.

William whispered, "What do want from me?"

"Give me all of it...all of it...," she growled.

Stiffening as an extreme wave of pleasure hit, her body left conscious control and was reduced to trembling when, without warning, electric spasms of delight jolted it. Lofting over previous barriers while leaving her suspended in rarified air was an intense orgasm, one that was low on her vocal Richter scale yet high in its intensity.

An entire torrent of affection left her, causing her man to leave her canal. Her honey felt good, but there was something about making her love come down that made William's thirst unquenchable.

"No, baby, put it back...please...put it back in..."

"In a minute, Keisha. I need a drink."

Going back downtown, an oral pleasure artist consumed her canvass with his paintbrush, massaging her triangle with lollipop licks. Needing to see the beauty of another cry-face from the lady in his life, desperate to reclaim her love over and over and over again, he slipped two fingers in her slick wetness, this action causing sensuous tentacles to touch Keisha's body.

Undone by an unfamiliar pleasure, every nerve, every fiber of her being was drowned by ecstasy.

With groovy-great glee, she panted, "I have some more for you..."

Moaning dynamically, her eyes rolled to the back of head and another rainfall came.

"There you go, baby," she screamed, her legs shaking violently.

Again William drank from her well.

Returning to her brim, his lizard hungrily found her lips. Entangling tongues, kissing ferociously in a rhythm that indicated primitive, poetically passionate pleasure, their bodies resumed the dance.

Varying the speed of his strokes, shifting the gears of his swollen stick, innately William seemed to know how to hit all the spots in her honey, when to beat it up with love, when to swerve his hips like he was dancing reggae, how to delicately glide as if dancing a waltz, and how to let her know how much he loved her by making her feel good all over...all over...all over...all over...and over.

Filling her, withdrawing, then filling her again, the way William was making love to the lady in his life was possessive, but not in the "Who's is it?" mode. Creating new G-spots within her, the determination of his motion, strong strokes emanating from love, need and urgency let her know, without words born from machismo that he wanted Keisha to be his queen, the lady of his life even in the afterlife when they returned to dust. He looked into her eyes, gave the deepest part of himself to this woman and received her soul in return.

And without words, she named her wet, watery, well *William*.

Feeling like the room was spinning in an orgasmic swirl, every muscle in her frame trembled. Years of pent-up tension left her and a sweet, sense of freedom shot through her, causing her toes to curl from pinpricks, then enormous rays of delight. Reaching that high score over and over, shuddering as if a personal trainer had worked her to exhaustion, her entire body throbbed from the joinder of heartbeats, and emotionally helpless sounds left her when she dug her nails into his brown flesh.

Staring deep into his eyes, the look on her face told a story words couldn't say.

With total transparency, it pleaded, *Please don't hurt me.*

That his eyes said the same thing sent a maddening delirium through them both.

"Give me more," she begged. "Give me more… Make me cry… Make me cry… I can't let you out of my life… I want to be yours so bad, baby…"

William whispered tenderly, "You already are, Keisha."

Hearing that made his queen clench her muscles even tighter; she wanted him inside of her forever.

Her rainforest again drenched the sheets.

Then the tears of many emotions ran from her, tears of complete vulnerability, tears of pain that mixed an empty past, a present ecstasy, and an eternal future all together.

And her man was in the same place: William shuddered, then released seven years of love by way of his own tears, milky-white tears captured by latex, and crystal tears from his eyes when he collapsed breathless, sobbing in her arms.

Gripping hard, Keisha experienced another orgasm and milked all the tears from his body. As she descended, she kissed his face, then held him as she wept as well.

Real love always cries together.

And two souls in search of each other became one while crying together.

FIFTEEN

At what point does a man realize that wanting all of a person after years of only loving part of them hurt? And at what point does a person justify the repercussions of such and come to the conclusion that such is life and let go?

Furious and downright miserable, Carl Austin refused to let go. He tossed and turned through the night as a living, breathing organism named despair took hold, growing larger in depression and irritability with each passing second.

Normally radiating invincibility in his walk and talk, this day seemed different; even the client noticed something awry in his spirit when they discussed an ongoing case over lunch on the East Side, at Smith & Wollensky.

"The pending Rolston matter is almost ready for trial. All conferences have been completed, and the depositions went smoothly," he said to Jerry Armstrong, the head of a multimillion-dollar construction firm and lifelong friend. "We'll be ready in a matter of weeks."

"Carl, you told me that earlier, before the meeting," Jerry said, a hint of exasperation invading his tone. "Brother, you've been repeating yourself a lot lately. Are you all right?"

"I've had a lot on my mind lately. My future."

"You know, you've established credibility as a top-flight lawyer and stabilizing force within the black community. Have you ever thought about politics, running for a state, then a national office? You could do even more in the public sector. If we pooled our resources and contacts, you could do some serious damage."

"It's a little too late for that, Jerry. I'm fifty-seven."

"But you look fifteen years younger. And you're successful, smart, well liked, and you've accomplished a lot without leaving a trail of enemies behind you. You're someone a whole nation could pay attention to."

"Come on, Jerry."

"Seriously, why don't you think about it? Winston Churchill was almost seventy years old when he first became Prime Minister of England, so what makes you think you can't do it? Besides, with Amanda by your side, you could…"

After ordering two martinis, Carl inhaled deeply.

He asked, "Can I speak to you off record?"

"Sure, man."

"I left Amanda on Sunday."

With wide eyes, Jerry asked, "What happened? She's your equal, a woman who stands on her own two feet. Plus, she's medium maintenance and has the class of a woman in power."

"I never loved her, Jerry."

"Don't you think that it's kind of late to be coming to that realization? You should try and make that work."

"Why should I stay with someone I don't love? I'm not Fitzgerald Grant."

"But you're creating a real-life scandal," Jerry countered, "Why are you sabotaging your legacy?" He paused. "Who is it, that school-teacher from Michigan?"

Carl's face had been slapped with surprise.

"How did you know?"

"Come on, Carl. People talk. So it's more than a fling, huh?"

"She makes me feel alive with wonder. But she doesn't want to see me anymore."

"So why don't you go back to your wife and learn to love her. You owe her that much. Hell, she gave up her life for you."

"It wouldn't be fair to either one of us."

"Are you sure you're not suffering from The Jelly Syndrome?"

"What in the hell is The Jelly Syndrome?"

Jerry Armstrong began a mature version of Storytime. "About twenty years ago there was a powerful man in the New York judicial system, a chief judge of the New York Court of Appeals. He could have run for President one day if not for an affair with a socialite. He ended up behind bars because he couldn't let go when it was over. He lost everything, his seat on the bench, his bar license, not to mention the disgrace he brought upon his family."

"How'd that happen?"

"The FBI picked him up on extortion and blackmail charges. Later, he was diagnosed as being bipolar, but in my opinion that was saving face for public embarrassment. His nose was so wide open that he lost control of everything."

"Pussy-whipped is what it's called."

"I like the jelly reference. It sounds better."

Jerry hit Carl close to home, but his ego wouldn't reveal any vulnerability, even though hearing this left words stuck in his throat.

His business partner cautioned, "Think this thing over, man. Amanda's a special lady, one who doesn't fall from the apple tree too often. It's kind of late in life to be chasing the unknown and you don't want to ruin your life over an out-of-state school-teacher."

Finally with a smug arrogance, Carl responded, "That's not going to happen to me."

His mouth said one thing, but his actions were of a man who suspended rational thinking. Excusing himself, he went into the men's room, popped more pills and called Keisha's cell.

No answer.

Then he called her home phone.

No answer there either.

She better not give my shit away.

Action always speaks louder than words, and that doesn't always mean in a good way.

In her dealings with Carl, Keisha had been content, but hopes she maintained for exclusiveness faded to the point that she couldn't remember them. Romanticizing about a love all hers and preserving certain inhibitions until she felt liberty, at fifty years of age, she thought that day had passed her by.

One night with William McCall changed all that.

Basking in the afterglow with a man that was solely hers shattered emotional barriers in a way that was foreign to what she had felt at any other time on this earth.

Liberated completely, Keisha exhaled like she'd released a burden that was difficult to shoulder. As sunshine brightened her eyes, a peaceful calm resided at her core. Extreme joy ruled her insides and the restless demons she knew were served eviction papers by a man who was completely invested in her happiness.

Knowing that made her feel free, uninhibited and sexy.

Knowing that made her want to please her man until he begged her to stop.

He's gonna get it, she thought.

Her meditation was amplified when she was greeted with a delightful aroma. Carrying a wooden tray, William brought food to his queen. On a plate were turkey bacon strips, two over-easy eggs, sugar-and-spice pancakes and a cup of coffee.

He greeted her with a kiss.

"I hope you didn't mind me making breakfast. You needed to eat."

"Now why would my husband feel uncomfortable in his house?"

William blushed.

"Well, I hope you like…"

Incredibly nervous, he watched with love as Keisha consumed her meal. Awaiting her judgment, he was stunned to see ambiguity; no raised brows in pleasant surprise, no finger-licking good response, nothing.

"So?"

"So what?"

"What do you think?"

"What do I think of what?"

"Of my breakfast."

"Oh, that. I'll let you know later what I think."

"What do you mean, *later?*"

She laughed. "You'll see."

"Why can't you tell me now?"

"You're like a little boy looking for approval from his mother."

"Well, they say that men marry women like their mothers."

"I've heard that before."

"Keisha, what would you like for dinner?"

"Dinner, too? I thought I was supposed to be taking you out."

"You don't have to."

"But I want to."

Keisha would do that, but first she would stop at a boutique on North Gratiot, near the Clinton Township mall.

With a sly smile, her voice was intoxicating when she purred, "I want you to wait in the car."

"What are you up to?"

"You'll see…"

The store's name, Lover's Lane, had always been a favorite of Keisha's; in fact she already owned a pair of stiletto knee-high boots she never wore.

I'm wearing them tonight, she thought.

Bypassing toys, gimmicks and other accessories, she immediately headed to the costume section of the store and purchased four leopard-print scarves and a blindfold. She left the store smiling mischievously and humming "Get Happy," a classic Judy Garland tune.

My man will definitely be happy after this.

When she tossed the package in the backseat, William asked, "What's in the bag?"

"You'll see."

"Why can't you tell me?"

"It's a surprise."

The intense look in her eyes made William's eyes drop to the floor of the car. Taking blatant possession of his body and soul, that she uttered those words in a trash-talking tone made him tense like a ball in need of release.

After eating at the Capital Grille in nearby Troy, they rushed home. Keisha said little over dinner, but an impish smirk accompanied steamy, seductive cat eyes.

Calling the shots from the minute they entered her home, a

vampire thirsty for a creamy wine was ready to devour her prey.

Like a tiny breeze of wind, she brushed her soft petals against his, pecking him affectionately. "Since you've been so good to me, Mama has a special treat for her hero," she said, her voice sounding demure, like calm before a storm. Placing the blindfold over William's eyes, she took his hand, leading him back into love.

There was something hypnotic about Keisha; something that indicated that an amorous aggression had taken hold.

Further proof came when she quickly undressed him, pushed him onto the queen-sized mattress and tied his arms and legs to the four posters.

With a seductive wickedness, she said, "Did I ever tell you that I'm an erotic rollercoaster? Well, tonight you're going on a ride. Now, I'll be right back."

"Keisha, wait…"

Left there naked, blindfolded and arms tied to a bed, William's breathing changed; his pants were full of anticipation and expectation.

Suddenly, he felt a heated drop on his chest, then a hot drizzle. Flinching, he shouted, "What the…"

"I always wanted to pour hot oil on my man."

"You get down like that?"

"I could, if you'd like."

"What I would like for you to do is to take the blindfold off so that I can see you."

"That's gonna cost you."

Knowing what that meant, William braced himself for more heat, and Keisha obliged, turning her drizzle to a steady pour from his chest to his torso.

The warm sensation aroused him even more.

"I knew my man would pass his initiation."

After kissing her hostage, her tongue slowly moved south, licking and sucking his neck, his collarbone, and his shoulders.

Squirming, a special part of William stood erect, down for whatever.

Keisha asked, "You like this, don't you?"

"Mmm…"

"That's not answering me." Continuing her achingly slow torture, she pinched his nipples, then sucked on them, causing an intense pleasure/pain sensation.

Finally William surrendered, saying, "Yes."

"Yes, what, Mr. McCall?"

"Yes, this feels good, Ms. Gray."

"Ooh, Mama likes that."

Finally, she removed the blindfold.

William was flummoxed, stunned to speechlessness. There was the lady in his life in a tuxedo jacket, black fedora, knee-high boots with fetish heels and fishnet nylons. Scrumptious and shapely, those cherry-red lips made his eyes luminous with want.

Gulping, he said, "Wow…"

"I take it you like."

"Yes. I do."

By presentation, Keisha made a powerful statement: that she was fearlessly on board to fully experience the love of her life. There wouldn't be any *I wonder if I showed enough class* anxieties; nor would questions like *can I keep him? Can I please him? Will he stick around even if I do?* have occupancy in her brain. Though she had only been in his life for a week, she knew the deal; the way he'd made love to her the night before told her so.

And her exhalation meant sexual freedom; that all bets were off.

Looking at her man with killer eyes, she went to her dresser, put on her Bose system, and said, "We're gonna do things a little different tonight."

Gulping, all William could do was nod his head yes.

A pulsating thump filled the room.

In a sexy purr, Keisha cooed, "Loving you makes me feel free."

William gulped again.

"That's right, William McCall, I love you. I know it's been a week, but I know who you are."

"I love…"

A long index finger stilled his lips.

"Let me dance for you, dear."

Inviting him to her body party, Usher's "Trading Places" was on and Keisha had again transformed. Melodically moving, her undulating hips and creative contortions cast a spell on her man. Removing her coat, she put her belly-dancing torso on display, mesmerizing William with the movement of her midriff.

Middle age had never been more mesmeric.

Mid-song, she further added to his distress when she unveiled something she rarely revealed. Keisha introduced William to that special part of a woman only exposed when she feels safe, comfortable and devoid of issues. Basking in her liberation and knowing this man would cuddle her with respect afterward, Keisha completely unleashed her inhibitions.

With a sexy growl, she crawled to him. Kneading the oil into his body, she took her breasts, squeezed them together and swallowed his sword in her canyon.

"Do you like that, baby?"

"Yes…"

If he enjoyed that portion of her striptease, then he would be saying "Ooo-wee" afterward…

Next, Keisha made a pleasurable mess of things when she rubbed her thick, flexible frame on top of his. The blend of oil and body scents, created an aroma that filled the room, an aphrodisiac that took Keisha even higher.

William's erection was singing a familiar song, one that needed release.

And music his hard flute made hypnotized his woman, so much so that she experienced a freedom she desperately needed to share.

She took him in her mouth with her freedom. Making her man feel the wetness that came with her liberation, she studied William's face while doing this. Pleased with the reaction, Keisha increased the motion of her bobbling, then used her tongue to polish his heated saber.

Basking in her power to please, that her man was helpless turned her on to the nth degree. Moaning while mastering oral pleasure, each flick of her tender tongue, every stroke of her eager lips distorted his face. Playing peek-a-boo with William's passion was a mind-blowing sensation, a this-feels-too-damn-good-feeling men know all too well when pushed to the brink.

Keisha's facial expression mixed affection, attentiveness and arousal.

Altering her intensity ever so slightly, she seductively slurped the head of his staff while wonderfully working his length with two hands.

In a deep Madame voice, she asked, "Does it feel good, baby?"

Moaning uncontrollably, William couldn't even answer, but the energy rising from his body told her all she needed to know. The transfer of power now complete, he was completely at her mercy.

And he loved it.

So did she.

Feeling powerful took Keisha's freedom to an otherworldly

level. Massaging his manliness with lustful lubrications, the motion of her mouth manipulation pushed him to the back of her throat again and again.

Meeting an urge to make him explode, she was exquisitely taming her tool, training it with freedom's frenetic foray, making it *her dick*. It knew when to stand at attention, when to swell and throb and ultimately, when to release a generous stream of satisfaction to a woman in love.

Giving a low sound of encouragement, William could barely take it, but did you think his woman was going to stop showing him what freedom felt like?

He had to take it all; as Keisha did the night they joined their love.

Soon, William's wood became steel as his back tensed up…

"That's right," Keisha said in a bold, salacious voice. "Give it all to me…"

Removing him from her oral cavern, she used her hand to finish him… First fast, as it swelled…then slowly as spurts of liquid love left it.

"There you go, baby…"

Her voice sounded soothing and sexy, both of which made William's body jerk violently as he lost all muscle control. He couldn't stop her from stroking, extracting every drop of love from his body.

Slowly, his muscles regained their sanity, and while his breathing remained hard, he had melted. Keisha untied her prisoner and watched him curl in a fetal position and twitch as he descended from orgasmic bliss.

When he touched down, he met a loving embrace.

"Does that feel better?" Keisha asked.

Breathlessly, he replied, "You're too much."

Their bodies now braided, as his masculine angles blended perfectly with her womanly curves, it seemed fitting that Usher would end their moment by announcing that he would switch things back and return the favor.

With a twinkle in his eyes, William looked at the love of his life.

"You've been a bad girl, Keisha, a very bad girl."

"I have?"

"Yes you have, and you know what happens to bad girls, right?"

"Do I get punished like a bad girl?"

"Yes, you most certainly do."

He'd been her and she'd been him.

For round two, William knew what he had to do; he would flip the script, return serve and kill it.

SIXTEEN

The lower East Side apartment where Carl stayed was as mangled as his emotions.

Carrying a week's worth of insecurities on his shoulders, he couldn't stop his meltdown. He walked around like a zombie, his bleary eyes and thoughts on Keisha. Bawling uncontrollably, he refused to relinquish memories of their passion; memories that were in the rearview mirror trying to escape his view.

The funk of a reality without her had taken hold, and the realization of this had left him demoralized.

Carl Austin sounded desperate. Calling her phones relentlessly, "Baby, I want to continue seeing you," he begged repeatedly. "Let me know what you think."

Another message indicated that he was afraid for her safety, a third revealed his anger.

"One fucking mistake and you're gonna do me like this? Well, fuck you, bitch! You were nothing more than a good fuck, do you hear me?"

His frustration mounting, also gathering momentum with each unanswered phone call was an internal storm. That the woman he loved didn't have the decency to respond made him want to explode.

Feelings like that made him want to inflict some serious pain.

Feelings like that made him want to kill.

His ego rode on the dogs of wounded pride. Circling his stomach, they traveled through his bloodstream to his brain, where, along with enablers known as prescription pills, crowded corridors in his head with havoc. Feeling empty and terribly lonely, not only did he love Keisha for who she was, but her spirit, love and energy always conjured memories of his mother.

In the seven years that Grace Austin was in Carl's life, she had been everything. All that changed on a fateful winter night in 1965 when she tried to avoid some debris in the middle of the westbound I-94. Swerving her Buick Skylark on an icy highway, she lost control of the vehicle and crossed the median. Crashing head-first into a tractor-trailer, the impact of the collision was so severe that it crushed the car, killing her instantly.

While swerving was a natural reaction, it cost Carl his mother. Devastated, he compensated for his loss by romanticizing a mother/son relationship. He attributed all his success to her, this despite having no more than a seven-year recollection of her existence.

Ultimately, not having his mother made him a depressed workaholic until that day he saw Keisha at the Palace. While he loved his wife, Amanda, those special qualities Keisha displayed renewed a deep longing for something maternally nurturing.

That reason, along with so many others, made Keisha Gray the most important woman of his life, a woman he had to hold onto.

Pulling out his phone, he tried again.

No answer on her cell.

No answer on the house phone.

Punching a closet door, the force of the blow created a hole the size of a fist. Inhaling deeply, his mind blazed a white-hot rage and insanity captured his nervous system, hatred kidnapped his face, and the heat of his anger immediately dried obsessive tears running down his cheeks.

That bolt of fury quickly turned to action.

She wants her house keys? Well, she'll get them, he thought.

Checking his schedule, he saw an opening and booked a first-class ticket to Detroit for later in the afternoon.

In Carl's eyes, the time was ripe for a sit-down in Motown. In spite of everything that happened over the past week—including his erratic behavior—he was optimistic the summit would restore good news to his life. The knife lodged in his heart would be removed, she'd return to his waiting arms, and bygones would be bygones.

That he had left his wife only made his offer of reconciliation to Keisha more enticing. Realizing that she was tired of all the secrecy, no longer would they sneak around corners as clandestine lovers, no longer would she be a backdoor woman. There would be no more inconsistencies or excuses, no more vacillating between wife and lover, and his eternal sweetheart would no longer be some shameful secret.

Carl Austin couldn't see any other result.

Keisha loved the Metropark on 16 Mile.

In the summer, she walked the two-mile paved road, admiring the breathtaking views of Lake St. Clair. In the winter, she followed a half-mile trail to a grassy meadow. There she would watch deer and other forms of wildlife feed from raspberry, wild roses and dogwood.

Sometimes she traveled along a winding trail that went past a cottonwood grove and sat along the edge of a huge cattail marsh.

She loved watching blue heron and other waterfowl wade in a swamp area, but not as much as she enjoyed feeding ducks and swans.

When thoughts ran deep, she would sit on a bench near a pond and reflect.

On this chilly February afternoon, the sun set on the west, a full moon rose east, and Keisha had company on her bench.

And her company thought he was on the brink of winning a long trivia contest.

William said, "Keisha, stop changing the rules so that you can catch up."

"Baby, you're two points away."

"It would have been over had you not changed the rules back to one point a question. You think you're slick, but it's all over. I'm winning."

"What's the score?"

"Ninety-eight to ninety."

"I told you I have a secret weapon."

"Well, you better use it, because you're running out of time."

"Okay, before I use it, I want to know this: which was your favorite Jackson concert tour?"

"The Bad Tour. He was at his athletic and creative peak and his dance moves were out-of-this world. I saw him at Madison Square Garden three times and in the Meadowlands once. In terms of showmanship and stage presence, he was at his best."

"I'm a little older than you, William. I loved the Triumph Tour, in 1981. The unity of him and his brothers was electrifying, the love between them strong. I can still feel the energy of that first song; the entire show for that matter. This was the template for all future Jackson tours."

"Oh, so you finally admit to it."

"Admit what, my age?"

William nodded.

"Yes, honey. I'll be fifty-one on December eighteenth." Without warning, Keisha moved close, and the luscious pout of her lips met his mouth, first with a teasing kiss, then one with intent. "I don't take care of you like I'm fifty-one, now do I?"

"You sure don't, baby. I love it when you unleash your inner Skyy Black."

"So, William loves my porn star skills."

"No, I love *you*, Keisha. I love your intelligence, your toughness and your compassion. You're a survivor and a fighter, like me. But I must also confess that I love it when you flick a switch and become that other woman. Every man wants a woman that has an inner Skyy Black, and a decent brother encourages and respects it."

Keisha said, "I'm so glad I met you…"

"You're the sun that creates my shine, my love."

After another kiss, they resumed battle.

William asked, "So, what's this surprise you keep saying that you have?"

"Are you sure you're ready for it?"

"Yes. I am."

"Tell you what, William. I'll ask you one more question. Name the Jacksons' biggest-selling single as a group."

"That's easy. 'Shake Your Body (Down To The Ground).' It sold over three million copies as a single."

"Correct."

"Yup. That's point game."

"You are so sure that you'll win."

"Keisha, give it up. You're down nine points and all I have to do is get one more. The only way I'll let you win is if you told me that you met him."

Pausing, Keisha smiled.

"No… No… Get outta here…"

Grinning now, she nodded.

"That's not possible… That's not possible… Get outta here."

"And it wasn't after a concert either. It was in a park."

"Get outta here… I don't believe you."

"Well, you better believe it."

"I gotta hear this… You really met Michael Jackson?"

On cue, Keisha returned to a time in her life when things were muddled, about five months after the death of her parents. On a college trip to USC, she stayed with a relative in nearby Encino and one evening in 1982 she happened to stroll to a park located on Ventura Boulevard.

"I needed to get away from it all; the memory of my parents, handling their estate and the decision whether to stay in Michigan or go to Southern Cal for college. My emotions were all over the place, so I decided to take a walk over to Genesta Park for a minute. I was on my way to a set of rust-colored picnic tables when I saw this guy lying in the grass, looking like he was waiting for the stars to come out. When I got closer, I couldn't believe my eyes."

"Weren't you excited? Didn't you want to scream?"

"No. I had too much stuff going on to be overly excited. Ironically, I think that's why he talked to me, because he saw that I wasn't awestruck."

"What'd you talk about?"

"Life. He was about to go into the studio to record *Thriller*, and William, there was a fire in his eyes when he talked about it because he felt the music industry tried to keep him in his place as an R&B singer. He wanted to kill it."

"I don't blame him. He only got one Grammy nomination for *Off the Wall*. What a freaking joke!"

"He was very down-to-earth. He offered me words of encouragement for my future, and was very compassionate when I told him about my parents. We could have talked longer than the fifteen minutes we did, but I didn't want to interrupt his creative flow. He even offered to drive me home, but I didn't want to draw any more attention to him."

"Wow," was all William could say.

"He looked so peaceful, yet so lonely."

"I can imagine. Speaking of lonely, can we shift gears for a second? Is Carl…"

"He's working my nerves, leaving all kinds of messages."

William's demeanor changed; a masculine dynamic that comes when a man loves a woman surfaced.

"Do I need to get involved in this?"

"No, baby, I can handle it."

"Are you sure? Many a jilted lover has behaved unreasonably after a break-up."

"When he put his hands on me, he made that 'love' word become null and void when it pertained to him."

"You know you're gonna have to face him, right?"

"And when I do, William, all I'll say is; now that I really know you, I'm no longer interested in you."

"It's not going to be that easy, Keisha. He's invested a lot of time."

"If he really loves me, he'll let me be." She paused, then asked, "Do you think we moved out of time?"

"No. You're a single woman."

"Hopefully not for long," she mumbled.

William took a deep breath and looked at Keisha. Creating a place of tranquility with his eyes, her affection doused the fires of fear and doubt. The outcome of the trivia contest was moot, the furthest thing from his mind. Centered on a moment he waited for all his life, he was walking in a new power.

That feeling made him feel free in newness.

"A penny for your thoughts, William."

"Keisha, I want to have a Super Soaker water gun fight."

"What?"

"I want to have a Super Soaker water gun fight with you."

"William, I'd love to do that, but not in the cold."

"Well, can we do it in the summertime?"

Recognizing his impulsiveness, Keisha smiled.

"We sure can, dear."

"And can we come back to this park on a night when the stars overhead feel so close we could stir them around?"

A bigger smile appeared, one that she had held inside all her life.

"We can even touch them, if you'd like."

"Can we argue about what movies we'll watch on Saturday nights?"

"*Holiday.*" Hearing a pause, she continued, "Cary Grant and…"

"Katharine Hepburn. From 1938. I also love *Stage Door.*"

"Me, too. I would love to dance with a partner like Fred and Ginger."

"I have all their movies, Keisha. We could learn their routines together."

"Can we watch Gene Kelly, too?"

"*On The Town, Anchors Away, Thousands Cheer, For Me and My Gal, Singin' in The Rain...*"

"I love *Cover Girl,* and *An American in Paris.*"

"I forgot about those two."

"You'll never forget those musicals again."

"Not after today I won't."

"Promise me one thing."

"What's that?"

"We always have to start movie night with Tyler Perry or a Blaxploitation flick."

"We can't forget our own, baby."

"No we can't, dear."

"We can't forget about each other's needs, baby."

"No we won't, dear."

"After they lay me off of this job…"

"Come home. Mama will have a big hug waiting."

"Forever?"

"Yes, William, I would love to be your wife."

Stunned, a man in love paused.

"How'd you know what I was thinking?"

"That look in your eyes told me you were tired of hearing your own heartbeat. I'm tired of hearing my own heartbeat, too. Let's make them dance together."

With the passion of a future man-and-wife connection, two warm mouths mingled in bliss.

After separating reluctantly, William said, "We have so much to talk about."

"And we'll figure it all out, because I believe in what's happening here."

"I believe in you."

"I believe in you, too, William."

"Keisha, we've only known each other for a week."

"I know, isn't this crazy?"

"But it feels so right, baby."

"I know, dear. It *is right*."

Sometimes, you know, William thought.

Sometimes, you know, Keisha thought.

Snuggling against one other, the heat of their love melted the chill away.

Arriving in Detroit at six, Carl Austin felt antsy.

Looking disturbed, he couldn't remember if he had called a limo service to pick him up from the airport, so he took a cab to his father's house.

Once Wallace Austin opened the door to his Orchard Lake home, he saw trouble. Seeing restlessness in his son's eyes, there was an eerie presence that was unsettling.

Watching him storm about while muttering "My life means nothing without her," through clenched teeth only heightened his concern.

He asked, "Is everything all right?"

Carl barked, "As fine as it's gonna be."

"Okay, I'm going to leave you to your thoughts for a second. I'll be right back."

He hid a growing sense of panic and called Amanda on her cell from another room in the house.

No answer.

He left a message and returned to another bizarre rant from his offspring.

Frantically pacing, Carl said to himself, "She's gonna walk away from me just like that? Why is she treating me this way? All I ever did was look after her and shower her with all my love. I'll tell you what…"

Bravely, his seventy-seven-year-old father tried to diffuse a ticking time bomb.

"Calm down, son. Have a seat."

Something in his voice moved through Carl like a jolt of sanity. Complying, the lunacy came to a standstill as he sat down on a sofa, eyes downcast, weary from a civil war within.

His father asked, "What's going on with you?"

"I got Keisha an engagement ring. I'm going to marry her."

Carl lifted his head. He looked deranged, as if the devil torturing his mind wanted him to dance with disorientation once more.

"Son, are you sure you know what you're doing?"

"I've never been more certain of anything in my life. I love Keisha and I came up here to be with her."

Trying to extract information, his father said, "You know, your wife, Amanda, said you've been acting weird lately, depressed, irritable and overly emotional. Maybe you should talk to someone about what you're experiencing."

Carl growled, "Did my wife also tell you that we separated over the weekend?"

The revelation was new, but after seeing his son's crazed look, Wallace calmly nodded *yes*.

"Then she shouldn't worry about me."

"I think you're making a mistake, son. You're making decisions under a lot of stress." He sighed. "Do you remember what I told you about dealing with people who don't stand to lose as much as you do when things get crazy? A high-profile divorce never looks good on a black man, especially in New York. There's a possibility that you'll lose the life you built, and for what, a woman who doesn't even live in your state? And how do you know that she still wants you, especially after you kept her waiting for years?"

In milliseconds, the brutality of their Marriott suite goodbye flashed through Carl's brain, taunting him back into madness. He couldn't will away the shame his soul felt nor the negative emotions that came from Keisha's announcement, one that caused a barbarian to beat a woman to the floor with his pain.

The volatility that moved through him transformed the logical—staying with his wife and going on with his life—into the illogical—

chasing after a woman who had had her fill with his waffling and moved on—and gave him a mask, a delusion which he would use to lie to his father.

With manipulative boldness, he said, "Keisha Gray is the only woman I ever loved, and she told me over the phone that she wanted to be my wife."

Wallace sat in his recliner, befuddled.

"Then what was all that ranting and raving about?"

"Amanda left me, Pop. She had an affair with another man, and told me that I worked too many hours. It bothered me for a second, and what you heard is closure. One person's trash is another's treasure."

"I see. Well, you have to do what you have to do. And know that I'm behind you all the way."

His lips said this, but his gut told him to try his daughter-in-law later for the truth.

Rising, Carl said, "That's good to know. Now if you'll excuse me, I'd like to go meet my new bride-to-be and go over some things."

A tale of deception had been masterfully woven, or so he thought.

Leaving the expansive home, he got into his black Hummer and sped off, but not before having another prescription cocktail and checking the utility truck's glove box.

Finding what he was looking for, a demented rage filled him.

If she doesn't take me back, there'll be a price to pay.

SEVENTEEN

I'd like to introduce myself.

I'm the third-person narrator's voice you've been following throughout this novel, the objective "Eye in the Sky." I apologize to those who find my intrusion a disturbance to the story's rhythm. Some might actually say that my invasion is akin to cutting in on a slow dance at a basement house party; a little awkward, yes, but as you'll read, there's a method to my narrative madness.

Now before I return to my point of view, I would like to discuss something called "A Whitley Gilbert Moment."

Let me explain this theory: *"A Whitley Gilbert Moment" is when the lives of two or more parties are permanently altered by the decision of a woman concerning love. Some people call it a choice, but a choice is made without reason. However, once you put reason behind a choice, it becomes a decision, one that's based on good, bad, familiarity, or unknown history.*

Why do I call it *"A Whitley Gilbert Moment?"*

Think about season five and the hour-long season finale of NBC's hit show in the 90's, *A Different World*. There, the namesake of my theory had to make a decision not based solely on love, but on history and the unknown. Quickly reasoning in a pressure-packed situation—A decision between a senator named Byron waiting for an "I Will" at the altar and a college sweetheart—Whitley chose Dwayne Wayne and love over the unknown.

Happily ever after for all, right?

What about Byron, the jilted senator? What ever happened to him? Were we privy to all the repercussions of the moment, all of its emotional fallout? Sure, we witnessed a dramatic "I Do" kiss from a loving couple and Diahann Carroll fainting, but did we see everything?

There's a flip side to "A Whitley Gilbert Moment," one that's not made for television; and sometimes those moments happen right in your own home.

As William and Keisha ventured downtown, the sparkle in their eyes was fierce and the peace in their souls surpassed normal understanding.

Filled with tremendous security, there was no doubt in William's mind that God answered his prayers when he turned years of lonely wrongs into one compatible right, and the elation flowing through him told him that he had finally found forever.

Looking at the man primed to love her eternally, Keisha Gray felt joy as well, and that made romantic passions run free. Balanced with a masculine completeness, she was empowered with boldness that only a woman touched by great emotion could fully understand.

Together, they celebrated their spontaneous engagement by going ring-shopping.

Allowing Keisha to take the wheel, William called his running buddy and put him on car speaker.

Steve answered, "I thought you were coming through."

"Man, I got redirected... I'm in Detroit."

Pause.

"Come on, give it up."

"What, Steve?"

"What'd you go do now, Black?"

"Well…"

There was another pause, one filled with giggles.

"William, what's going on, man?"

A female voice intervened.

"Steve? I've heard so much about you."

"Who's this?"

"Keisha Gray. I'm William's fiancée. We want to know if you'll be the best man at our wedding."

There was another pause.

Keisha said, "Steve, or is it, Black? That's what you call each other, am I correct?"

"Yes."

With a sexy Midwestern drawl, a lady in love said, "Now don't go worrying about William. His plane has landed safely in the arms of a woman who promises to love him forever."

Steve said, "Wow. I'm amazed at how quickly it happened."

"So am I. But he made it easy for me to give my heart to him."

"He's a very special guy, Keisha."

"And I'm a different kind of lady, Steve. Like the Jacksons song."

"Let me guess; you're a Michael Jackson fan, too."

"I'm a bigger one than William. I kicked his ass in a trivia contest!"

"You did?"

The vanquished said, "Yes, she did."

"Damn, Black!"

"Steve, I'm going to let you catch up with my man now."

"It was a pleasure, Keisha."

"Likewise."

Immediately, William asked, "So, what do you think, Black?"

"John McClane has finally hooked up with Holly, huh?"

"I think so, Steve. It feels right."

With emphasis, "It is right," Keisha shouted.

Chuckling, William said, "I guess that settles it."

Steve added, "Yeah, I guess it does. So when are you two love-birds coming to Delaware?"

"The first chance we get, Black. We're getting the ring now."

"Wow. You two are serious."

In unison, two heartbeats said, "And you know this, man!!!"

More laughter.

Resuming the conversation, William said, "The past week has been the most fun I've had in years and it's all because of Keisha. I'm so grateful she ordered that cup of coffee for me on Valentine's Day."

"You two met in New York?" Steve asked.

"Yes, we most certainly did," Keisha said, "And we've been on the road since and Steve, I haven't stopped smiling. It seems like I've known my husband forever."

William quipped, "It took a minute, but...*I found her.*"

"Yes, baby, you have... And I'll never leave your side."

Steve asked the couple to hold for a full minute.

Finally he said, "Let me tell you about the sound I hear: I hear the music of matching moods creating love. I hear the melody of two people finally finding something they've searched for desperately. I hear two people thinking together as if they've known each other forever. I don't have to be there to see the gazing or to know that you have each other's best interests at heart and will do anything to bring happiness to one another. It's a miracle, something brought together by a Higher Power, a union formed by God.

"At first when Keisha dropped her status, my mind screamed, 'Not again, William.' But in a few minutes what I initially opposed I now celebrate. What you two have is powerful, beautiful and real, and other than the birth of my children, being the best man at the wedding will be the highlight of my life. Congratulations to you both."

Silence.

"My name is William McCall."

His fiancée added, "And I'm Keisha McCall."

"And together we approve this message."

Their chemistry was so uniquely in sync that the only thing missing was Skype, so they could have seen the future best man shaking his head in disbelief.

Steve said, "I'm gonna let you two lovebirds find that ring. Make it a nice one, Black."

Keisha shouted, "Bling, bling, baby."

"William, she's as crazy as you are."

"That's why I love her, Steve."

"Talk to you later."

"No doubt."

Their transparent white-hot energy had magical powers. Totally caught up in their love, the manager at the jeweler had given them a special rate on a stunning engagement ring. Looking impressive in 10K white gold was a beautiful flower-shaped cluster of round diamonds accented by smaller circular diamonds. Princess-cut diamonds flanked the center arrangement and the shiny shank was filled with even more.

William was about to get on bended knee when Keisha stopped him, saying, "You don't have to, baby. You already know the answer."

"So much for tradition."

"Baby, you know I'm different."

"I love your different, Keisha."

What *wasn't* different, however, was the actual moment William placed the bauble on her left finger. Overcome with emotion, Keisha felt a surge of electricity jolt her heart and the tears that made her vision blurry were for her parents; they would have loved this moment, she reasoned.

Mommy, you would love William. He's everything in a man you wanted for me. Daddy would have loved him, too. He's kind, patient, compassionate, warm and humble. The love in his heart is so open, Mommy. He's a real sweetie.

"Now it's official," she said, fighting sniffles. "I wish my parents…"

"They're in heaven, watching us. I pray they're happy with your choice."

"I know I am."

"Keisha, if you feel like we're rushing…"

Her engagement ring finger stilled his lips.

"I have never been happier in my life than I am right now. And it's because of you, dear."

Wrapped in his embrace, she joined her future husband in heaven on earth. Placing her hand on his heart, in a soft, soothing voice, William asked, "Can you feel it beating?"

"Yes."

"It hasn't ticked with this kind of love in years, and I have the next fifty to build on the permanence I feel in my soul. I love you so much, Keisha."

"Fifty years. Is that all? I plan to live to be a hundred and ten and I expect you to be around just as long, Mister."

"I guess you done told me."

Generating enough electricity to illuminate all of Michigan, their starry-eyes were a strong indicator of what would happen later.

The anticipation of their bedroom magic grew over dinner at The Rattlesnake Club. Taking in Canada from a breathtaking view, the Detroit River sparkled from the full moon above.

Without question this night, this moment and these two people seemed meant to be. While they tried to exhibit public cool, the overwhelming joy they shared manifested itself in playing footsies under the table, sharing tender kisses, and hugging each other.

In each other they saw the incredible, the irresistible and irreplaceable.

Keisha said, "Our love is so powerful that it needs an international skyline."

William beamed another beautiful smile. "Baby, I've never been so consumed. You entered my life like a sexy tornado and blew down every single defense mechanism I had built around my heart. My spirit was in exile and I buried myself into my work and into making others happy. I had completely forgotten what those love bolts felt like. Now, I can't rid myself of this amazing feeling."

"And you don't have to, either."

"I feel like I'm on a natural high all the time and I don't ever want to come down."

"William, take that feeling and intensify it a million times over. It's like fireworks are exploding in my soul and I don't want them to stop. I love you, William, and I'm never letting you go."

"You won't have to, Keisha. You won't have to."

He was a man worth millions, but his entire sense of worth seemed contingent on Keisha's love.

Parking his Hummer out of sight, Carl took the liberty of letting himself into her house, and for an hour he sat in the low-legged recliner with roses in hand.

With each passing minute, he grew more frustrated. Deflated in disappointment, into his mouth went more pills.

There's an old saying that when you go looking through a woman's purse, you'll always find something that you're not supposed to see. Apparently Carl failed to realize the application is magnified a million times over when you go through her home when she's not there. Enraged, he went into the bedroom and saw a white pair of Nike Air Flight basketball shoes at the foot of her sleeping place. He stood there motionless, battling flames of fury while cursing under his breath.

The heat of those flames brought his blood to a boil at warp speed.

Another thing was happening: An ugly transformation had begun. During the drive to Keisha's home he would hope; hope that ten years of memories would expunge one regrettable moment, and hope that ten years of touching her deep with all he had inside would plant forgiveness in her soul.

He wanted to go ballistic, but he told himself he would give it one last try.

One last try to keep the barrage of emotions from going haywire.

One last try to keep that barbarian from going postal.

That one last try would be put to the test; he heard a click, a jingle and the laughter of two in the living room.

"Honey, you need to stop," William said.

"No, you need to. After what I just saw, I might have to share my trivia contest victory. I didn't know you could move like Michael."

"Didn't I tell you that I studied every dance step? But I'm getting a little old to be doing him all the time. People will think I haven't grown up."

Keisha snuggled against his chest and kissed him.

"You should stop worrying about what people think and be yourself. Besides, I love all that energy."

"It might be better served in another place."

"I know that's right."

"By the way, I'm glad you took me by Iron Street and showed me where you got your slammin' hat from. Stef and Ty Dickey are really cool people."

"I know, right?"

"Keisha, I felt a positive aura from the minute we entered their store, and they made us feel so welcome. I love their working chemistry. They're soul teammates."

"There's nothing like watching harmony between black business and love."

"Black love, baby. There's nothing quite like it."

From the bedroom, Carl heard their affection, each word sending him perilously close to his breaking point. The tenderness from another man directed toward Keisha was like lighting the wick to a barrel of dynamite. The fuse would burn close to the powder keg, closer to explosive destruction...closer...closer...

Keisha, looking at her finger, said, "The ring is so beautiful, William."

"That ring means that I'll be subservient and true to your heart. Meeting you on Valentine's Day was the greatest moment of my life."

That bitch was fucking him!

The lit wick was now tantalizingly close to detonation.

From the bedroom doorway, Carl watched the unthinkable; an emotionally available man treating his Keisha as if nothing else mattered in the world but her. Shared looks told him that words didn't need to describe the love they had found; it was the stuff that constructed skyscrapers entitled forever. Not only were serious fires burning, but also there was silliness when they talked of tomorrow. Seeing them caress each other's hearts, somehow Carl knew the orgasms Keisha felt with him had been overpowered. Carl knew that a heart once his had been transported to a new galaxy, one where Keisha didn't mind being submissive or subjective, for she knew without a shadow of doubt that her man had surrendered. She'd been claimed by a man not only strong enough to lead but bold enough to smack down Jesus if he tried to disrespect her. Carl saw something richer than all the Benjamins he possessed, something more valuable than all the jewelry he'd brought her, something more expansive than all the worlds they'd traveled together. A splendid, spectacular sensation gripped her spirit, something sudden, startling and surprisingly simple; a man whose fabric was tailored with character.

In seconds, Carl Austin saw all this.

But still, he gave it one last try.

Disrupting their peace, he brought anger and disbelief to their moment.

The smile of Keisha's face dropped.

Leaving William's arms, she was stunned, dumbfounded with mouth agape. Bombarded with mixed emotions, her heart was beating fast as the tension that gripped her senses.

"Carl? What in the hell are you doing here?"

"Baby, we need to talk."

"I don't believe this. You can't do this to me!"

All it took was one chord of distress, and William, numbed for a second by the intrusion, warmed to his responsibility. He'd never been much of a fighter, but something about Keisha brought about a fearless dynamic he'd never known before.

And it couldn't have come at a better time; with authority, he stepped in front of his woman.

"My man, you need to check yourself."

"This doesn't concern you, Brother."

"When you show up in her house unannounced, it becomes my concern!"

When Carl moved to grab Keisha's hand, he smacked it down.

"I saw what you did to her face, so don't even think about touching her. We can handle this!"

To emphasize his point, he stepped to the taller, bigger man.

"Keisha, you need to do something with this," Carl said.

"Brotha, there's plenty of space and opportunity for *this* to fuck you up!"

Shoulders squared, fists clenched and ready for battle, William was about to take another step when he felt Keisha hold him back.

"William, please don't. Calm down…please. Let me handle it."

Looking in her face, he saw fear in her eyes, not only what could happen if the situation escalated, but the fear of living through another tragedy; something happening to another person she loved.

Reluctantly, he stood down.

Carl said, "Keisha, I need to talk to you. Can we go somewhere private?"

"No," William announced. "Whatever you have to say, you can do it in front of me. I know all about you, brother, and you need to know that Keisha deserves more than part-time love."

Carl looked at Keisha like he'd been betrayed.

"What doesn't he know?" he asked, the ire in his voice growing. "Is he the reason why you haven't returned my calls?"

"Carl, what else is there to say? You put your hands on me."

"Keisha, why can't you forgive me?"

"I've already forgiven you, but I won't let you hurt me anymore. Besides, you're still married and I'm a single woman entitled to do whatever and see whomever I want to."

"I left Amanda over the weekend. I want to be with you."

Stopped dead in her tracks with shock, his former lover paused. Now confused, every single emotion in her body was at war.

If Facebook had a status option for this scenario, it would simply say *TORN*.

William tried to remain calm and looked in Keisha's eyes, trying to gauge what she would say next. All he saw was bewilderment.

Sensing daylight, Carl felt the emotional pendulum shift and went for broke. He pulled out his own blue velvet box and opened it.

His bling was bigger than the bling on her left hand.

"Look, I know I messed up pretty bad, but I'm willing to do whatever I can to fix things. Forgive me, Keisha. You know what we had. Focus on our memories and the good times...didn't I treat you right? I can give you everything; my heart, my soul, my spirit, anything you want. I'm willing to do whatever it takes. My life means nothing without you."

Keisha paused. That she allowed him to plead his case meant the door to her heart was slightly ajar; she'd given in ever so slightly. And now she had a decision to make.

Her Whitley Gilbert moment had arrived.

For three minutes the room remained silent, the longest one hundred-eighty seconds of three lives.

William stood there, emotionless. Having witnessed a desperate man's petition to stay in the life of someone he loved, the initial burst of anger he felt when he first saw Carl was now a resigned calm.

He closed his eyes and took a deep breath. So many words came to mind, but three decades of ups and downs with his heart afforded him a strength that told him no matter what happened he would be okay. Life had dealt him many tough breaks; this would simply be another one, he thought. He would find solace in the fact that he showed a woman what love meant to him and be on his way.

She can keep the ring, he thought.

Opening his eyes, he again looked at Keisha. Though clouds of disappointment surrounded his spirit and he felt the pain that comes before tremendous heartbreak, strangely, all he could think of was a song composed by Charlie Chaplin.

It was a song that was remade by, of all people, Michael Jackson. *When you've done all you can do*, William thought, *you simply smile*.

Bravely concealing sadness, his glowing smile said: *You should have listened to me when I said that "goodbye" would be even harder in person. You're in a tough spot, and if you change your mind about us, then I understand. All that matters to me is your happiness.*

Sensing that he had given up, Carl exhaled.

Somehow, Keisha knew what his smile meant; in milliseconds, her mind flashed through a decade of Carl, then of the past week.

Then she spoke.

"Like I said earlier, I forgive you, Carl, because I know you didn't mean to hurt me. We have so much history, some tremendous moments that I cherish so much."

Tossing aside his guilt, boldly he said, "And I'm ready to create more, baby. Give him his ring back, let's put this week behind us and move on."

Keisha paused.

"It's not that simple, Carl. While I've forgiven you, my life is headed in a new direction. I'm William's wife."

In seconds, Carl's confidence returned to desperation. Incomprehension gripped his psyche, and he couldn't rationalize what had happened. He had jumped out of a plane knowing that his heart would land safely because of a familiar parachute.

The problem was this time, the parachute hadn't opened.

"What are you talking about? I said I was sorry... I said I was sorry... I was confused, hurt... All I want is things to be right, like they once were... Why are you doing this to me, to us?"

"Carl, what we put Amanda through was unfair. I want you to come to your senses, go home and salvage what you have there. I want to put this behind me so that I can receive the love I deserve."

SPLAT!

Because he couldn't distinguish the difference between a woman being his lover and her being exclusively committed in love, Carl landed face-first into a concrete-hard reality. Cracking his rose-colored lenses, the fantasy of being husband-and-wife with Keisha had been destroyed. The intensity of his sorrow unbearable, her dismissal of his emotions brought about the emergence of a deep-rooted pathological fear.

He had left Amanda, a woman he didn't love, but the two who had captured his soul had *left him;* his mother by tragedy, and the woman he loved by way of decision. In his mind, he felt abandoned, and money and power couldn't bring him the one thing he desperately craved.

A man with the world as his oyster had been hoodwinked.

Calmly, Carl asked, "Are you telling me that after all we shared that you don't feel anything anymore?"

Keisha responded, "I didn't say I don't feel anything for you. I'll always remember the time we shared. But I meant what I said in the hotel room, Carl."

His frustration paired with the excruciating pain of rejection. Too agonizing to stomach and too hypersensitive to let go, a wicked illusion kidnapped Carl's senses, one that wouldn't go away.

Observing the exchange, there was no victory in William's eyes. While happy that his bride-to-be made the right decision, too many times in his past he was the one devastated by choice, too many times he was the one left kicking rocks while others danced a happily ever after jig.

Watching someone get their heart broken is not a cause for celebration, he thought.

Carl paused.

He asked, "So, it's over, just like that?"

Keisha lowered her head and William felt the tension ease. Moving away from his fiancée, he started toward the kitchen.

These were two gargantuan mistakes.

Detonated by total devastation, uncontrollable rage got the best of a man faced with total hopelessness.

Carl took three steps toward the front door, stopped, turned and reached into his jacket for the object on his belt, a 9mm Glock.

Turning back, William saw the gun pointed in Keisha's direction, right at her head.

"Keisha!"

"Stay right there, or she's gone." The barbarian shouted through eyes that announced the suspension of clear thinking.

Keisha was frozen. Her cat eyes wide, she thought she was about to see her parents again.

"Don't do it," she begged.

Redirecting the gun at William, the barbarian said, "Keisha, don't fight me on this."

"Please, Carl, you don't have to do this! I know you're hurting right now, but you'll lose everything."

His senses left him and all a tortured soul could see was killing somebody so the pain would cease to exist.

"Carl," William said, staring at him eye-to-eye, "Don't throw it all away. You're better than this. Think about what you're doing, man. You don't want to do this."

"All I wanted was for things to be right, like they were."

Seeing death in his eyes, Keisha pleaded, "Think about your son. Please think about him."

Again Carl pointed the gun at her temple, moving closer so that it meshed with flesh. He wrestled with wounded emotions, but his trigger hand remained firm.

"How could you betray me this way? How could you betray us?"

Keisha's body trembled while her heart leaped from her chest. Terror and panic held her eyes and she felt like she had already stopped breathing.

The barbarian distorted reality further when he said, "We can get married tomorrow."

"Yes we can, dear."

Keisha hoped her answer would untangle his psychotic entanglement as well as be her bulletproof shield.

Carl's frown was upside down in an evil way, and an opaque look in his eyes meant he now lacked remorse.

He said, "We sure can, Mrs. Austin. But first, we must take care of something."

A loud boom pierced the tension.

Amazingly, Keisha was still alive.

Looking right, a scream erupted from her when she saw a body pitch forward.

Landing hard, William hit the floor face-first and somehow rolled onto his back.

Seeing crimson flow from his chest didn't stop the flood of adrenaline rushing through the barbarian; he had sixteen rounds left in the clip and one in the chamber. Calmly, he turned to Keisha.

"He looks like he needs more."

"Oh, no, Carl, don't!"

Three more booms filled the air, three more screams for Keisha.

The body of her fiancé twitched.

"What did you do?!" she sobbed, yelling at him. "What did you do?!!"

"Shut up, Keisha, shut up!"

Somehow, the question halted the toxic rage Carl felt.

But insanity remained.

"This is your fault, Keisha," he said, "How could you do that to him?"

Before she could answer, she saw Carl Austin point the gun at her.

"Carl, please don't do this. We can fix things. Put the gun down."

The barbarian knew better. As successful as he was, Carl Austin was a tragic Greek figure, a man who allowed his anger, an obsessive disorder and a deep-rooted fear of rejection shape a surrealistic moment that cost him everything; his money, his power and peace of mind.

And another life would follow.

Flawed by his frailties, all logic had abandoned him.

Father, forgive me for what I've done. To be absent from the body is to be present with You.

He turned the gun on himself, pushing it hard into his temple.

Keisha saw honesty in his eyes. But before she drew her next breath, the barbarian pulled the trigger.

A lifeless corpse hit the floor hard. Like an unhinged marionette with its eyes wide open, Keisha could see a strange calm in them; he had found what he was looking for in permanent darkness.

But she couldn't grieve his demise; to her right, a man in love with her was still alive, albeit barely.

Rushing to William's side, she checked his pulse, then cradled his head in her arms. Too numb to scream, her tears mingled with a torrent of blood pouring from his wounds.

"Oh my God, please don't do this to me again. Don't take another one away from me. ARE YOU LISTENING TO ME?! God, please…," she cried.

She felt a hand weakly caress her face, then fall limp. Looking down, she saw another glowing smile.

William perused her face as if to memorize every line and pore. Feebly, he tried to console the Lady in His Life. Through ragged breaths, he said, "We're going…to be fine…Keisha…please don't…don't cry."

A cough spewed crimson on Keisha.

He tried to apologize, but an index finger stilled him.

"Please don't leave me, William. I love you."

Ignoring the red life pouring from him, she gently propped his head against a pillow and rose, trembling even as she offered a brave smile.

"Don't you go anywhere, you hear me?"

Slowly nodding, William's eyes fluttered between awareness and an unconscious state, then succumbed to the latter when he closed them. In case they never opened again, he asked God to forgive his sins.

At peace with whatever outcome his Father chose, he was not afraid of death.

But the lady in his life was afraid of losing him. Pulling out a smartphone, she revisited her past with a familiar call.

"*Nine-one-one. What's your emergency?*"

Covered and surrounded by blood, her body rocked in shock and she had trouble breathing. Yet there was an eerie calm to her tone.

Gasping, she spoke slowly, saying, "I need help, please come quickly."

Tears escaped her when she gave horrific particulars, even more tears when the flashing lights and crying screams of sirens invaded her numbness. EMTs and police appeared, asking questions as they strapped two bodies onto portable gurneys, one man with closed eyes still fighting, the other with eyes wide open having conceded to his demons.

If Carl Austin had had breath, his tortured heart would have danced with glee, for he accomplished what he had set out to do.

For giving his shit away, Keisha Gray paid the ultimate price.

He had killed her, all right; experiencing the worst kind of death, she remained alive physically, but her insides were hollow.

A Whitley Gilbert moment not made for television can do that to a person.

EIGHTEEN

Their friendship defined brotherhood; it had been that way since a skinny chocolate kid waited his turn at bat during a kickball game.

A cream-colored kid with bowed legs and bushy eyebrows vividly remembered the particulars; *June 1978. West Brighton Projects on Staten Island, in front of my building at 820 Henderson Avenue. He was sitting on a bench, because he batted third.*

With a confidence that belied his years, the cream-colored kid with bow-legs and bushy brows walked up and introduced himself.

"You're new around here," he said, extending a hand. "My name's Steve."

"I'm William."

Then the skinny chocolate kid rose from the bench, kicked the red ball into the parking lot, quickly sped around the bases and sat down.

Not bad, Steve Randall thought.

Instantly, they talked sports.

Steve asked, "Do you play basketball as well as kickball?"

"I try."

The first time they played one-on-one he tried; but the skinny chocolate kid got killed, 15 to nothing.

He was in over his head, Steve recalled, smiling. *He didn't know my athletic reputation.* Evoking memories of the summer free lunch program and 3-man leagues at PS 18, he remembered his new friend being terrified, afraid to play.

His greatest enemy had always been confidence. He never realized his ability until he was backed into a corner and had to fight his way out.

They grew closer in intermediate school, when the skinny chocolate kid needed direction to the principal's office. Soon, paper football games, lunchtime hockey leagues, chess club competition, neighborhood paper routes and girls followed.

Through it all, there was basketball.

Athletically gifted, Steve was an accomplished wizard with the rock and even more patient with the overachieving skinny chocolate kid. After long practices, the captain of the basketball team taught William the fundamentals; ball-handling, defensive slides, give-and-go's, backdoor cuts and pick and rolls, and watched the team manager slowly develop.

He thought his student was ready for a spot on the eighth-grade team, but had to be the bearer of bad news when he learned William was the final cut. *That moment was more painful than when I beat him out for the last spot in the school spelling bee*, Steve thought. *I remember the anguish on his face as if it were yesterday.*

They maintained their closeness, even as they went to separate high schools. Steve, now an all-city point guard in the Private School leagues, still found time to hone the skinny his pupil's skills.

Though he never beat his mentor, William was gaining; the games got closer and closer.

So did their friendship.

Transcending the hardwood, they celebrated blessings and burdens as they shared a rhythmic union. Starting and finishing each other's sentences, with brotherly bravado they even shared a nickname—Black—and were each other's voice of reason when life's struggles filled their cups with doubt.

Warring with cold feet, "William, should I marry Anita?" Steve had asked weeks before taking the plunge.

In his response, his best man didn't pull any punches.

"Black, are you stupid?? You have a woman who stood by you when you were at your lowest. Remember when you lost your job at the post office? All she said was 'Let's see what happens.' Then she guided you through a storm by cooking your meals and paying your bills. How many women do that? Man, you better go down that aisle. Look at my life... You don't want any of my drama."

His drama. Steve smiled.

With endless patience and an abundance of hope that one day "John McClane" would find the one thing he truly wanted, Steve was his ride-or-die partner through stories of tremendous heartbreak and fleeting happiness.

He had been through it all with that skinny chocolate kid...

But nothing, absolutely nothing they had experienced together could have prepared him for *the phone call, the long drive,* and *the talk.*

The phone call came at midnight.

Anita Randall rushed into the man cave of their Delaware home, her watery eyes speaking what words didn't say.

She handed him the cell phone, the keys to an unconscionable chaos.

Immediately her husband knew something was wrong.

Keisha had used William's cell phone to make the call, and Steve heard panic.

"William's been shot! Oh my God! What did he do to deserve this? What did he do to deserve this?" Her moans were woeful cries that disrupted sanity; each scream like a wrecking ball crashing against the foundation of their emotional landscape.

The wrecking ball traveled six hundred miles to Delaware, joining a team of evil demolition experts conspiring to destroy a thirty-five-year friendship.

Steve's first reaction was that of a person in great distress: His body went limp with shock. Instantly recovering, his next thought was to protect his wounded friend.

His ride-or-die brother William had fallen, and Steve prayed that God would fill him with enough life to get up.

Booking a flight to Motown wouldn't do; he quickly decided that he would drive through the shadows of the night. Within a half-hour he packed a bag, hopped into a sunset-brown Explorer, turned on the GPS and saw ten hours and six hundred miles before a shoulder was there for his friend to lean on.

During *the long ride*, he experienced the emotional gamut. Moving through Pennsylvania and Ohio, memories flooded his heart and mind, vivid recollections that decorated a canvass with abstract colors that would have made Picasso jealous: How they shared sex secrets to drive women crazy… Crashing frat parties and rocking to go-go beats at Howard… Delaware State and KRS-One… Trips to Chester, Pennsylvania; Virginia Beach… The many basketball wars…

Despite the distance life put between them, their connection grew as strong as the responsibilities manhood had brought into their lives. Steve had a son and named him after his uncle William, and when he battled with depression in Oklahoma, it was his friend who encouraged him to approach his bosses about expanding their trucking company.

A few months later, the company gave Steve unprecedented authority to start a branch in New Castle, Delaware, and it quickly became its most profitable enterprise.

God has used William in my life in so many ways, he thought.

And the favor was returned in spades. For three decades, Steve had been William's sounding board when it came to his heart. Sharing laughter, elation, anger, frustration, tears of pain and joyful screams, without being preachy, he offered advice through brutally honest opinions, truths that made him think.

One of those truths may have gotten my best friend killed.

That thought brought a feeling of devastation so profound that he pulled over twice—on I-76 West and on I-80 West near Akron—to compose himself. Tears filled his pupils and guilt threatened to rip his soul from his core.

Seven days earlier, he had suggested to William that he reemerge from solitude and learn to love anew.

Seven days ago, he had encouraged his Ride-or-Die to live again.

Seven days later, Steve didn't think that living again entailed physically leaving this earth.

That thought evaporated moisture from his eyes, but the redness of driving through the night remained as he trimmed two hours off the trip. Hitting Michigan by eight, he zoomed through two miles on I-96 West, and sped eighteen more, to Exit 190 A, the Gratiot Avenue exit.

Ten minutes, later, he arrived at the Emergency Service Center of McLaren Macomb Hospital.

Rushing through the automatic doors, the only face he saw in the family waiting area was a woman holding on to a black cashmere coat. Wearing tight black leggings and Minnetonka suede fringe boots, the huge blood stains on her blue denim shirt gave Steve a visual of what happened hours earlier.

Keisha was there physically, but emotionally she was still in grief; her gaze seemed distant, as if she were searching for a new reality to replace her nightmarish being.

Steve knew by her exhausted, brokenhearted presence that she was still numb.

She must have done the police report already, he thought.

The woman in despair took one look at the concern in his face and knew who he was.

She rose when he approached her. In an expression of humility and thanks, she pressed her cheek against his as they embraced.

He asked, "How's he doing?"

"They're working on him in the trauma center."

Concealing his worry, William's best friend bit his lip.

"Are you okay?"

Those words sent pain coursing through her, a pain so strong it forced her to sit down and bury her head in her hands.

Keisha finally fell apart, crying openly.

"He might be dead because of me. I already have one man's blood on my hands."

Join the club, Steve thought, pulling her into his arms. "Don't say that. Your man's a fighter. He'll pull through."

For the next hour, Keisha emptied her soul. From her parents' double murder to the fear of losing the best thing that ever happened to her, the recitation of her battle-tested existence brought empathy from Steve.

They're made for each other, he thought.

When she revealed her affair with Carl, the weight of remorse and regret consumed her, producing tears as heavy as her sorrow.

"I never should have gotten involved with him," she cried. "His wife will hate me."

Speechless, all Steve saw was red, the color of fury. With his if-I-can't-have-you-I'll-kill-the-next-man brand of bitch-ass-ness, Carl Austin had thrown shade at William in the worst kind of way.

Anger had found Steve and he prayed she would change topics before he lost it.

She must have heard his mind rumbling; shifting gears, Keisha thought of William and her eyes glowed lovingly. Like the impact of two meteors colliding, the uncharted meeting brought unforgettable light to each other.

"I didn't think the type of love he shared even existed. Steve, he's so open and caring, so…"

"Solid," Steve added.

"It's a solidness that I can't live without."

"Unfortunately, that same solidness made Carl lose it."

Crashing back to Earth, the statement returned them to a tense reality where the life of a loved one was hanging by a thread. A pause ensued, during which the blood of two lives again messed with Keisha.

Ten minutes passed before she spoke.

"Steve, please don't hate me. I didn't know that it would turn…"

"Keisha, please stop beating yourself up. Behind all his kindness, William is one tough hombre. He's gonna be fine, watch." He paused. "But it wouldn't hurt if we prayed for him."

Grabbing hands, they bowed their heads.

Right as they finished, an older white gentleman wearing surgical scrubs approached them.

"Ms. Gray," he said, "William McCall has been out of surgery for a half-hour. He's in a chemically induced sleep."

He was careful not to use the word "coma" so as not to alarm them.

Steve extended his hand. "I'm Steve Randall, his…"

"Dr. Horace Vogel, the orthopedic surgeon. Ms. Gray told me all about you. We're glad that you made it here safely."

A small smile cracked through both Steve's and Keisha's pins-and-needles look.

Studying their reactions, Dr. Vogel lowered his head, as if in deep thought. Then he picked it up and delivered the grim news straight, no chaser.

The news made Keisha so upset that she immediately rushed from the hospital.

The news made Steve's knees so weak he had to sit down.

Amanda Austin had decided to wait until dawn to return the call to her father-in-law and had actually been in the midst of a good night sleep when the annoying shrill of her house phone disturbed her peace.

Seconds later, the doorbell rang.

Looking at a wall clock, she noted the time.

Three a.m.

What in the world?

The doorbell, she decided, was more important.

Maybe Carl has come to his senses, she thought.

Since he had left her, Amanda had struggled with her sudden, strange new way of life. With each hour that passed, she was an hour removed from the indifference she saw in her husband's eyes when his bulletin blasted her emotions. Though her new existence created strain, somehow she had found her peace and refused to succumb to the sadness.

Slipping on the rose-colored robe of a stunning peignoir set, even in the wee hours, she was a vision of elegance and maturity.

When she opened the door to her brownstone, she became suspicious when she saw two of New York's finest.

She asked, "Can I help you?"

"Mrs. Austin, can we come inside?" the older officer asked.

"Sure."

The house phone kept ringing.

"Excuse me, officers," she said politely.

Picking up a living room receiver, she heard her father-in-law sounding like he'd been swallowed by a heavy spell of sorrow.

"Is everything okay?" Amanda asked.

All Wallace Austin did was ask a question. "Are the police at your home?"

"They're right here..."

They're right here. Oh my God... My husband... My husband...

Those three words triggered everything. *They're right here* caused her to hang up the phone without realizing it, before he could give her the painful particulars. *They're right here* filled her face with grief, then produced profound agony through a horrific wail. *They're right here* made her wish her husband were there to hold her and ease the pain, but *They're right here* meant that he was elsewhere; perhaps on a table in the morgue.

Sitting down on the sofa, she tried to keep the tears at bay by fluttering her lids, but the words *They're right here* were too formidable an opponent; the flood came, along with moans and screams from a person who didn't realize they were coming from her soul.

Soon, another type of shock surfaced; a silent one that numbed the depths of her spirit. Her head was spinning as she stared ahead, lost in deep thought.

After a while, she returned from the traumatic blankness and she shielded her disbelief with bravery. Amanda didn't collapse completely, but her voice fractured when she said, "Tell me what happened."

The younger officer took a breath. "We're sorry, Mrs. Austin, but the only information we received from the Roseville Police..."

"Wait, are you telling me this didn't happen in New York?"

Pause.

After shaking her head, more tears fell.

The policeman continued. "He died of a self-inflicted gunshot wound at the home of a Keisha Gray. There was another man wounded on the scene."

"My goodness, Carl!" she screamed. "What were you into? What were you into?"

"Ma'am, we're really sorry. Are you going to be all right?"

By this time, Amanda had switched to autopilot. Once the officers left, she immediately called her father-in-law. Though he had just experienced a parent's worst nightmare, his emotional condition was not a priority to her; in the alternative, once she heard his voice, she became investigative.

"How long have you known about Keisha?"

Pause.

The silent air gave her a truth she wanted but not really.

Continuing her deposition, her demeanor was as cool as Clint Eastwood in those spaghetti western movies, her tone blunt.

"Did he ever stop and think that his actions might have serious consequences? Did you ever stop and think about my feelings?"

"At the very beginning, I warned him, but Carl was his own man."

"And you smiled in my face this whole time…"

More silence.

"Wallace Austin, you were an accessory to my husband's death, but I forgive you. If I haven't told you already, thanks for all you've done in my life. After the funeral, we'll sort things out legally and once we're done, you're never to communicate with me again. I hope God has mercy on your soul."

She hung up.

There was another person Amanda had words for, but that would come face-to-face after making a call to Carl, Jr., after going to Michigan to identify the body, after the funeral and all of the madness was buried six feet under.

But until then, she embraced the sadness that came with mourning so that she could begin to comprehend the incomprehensible. Turning off the auto-pilot, she collapsed on her bed and wept.

A week had passed before he opened his eyes; seven days in that ambiguous touch-and-go area which separates life from death.

Heavily medicated, William fought grogginess. Thinking the bright lights in the room meant that he was awaiting judgment at the gates of heaven, the smell of hospital room disinfectants and machines beeping in every corner told him that he was still on earth, albeit barely. Breathing through tubes in his throat, he was attached to a catheter and a ventilator. An IV was hooked to his arm, feeding him liquid that he wished he could drink.

Weakly, he tried to sit up, but his body wasn't responding.

Again, he tried.

No response, no feeling.

A third time he tried; still, nothing.

Watching his struggle from a seat near his bed was his best friend. During the past week, many of William's relatives had taken the trip to Michigan and left, but Steve refused to leave his side. Delegating the work at his Delaware trucking company, he called the main hub in Oklahoma and explained his situation.

"We understand totally. Take as much time as you need and do what you have to do," they said.

And he would.

Speaking to specialists on William's behalf, when he received grim prognoses for his efforts, the competitive fire he displayed on the steamy asphalt of many New York City blacktops resurfaced. He would not give up until he found a positive opinion, a glimmer of hope to offer his best friend about his condition.

But first he had to have *the talk*, the toughest conversation of his life. There would be nothing cool about it; simply one comrade hoping another would be able to handle a new truth, an unfortunate game-changer.

Rising from his chair, he walked to a position where he could look his friend in his face.

William, trying to speak his first words in a week, mumbled weakly.

Steve hushed him.

"The doctors want you to concentrate on getting your strength back, so try not to talk. There's something I have to tell you, but first I need to know if you can hear me. I want you to blink once if you can hear me."

William slowly blinked once.

Steve sighed with a mixture of relief and sadness. Dropping his head for a second to gather strength, when he returned to his best friend, he saw peace and clarity in his eyes, a brave gaze that spoke words he couldn't say.

You know how we do. Keep it one hundred, Black.

Steve saw that look and smiled. In milliseconds, he remembered an overcast summer morning in Brooklyn when they were going at it on the hardwood. Then in their early twenties, their one-on-one battles had evolved into psychological wars, intense physically, but even tougher mentally. Friendship be damned once they stepped on the basketball court; the games became personal, yet Steve had never lost to his student… Until that day.

There was a look in his eyes, Steve recalled, *one of determination that I had never seen before.* During the battle, the teacher knocked William on his ass repeatedly, but the look in his student's eyes remained the same as it said, "I've got to be strong. Because I get knocked down doesn't mean I've got to stay down. If I get knocked down, I'll get back up and stand tall."

William stood tall that day, finally defeating his athletic mentor.

I never knew how badly he wanted to win until that day, Steve remembered.

William had that same look as he lay in a hospital bed nearly three decades later, a look that made Steve snicker.

"Well, Black," he joked, his humor barely hiding his devastation, "You really did it this time. You took two in the chest, one in the abdomen and one traveled through your body. By the time you made it to the hospital, you had lost over a pint of blood. The good news is the bullets the doctors removed from your chest missed all the major arteries."

Taking a deep breath, Steve peered at his friend once more.

Keep it one hundred, Black, all the way through.

Sighing, he continued. "William, the bad news is that you have severe nerve damage to your spine. It happened when you fell or when the bullet traveled through you. It's badly swollen." Steve rubbed him. "Blink your eyes twice if you can feel me touching your forearm, and once if..."

William McCall blinked slowly...once.

Quivering with emotion, he asked again and William complied, only blinking once.

In three decades of friendship, Steven Randall never cried in front of his friend.

All that changed with two blinks of an eye.

Watching his friend's pain, the look in his eyes remained determined. Somehow through the sedation he understood his condition, that he was paralyzed. The extent of his paralysis was not yet known; Steve composed himself and told him the doctors weren't making any guarantees he would regain motor or sensory functions, but would do everything within their medical power.

"Basically, it's up to God," Steve said.

William was valiant in front of his best friend, yet in the wee hours when no one was present but the beeping sounds of machines aiding his tragic state, he finally let his guard down.

Once again he had been hammered by the subjective cruelty of life, and this time he was damaged physically as well as emotionally.

Struggling with his spirit, a man who had lost everything in a thirty-year quest for the one thing he truly wanted, closed his eyes. Battling every single emotion a human could feel, his mind and heart spoke truth.

God, I am grateful that you spared my life, but is this what it's come to? Is this how I'm supposed to recognize You? If You wanted to get my attention, You could have given me two in the shoulder and called it a day. But to take the ability to control my body, Father... WHY? Why would You leave me a cripple? Why would You take away my ability to take care of myself?

Father, You have tested me so much, and all I ever wanted from life was LOVE; Your love and love from what you created from a man's rib. Lord knows, I do all I can to show Your greatest energy in all I do, and I know I'm not supposed to ask why or claim a victim mentality, but all this crap, God... Why have I been subjected to all of this crap? I held my head up when women thought I was gay, never wavered when I was in a homeless shelter. I've had my heart broken, made the mistake of breaking a few hearts, learned my lessons along the way, endured the loss of a loved one to cancer and I have never complained. But God, what did I ever do to deserve this? Why have You forsaken me?

All I've ever tried to do is give love like You commanded us to, and now I feel like I have nothing left. What have I done to deserve this? What have I done wrong?

The tears streamed from his eyes, and he hoped he wouldn't drown in them.

Father, I've been knocked down so many times, and I always found a way to rise. But I'm in a bad place right now. The walls of my strength are crumbling down on my spirit, and I don't have much fight left. My soul is bent and my heart feels pain. Yet somehow I know there's a purpose for my present state. The rain can't come any harder than this, and if it does, I'll be okay, because for some reason I can't put my finger on it, I trust You.

The doctors have painted a bleak picture. I may never move again for the rest of my life, but I refuse to let their outlook be the final word. But in order to stand tall, I need You, Father. I need You to rebuild me. I know this will be hard, because I know part of me is dead, and maybe it's for the best, so that You can reconstruct me in a way that best serves You.

All I'm asking for is my body back, so that I can stand tall.

Give me my body back, God.

I want to stand tall again, Father.

Please, Father, give me my body back...

After pouring his heart out, William tried to make a fist with his right hand and felt a twinge.

A single finger moved, barely.

All he asked for was a chance and God had answered his prayer.

The rest would be up to him.

NINETEEN

She tried to suppress the growing storm, but it had been unleashed. Attacking her core, the horrors of past and present paralyzed her mentally, so much so that she couldn't sleep, eat or think. Her cat-eyes, once lively and filled with hope, were blank and blood-shot. The dam holding tear ducts was empty, for she had cried so much and so often that her sobs became tearless. A deep heaviness captured her soul, weighing it down with a tremendous burden.

Keisha Gray was in a daze; a daze that made her head swell with an ache that wouldn't go away. Barely able to put one foot in front of the next, her strength, spirit and love had been robbed by a bandit named guilt.

If it hadn't been for her best friend Theresa Newsome, she might have taken the gun that Carl used to destroy her spirit and added her name to a long list of people who couldn't take it anymore. Rushing to her aide, she immediately moved her to Motown, into her Riverfront condo.

The sister that Keisha never had was found in Theresa, a thick, chocolate woman of strength who not only was a college classmate, but worked as a principal in the Detroit Public School System. A brutally honest straight shooter, she had never approved of Carl but always kept her opinions about their relationship to herself.

She regretted that decision the minute she arrived home from vacationing. The local news crews converged at the front of her building, launching a full-fledged assault for information like vultures picking the last bit of flesh off a carcass.

"Was Ms. Gray planning to keep both men? What was William McCall's relationship to Mr. Austin? Was it his gun?" a reporter asked.

Another asked, "We heard the love triangle lasted ten years. Can you confirm that?"

Shielding her eyes from the glare of lights and camera, Theresa said, "I have no comment. Why am I being questioned? What does this have to do with me?"

With irritating smugness, a smart-ass had an answer that stopped her dead in her tracks.

"You're her best friend," he announced.

"Who told you that?"

"We find out everything, Ms. Newsome."

"You're like parasites, you know that?"

"We only want the story. The people have a right to know."

"People also have the right to mind their own business, so please, leave me alone!"

With that, she rushed past building security to her apartment.

Keisha finally contacted her later that night and told her everything: the letter, the hotel room incident and how it all led to the greatest experience of her life, a great week that ended in unbearable pain.

"Carl killed himself, and a good man is paralyzed, all because of me," she sobbed.

"Damn, Keisha."

"How am I going to make it through?"

"Come stay with me, girl," Theresa directed. "I'll meet you at the back entrance."

Keisha fell apart once she saw her best friend, literally collapsing in her arms.

Theresa then started the healing process. When Keisha found it difficult to function, she cooked and bathed her, and when she paced the hardwood floors crying and searching for answers, she found a seat on her chocolate sectional and listened to her anguish. Consoling her when she stared at the Detroit skyline through twenty-seventh-floor windows, Theresa rocked her to sleep when nightmares made her moan in agony and held her tight when her body thawed out the shock and shivered from the pain.

Silently, she hoped her friend would digest the tragedy and do something she suggested many times throughout their friendship: Find a good church and cultivate a relationship with God.

Two days later, she revisited the subject over breakfast.

She asked, "Have you ever thought about the opportunity amidst your storm?"

Keisha looked stunned. The question made her stop chewing her scrambled eggs. She was so upset that her leg twitched underneath the table.

"Opportunity? What opportunity? I've destroyed the lives of innocent people. Where's the opportunity in that?"

"Keisha, opportunity is created when you move forward and forgive yourself for everything that's happened. God has already forgiven you."

"Has he really?"

"Yeah. There are human consequences you'll have to endure, but He'll bring you through. He's with you."

"It sure doesn't feel that way," Keisha quipped.

"You're kidding me, right? For twenty-five years, you've been a successful schoolteacher in an economically challenged city, and you survived the tragic loss of your parents. And two weeks ago you should have been dead. If I were you, I'd be on my knees thanking God for all He's brought me through, and praying for that paralyzed man in the hospital."

Looking at the engagement ring on her hand, Keisha took a deep breath. She couldn't stop fidgeting, or keep the lump from forming in her throat. Rising, she walked over to the living room windows and looked for comfort in an outstanding panoramic view.

Instead, a suffocating feeling clung to her. She wanted to be held, but the strong hands she wanted comfort from lay unmoving in a hospital bed; and she was the reason why.

Guilt kicked down the front door to her heart, causing her to collapse into her best friend's arms once more.

"William's going to be okay," Theresa said. "You should go see him."

"I can't bear to look at him that way. He'll never forgive me."

"If he's the man you say he is, then should there be any worry?"

"I know, but…"

Their conversation was interrupted by a ringing bell.

Immediately, Theresa's jaw tightened, and there was irritation in her tone when she went to the door.

"I thought I told security…"

Her anger turned to amazement once she opened it and saw a tall, elegant-looking woman. Wearing a collarless fit-and-flared swing coat, the cinched belt around her waist made the berry-hued outerwear mimic a dress. The matching black leggings and cardigan sweater she wore underneath accentuated an outfit that screamed sexy, super-fit sophistication.

Sophistication was not in the face of this woman; her red-rimmed eyes were puffy and sleepless, much like the woman at the window. It looked like she'd been crying for two weeks straight.

Theresa didn't even have to ask who she was.

She yelled, "There's someone at the door for you."

Embarrassment piled onto guilt once Keisha turned and saw the woman checking her out from head to toe with a grief as deep as hers. She didn't see anger in her eyes, even though her violation of sisterhood could have justified it. Nor, in the alternative, did she feel any condescension. She saw a woman like her, sharing a common thread.

For ten years they had loved the same man, shared in his emotions, dreams and desires.

But they also shared an open wound.

While bonded in trauma, they were hurting on different sides of the fence. An ex-mistress had lost a man she loved, but Amanda Austin had lost her husband, a man she had devoted over three decades of her life to, and all the money he left behind couldn't bring him back.

Keisha was about to say something when the widow read the remorse in her eyes and lines of guilt in her face.

"Please," Amanda said, stopping her. "There's nothing either one of us could say that will change things."

"Why did you come here?"

"I needed to see the woman my husband left me for. You are who I thought you were."

"I beg your pardon?"

Sensing the tension, Theresa quickly excused herself by moving to the bedroom. In turn, the women sharing history moved to the chocolate sectional.

"Listen," Amanda said, sitting. "I didn't come here for trouble. We're mature women and we can't fight over a dead man. I think the local media has done a good job at falsifying reality, and handling things like chickenheads wouldn't be good for either one of us."

Echoing the sentiment, Keisha nodded. Under different circumstances, she would have high-fived her, but instead she sat there swallowing the awkwardness for a full minute.

Then humbly, she attempted to reattach a severed cord.

Unsteady, with vulnerability, "Amanda, please forgive me," she said apologetically. "In the end, I told him we were unfair to you and that he should save his marriage."

The widow began rocking her body. Longing to be embraced in familiar arms, depression reappeared in her eyes as she pulled tissue from her purse.

Bravely, she tried to keep stubborn tears from falling, but they were as obstinate as she was dignified.

"Excuse me," she said, dabbing, trying to remain composed.

Keisha said, "I understand."

Rubbing her own eyes, a stubborn rainfall soaked her cheekbones as well.

Remorsefully, "Amanda, please forgive me," she repeated. "I didn't know it would evolve into all of this."

"Even if I didn't want to forgive you…even if God had not instructed me to, I have to."

Perplexity mingled with Keisha's sadness, causing her to search a widow's eyes for clarification.

Swallowing her emotions, Amanda read her non-verbal inquiry and sighed. Then she sat for a full minute, gathering herself and words she needed, ones she hoped would come without wailing and weeping.

Turning the pages of her personal journal, she began talking about her older sister, a beautiful woman with honey-brown eyes; powerful, piercing pupils that made men aware of the expansion and tightening of their lungs.

"Her eyes were breathtaking," Amanda said, desperately trying to remain composed. "Her lips were rich and red, her milk chocolate skin was filled with life, and her heart was full of love. But her greatest gift was her mind."

Her older sister had graduated summa cum laude from Michigan, had pledged Delta Sigma Theta and had designs on divinity school when she had succumbed to her weakness.

"As much beauty was in her spirit, she always felt like love was missing from her life and often made the wrong choices in men. She was so desperate to find the love of her life…"

Keisha asked, "Did your father encourage her to love herself? Did he ever tell her that she was the prize?"

"My father left my mother for a white woman when I was three, and my sister was seven. My mother remarried but that ended in divorce as well."

"I'm sorry, Amanda."

"I'm not. He was physically abusive to my mother and tried to molest my sister when she was ten."

"My mother was killed by an abusive man," Keisha announced.

Amanda's voice nearly cracked when she said, "I know. I remember the exact time it happened."

"I can imagine. It was all over the news, so everybody in Detroit knew back then."

"The newspapers didn't tell me, nor did CBS or the other affiliates."

Again, Keisha looked bewildered.

Continuing, Amanda told her about a relationship her older sister had when she was the Vice President of Trustees of a church in Pontiac. Her sister used to come home raving about an exciting man she had met, one that was the perfect mixture of strength, character and wisdom.

"He was significantly older and a beacon in the community," Amanda said.

"There was nothing wrong with that," Keisha declared.

"He was married."

Keisha's eyes widened. She couldn't help but think about the nightmare that tormented her soul. Covering her eyes, what was once unthinkable began filling her thought capacity at an alarming rate.

Amanda resumed her tale, saying that her sister used to call her at Syracuse announcing her love and she thought the feelings were mutual. She said, "Yet once I was made aware of his status, I listened for confusion in her tone. She was conflicted, torn between euphoria and being ashamed when she saw him with his wife worshipping. I tried to persuade her to find a man of her own, but she wouldn't listen. My sister could be so damn stubborn."

"Sometimes the human mind wants love so bad that it plants itself in denial," Keisha added.

"Tell me about it. Between their hotel room rendezvous where he made her toes curl, the lavish dinner date in downtown Detroit and the nights when she was high on cocaine, she held on to the promise that he would leave his wife."

The cocaine, Keisha thought, with her mouth opened wide. The truth of a possible reality smashed into her like a blow, staggering her spirit.

God, please don't do this to me.

It took her a minute, but in a struggling tone, she asked, "Do you remember the man's line of work?"

"He was with the Detroit Police Department."

Keisha swallowed hard and her heart stopped. Wincing, her brain felt like it was attached to a pump and the memory of an awful tragedy was inflating it with hot air. Her head throbbed unceasingly, yet she remained calm as Amanda continued.

"On the night your father murdered your family, the soul of someone else died; my older sister, Karen."

Keisha closed her eyes and tried to will the tears from falling. Her hands shook and nausea gripped her as she sniffled once, then twice.

She asked, "The child she was carrying?"

Amanda's lips quivered. She, too, was losing her composure.

"She lost it in a miscarriage a month later. It must have been the cocaine. The traumatic trinity sent her over the edge. Soon, cocaine turned to crack, then heroin and prostitution to support her habit. She caught the AIDS monster from the needle and held on 'til 1991, right before Magic Johnson's HIV announcement."

"What did Carl say about all this?"

"He knew my sister was a drug addict, but he never knew why. I never told him." After a pause, Amanda said, "She's the reason why I'm a drug counselor in Harlem. Each person I save from drug abuse keeps her spirit alive."

Finally succumbing to the enormous grief she'd been carrying, the widow's body trembled like she was still mourning both Carl and Karen. Then she placed her dignity down for a respite to weep.

Clutching Amanda's free hand, Keisha's eyes filled with tears from her own memories.

"Please accept my sincerest apologies. I never meant to hurt you."

Just as quickly, the tears stopped, and incredible grace and grandeur returned to Amanda's spirit, causing her to straighten up after she wiped her eyes.

"It's been a few weeks for us both. How are you holding up?"

Through more sniffles, Keisha said, "Like you, I've had my moments, but somehow I find a way to press forward. I can only imagine what you've been hearing about Carl and that night."

"Between the press, the police and his father, I've heard speculation and theories. I think I'm ready for the truth now."

Her mouth uttered this, yet there was caution in Amanda's tone. If the information proved too blunt for her sensibilities, she feared how she might react.

Keisha reclined on the couch, her eyes locked on to Amanda's, making sure she would be okay. Then with extreme difficulty, she spoke slowly.

"I went to New York to break it off with him, face-to-face, on Valentine's Day. I felt guilty and I didn't want to see him conflicted anymore, so I took the decision out of his hands. When I announced my intentions, he beat me up in a hotel room."

Rocking to control her nerves, Amanda lowered her gaze to the hardwood floor.

Keisha continued.

"I went to a restaurant that morning and met a man…"

The climate in the room instantly changed when Amanda looked up.

With a hint of sarcasm in her tone, she mumbled, "William McCall, the man that's paralyzed. Reports say that you ran from the hospital once you found out and haven't been back since."

I deserved that, Keisha thought, slightly riled yet understanding her part in a horrific stage play where two-thirds of the cast were silenced. She had to read all the parts while sidestepping the ex-mistress/widow landmine. One misread line and she could ignite an explosion, an ugly unscripted scene.

Bravely, she took a deep breath, exhaled slowly, masked her irritation and continued. "William saw my pain and took me away. Days later, we arrived home and Carl was there."

There was a pause, during which Keisha could see Amanda fighting with a wide range of emotions.

Finally, she spoke.

"Was there a fight between my husband and William?"

"No."

"Did he try to attack you?"

"No."

Amanda let out a long, exasperated sigh.

"Then what on earth provoked my husband to kill himself?"

Keisha again paused. Within milliseconds a litany of explanations popped in her head: excuses, fabrications, cop-outs, even truths minus the meticulous scenery. But she couldn't frame the picture; she couldn't bring herself to admit that Carl was so desperate for her affection that he lost his mind.

Speechless, she didn't know what to say.

Suddenly, she noticed that Amanda's eyes went to the engagement ring on her left hand.

"Was that my husband's handiwork?" she asked.

"No."

"Were you in love with my husband when he died?"

Once again Keisha's silence became her communication, her language of choice.

Without words, the jigsaw puzzle came together, and the result of its completion was etched all over Amanda's face. Shaking her head in denial, she tried to pull it together quickly, but her dignity had been stolen. In an instant her eyes fought embarrassment, hurt, anger and the reemerging pain of an immeasurable loss all at once.

Adding insult to injury, however, was a stinging reality: Her husband killed himself over a woman who had moved on. He killed himself over a woman who loved him but wasn't *in love* with him, a woman he loved more than she loved him.

Desperation caused Amanda to shout, "He must have been sick, mentally ill. It was the pills, wasn't it?" The manner in which she asked the question was begging for Keisha to agree, begging for her to provide a lifeline.

She asked again with even more conviction.

"It was those damn pills, wasn't it?"

Keisha nodded yes, even though she knew better.

Within minutes, a familiar fiber was restored in Amanda, one that told her that she would be okay. While her lips trembled, she felt her strength coming back.

"In those last few months," she announced, "my husband was acting strange. He was depressed, irritable, hadn't slept in weeks, lost weight and the ability to concentrate. It was those pills."

In her silence, Keisha wondered how she, a woman centered in truth, could build a tower of strength with pillars of delusion; a story she didn't really believe herself.

Continuing her reconstruction, Amanda said, "I begged him to seek psychiatric help. I even had doctors prescribe him with pills that would enliven his mood, but he grew more depressed. We fought over trivial things like chores around the house and Carl Jr.'s education after undergrad. As a last gasp to save our marriage, I suggested separation until he sorted things out because I hated the condition that he was in. He refused. Finally, it got to the point where I couldn't take it anymore, so I asked him to leave. By that time my husband was broken, a shell of the man I fell in love with. Over the last ten years, that was the man that you knew."

Keisha digested the desperate ramble with diplomacy.

"I'm really sorry you had to endure all of this. Your healing process has already begun, and I'm sure that Carl wouldn't want you to grieve his loss forever."

"You sure, well, don't seem to be missing him very much," Amanda snapped. "I'm amazed at how your feelings moved from one man to the next and how ignorant you were to think there wouldn't be any fallout."

Feeling a sudden uneasiness grip the space between them, Keisha felt her chest rise in irritation, especially when she saw a slither of evilness escape Amanda by way of a smirk.

But she refused to take the bait; she refused to match the sophisticate's snipe with darts of her own. In spite of her pain, she refused to reveal her truth: that she, too, battled conflicting emotions; that her memories with Carl were vivid in color and passion.

Other than that tragic last week, her season with Carl had been wonderful. But it was simply that, a season, a temporary pass in a world that in the end showed that money, power and prestige would never have a seat at the same table with exclusive love.

And within the burnt ashes of her season, within the wreckage of a painful lesson, she found someone warm, tender and completely new. In some surrealistic way, she had found love amidst pain and tragedy; provided she muster the courage to see the man who planted the heels of her sexy shoe boots on solid ground.

Instead of saying any of this, she disarmed Amanda with humility.

"When you commit adultery like I did, there are repercussions for your actions, and your presence has made me fully aware of the pain that I caused. I had a relationship with your husband behind your back and paid a horrible price not only with his death, but by watching a totally innocent man whom I love dearly lose his fundamental way of life. Again, for what it's worth, I'm sorry."

"You should be," Amanda said.

At that moment, the grandfather clock in Theresa's living room struck twelve, meaning high noon was midnight in Keisha's eyes.

High noon also meant that the confrontation was over, and with it, Keisha's patience.

Rising, she said, "I think it's time for you to leave, Mrs. Austin."

As they walked to the front door, Amanda said, "Maybe down the road we'll be able to discuss things further."

"Maybe," Keisha replied, knowing that their paths would never cross again.

"Maybe we'll even become friends."

Keisha's silence allowed the statement to linger only long enough for the woman that said it to realize its absurdity.

Now in the hallway, Amanda couldn't resist throwing one last jab.

With a sardonic look, she said, "You really should see about William."

Keisha flashed an angry smile. "I'll do that."

Hearing the front door slam, Theresa reemerged with a look on her face indicating that she had been ear hustling the whole time. Taking her best friend's hand, she rejoined Keisha in her valley of pain.

She asked, "Do you remember what I said about human consequences?"

Sadly, Keisha nodded. She was hurting in many ways, and while Theresa offered a comforting shoulder, it wasn't nearly enough.

It would never be enough as long as she was afraid to look into the eyes of the man she loved, an invalid in a hospital bed.

TWENTY
Three Months Later...

Keep your chin up, even when things don't look too good.

William McCall told himself this, but when applying the mantra to his recovery, he fell short in many ways.

It was difficult for him to be positive when he looked down and saw unmoving, atrophied legs and a diaper at his groin.

Further degradation came when the nurse aides changed him. Using latex gloves and digital stimulation to remove feces from his rectum, he had no bowel or bladder control and needed their help; so as not to get an infection from fecal compaction.

Humiliated to tears, the words "I'm sorry," meekly escaped his lips whenever a nurse performed this unpleasant task.

While "incontinence" was the clinical description of his state, the indignity filling his head could not be defined, nor could the wide range of emotions he experienced. The fact that Carl Austin, the reason for his physical condition, had escaped his wrath when he killed himself, infuriated him.

What a freaking coward, William thought.

Carl's exit reminded him of the Nazis who cheated the gallows at Nuremberg with cyanide capsules. If he still had breath, William would have clasped his hands around his neck and squeezed until there was no life left.

That he could think about using his hands was a miracle in itself;

two days after he moved a single finger, he was able to open and close his hands. A couple of weeks later, he could lift his arms chest high.

That alone changed his anger to hope.

Doctor Vogel, who had predicted less than a 5 percent chance that William would regain utilization of his physical abilities, was cautiously optimistic.

"It's possible that William could resume a normal life," he had told Steve Randall. "But he's going to have to work hard."

That's all the news his running partner needed to hear.

After William showed range and motion in his upper body, he was transferred to the Henry Ford Rehabilitation Center in Warren, Michigan and was classified as a paraplegic.

But the Ride-or-Die brothers were determined to rid themselves of that title as well.

Steve was hopeful, in large part because of the health system's sterling reputation. The highly certified physicians, trained nurses and skilled professionals took great pride in the fact that they worked with patients of all ages while halting the psychological tumbling process that came with severe trauma.

Yet at the end of the day, it's up to him, he thought. *It's that simple.*

But, Steve decided, he would need help. Talking to his wife one day, Anita reminded him of a guy who he competed with back in high school, one whom he talked about constantly through the years.

She said, "Christian Spencer, honey. Do you remember him?"

"Yes I do. Back in the day, he dunked hard on me once."

"Well, I saw his name on television recently. He traded his tennis shoes for a stethoscope. He's an orthopedic specialist in the Michigan area now. Maybe he can help."

After searching online for his particulars, Steve came up with a number. If he could have pressed the numbers on his smartphone with his fingers crossed, he would have.

He heard, "Christian Spencer, here."

"Chris? This is Steve. Steve Randall. "

"I must be hearing things. This can't be The Wizard?"

"In full mind and voice…"

"Man, how's your head doing after all these years? I got you good, didn't I? We should have put that one on a poster and made a truckload of money."

"Yeah, you got me, dawg."

"I had to do something to ignite my team that day. You dropped forty on us that day."

Steve laughed. "Yet all everyone remembered was that vicious dunk. It was like when Blake Griffin caught Kendrick Perkins."

"Tell me about it. Anyway, what are you up to these days? Are you still balling?"

"Man, not as much. I own a trucking company in Delaware and my wife and kids take up the rest of my time. But I still catch fools slipping when they call me old."

"I hear you. I haven't played much since I blew my knee out."

"I heard about that, Chris. I thought you were NBA material, man."

"When one door closes, God opens another one even wider than the one that shut. I transferred that same tenacity I used on the court into medicine and therapy. I wanted to be the best in my profession, Steve. Sprinkle in a little faith, and dreams come true." After a pause, Christian asked, "What's up, man?"

As unflappable as Steve's demeanor was on the basketball, when it came to his best friend, he struggled with his composure: He fought through tears to talk.

"Chris, you gotta help me. I have a friend who needs your services." Telling him about William and his condition, when finished he told him, "I'm sorry, I don't meant to beg and I know that you're busy, but you must help me help him. Please."

Dr. Spencer said calmly, "Steve. I'll do all I can, but I can't make any guarantees. It's going to be hard as hell. The rehabilitation process is not for the weak-minded. It is a humbling progression where self-pity is exposed quickly. I hope William understands that in spite of his circumstance, he still has power."

When Steve mentioned this to his best friend, William asked, "Steve, do you think I can do it?"

"Black, your faith kept you alive when Carl pumped those bullets into you, and your faith caused you to move your body when at first, all you could move was your eyelids. The doctors haven't made any promises, and neither did the specialist being brought in. But I will say this: God knows your spirit, and He knows that no matter what hand you've been dealt, you've always made the best of the situation."

William closed his eyes. Recalling the night where everything had changed, then how far he'd come, he opened them and smiled.

There was a twinkle in his eyes, a twinkle of thanks.

He felt thankful for every day he saw sunrise. He felt thankful for progress: Three months earlier, doctors had called him a quadriplegic. A month after that, he struggled doing bicep curls with a one-pound weight. Now, he was in a motorized wheelchair gliding around.

Steve asked, "What were you thinking about?"

"I'm basking in how much God loves me. There's no love like His, and He showed me this by sparing my life. Even in the state I'm in, I own strength I've never known before, and that's because of Him. Maybe all of this happened so that I can look at life differently. I'm bent, but I'm not broken, Steve. I'll walk again... "

"And you'll dance again, Black. I can't wait to see you moonwalk again like Michael."

"No, Steve... Like William."

"I heard that!"

"There's another way I know that God really loves me." Barely lifting his arm, he weakly grabbed Steve's hand. "He gave me you, Black."

"C'mon, man, you know the drill. We ride together..."

"We die together..."

"We're bold brothers in life..."

Verbal and mental transformation was one thing, but his heart remained in a place where mysteries were embalmed with enigmatic fluids, wrapped in riddles and buried in befuddling bewilderment.

When William thought of Keisha, a pang of sadness tugged at his core. While he didn't want to believe that she was a sunshine soldier who only appeared when skies bled a generous blue, he had trouble comprehending why she hadn't visited him. He wanted to see her face, to know that she was okay. Then from a place of deep love, he would tell her that if she needed to wash away the pain with a fresh start, he'd survive, because as long as God loved him, he was never alone. He would accept if she moved on and she would always remain in his heart.

All he wanted to say is thank you for reawakening his soul with love, and ask one thing of her: to remember him.

That she didn't afford him that opportunity mystified him.

So did one question.

Why hasn't she come to see me?

The hard work started with a little prodding.

Poking his legs, "Do you feel this?" Dr. Spencer asked his newest patient.

To this point, it had been a daily routine which threatened his fighting spirit. For three months, William would be asked this question by a physical therapist, and after responding "no," he would wait until they left the room to emote.

And the anguish he felt was deep. Because of his active spirit, having lifeless legs was like Wynton Marsalis losing the ability to play the trumpet.

Courageously, he combatted this helpless feeling with constant prayer and meditation. Inspired by what he saw, Steve had purchased a Bible and read with him daily. While William didn't memorize scriptures, a couple of passages had special meaning. In the fourth chapter of the Apostle Paul's letter to the Philippians, he read how he could do anything with the strength of Christ.

That includes standing tall, he thought as he finished verse thirteen.

Yet every morning, William prayed for some sort of feeling below his groin, and every day produced the same result.

However, there was something different about that Wednesday morning in late May. When Dr. Spencer asked if he felt something in his legs, William thought of the Apostle Paul once more, and the fourth chapter of his Second Epistle to the Corinthian congregation. The seventh through ninth verses always spoke to his soul. For years the troubles of life pressured, perplexed and punished him, but somehow he always maintained his benevolence, compassion and love.

William had been knocked down repeatedly, but he never stayed down.

And when Dr. Spencer asked him if he could feel his poke, a

power that was always within his frame but not his own, began helping him to his feet.

"Yes," he said softly.

"Now, I want you to try lifting your right leg," the doctor instructed.

William complied, and nothing happened.

"Can I try again?" he asked.

Dr. Spencer nodded, and in return he saw an ugly grimace from his patient.

He saw something else as well: His right leg moved barely. So did his left leg after a couple more ugly grimaces.

After seeing his effort, the doctor said, "Okay, William, you might be able to do this. But I'm not going to make you any promises. This will be the toughest thing you'll ever do. And I'm not going to be easy on you. Steve told me that you had a pretty good basketball game."

Through ragged breaths, "Yeah, well, he taught me everything I know," William said proudly.

The doctor showed no emotion.

"Well, I dunked it hard on his ass when we played. So I want you to imagine what's in store, and get some rest. Today's your birthday, and that's the only reason why we didn't start immediately."

William had completely forgotten it was his special day, but he would never forget the present his Heavenly Father had given him.

The assigned physical therapist surprised him at five the next morning; only it wasn't the one he was used to having.

It was Christian Spencer himself.

"Let's find out your deficits," he said firmly. "Can you roll in the bed?"

Weakly, William tried and failed.

He received no sympathy.

"Push, dammit!" the doctor barked out. "I told you I was going to be hard on your ass."

Once again William tried, and failed.

"We'll have to rebuild you from your core, William."

With that, the doctor and his team of therapists went to work. Twisting and turning him, they rolled him from side to side, propped him up, then laid him back down on the bed. When they saw William had control of his upper torso, they focused their attention on his legs. A sharp pain made his whole body hurt when they manipulated them.

"Pain is good," they said. "That means that you have feeling in your legs."

They continued with the bending and stretching exercises. Lifting his legs, they heard a scream so loud that it vibrated through the fourth-floor facility.

Studying his reactions, Dr. Spencer saw that his legs were immobile, but he still had nerve activity.

"While I can't make you any promises," he again told his patient, "There's hope. But I must be honest with you. Because your legs retain feeling, every therapy session from here on out will test your pain threshold. If you can stand the pain, you'll be a major contributor to your own miracle. If not, then you'll be stuck in a wheelchair."

William could deal with the pain, but over the course of the next few weeks, the mental struggle was worse than anything physical. Battling bouts of self-pity, he still had to deal with the awful humiliation of relieving his bowels. And he felt badly that Doctor Spencer spent hours with him.

"That time could be spent with other patients," he told him.

"You let me worry about that," the doctor said dismissively. Then, he punished his patient for having compassion by instructing his therapy team to be even more brutal in their workout sessions.

"Wear his ass out," he told them. "He'll respond. He's a lot tougher than he thinks. But he's gotta believe that."

Almost every night, William apologized to his best friend about being a burden.

One night he said, "Black, you should be in Delaware, with your family. Doesn't your job need you?"

"William, I run my own business, so I can do whatever I want. And you *are* family," Steve assured.

"I know we're Ride-or-Die, but…"

"No buts, Black. The way you can express your appreciation is by walking out of this hospital without the aid of a walker or cane."

William was trying with everything he had, but the process had him so frustrated that one summer evening it all came out.

Seated on his bed after another day of futility, the tears fell at nightfall. Peering upward, he screamed at his Father.

God, why didn't you take me, too? If someone handed me a gun right now, I might be joining Carl, wherever he is. What did I ever do to deserve this? I mean really…I can't take it anymore.

Watching his exasperation from the doorway was Christian Spencer. While he was brutal during the therapy sessions, silently he had become his biggest fan. Watching tearful rain drench the cheeks of a man whose hope was frail, he thought of how depression swallowed him when his knee, part of his lasting significance as an athlete, gave out. While it paled in comparison to paralysis, the emotional demoralization could have sent him over the edge. But he didn't allow his pain to blind or bind him, nor did he allow pain to become a roadblock between him and new reality.

Not only did he accept his new reality, but he embraced it by becoming the most prolific orthopedic surgeon in Michigan.

Now he had to convince his favorite patient to accept a reality that he hoped would be greater than what he was experiencing now.

Entering the room, Dr. Spencer said, "William, I need you to do me a favor. Remember that guy that used to play basketball and dance his ass off, that guy named William McCall? Well, that person is never coming back. The only way to walk again...The only way you'll *live* again is if you let that person go. He's not coming back."

William nodded, but also wondered to himself if losing that person also meant losing the love he possessed for a woman who hadn't returned.

"Keisha, I'm glad that you finally decided to come with me. It'll be good for your soul."

"Thanks for inviting me, Theresa. I've enjoyed the sermons at church, and I thought that the Women's Retreat would help me."

"It's going to be a life-changing experience. And to think, a few months ago I literally had to twist your arm to attend a service."

"To be quite honest with you, ever since I lost my parents, I used to relegate church time to funerals and weddings, nothing else. All that talk about church being a place of healing went out the window once I found out about my father's affair."

"Sinners still sit in those pews, girl. Our walk with God is not without temptation. People still make mistakes. We ask God for forgiveness, and more of Him."

"I know that now. I also used to think that all your talk about God was hot air. But the more I've been hearing the Word of

God, the more I need it. Like the song the choir sang the other day, His word is like the sun on my mornings; my entire day, actually."

"You not only need His Word, Keisha, you need Him. You can't live without Him."

Traveling along I-75 North, then US-10 West, a woman finding her way pondered the words of her best friend, and for the first time in months, a smile formed at the corners of her mouth. Although feeling nervousness about attending the retreat, she was determined to give her mind, heart and soul to the spiritual food she hoped to receive.

When they arrived at the Lake Ann Camp facility, Keisha received more than spiritual meals. Feeling as if she had been taken to a holy place, being surrounded by so many women in worship, changed her. Feeling reconnected with an important part of her existence, she felt God's presence throughout the beautiful 300-plus-acre campus.

God's presence within her allowed her to share her life amongst 150 God-fearing sisters. In a powerful testimony, she spoke of coping with two brutalities separated by three decades of fear; a fear that left her frozen in the quest for the one thing she truly wanted: love.

"I've wandered in a dark maze searching for light, and I've known deep pain," she said, addressing her sisters that Saturday night. "Yet until I found the switch, the one that turned on the light and brought me here today, God has always provided for a flashlight for me. Sometimes the batteries shut off and I bumped into things that knocked me down, but the Lord would pick me up, dust me off and give me the batteries needed to complete the journey. I'm here, God. I'm here. There will be other mazes to find my way through, but they'll be easier to navigate through, for I've found the switch and the lights are on. And when the enemy tries to shut them off, I know that God has a flashlight for me."

From the back of the worship center, she heard a woman sing a modified version of Parliament's R&B classic.

"Flashlight… God's light… Lord's light…Right light…Everybody needs a little light, under God's sun," she screamed.

The place went crazy.

The Women's Ministry had found the retreat's anthem.

And the following Sunday, Keisha confirmed that she had found the place she was supposed to be. When the doors of the church opened the following Sunday, she up went to the pulpit and gave her right hand to the pastor.

But her heart was now God's.

Well, almost all of it…

There was a special part of her core in a rehabilitation center in Warren, desperately trying to walk again. Never able to shake the guilt she felt, that she still couldn't muster the courage to face William had her feeling conflicted.

So did the following Sunday's sermon. To celebrate the twentieth anniversary of Greater Destiny Baptist Church, the church brought in a special pastor to deliver a message about God's greatest gift between man and woman.

Keisha had her head down when she heard a powerful statement, "Every human being who's ever lived, who's ever taken a breath, has longed to be loved."

Looking up, she almost fainted.

It was the Reverend from the South, Tim McCann.

In a booming voice, he began his sermon by asking a question. "What do people desperate for love and the Apostle Peter have in common?"

Hearing silence, the pastor continued.

"So many couples start out with great intentions, like Peter did when he jumped out the boat and walked on water. But he began to sink when he lost confidence in himself and the abilities God gave him. With every step he took, he lost faith. He took his eyes off Jesus and started looking around at huge winds and all the large waves. Doing that illustrated a confidence crisis, one that Peter had then, and one people searching for love have today.

"So many times we're like Peter walking on water. At first everything is fine, but once we lose confidence in our mates and ourselves, our faith falters. That makes us susceptible to the high winds and huge waves of life; the difficult circumstances that plague God's greatest gift to humankind, love. Whereas Peter started to sink, we allow fear and pain to redirect our paths back to the boat of single selfishness. It's either that, or we search someone else's murky waters for love and affection. Other than the temporary easement of pain, doing that perpetuates the cycle all over.

"How do we break this cycle? By learning to love the God in our mates and us, while keeping our eyes focused on God. When we lean on Him, the storms that often swallow our best intentions cease, and we find peace. When we cry out to the Jesus, He puts the hands of two wavering souls together and fastens them with His Love, which is the greatest love of all. His love lives in us, and when we recognize this, it gives two in love the confidence to survive even the most impossible circumstances. Trust His Love and He will bring you the love you deserve."

The Pastor from the South had more than done his job; he left a woman in the fourth pew sobbing uncontrollably. Keisha's vision was so blurred that Theresa eventually had to help her leave the sanctuary.

Her crying continued at home, as she tried to write in her journal. As she sniveled and placed her prose on paper, the pages got wet, forcing her to stop. Burying her head into her hands, the boohooing went on for a solid hour.

She couldn't stop crying, and she knew why.

William.

God had reached inside His enormous bag of blessings and given her what she always wanted, and at a time when she needed him the most. And at a time when he needed her, she was nowhere to be found.

Unable to shake the guilt that tormented her soul, she still couldn't face him.

Her watershed finally stopped, and for three hours, she sat on the bed in Theresa's guest room, trying to figure out how to let this man know *something*.

Suddenly, a whisper interrupted her confusion.

I am here with you always, the voice said.

A God moment had filled her soul with peace; a peace that washed away her pain and brought sunshine along with a rainbow.

Deciding that her rainbow would be colored with spirit and truth, she moved into the living room and turned on the stereo.

The first sound she heard sent chills through her.

"You and I must make a pact," the youthful genius sang.

I love you, William, and I'll always be there.

William remembered what Dr. Spencer had told him, yet his struggles continued. But there was now a steely resolve that lived inside of him.

Part of that came from the happiness he saw in the eyes of others in the struggle. Talking to a brother as he was being lifted onto a soft mat, he asked, "How do you remain positive?"

"A good attitude will take you places," he replied. "Besides, to-morrow's not promised to any of us. Being alive is a blessing in itself."

"How long did it take you to get comfortable with your situation?" he asked another.

"Not long. I put my faith in God and allowed him to show me the way."

Both those instances were uplifting, yet when he met a man whose wife left him because of a spinal cord injury, he remembered Keisha.

She still hadn't come to see him.

Maybe she doesn't want to see me this way… Maybe she's moved on and is scared to tell me so… Maybe…

A tap on the shoulder interrupted his maybe musings.

Handing him an envelope, Steve said, "This came for you."

Opening the envelope, William saw a neatly folded letter on orange paper.

After reading it, he handed it to his best friend, who also read it.

Then they looked at one another.

The next day, William upped his rehab hours from one to five. His next rehab week was increased to six days instead of his normal five. When the therapist ordered five sets of painful leg lifts and stretches, he demanded five more, then another five.

Watching in shock, Dr. Spencer had never seen him so focused.

Steve helped him with regaining upper body strength and within two weeks of the extra work, he was sitting up and rolling over.

"Let me see if I can stand," William told Dr. Spencer two weeks later.

"Are you sure you're ready?" Steve asked.

"Let's give it a shot."

After motor wheeling over to the facility's main workout room, William sat alone between the parallel bars. Closing his eyes, he remembered what Dr. Spencer had said about letting go of his old body to resume his life.

Lowering his head, he thanked God for bringing him this far; not only through the tragedy, but his entire journey through life.

Father, if your purpose is not for me to take another step, then I understand.

Then two nurses came over. To ensure his safety, they fit his lower legs in KAFOs, custom-fit braces for support.

"These are to prevent toe drag and your feet from dropping," one said.

The other, an older woman named Gail, told him a story about her son. Ten years earlier while driving in a Michigan snowstorm, he got into an accident, which left him paralyzed from the neck down. One morning while being transferred to Henry Ford for therapy, he told her he wasn't feeling well. Then his eyes closed, and sadly, never opened again. He died from a pulmonary embolism; a massive blood clot that traveled from his lower cavity into his lungs and created cardio-arrest.

"That's why what you're attempting to do may save your life," she said, dabbing at her eyes.

William nodded. Then, as one therapist positioned herself in front of him, he placed his arms on the railings, which were chest-high from his seated position.

And with all the strength he owned in his life, he pushed up. Wobbling, his legs were overcooked noodles, soggy and slightly rubbery. He felt himself falling backward into the wheelchair, but he was determined not to fall again… ever.

He pushed even harder, and wobbled again. Closing his eyes, he grimaced and screamed. A third time he tried...

At first he buckled, but then the wobbling stopped. Holding his head straight, he stiffened his back and put his body weight on his legs. Biting his lower lip, he lifted his left foot, dragged it across the tiled floor, and slowly planted it a few inches in front of the rest of him. Then he did it with his right foot. Trembling, he paused long enough to allow Gail to wipe the sweat that poured from him.

Then his left foot went forward again, and he planted.

His right foot, forward, then planted.

Wobbling, his legs finally gave way, and Dr. Spencer, having wheeled his chair beneath him, eased him down gently and placed a towel over his head.

He didn't want his favorite patient to see an entire room crying.

THE OUTRO

Valentine's Day, one year later...

Each step he took was cherished more than the one before; every movement he made was appreciated like a precious gift.

Striding easily, you never would have known that the man who was about to enter Friday's was told by doctors that he'd never walk again; hell, they didn't even know if he would ever be able to sit on the toilet and relieve himself.

Following Dr. Spencer's instructions, William McCall did let go of his old body. And when he did that, God smiled and gave it back, better than ever. Miraculously, the swelling in his spine disappeared and the damaged nerves healed, confounding all the specialists. His bodily functions returned, and, after more stretching and screaming, so did the strength in his legs.

He started out between parallel bars, struggling to rise. But with God's grace, a little effort and love, he'd been taken to a higher place, one where he could walk, run and dance again.

But more importantly, the higher place allowed him to stand tall.

Mentally tough and spiritually sound, he was wealthy in a way he'd never been. His faith in life had been tested, and by passing the test, he found out who he was as a man.

And also, "Whose" he was revealed.

Establishing a relationship with God, he examined his life, all that he'd endured and overcome, and came to the realization that his salvation was not of his doing. When he was left heartbroken in those formative years, it was his heavenly Father who put him back together time and time again. When he struggled to live, God had sent an angel named Linda to help him back to his feet. And when he was left a cripple, God gave him his body back.

He really loves me, he thought. *At the very least I can find a church to attend.*

Soon, merely attending a church turned into membership and an active role in creating basketball leagues that focused on the knowledge of two games; one that was played on hardwood and asphalt, and, more importantly, the game of life. He found joy in lighting up the lives of the younger kids, and an even greater joy when a college-bound kid openly challenged his teachings one Saturday in late-January.

"Having an effective jump shot opens up so many things. It makes your first step quicker," he said, draining a set-shot in a Harlem gym.

The tall, cocky kid visiting his practice tried to show him up in front of his church friends.

"C'mon, old school, what do you know about the game?"

"I know enough to know what I'm talking about," William replied calmly.

The six-foot-two, All-City shooting guard named Shawn then shouted, "Let's see if you know."

Stepping to the foul line, he put a ball in the old man's hand.

"Check it up, old school. Game is three. If you can hit three on me, I'll do whatever you say."

William closed his eyes. Since his amazing recovery, he had only shot around when instructing, and to that point hadn't tested his knees or ankles by playing hard. So he said a quick prayer, one which drew laughter from others watching.

Opening his eyes, he had a focused look and a swagger about him.

"Which side do you want it from, left or right?"

"Left."

Two quick dribbles left and a jump shot later and the kid was down one-zip.

Taking the ball out again, William said, "That was my weak side. I'll go right next."

After two quick dribbles right, he pulled up for another jumper. Point game.

Shawn's friends stopped laughing. Actually, one of them mocked his boy by asking if he needed some water.

"Yo, man," another one shouted, "That dude used to be a cripple."

Then came the shout, "Yo, you gonna let a cripple school you?"

Shawn grew angry when he heard that. Now playing suffocating defense, he could smell William's toothpaste, he was so close.

As they body-bumped and jostled for manhood, William smiled. "Do you remember what I said earlier about first steps, Shawn?"

"You're not scoring anymore, old school."

"Well, I forgot to mention…"

After a ball-fake and a dribble-drive, it was over.

Handing Shawn the ball, William said, "I forgot to mention that with a ball-fake and Christ, I can do all things." His directive for the humbled kid was to read Philippians 4:13, and to work on his "J."

Not only had God showed up, but he showed out when revealing to William that He returned everything to him, including a jump shot and dribble drive.

What He's done with me is amazing, he thought. Smiling as he opened the restaurant door, he strolled past couples holding hands at their tables and sat at his favorite seat at the bar.

Donald, his favorite bartender, was fixing a drink with his back to the patrons when he heard a familiar request.

"May I have the Chicken Alfredo entree? From what I hear, it's pretty good. "

Turning, Donald's eyes widened with cheer. Coming from behind the bar, he embraced his brother.

"I heard about what happened," he said. "I prayed for you."

"Thanks, man. Hearing that means everything."

"Listen, whatever you want tonight, it's on the house. Do you want your Long Island Iced Tea with a tequila shot?"

"A glass of Merlot is fine. My taste for the hard stuff has diminished considerably."

"I can imagine."

After fixing the drink, Donald asked, "So whatever happened to Keisha?"

William sighed; his deep sigh uttered words his mouth couldn't say.

"Man, I'm sorry. I really thought you two would make it."

William sighed again.

"Donald, what I learned from knowing her is certain people will always be there, and that doesn't mean physically. The experience of knowing presence in memory keeps them here. We may selfishly want the physical interaction, that face-to-face, soul-connecting chemistry, but sometimes the journey together is but an instant, and you cherish it for what it was."

"I feel you, man. They'll be others."

As the bartender tended other patrons, William went to the jukebox and placed two dollars in. He requested two different versions of the same song; one with the musical arrangement and one sung a cappella.

Returning to his seat at the bar, he pulled out the orange letter that he received while at Henry Ford. At the precise moment in which he started reading, the voices of five brothers blended tenderness, grace, authority and inspiration to deliver a soul-stirring sonnet.

Marlon, Tito and Jackie harmonized God's greatest energy with gentle beauty.

Jermaine Jackson spoke of its comfort, being glad he found it, and how he would hold on to it for dear life.

And the one in the middle, the child prodigy who brought two people together some thirty-five years later for an incredible experience, made a very special vow.

I'll be there, Michael Jackson said.

Bravely, William started reading the letter.

William, I am hoping that you respect the course of action I've taken, as it comes from the deepest place of my existence. While I'm aware that you might discard this immediately, please know that I would take no offense in you doing so. If you've read this far, then I am grateful.

I've cried myself to sleep many nights since that fateful experience, and many nights thereafter when realizing that the arms I needed to comfort me would never hold me again. That I was the reason behind your paralysis buried me with guilt so deep that I couldn't bear to look in your eyes. You didn't deserve what happened to you.

William, words cannot fully express the joy you brought to my life. During that week we spent together, I was happily married to the man I always wanted to share the world with. You helped me put things in perspective regarding the death of my parents when you told me I was a star because of my scars. You saw my pain regarding Carl and offered a total stranger love. That you exhibited such selfless faith told me so much about your strength, strength you don't even know you have. And when love woke me up at dawn, you had your arms around me, arms that I knew, without a shadow of a doubt, would love me forever. How did I know that? By the way you made love to me. You gave your soul to me, William, and even if it was for that incredibly brief moment, I'm eternally humbled to have been graced by a comet; a wondrous comet of love with an unconquerable soul and unbreakable spirit.

You're a beautiful man with a beautiful heart, surrounded by amazing people that fill you with a love that overflows. And once you recover from this awful condition (I HAVE COMPLETE FAITH IN YOU), I truly hope God blesses you with an amazing woman that brings joy and laughter to your life. And if she doesn't… Well, our matchmaker Michael said it best…I'll be there. I'll always be there, if you promise to keep the memories of our experience alive in your heart.

William, I'm in a period of transformation. (Ergo, the paper color orange—it signifies transformation.) God has come into my life and rearranged things so that I look first and foremost at Him. While I am grateful for all He has and is doing in my life, the only thing I asked of Him is to let the love I possessed for my husband William never die, even if our paths in life never cross again. And no matter what happens, whenever I think of you, I'll see my husband: his smile, his warmth, his tender compassion and his love of everything good. And whenever I think of you, my hope is that I'll be there always, in your heart.

I love you, William, Forever and For Always.

Keisha McCall

Closing the letter, William placed it in its envelope. Then after wiping his eyes, he closed them.

Father, I humbly thank you for life and the air that You breathe into my dust… You have blessed me in ways that I can't even imagine, and You keep blessing me. I wish I could count them all, but Lord knows I don't want you to think I'm keeping score. To the very second, I am not worthy of all you've done in my life.

Father, I feel I'm going to the well with this request, and please forgive my bluntness. You know my track record with my heart; it took me years to realize that I'm not in control. You are. I know we have freedom of choice, but I really need your help, as I can't guess on this one. Is Keisha Gray the Lady in My Life? Give me one sign, and I'll leave this chair, pack my bags and go to her. And if she's not, then please give her a man that'll love her unconditionally, as she deserves Your very best. Either way, hit me over the head with a brick, so the message is crystal clear. I need to know: Is she the one for me, God? Please, please help a brother out. Amen.

As his eyes remained closed, a violin followed by a Caribbean-mixed sound filled the room. Then a familiar voice blended with someone new. Creating beauty with lush harmonies and an infectious melody, the song communicated joy, longing and a tinge of sadness, for the lead singer had passed away before its commercial release.

Yet there he was, sharing the stage with Akon while speaking from heaven.

You've both been there before, so together it'll work.

When cold darkness threatens love, embrace each other until sunrise.

Hold each other's hands and nothing will come between you, Michael Jackson sang.

Then he heard another familiar sound.

"I couldn't stay away any longer," the sweet voice said.

William's eyes opened wide and Donald placed another glass of Merlot in front of him.

"You know," he said, smiling, "There's another person I know who loves Michael Jackson as much as you do. As a matter of fact, you should look over your shoulder."

William McCall turned around and saw a woman with beautiful

cat eyes, wearing black jeans, a black sweater and an engagement ring.

Giving him an immediate answer, God had given him everything back, plus interest.

With tear-stained cheeks, Keisha asked, "Well, are you going to hold my hand, or do you want it to fall off?"

THE MAGNIFICENT SEVEN REMIX

UNBREAKABLE: THE MAGNIFICENT SEVEN REMIX...

"I remember when Michael Jackson died. Though saddened, people from all walks of life, Black, White, Hispanic and Asian, celebrated the entire week on 125th Street in front of the Apollo, dancing, singing and crying on each other's shoulders. It was magic! You can't beat that love for a Legend."

—NATIONAL BESTSELLING AUTHOR TREASURE BLUE

God Bless You, Treasure Blue... Generations gathered, delivering spirit-shaking emotions from their souls, bringing flowers, candles, letters and lyrics. We sang, we danced, we cried as if we all lost a family member, and with brave yet broken hearts, we smiled, for we remembered the time. Years later, we still remember a time when all impossibilities seem realistically within our reach. With faith and love, Michael Jackson made us all believe.

In his own unique way, he made us feel UNBREAKABLE. Yet as great as his gifts were to the world, so were some of his flaws. Lord knows, I wish he were still here, but perhaps my literary brother Alvin L.A. Horn captured it best when he asked me to close my eyes and try to imagine Michael Jackson alive at seventy or eighty years of age. Selfishly, we all want him to always be here physically, but when we listen to his music, sing his songs and spread love throughout the world, he still lives... His legacy inspired triumph through talent. The following piece is a prime example of such. From the bottom of my heart, I want to express heartfelt thanks to the contributors, all of whom saw my vision and selflessly gave of their time and talents...

Picture this: We've returned to South Beach and the Hit Factory Recording Studio. The novel had been mixed and remixed and was now complete, ready for the crazy world of readers to laud or loathe the effort. A feel-good vibe filled the air, much like what John, Paul, Ringo and George must have felt in 1963, the year *before* their life-altering Ed Sullivan experience. It was then the Beatles realized that they were on to something, and it was only a matter of time before America and the entire globe knew what they realized.

Author William Fredrick Cooper wouldn't go that far, but he experienced a wonderful sensation, one that told him that he'd been cleansed. In realizing that life had bent him in the shape of a pretzel, like his fictional namesake, he was not broken.

God had to take me through some things so that he could mold me. He forgave my missteps, and was with me through the consequences of some of my actions. He removed things that hindered my growth, shielded my heart from those who meant harm, tested me so that I put all my faith in Him, and pruned me so that He could use me in a way that made a difference.

While feeling triumphant, the author accepted his transformation with humility, for he knew the struggles of life are always one step behind. He also knew, as a flawed man, that he would continue to be a work in progress.

Peering upward at the heavens, "I'm trying, Father. I'm still trying," he mumbled.

He opened the door to the control room.

"SURPRISE!!!"

Seven of his friends had made the trip; some from near, others from far.

His best friend for over thirty-five years, Steven McGoy (a/k/a Scorpio Sessions) took the lead. Turning on "Unbreakable's" potent, persistently pulsating instrumental, he allowed the relentless piano-bass hook to fill the room.

Then he spoke for them all.

"While you were writing, we all listened to this. It inspired us all to create our own magic. Sit back and listen to what the groove did. I'll go first."

Suddenly, the music stopped.

And Scorpio Sessions stepped to the mike.

UNBREAKABLE
by Scorpio Sessions

Unbreakable
Unshakeable
Incorruptible
Not forsake-able
made in his image more than capable
sleeping slumped over some not wake able
lost in life's sauce the insatiable
melt hearts desires inescapable
UNBREAKABLE, UNBREAKABLE

No weapon formed against me prospers
Full attention to details erasable
Mistakes made forgiven unmistakable
Stumbled now humbled relatable
SO GRATEFUL, SO GRATEFUL
Come through it all now unbreakable
Why SO HATEFUL, SO HATEFUL
I made it through not debatable
NOT DEBATABLE NOT DEBATABLE
Glory to the one that makes me unbreakable
I am unbreakable
You are unbreakable
We are unbreakable!

Snaps filled the air as the groove returned.

"That was hot, Black!" William said.

"That's simply the beginning, Will. There's plenty more in store."

On cue, Tunde Dike, (a/k/a Thick Code) approached William with a warm hug.

He said, "Your distant relatives from Nigeria, West Africa salute your purpose, my brother. To be unbreakable means summoning the courage to conquer the hard times in life with determination. If I may…"

Once again, the music stopped, and a different yet potent flow captured the spirit of the room.

UNBREAKABLE (Spoken Word Poetry)
by Thick Code

Naked in the ghost town of this cold world
Like an echo all I hear is my word
My audible pain hurts like a sword
Footsteps of bogeyman in the night
In the night no bright light to my sight
Then fear terrorizes the night with nightmares
My sweet dream is my dream and my everyday dream
Walked miles not with frown with smiles
Then I see clearer
I see the shining stars in the night sky
So I fly so high and kiss the blue sky
Craziest moment I lost my dearest
The craziness of unhappiness and Sadness
Decided survivor in the wilderness
Nobody by my side
All I see is myself by my side
Loneliness whispers suicide
I choose life not to kill with gun or knife
Then I hear the voice of hope in the midst of no hope
My hope like a sun casts the shadow of burden behind me
I'm hopeful because I can feel the power of hope in me
I can see the more beautiful me
The more powerful me living in me
Poverty has spoken
The wings are broken
Our rights are stolen
Poverty is a terrorist
No good living on the list

Lost beautiful dreams to it
But mine is immortal
Secured in a sacred altar
In fact my dream is intact
As old as time
Spending days without dime
So empty like a lost rhyme
The only alternative is crime
Will never because I've seen my prime time
So beautiful like beat and rhyme
Days of rumble in the jungle
I stay humble not to stumble
Enable to face the trouble
My future is predictable despite the global unstable
The incredible streetwise
Sensible, reasonable and knowledgeable
The impossible is now possible and life is now edible
With success I'm inseparable
My dream is irreplaceable
Seen pains and undesirable
Conquered all my power is irresistible
Now stepping into the limelight they all tremble
Small minds called me a rebel
Because I'm undisputed
I'm unbreakable
Still....Unbreakable!

Snaps, then music...
Pointing in the direction of some powerful women, Steve con-

tinued the narration. "Before you got here, I asked the ladies if they wanted to start things off. All of them said fire before finesse. But once you hear them, you'll agree that they're on fire."

"The perfect segue," Cezanne Poetess said. "William, London, England sends its love from across the pond. To me, the definition of unbreakable is knowledge of oneself. Take a listen."

I Am What I WILL to Be!
by Cezanne

"I am...Cezanne!"
I can write
I can paint
I can dance
I can sing
I can do anything I put my *mind* to!
And so can you...

Years ago (long before it was actually so)
I began telling my Self;
"I am a brilliant and successful artist"
"I am a prolific writer"
"I am a first-class performer"
"I am mentally free"
And now,
I am what I *willed* to be!

Now, let me give you an idea how I train my subconscious mind
to believe the suggestions I make to it
So that *it* co-operates with *me*

By using my will-power with the power of **"I am..."**
I am in the process of changing everything about me
Recreating Who I Am and Who I wish to be
So listen carefully...

"I am the master of all my thoughts and feelings"
Whatever I say my *mind* has to follow—I am the one in control!

"I am in a constant state of bliss"
By keeping my Self feeling happy,
I am attracting good things to me!

"I am grateful for every little thing that happens to me"
My positive mental attitude of gratitude
Helps me to see the good in every situation,
And God opens the doors for me.

"I am in control of my destiny"
I don't have a victim mentality
Every experience I go through
Only serves to give me the opportunity
To decide *Who* and *What* I will to be.

"I am strong"
I bend but I don't break.
I rise above every challenge that life throws at me

"I am a born leader"
I have the ability to influence many
Through the various gifts and talents that have been given to me.

"I am a natural healer"
I have the power to heal with my hands,
My voice and the words I speak
My work sends out a healing energy

"I am spiritual"
There's more to me than meets the eye
99% of me you cannot even see!
I am a Spirit, living in this body,
More Divine than human
Yet I use my body to express my Self perfectly
I study Ancient Wisdom like a religion
Yet this 'Higher Education' cannot be gained from any university;

"I am a great creator"
I can create from nothing but the raw materials of mental
principles!
My sexual energy is the key to my creativity
I am what I *WILL* to be!

"I am a freedom-fighter"
I fight for the right to be free, daily!
I'm constantly breaking free from the mental chains of religion,
Mis-education and how society tells me I should be
I'm always breaking boundaries
Thinking *outside* of the box
So don't try to cage me in to *your* way of thinking;
Who are *you* to tell *me* what I should think, do and expect
Don't you know I have my own spirit guides and intellect?
I will *not* be controlled by the will of another,

Not even my own Black brother!
I have a mind of my own, and a free will to use it
My mind, I am the only one to control it!
If I didn't ask for your advice
What makes you think you should give it?
So you master your mind
And let me master mine
My will, not your will, be done!

"I am being the change I want to see"
As taught by Mahatma Gandhi,
Changing my world from the inside out
I am what I WILL to be.

I WILL my Self to wellness!
I WILL my Self to transformation!
I WILL my Self to claim the riches of God's Kingdom!

What I will for my Self,
You can be too
All you have to do is tell your Self that you're 'it' already
And soon you'll become what you WILL to be!

Marcus Garvey gave the call for liberation
And now his place I fill

"Up you mighty people,
You can accomplish what you WILL!"
© Cezanne 2010

"Now, William," the poetess concluded, taking her seat. "You add all that up, and it makes you unbreakable."

The whole room shouted a collective "DAMMNNNNN!!!!"

Steve didn't even put the music back on.

He said, "Cezanne brought along some company, Fred…"

"Fred?" Cezanne asked, "Who's Fred?"

Suddenly, someone knocked on the studio door.

A familiar voice dropped in with the answer.

"Fred is what his family calls him. I call him William."

At that moment William and the woman locked eyes. So much could have been said, but no words were necessary, for their history spoke so many wordless emotions.

"Can I?" the woman respectfully asked.

"You may." William nodded.

"Thanks. To me, being unbreakable means that you acknowledge the bumps in the road, and understand that the trials of life bring triumph and the tests produce testimonies. But before you realize all this, sometimes you have to ask yourself a question."

Who Said It Would Be Easy?
by Cheryl Faye

Life is like a box of chocolates
You never know what you're gonna get.
Sometimes joy, sometimes pain,
Sometimes sunshine, sometimes rain,
Sometimes it's all good, other times it's not.
Sometimes you'll feel like the fire's extra hot.
Sometimes when you think you just can't take no more

Circumstances will knock your behind right down to the floor
It's in those times we begin to wonder
If God truly, truly cares
Because so much is coming at us
And we learn that life's no crystal stair.
But who said it would be easy
Just because we believe in God
Do you really think that's a guarantee?
That life won't be so hard
It's largely due to our belief
In a wonder working Majesty
That the enemy will mess with us
To shake up our faith and disprove our trust.
But it's times like these that we must cling
Ever stronger to our peace and joy
Because fire cleanses, purifies and makes us precious
Just like a child's favorite toy.
So don't you be discouraged
Because nothing seems to go your way
Consider that when the storm is over
You'll be standing in a brand new day.
It's true that what God has for you
Is for you and you alone
Can't no one take it from you
And they can do nothing to postpone
God's promise for your life
Your day of victory is near
But if we're not ready to receive
That which He whispered in our ear
You can be sure God will do

Whatever it is God must
Until we're solid like stainless steel
No longer prone to rust.
Who said it would be easy
This journey we call life
But if we hold tight to our hope in God
We'll be able to manage the strife.
The fire, the trials and the tests
All help to make us stronger
So that when God is ready to use us
For His glory, we'll be able to stand much longer
So don't be discouraged just because
Right now you've got to go through it
In order for a pearl to become what it is
Irritation for a time must be endured
But when the irksome time has passed
You'll emerge as a precious, precious gem
More useful, much stronger
And if you can imagine
Even more loved by Him.

The snaps rained down, but Cheryl Faye didn't stick around for the applause. Placing the mike on the stand, she left the room quickly.

"She always had a style of her own," William said.

"I, too, know about adversity," a meek voice in the back announced. Striding up to William, she greeted him with a familiar refrain.

"Hey, Pumpkin," Minister Utrena Johnson said. "Now you know I represent the South. Actually, I represent anyone who had to look at the person in the mirror and remember that God made us to be more than conquerors. Sometimes we have to remind ourselves that the God in you may allow you to bend with your own imperfections, but He'll never let you break."

The Search For Unbreakable
by Minister Utrena Johnson

Fragile was the piece
That disturbed my peace
Wound in deceit
I chose to cheat
His lies made me lie down
Tarnishing my crown
Explosive, he erupted
My marriage interrupted
Bleeding God's presence retreating
My reach couldn't stretch
My being a wretch
This female dog
Who Fetched fame...
More like, I was being played by the game...
Her lies
Spread like cancer
Betrayal held my heart
For ransom
Solo was no longer a song
It was my home So Low seemed high
Irony...

So Low was my view to the sky
My stare now a stair
Above my self-destruction
Was the peace that
Disturbed my piece of hell
And He whispered
Get up, My child
You can't fail
You're Unbreakable

When finished, "You like, Sweetie?" she asked.

The rooms snapped its approval.

The theme music returned, and with it, Steve at the controls.

He asked, "Fred, are you digging this?"

"I sure am."

"Cool… This next brother has been waiting for a minute. You met him in Canada years ago, and while he was in England, Cezanne convinced him to flow through."

"He sees me, Steve," said Kwame McPherson.

William smiled. "Man, how are you? It's been a minute."

"God is so good, William. I live in Jamaica, but I travel across the pond a lot."

"I can tell from your writing. It's amazing."

"It's all love, man. Like the piece I wrote for you. Sometimes being unbreakable means that you're indissoluble, too."

Indissoluble...
by Kwame McPherson

I felt the stress
I remember the trauma
The scars are there for all to see
My tears trails, embedded in my cheeks
Disappearing like train tracks
Evidence of the years, months and not just weeks
Of trying to be in a world so incomplete
Being beaten all over, 'til I am so weak

I feel the whip on my back
Tearing my flesh, ripping my soul
Clawing at my essence
Shredding my organs, dismantling my mind
Taking its toll
My thoughts
My consciousness
Empty
Vacant
A space

Shackles bite my ankles
Decimate my wrists
My life blood seeps
A small stream untapped
Like my mind when I see my Queen
But she's bound like me
Torn from my side

A trophy for someone, who isn't me
My eyes blind
I no longer see

My muscles pulse
My limbs throb
A light brightens within me
Starting from a seed
Filling me, touching my cells
Filling my bones
Transforming my organs
Within me our story returns to life
Ghostly shadows dissipate the hurt
Remove the pain, the strife
I feel their power
It beats
It pounds
I'm alive
I'm alive
I haven't stopped

I am solid, I am sound
I'm incredible
I'm alive
I'm alive
I'm indissoluble
And I'm unbreakable…

"Wow," William said, wiping his eyes.

"It's all love, bro."

Steve said, "I saved these next two for last. They made us all aware of your struggles while writing this book, and they're the reason why we're all here. They really love you, as do we all. You've never met them before, and we'd like for them to take us home with each of their pieces. So without introduction, I'm gonna let them fly."

The statuesque woman that rose in the sound room was elegance in motion; a portrait of calm. Her award-winning publishing company illustrated what happened when agape love met business and talent. Aptly defined, her tranquility created a Peace within the Storm of a literary world that sorely needs her kind of love.

The God in her illuminated the recording studio.

Approaching the mike, in a humble voice, she uttered, "This is for you, William."

For All We Know...
by Elissa Gabrielle

Through veins that carried mighty blood.
Through tears that sustained heartache and washed away fear.
Through wading of the ocean and surviving the flood.
Through uprooted roots and unbridled resistance.
For all we know,
this is the foundation for your existence.

You have not blown an uncertain trumpet.
You have not crumbled under the guise of defeat.
You have not lost in the midst of assumption.

You have not failed to deal in hope.
For all we know,
you secured that knot at the end of your rope.

You've gone from failure to failure and smiled your way through.
You've gone from the vision to the dream to the glory and
everything in between.
You've gone from the let down to the knock down but
you didn't stay down and still found the strength to rise.
You've gone from knowing that success is just hard work
in disguise.
For all we know,
you were born of blessed seed and inherited the wise.

You smiled in the face of adversity.
You laughed when they called for your demise.
You sang to the heavens while they plotted your downfall.
You raised your fist, arched your back, stood tall when you
were told you would not rise.
For all we know,
you were answering that God-given call.

With step triumphant and a soul of cheer.
Go'on and win the daily battle without fear.
True worth is in being, not seeming.
And you've faced what you must.
Seen some hopes fail, yet kept unfaltering trust,
that God is God.
For all we know,
He is always true and just.

Thank you for standing up in your own life.

Thank you for encouraging us through the profound collective power of our reflection.

Thank you for informing us of our own best vision.

Thank you for never yielding to submission.

For all we know,

your courage, your strength, your battle, your hunger has inspired another's mission.

...and perhaps a nation of millions.

When she finished, there wasn't a dry eye in the room.

"God bless you," were her parting words.

Without an introduction, the next brother, a victor of adversities of his own, stepped up. Under normal conditions, this master of words, rhythm and narrative detail would have dropped something so sensuously smooth that all the women in the world would have been throwing their panties at him.

But this occasion caused him to reach deep and show another side.

Rubbing his salt-and-peppered goatee, "I do many things, William," the distinguished brother from Seattle said. "Now, through words, I want to show you what being unbreakable means to me."

TORTURED BUT NOT BROKEN—
I'M UNBREAKABLE...
by Alvin L.A. Horn

The West Coast (Tupac Shakur)-like response, hear his voice

The legacy
A beat down, yeah, ah-huh
The news of a soul tortured
Me and you, and friends and foes
Lovers
Strangers
Associates
Family
Blood and the cuz-ins, yeah, ah-huh
Whatever you think you are to me
You and I have slayed, sliced, and been cut
You and I have funked all over each other
It's all torture to every aspect of our walk and the talk
From our birth to death we torture ourselves with hurt, yeah,
ah-huh
Until we learn to do right, and understand what rights should
be done to us
Even then when it's not to our liking; we survive in the jungle
of *Human Nature...and then we know*
I'm never broken, I'm *Unbreakable...*

Yeah, it's self-inflicted torture if you lie to yourself
If we don't maintain love
I said love

Not lies, yeah, ah-huh

There are no shades of grey of weak thoughts and words and actions; it's either *Black or White*...you hear me

When we maintain love

When we drop the funny face; the phony race to be on top of each other

We all come up

I know folks *Wanna Be Startin' Something*...

But if they try to fast track using me

Haha-yeah, they'll be breakin' their own asses on hard cement on a rainy day

Yeah it's gonna get *Bad*...

I'll be leavin' them wet and maybe embarrassed because they're assed out

Exposed, yeah, ah-huh exposed

Aged-out shit starters, behind my back they stab and in my face they *Scream*...how great I am

Yeah go ahead, *Don't Stop 'Til You Get Enough*...

The rest of us know *Billie Jean*...*got impregnated* with lies and game, she's their ultra-ego-*Dirty Diana* groupie

Trying to win at all costs is self-infliction of pain

It leaves hearts and souls in pouring down drains of mental waste

Hard cases I felt them, yeah

Of torture I felt from them, and those other ones

But I'm not broken

Simply put, I'm *Unbreakable*...

I'm faithful to God and asking Him to forgive my missteps

Reason being, those around have faked the funk of realities, yeah, ah-huh

They went up for a nasty dunk in my face and got rejected, you heard me!

I didn't need mama to tell me to knock them out, you heard me!

My stare alone into fools living in ghetto paradise mind-sets lets me drive by corrupt minds and surpass their asses in the slow lane

Why because, their Pinto-driving asses are broken down alongside the path ways to success in living the right way to live

Me, yeah

I'm never broken, I'm *Unbreakable*...

That lover

Lovers

Yes it was good while it lasted

What, did I do wrong?

Or was or you?

We left our souls at *Heartbreak Hotel*...

Don't Matter Time Waits For No One...

Never Can Say Goodbye...

Got To Be There...When we grow-up

And live by the *ABC*...of love

Maybe Tomorrow...

Why?

All I Do Is Think Of You...

So if you're not broken

I'll Be There...

Ask The Lonely...

Them folks who smile in your face, yeah, ah-huh

Slinging wrong notes of auto tuned fake relationships, like a lot of those Facebook relationships

Sounding almost right, but so wrong

Slim slimy rat looking like a friendly rat named *Ben*...but carrying foulness

Saw them coming they weren't a *Smooth Criminal*...

They couldn't I wouldn't let them break me, I'm *Unbreakable*...

Body Language...and verbal detraction told and tells me of their crimes like Daddy Joe whooping that ass, and taking money they didn't earn

Hell nah'

The Boogie Man...ain't dealing with no scarecrow here

This ain't the Wiz, I'm alive in reality

I'm *Unbreakable*...because I use me, and not them to be a *Bridge Over Troubled Water*...

Checking them once and checking them twice and every single damn time

So they can't break me, and that leaves me *Unbreakable*...

Every man and woman knows how a potential dangerous situation can end one's dream

Me I'm a *Dancing Machine*...away from those who play broken records of cracked lifestyles

If you're an 8track of the same thing repeating what's wrong

I eject you from my groove, yeah, ah-huh

Now shake that ass one time

Or at least your mind to be free

Why, you can't get over on me *Beat It*...

Because, I'm never broken, *I'm Unbreakable*...

You can't undo what God wants me to do

You may get in the way

But I will step over you or on you, and maybe break you

© ALVIN L.A. HORN, 2013

The distinctive beat invaded the moment one last time, causing the Magnificent Seven to form a circle. Smiling, joy filled the room as they danced, each moving in their own unique way. Together, they created a moment that best exemplified the spirit of not only the new man before them, but, more importantly, of a man whose music was the soundtrack of their lives.

"So," Steve asked, "That is what 'Unbreakable' means to us. Now what we want to know is what does it mean to you?"

Moving into the center of the circle, a tearful author could only muster one word, a word that best represented what he felt for all of them.

"Love."

THE MICHAEL JACKSON TRIBUTES

IT'S BETTER ON THE OTHER SIDE, MICHAEL...

(Written July 1, 2009)

(Inspired by "Better on the Other Side"—A MJ TRIBUTE by The Game featuring Diddy, Chris Brown, Polow DaDon, Mario Winans, Usher and Boyz II Men)

Down here on earth, we still cry;
Fifty years of age, too young to die.
Tears ran down my cheeks as I asked why;
Then words from an angel came from the sky.

It's better on the other side, Michael;
In God's arms you'll find peace.
A job well done brings an eternal smile;
The lonely feelings of pain will cease.

As the candles flicker, then fade in sadness;
Millions receive a message from above,
He was more than a King of Pop, God proclaimed;
He was a soldier of Peace and Love.

L
eaving behind generations of many screaming, gasping for air and crying tears of joy, my idol Michael Joseph Jackson was a gravity-defying force of nature not of this world. Embedding himself in our emotional, spiritual and cultural DNA for four decades, his global adoration was messianic. Transcending races long before *The Cosby Show*, Oprah Winfrey, Michael Jordan, Tiger Woods and Barack Obama (!), he painted intense portraits of peace and love through song and dance. And like one of his vibrant vocal harmonies, he brought musical genres, creeds and colors together when he put his heart and soul on display for all to see.

Like Picasso, Mozart, and Beethoven, the creations during Michael's artistic journey on earth rendered the talkative speechless, and served as an inspiration to many walks of life. Making us believe all was possible with a little faith and self-esteem, the gifts from above he left behind still have us unable to look away; for we might miss something.

He gave us soul as a mezzo-soprano prodigy, playing his tender tenor tone as sweet as a musical instrument. And when he grew older, Michael moved majestically, magnificently meshing smooth-as-silk falsettos, gritty growls and gulps, electrifying emotional urgency and feather-timbre sensitivity to create something enchanting. Combining purity, power, precision and pitch, his gift was not one you saw on *American Idol* vying for fifteen minutes of fame. Rather, it's akin to an incandescent meteor spaceship falling from a generous blue sky crashing near unsuspecting farmers driving on a country road.

He was a real-life son of Jor-El, only tragically, he never seemed to fit a Clark Kent disguise.

Possessing that it factor from GO, his gift from God was so

different; the force of it incomprehensible to this very day. His voice kicked in the door of music normalcy, waved a "four-four" of freakish talent, announced itself to a world's soundtrack, and would never leave us.

That's why it hurt so much to see him go home.

Down here on earth, we still cry;
Fifty years of age, too young to die.
Tears ran down my cheeks as I asked why;
Then words from an angel came from the sky.

It's better on the other side, Michael;
In God's arms you'll find peace.
A job well done brings an eternal smile;
The lonely feelings of pain will cease.

As the candles flicker, then fade in sadness;
Millions receive a message from above,
He was more than a King of Pop, God proclaimed;
He was a soldier of Peace and Love.

A towering figure with universal appeal, he was chosen by God to bring joy to us all; a magical man of miracles by way of song who breathed life into music. Confident in his gift of communication, from early on he spoke to our hearts. Soaring with youthful pipes, he sang songs that spoke with emotions unheard of from one so young. Inventing infectious melodies that will never be outdated, his voice was a throwback, an era-blending tribute to

Ray Charles, Frank Sinatra, Elvis Presley and others who lent a distinct personality to timeless tunes. What separated him from those and other musical geniuses is that he started way before puberty. Integrity and fidelity was preached in *I'll Be There*, playground rhymes in *ABC*, and determination in righting hopeful wrongs in *I Want You Back*. Singing those songs with his brothers with maturity and feeling, Michael's vocals invaded our veins, giving our bloodstreams a new type of oxygen. Graciously placing his soul in our hands to hold, he made us realize that we are the world by unselfishly blessing us with his blessing.

Love does that.

That's why it's so hard to say goodbye.

Down here on earth, we still cry;
Fifty years of age, too young to die.
Tears ran down my cheeks as I asked why;
Then words from an angel came from the sky.

It's better on the other side, Michael;
In God's arms you'll find peace.
A job well done brings an eternal smile;
And lonely feelings of pain will cease.

As the candles flicker, then fade in sadness;
Millions receive a message from above,
He was more than a King of Pop, God proclaimed;
He was a soldier of Peace and Love.

Declaring his manhood by going *Off the Wall*, the tenderness of Michael's tone never changed. Capturing vulnerability while maintaining his self-assurance, hees, hoos and hiccups became vocal trademarks as his musical maturity grabbed, then took you on a passionate rendezvous through the wonders of his heart. Sensitive yet seductive, ambitious and hard as it was sophisticated and smooth, you can see Michael standing tall as he vocalized his every emotion. Easing down many roads of creative freedom by mixing funk with jazz, disco with old-school soul, *Off the Wall* was merely an appetizer for an entrée of Kings.

Thriller made the world dance joyously. Aligning the sun, moon and stars with the fusion of talent, material and production, God placed a hand on his chosen one's shoulder and said, "Let's rock, son."

The standard bearer of today's pop culture, simply put, Michael killed *Thriller*.

He killed it.

Begging lovely in "The Lady in My Life," he had many brothers pleading to their ladies "Don't You Go Nowhere" or "Ooh girl, lemme keep you warm." Hell, horror movie star Vincent Price rapped on the album's eerily interesting title track. *Beat It*, bridging moods and music genres with its edginess, made even the most hardcore R&B lovers dig Eddie Van Halen and his blistering guitar solo.

"Billie Jean" was recorded in one take. All you needed to hear was that insistent, thumping drumbeat, a perfect, percolating groove, Louis Johnson's bass line, Jerry Hey's string arrangement and yelps from a scintillating voice conveying depth in its rawness when screaming, "The kid is not my son…," and you know why angels rejoice in the arrival of a King.

But why, I asked God with bloodshot eyes from my constant sobbing, why did he have to leave us now?

Down here on earth, we still cry;
Fifty years of age, too young to die.
Tears ran down my cheeks as I asked why;
Then words from an angel came from the sky.

It's better on the other side, Michael;
In God's arms you'll find peace.
A job well done brings an eternal smile;
And lonely feelings of pain will cease.

As the candles flicker, then fade in sadness;
Millions receive a message from above,
He was more than a King of Pop, God proclaimed;
He was a soldier of Peace and Love

The lights are dim on Broadway today, as the Great White Way weeps with regret on the opportunity it missed when a supernova chose popular music over its riches. Their loss was the gain of us all, for in Michael Jackson, we saw the miracle of dance. Paying homage to the souls of "Mr. Bojangles," Jackie Wilson and James Brown, the grace of Gene Kelly, the flair of Bob Fosse, and the angular agility of Astaire and Ailey, his intricate inventiveness through footwork and body movement was a mixture of everything. Merging elements of pop, R&B and rock, artistically adding tap, jazz, vaudeville to a blend of ballet, breathtaking boogie and breakdancing, fusing fantastic fluidity with tense twitches, sudden stops and starts, as a physical engineer he always left us wanting more as he made the world dance with him.

He was a one-man virtuoso. You don't believe me? Try this: Think of this dancing machine's legacy; an absolute, awesome mastery of music and movement. Think of the creation of a mechanical robot that moved Michael from childhood prodigy to superior showman. Next, a percussive pelvis thrust to the time of a tick; then a sexually charged crotch grab. Picture him rising on his toes *en pointe* after a series of spectacular spins. Watch a leg kick after executing fast, fancy footwork. Wonder at the many abstract forays within the beat of song that created its own rhythm. Think of the memorable rides through a world of escapism by way of landmark videos and groundbreaking short films.

And of course, there was something so simple yet special in its sophistication: a smooth, sensationally slick slide backward that deftly defied logic and gravity all at once.

That was the moonwalk to us all.

But to Michael Jackson, it was much more.

It was a piece of his soul.

His was a soul that garnered an outpouring of adoration from peers past and present, celebrities and millions of fans worldwide. (A love he never felt because of his own troubles the media wants us to remember him by. NOT!) It was a soul that stopped the world every time he moved, even in death. It was a soul that breathed love through song and dance; through countless millions given in charitable assistance worldwide both known and unknown, a soul that implored the ceasing of hip-hop beefs, sometimes successful (The Game and 50 Cent), other times tragically not (2Pac and Biggie). It was a soul that dominated music charts, obliterated sales records, broke racial barriers and changed music forever.

Remembering the time when he rocked our worlds and showed us miracles with *HIStory*, his soul was *Bad, Invincible* and *Dangerous* as it gave us thunderbolt-like chills on stage, in dance, and in song.

At his best, the soul of Michael Jackson gave us all love.

God's Love.

Down here on earth, we still cry;
Fifty years of age, too young to die.
Tears ran down my cheeks as I asked why;
Then words from an angel came from the sky.

It's better on the other side, Michael;
In God's arms you'll find peace.
A job well done brings an eternal smile;
And lonely feelings of pain will cease.

As the candles flicker, then fade in sadness;
Millions receive a message from above,
He was more than a King of Pop, God proclaimed;
He was a soldier of Peace and Love.

While hearts on earth feel a true loss,
Joy rises with the morning sun
For a soldier of Peace and Love returns home
To His Father, and the words that bring glory to His name
Well Done.

Rest in peace on that other side, my friend. It's better there.

WILLIAM'S NOTE:

Thank you, Michael Jackson, for teaching me how to dance when I had no dexterity; showing me perfectionism if I study a craft, and showing me sensitivity and love through your music; for giving me confidence in myself when I had none. While I cry today as our spirits disconnect, I know that God has you. Know that you take rest in a place where no one will judge or hate you; a place where there is no strife, no issues and insecurities and most importantly, you are safe. Thank you so much for being such an inspiration to all my dreams and desires, and leaving so much of yourself behind. May God continue to bless you, and the overflow of such brings love to us here on earth. God Bless You, Man.

NEVER CAN SAY GOODBYE: WILLIAM'S TOP 100 MICHAEL JACKSON SONGS

(Originally Written July 25, 2009; Updated July 2012)

The magic was in his music, and we can never forget that. Majestically moving through our souls while going where no performer ever ventured—and never will again—he made us all proud. Imposing his artistic will on the world, he made all creeds and colors acknowledge the fact that the best entertainer this world has ever seen could actually be someone with bronze skin.

Michael Jackson embodied everything right with musical history on the planet.

Running through a wide range of emotions while compiling this list, I never realized the stranglehold he had on everything I knew over the past forty years. Whenever the joy of a puppy love captured my soul, I grooved to Michael. Whenever feelings of rejection and ridicule threatened to take me to a negative place, I was soothed by the whispers of someone who identified with my emotionally sensitive state.

Lord knows, I had it bad. From being a monster in a *Thriller* dance routine and performing "Beat It" to a sold-out high school audience (I distinctly remember a moment when the microphone came apart and I had to dance my ass off. ROFLMAO!!!!) to my boys ripping apart my *Thriller* cassette after I performed the Motown

25 version of "Billie Jean" at summer camp, to even having…an MJ picture on my name belt and a black *Thriller* jacket…

I think you get the picture.

Why my insanity was never checked is anyone's guess.

When a dexterity-challenged teenager lacking confidence needed to learn how to dance, there was the gloved one, moonwalking to another breathtaking jam. Forcing me to look somewhere within, the melodious mixture of voice, beat and hook gave me attitude through expression. Soon after I learned his signature steps, other dances followed: Intricate pop-locking within the beat of a song. Salsa, Meringue or Bachata steps. A pirouette while dancing house. Ticking, swaying calypso hip movement that made ladies think I was Jamaican. Doing the Hustle, then Stepping. Moving from grace to aggression by way of body movement, the rhythmic beast in me was finally unleashed as I totally identified with the freeness dancers speak of.

Michael Jackson gave me that soul, and I haven't stopped dancing since.

But perhaps the greatest thing my fascination with Michael Jackson allowed was in what he did so effortlessly: spread joy and kindness, and unselfishly made others feel good by turning love into action. Working overtime for weeks in late 1987, I saved about four hundred dollars, then joined hundreds of fans on line at Madison Square Garden in twenty-degree weather. For thirty-nine hours over a January weekend, I went toe-to-toe with frostbite. That Monday morning produced victory: I got six tickets to the *Bad Tour* concert and immediately called my family and my puppy love Audra.

(NOTE: I also received two more for a United Negro College Fund benefit performance from an attorney in my office; and would go again when he returned to the tri-state area in the fall one day after going to

see Prince's Lovesexy Tour at the Garden—MJ got jealous and sent me tickets—Psyche!)

For three nights in March, we would see magic.

Seeing the joy on their faces as green lasers shot off the King of Pop when he was "Another Part of Me," enjoying the high-fives we gave each other after emulating the video steps (okay, my brothers can't dance like me...LOL), and feeling the love Michael gave nineteen thousand New Yorkers each night made it all worthwhile.

Like him, I brought people together with all the love I owned in my heart.

Damn, I'm still smiling.

In addition to leaving behind so many fond memories, I also inherited a demand of self-excellence. Studying his perfectionism in terms of artistic invention, Michael helps me with my writing as well. Lighting a fire in the pit of my belly, as he was a student of James Brown, Fred Astaire, Bob Fosse and other timeless throwbacks, I, too, have reviewed, dissected and admired my writing forefathers in the hopes that one day I'll be fortunate to push my literary boundaries to an otherworldly level.

Study the best and become greater, Michael said.

I live, breathe and act on that statement. Watch carefully the charted path: Adopting a *less is more* philosophy (meaning a book every three to four years), I'm a strong believer in the quality of black penmanship in lieu of saturating a craft growing more diluted with each passing day. Competing against history as opposed to volume, the current fads and book sales, I am praying God touches my soul with that freakishly powerful, one-of-a-kind brilliance that defies logic.

If blessed with that fortune, then I owe it all to Michael Jackson, for he taught me an unrelenting commitment to excellence.

My idol Michael Jackson gave so much to me, and it's still hard to say goodbye. However, with this list, I have finally grasped a sense of closure. The following are my 100-plus favorite songs that Michael Jackson recorded as a solo artist, with his brothers, and others. I truly hope you have as much fun reviewing this collection as I had in composing it.

WILLIAM'S TOP 100 MICHAEL JACKSON SONGS

101. Hollywood Tonight (*Michael* CD, 2010)

100. Take me Back (*Forever, Michael* LP, 1975)

99. Maybe Tomorrow (w/The Jackson Five, *Maybe Tomorrow* LP, 1971)

98. P.Y.T.—Pretty Young Thing (*Thriller* LP, 1982)

97. Farewell My Summer Love (Recorded in 1973 or 1975, released in 1984)

96. Style Of Life (w/The Jacksons, *The Jacksons* LP, 1976)

95. Time Waits For No One (w/the Jacksons, *Triumph* LP, 1980)

94. Body Language (w/the Jackson Five, *Dancing Machine* LP, 1974)

93. *(tie)* Maria—You Were The Only One (*Got To Be There* LP, 1972)

    All I Do Is Think Of You (w/the Jackson Five, *Moving Violation* LP, 1975)

92. Do What You Wanna (w/The Jacksons, *Goin' Places* LP, 1977)

91. Don't Say Goodbye Again (w/The Jackson Five, *Get it Together* LP, 1973)

90. Even Though You're Gone (w/The Jacksons, *Goin' Places* LP, 1977)

89. Burn This Disco Out (*Off the Wall*, 1979)

88. Push Me Away (w/The Jacksons, *Destiny* LP, 1978)

87. Moving Violation (w/The Jackson Five, *Moving Violation* LP, 1975)

86. Heaven Can Wait (*Invincible* CD, 2001)

85. Whatever Happens (w/Carlos Santana, *Invincible* CD, 2001)

84. If I Don't Love You This Way (w/The Jackson Five, *Dancing Machine* LP 1974)

83. Hold My Hand (w/Akon, *Michael* CD, 2010)

82. Somebody's Watching Me (w/Rockwell, 1984)

81. Who Is It- Brothers In Rhythm 12" Remix (*Dangerous* CD, 1991)

80. Stranger In Moscow (*HIStory* CD, 1995)

79. Good Times (w/The Jacksons, *The Jacksons*, LP, 1976)

78. Be Not Always (w/The Jacksons, *Victory* LP, 1984)

77. Walk Right Now (w/The Jacksons, *Triumph* LP, 1980)

76. Life Of The Party (w/The Jackson Five, *Dancing Machine* LP, 1974)

75. In The Closet (*Dangerous* CD, 1991)

74. I Just Can't Stop Loving You (w/Siedah Garrett, *Bad* CD, 1987)

73. I Can't Help It (*Off the Wall* LP, 1979)

72. I Am Love (w/The Jackson Five, *Dancing Machine* LP, 1974)

71. You Can't Win (*The Wiz* Soundtrack, 1978)

70. Off the Wall (*Off the Wall* LP, 1979)

69. Forever Came Today (w/ The Jackson Five, *Moving Violation* LP, 1975)

68. Get On The Floor (*Off the Wall* LP, 1979)

67. Scream (Duet w/Janet Jackson, *HIStory* CD, 1995)

66. Torture (w/The Jacksons, *Victory* LP, 1984)

65. Jam (*Dangerous* CD, 1992)

64. Break Of Dawn (*Invincible* CD, 2001)

63. Mama's Pearl (w/The Jackson Five, Third Album, 1970)

62. The Girl Is Mine (Duet w/Paul McCartney, *Thriller* LP, 1982)

61. Get It Together (w/The Jackson Five, *Get It Together* LP, 1973)

60. Say, Say, Say (Duet w/Paul McCartney, *Pipes Of Peace* LP, 1983)

59. Lovely One (w/The Jacksons, *Triumph* LP, 1980)

58. Sugar Daddy (w/The Jackson Five, *Greatest Hits* LP, 1971)

57. Just A Little Bit Of You (*Forever, Michael* LP, 1975)

56. Tell Me I'm Not Dreaming (w/Jermaine Jackson, *Jermaine Jackson* LP, 1984)

55. Thriller (*Thriller* LP, 1982)

54. BAD (Bad CD, 1987)

53. Earth Song (*HIStory*, CD, 1995)

52. ABC (w/The Jackson Five, *ABC* LP, 1970)

51. Enjoy Yourself (w/The Jacksons, *The Jacksons* LP, 1976)

50. This Time Around (w/The Notorious B.I.G., *HIStory* CD, 1995)

49. Blood On The Dance Floor (*Blood On The Dance Floor* Remix CD, 1997)

48. Why You Wanna Trip On Me (*Dangerous* CD, 1991)

47. You Were There (*Sammy Davis 60th Anniversary Tribute*, 1990)

46. Get It (duet w/Stevie Wonder, *Characters* CD, 1987)

45. The Love You Save (w/The Jackson Five, *ABC* LP, 1970)

44.   Wanna Be Starting Something (*Thriller* LP, 1982)

43.   Blues Away (w/The Jacksons, *The Jacksons* LP, 1976)

42.   Ghosts (*Blood On The Dance Floor* Remix CD, 1997)

41.   Shake Your Body Down To The Ground (w/The Jacksons, *Destiny* LP, 1978)

40.   *(tie)* Ben (*Ben*, 1972)
       We're Almost There (*Forever, Michael* LP, 1975)

39.   Xscape (unreleased song, 2007)

38.   I Want You Back (*Diana Ross Presents The Jackson Five* LP, 1969)

37.   Someone Put Your Hand Out (*Ultimate Collection* CD, 2004)

36.   I Can't Make It Another Day (w/Lenny Kravitz, *Michael* CD, 2010)

35.   *(tie)* Never Can Say Goodbye (w/The Jackson Five, *Maybe Tomorrow* LP, 1971)
       Up Again (*Music and Me*, 1973)

34.   She's Out Of My Life (*Off the Wall* LP, 1979)

33.   Blame it on The Boogie (w/The Jacksons, *Destiny* LP, 1978)

32.   Dangerous (*Dangerous* CD, 1991)

31.   Rockin' Robin (*Got To Be There* LP, 1972)

30.   State Of Shock (w/Mick Jagger and The Jacksons, *Victory* LP, 1984)

29.   Goin' Back To Indiana (w/The Jackson Five, Third Album, 1970)

28.   (tie) One Day in Your Life (*Forever, Michael* LP, 1975)
       Ain't No Sunshine (*Got To Be There* LP, 1972)

27.   Gone Too Soon (*Dangerous* CD, 1991)

26.   Who's Loving You (*Diana Ross Presents The Jackson Five* LP, 1969)

25. The Way You Make Me Feel (*Bad* CD, 1987)

24. You Are Not Alone (*HIStory* CD, 1995)

23. I'll Be There (w/The Jackson Five, Third Album, 1970)

22. Another Part Of Me—Live Version (*Bad 25* CD, 2012)

21. *(tie)* She Drives Me Wild (*Dangerous* CD, 1991)
    Eaten Alive (w/Diana Ross & Bee Gees, *Eaten Alive* LP, 1985)

20. *(tie)* Will You Be There (*Dangerous* CD, 1991)
    Can You Feel It (w/The Jacksons, *Triumph* LP, 1980)

19. *(tie)* Smooth Criminal (*Bad* CD, 1987)
    I Wanna Be Where You Are (*Got to Be There* LP, 1972)

18. Human Nature (*Thriller* LP, 1982)

17. Rock With You (*Off the Wall* LP, 1979)

16. Beat It (*Thriller* LP, 1982)

15. It's Too Late To Change The Time (w/The Jackson Five, *Get It Together* LP, 1973)

14. Don't Stop 'Til You Get Enough (*Off the Wall* LP, 1979)

13. Dancing Machine (w/The Jackson Five, *Get It Together* LP, 1973)

12. You Were Made Especially For Me (w/The Jackson Five, *Moving Violation* LP, 1975)

11. Butterflies (*Invincible* CD, 2001)

10. Find Me A Girl (w/The Jacksons, *Goin' Places* LP, 1977)

9. Show You The Way To Go (w/The Jacksons, *The Jacksons*, LP, 1976)

8. The Lady In My Life (*Thriller* LP, 1982)

7. Lookin' Through The Windows (w/The Jackson Five, *Lookin' Through The Windows* LP, 1972)

6. *(tie)* Heartbreak Hotel (also known as This Place Hotel, *Triumph* LP, 1980)
   You Rock My World (*Invincible* CD, 2001)

5.   Man In The Mirror (*Bad* CD, 1987)
4.   Billie Jean (*Thriller* LP, 1982)
3.   Got To Be There (*Got To Be There* LP, 1972)
2.   Remember The Time (*Dangerous* CD, 1991)
1.   Unbreakable (*Invincible* CD, 2001)

WILLIAM'S TOP TWELVE MICHAEL JACKSON ALBUMS

12. *The Jacksons* (w/ The Jacksons, EPIC/CBS RECORDS, 1976)

11. *Invincible* (CBS/SONY RECORDS, 2001)

10. *Going Places* (w/The Jacksons, EPIC/CBS RECORDS, 1977)

9. *Moving Violation* (w/The Jackson Five, MOTOWN, 1975)

8. *Bad* (CBS/SONY RECORDS, 1987)

7. *The Jacksons Live* (EPIC/CBS RECORDS, 1981)

6. *Dancing Machine* (w/The Jackson Five, MOTOWN, 1974)

5. *Get It Together* (w/The Jackson Five, MOTOWN, 1973)

4. *Triumph* (w/The Jacksons, EPIC/CBS RECORDS, 1980)

3. *Off the Wall* (EPIC/CBS RECORDS, 1979)

2. *Thriller* (EPIC/CBS RECORDS, 1982)

1. *Dangerous* (EPIC/CBS RECORDS, 1991)

EVEN THOUGH YOU'RE GONE...

(Remembering Michael, One Year Later)
Written June 28, 2010

A year later, tears race down my cheeks.

Meeting at my chin, the pain of them wage constant war with my need to rejoice and celebrate the electrifying legacy you left behind. Sure, there were unexplained eccentricities along the way, not to mention a never-ending battle for respect; then redemption. While pockets of cynics fossilized your power and ridiculed your need to be different, millions of us who knew your heart agree on this:

Because, you're not here, Michael Jackson, a significant amount of love is missing all over the globe.

We live in a sick world. Anytime the real definition of capitalism—in order for people to be rich, others must be rock bottom poor—is considered normal, anytime a world takes pride in dysfunction that leaves people wrecked, anytime we glorify greediness and selfishness—The more self-centered we become, the less human we are—we validate the footprints of a universal system gone cockeyed.

Michael, you were not God, yet you allowed a glimpse of His love to shine when you said the "Man In The Mirror" needs to make a change. Through millions of dollars given in charitable assistance, you showed truth in the adage "To whom much is given, much more is required." You gave from your soul sans expectation and remuneration, and when it was lonely and empty, you reached deeper inside and gave more.

Love covers a multitude of sins, and while many in a sick world remember you as a tragic identity of problematic confusion—with millions starving and countries ravaged by war, disease and greed, could you say negative depictions of Michael Jackson by the media and cynics mirror an imperfection in themselves they refuse to see?—I knew that once you left this problem world, positive memories would reign supreme. That you left so much of your heart behind in song and dance renders doubters dwelling in derision moot.

We remember the music that made us move.

We remember the motion that made us marvel in your magic.

Even though you're gone, your love for us all conquered jealousy and hatred.

I learned that would be the case a long time ago…like I learned to understand things that are incomprehensible to others. Your pigmentation problem was akin to the Black Experience in America: many of us are still uncomfortable in our own skin, a skin that, in spite of the fact that Obama won, is still being assaulted daily by the ignorance of white supremacists. Those Band-Aids on your fingers may have been centuries of wounds that still need treatment; wounds of a world in denial of its many problems: dishonor, distrust, subtle and blatant racism, inner-city crime, large-scale wars and terrorism, overcrowded prison systems and waste of natural resources.

Only Father knows where this planet of pain is headed…

However every now and then, God provides us with an angel in human form, a gift so blinding in its beauty that its mere presence makes the world a better place. Michael, you weren't the ultimate physician or doctor, but you provided joy when we felt pain and smiles when those tears came from an unforgiving world. Softly, then boldly carrying us into your dreams of escapism, ones filled with joy and bliss, as our eyes remained transfixed on your mesmerizing gifts from above, we watched the impossible become possible, then rejoiced and celebrated the massive impact of goodness that invaded our hearts.

You gave us that, Michael, by showing us how to heal with the divine in you. Not to mention a talent so unique that even after your death, it still needs its own space in history.

That's what usually happens when you've witnessed the greatest there ever was.

There have always been others superstars, and there will be many more.

But they'll never be another Michael Jackson.

One year after your untimely journey home, much of the music industry is left with one-trick ponies that have little definition of history and its importance to our future. Failing to draw on their own creativity, many think sampling is substance, image is everything, and, in some recent instances, prefer idiotic ways of self-marketing as opposed to establishing a body of work that transcends time. That a slew of mercenaries lacking self-control have replaced timeless acts of artistic creativity in so many entertainment arenas further emphasizes your journey home.

But many of us still remember the time. Friday night, at a dance spot in downtown Manhattan, someone noticed the red T-shirt I wore in tribute, pointed me out to the DJ, and instantly a couple of jams came. I never knew how good "Heartbreak Hotel" sounded in a club until I heard that Gothic groove thump from the speakers; or "Enjoy Yourself." A couple of hours later, the DJ went in, and people who saw me dance Salsa with the Latin women, House with the old Paradise Garage heads, and hip-hop with the younger generation, smiled. Singing Jackson Five songs, people of all ages were doing the robot to "Dancing Machine," and the old J5 steps.

Then "Billie Jean" came on. In that same instant, a brother approached me and asked if I knew the Motown 25 routine. To that point, I was like Jimmy Swaggart, merely watching everyone enjoy your music.

Then, as if you touched me with your hand, something came over me.

The motorized shuffle during the first verse was followed by snapping leg kicks leading to the chorus. Pleading like you did on Motown 25, I rocked that camel walk between spin-and freeze poses that made Fred Astaire call you "an angry dancer." And of course mid-song, I took what "Caszper" and Jeffrey Daniel taught you and made it my own for a night.

First, I moonwalked backward, in a circular motion, and finally, Neil Armstrong style forward. Combining mechanical movements with mime, the place went crazy, and the manager was so moved visibly that he brought me dinner later. But that was not before a few of us did the "Thriller" dance and Chicago-stepped to "You Rock My World."

Wiping away tears, a few of us nodded.

Without words, we all knew.

Even though you're gone, the love you showed us remains in us all.

And for that, we give heartfelt thanks to God for bringing you into our lives to make the world a better place.

LOVE IS ALL WE NEED

(Let me preface my statement by saying that if this is misinterpreted as anything more than a humble opinion, then the message and its heartfelt sincerity was misunderstood. I prayed for guidance in the hope that I could utter words that might lend objectivity to our issues regarding dating. Trust me, I don't have all the answers and this is counsel for me as well. Here's what God provided. Hope this helps.)

A while back, I read two lists: "25 Things Brothers Should Be Saying to Sisters" and "Top Ten Reasons Why It's Hard To Date A Black Women," then the follow-up online posts and the follow-up responses in a readers group that exhibited so much fear and pain when pertaining to LOVE, God's most precious gift to us all.

Tears streamed down my cheeks.

It still hurts to see the bitterness and pain that exists when speaking of Black Love.

Who's at fault for all the madness? Are the brothers to blame for not being fathers and teaching their sons to respect? Are women culpable for not training their daughters how to recognize substance? Sisters, for emasculating brothers by broadcasting their deficiencies, while making them feel unappreciated? Are the men at fault for singing love songs that in words carry passion and depth, but in actions providing nothing but misery? Are women using the infamous attitude as a defense mechanism? Are brothers not recognizing the virtues and strength of women?

How about both genders, for not listening to one another and searching for unrealistic images while overlooking what God has provided for you?

As evidenced by the above, the back-and-forth in-fighting could go on endlessly. A painful indifference in regard to God's most precious gift and its correlation with dating rendered moot by all the dissension, empty experiences come and go, further exacerbating the jaded genders. Instead of inspiration and hope, Brothers and Sisters wear armor for combat.

At what point do we realize Love is truly all we need? The Apostle Paul, in 1 Corinthians 13:13, indicates that we should abide by faith, hope and love when it comes to everything life has to offer, and its relevance to relationships of the heart is a mandate.

"The greatest of these is Love," the Apostle continued.

Love really is all we need.

Given the state of relationships today: Its weird dating principles, painful outcomes, and negative in-fighting between the sexes— do we even truly believe in it?

And why not?

Maybe the solutions lie deep within ourselves, provided we conquer the traits that fuel unreasonable conditions unconsciously affecting our hearts. These pathologies threaten our positive mentality with regards to Love and our helpmate, as it constrains the energy that generates optimistic feelings about the opposite gender. Refusing to let go of the negativity birthed by this affliction only inflames the defense mechanisms that keep the hopeful, faithful and loving spirits we so desperately want to share mired in the darkness of our souls, never to see the light of day.

What is this conditioning? It's men and women wailing and weeping in emotional misery, anger and frustration because our distorted view of Love has us tied up in knots. Our jaded experiences, coupled with pessimistic outlooks on interpersonal relationships, have us acting like men and women who don't need each other. In our refusal to see how entrenched we are in a negative eventuality, our issues and jaded experiences concerning Love become one. WE BECOME OUR ISSUES AS OPPOSED TO MERELY POSSESSING THEM. The things that pain and plague our souls concerning matters of the heart usurp our body, disrupt our mindsets and entrench themselves within our existence, thereby giving us a cynical view of every aspect of Love and our association with a hopeful mate.

Instead of positive hope and faith being spoken from our mouths, resentment, cynicism, drama and fear poorly disguised as "nuggets of information" escape angry lips. Periodicals, talk shows, Internet posts like the aforementioned and drama-related novels with nary an uplifting word serve as a negative backdrop to a predetermined failure felt by both genders. Belief systems now slanted in subjectivity, we stand on opposite ends of the spectrum without ever moving close to one another to solve problems.

In short, we defeat ourselves with BS before we even suit up and run the race. Brothers refuse to open up completely. Sisters have their guards up all the time, expecting the shoe to drop. Nobody concedes even an apology. Both sexes give no quarter by way of praise. In the alternative, they'd rather talk at each other through personal issues and experiences, arguing about who's right and wrong as opposed to coming together in an effort to bridge acrimonious chasms with solutions.

Do you feel me? This is not good. And try as one might to escape the conditioning, we find ourselves consumed and confused with this state of mind, sometimes defending its miserable existence with anger and fear by way of preconceived notions, thereby justifying our inability to conquer the detrimental nature of it. And if we do summon the wherewithal to leave the negative cycle, then we think we've lost ourselves because we're doing something different. Something's wrong if we slip and give praise to a good Brother or Sister, and heaven forbid we exhibit a glimpse of emotional vulnerability, we think.

Quite the contrary. Overcoming issues and experiences that haunt us presents limitless possibilities to enjoy love as the Apostle Paul spoke of it. We begin to judge each experience as an individual case and are willing to give from the depths of our souls without expectation. Love of any color is about giving, isn't it? That strange feeling of conquering issues is non-existent, because we have learned agape love, the unconditional devotion that fosters pure, fruitful Black Love.

But how many of us are willing to overcome these fears, put away the litany of excuses and insecure thoughts of the "other shoe dropping"? How many of us not only believe in ourselves enough to escape those fears and insecurities, but in the ancestors who have produced modern-day kings and queens yet to touch our hearts? How many of us are willing to let go of the fears that shape, pollute and deter Love? How much anger do we have to relinquish before the three little words—I LOVE YOU—bring tears of joy as opposed to sobs of pain?

How can we ease the pain that exists between us?

With a little love.

True Love is really all we need, family.

THE BIG-UPS...

UNBREAKABLE: THE BIG-UPS

"Greatness lives on the edge of destruction... You are here, because in the face of destruction, on the brink of almost being destroyed you pound on your chest and said...I'M STILL STANDING, BRING IT! You learn that you don't break... You learn that you're unbreakable..."

—WILL SMITH

Heavenly Father, you allowed me to finish another one, and I am grateful. You knew my struggles, what I faced in terms of adversity, yet You showed me how tough I am in the face of tremendous pressure. You have been with me in some valleys, when I didn't know if I would see the next day, and have always loved me when I felt no one else did.

I often wondered why my life goes haywire every time I write a book, but I look at it now with great respect and humility. If this brings out the very best in me—YOU—then all I humbly ask of You is to give me strength to complete the tasks in a way that helps others. Thank you so much for the gift You gave me. It's in perfect concert with my heart and spirit to make a difference in all that I do. I pray that I gave You honor with my ballad *UNBREAKABLE*. My apologies about some of the steam and color, but hopefully I conveyed Your greatest gift to us all, Love.

Again, my heart is in all that I do.

Not only is my heart there, but my goal remains: I hope to write that perfect story. And if I fall short in my quest for perfection, Vince Lombardi said that I still might have a shot at excellence.

Hell, I'll settle for that.

Father, these Big-ups are from my heart, because there are so many that have touched my life. My daughter, Maranda: You have made me so proud. You're a young college woman, now, one who has embarked on her adult journey with the grace of a princess. Remember: YOU ARE THE PRIZE!!! Always demand respect, continue to give love to others from your spirit, check that outspoken, opinionated tongue of yours (something your father and mother still struggle with), and keep your eyes on God and all he has in store for you. Remember, the only lesson Daddy is trying to show you is that when God has a purpose for your life, you never give up, no matter what obstacles you may encounter, no matter where the destination leaves you. I love you so much.

Audrey: God used you to be an awesome mother. I am so thankful to you that our daughter hasn't caused us many sleepless nights. Thank you for being strong in areas where I sucked (no other way to put it) and for being the special woman you are.

Grandma: You are my biggest supporter, my best friend, my biggest fan and cheerleader; my everything. I find joy in knowing that you are at peace with your journey through life, and your words of wisdom have helped my personal growth more than you'll ever know. I love you so much!!!

To my Grandfather, Rufus Royster: I know you're in good health, now that God has you. I miss your stories and being able to cook breakfast for you. Thank you for being a man in every sense of the word, and thank you for the one last blessing: I wrote *UNBREAK-*

ABLE at your desktop in the basement!!! Rest in Peace, Grandpa.

To Pastor Tony Baker and my St. Philips Baptist Church Family: Thank you for taking me as I am. Your sermons have inspired me more than you'll ever know. Reverend Horace Sheffield and my New Destiny Baptist Church Family: You guys made a stranger in a new city feel right at home with your love…I love you guys. Bishop T.D. Jakes, Joel Osteen and Charles Stanley: Thank goodness for your online services. When I couldn't fellowship, your online sermons brought it to me. I am so grateful.

Ma: I love you so much. You're ten times the better writer than me, and I'm fortunate you (through God) passed this along when you gave me life. I love you. My Family: brothers and sisters, Stephanie, Adrian, Jeffrey, Gerald, Janessa, Alvin, Allan, Darlene; my cousins, Desiree, Sherman Jr., Shawn, Alexis, Charles Jr., Jamar, Darren and Shernay; Uncles Charles, Larry and Sherman, Aunts Susan, Grace and Ruth: I am so proud of each and every one of you. Pop: you know how we do.

To David McGoy: Thank you so much for introducing me to the works of Colson Whitehead. I've been reading a lot of Richard Wright lately, as I love his eloquence. (I loved *Savage Holiday*— Erskine was a trip…) To be honest: I wouldn't be doing any of this if it weren't for you. You've always been my primary inspiration, and I hope my stories make you proud. That sixth-grade water gun fight was a blessing from God, because he gave me another brother.

Steven (Randall) McGoy: God gave you something real, something special, and something that will touch, change and help so many people. From Langston, to Nikki and Sonja Sanchez, the torch has been passed to my boy. With God, all things are possible.

To Pardeice McGoy, Allen and Tammi Greer Brown, Askia Farrell, Bobby/Darlene Moore, Al Harrison, Daniel/Cheryl Marks and Melody Hawkins: I love all of you very much, and have never stopped in spite of our different journeys through life. I appreciate the village from afar and all that you've done for my daughter. Ms. Atherline Smith and Josephine Tucker: Thank you for fully understanding the depths of my journey. It's lonely sometimes, but I'm never completely alone, because God is in my corner.

To the Force: Katrina Spicer, Joyce Powell, Anita Turner, Marc Coleman, Memphis Vaughan, Jr. Christian Davis, Tad and Stacey Spencer, Darren McCalla, Matthew Fudge, Arminta Theodosia Barriero, Brian (B.K.) Simpson, Torin Cotten, Spencer Sally, James E. Smith, Jr., Richard Egan, Hector and Martha Gonzalez, Samuel DeLeon, Daren Hunter, John Fleming, Anthony and Debbie Lopez, Melonn Blue, Kevin Walton, Michael "R.D." Cooper, Nashaun Pass, Carlton Watler, Terry Benjamin, Icsom Jones, James Bethea, Jesus Hernandez, Gail and Lisa Carr: No matter where I go, no matter what I do, all of my heart, mind, body and soul will treasure each of you. You guys are the pulse of my dreams, and I only hope to make you all proud with the end result. To my second Grandmother, Stella Venner: I enjoyed those shopping runs. Thank you so much for allowing me to help. Your spirit is amazing.

To Vivian Cacal Perry: God bless you so much for your love and heartfelt support. I never would have made it without you, and to think, a simple YES, YES, YES started it all. Aloha is not enough, babe.

Deacon Tracy Brown and family: at my lowest, you guys showed me what Love is all about. I will never, ever forget that. Tracy, you are an amazing woman and the inspiration behind so much. Thank you for fixing things.

Zane and Charmaine: I am here, because you two were there,

through it all. God Bless You for all you are doing. Zane... You know the deal.

Charene Thornton: Smile. A response to a simple email back in 1999, and look what it's turned into. You were, are, and always will be an angel.

To the many readers and bookclubs that have supported my novels: God bless you, all. Lord knows I try to make every word count. And if I slip in substance, keep it real with me. I want no fall-off!! Tee C. Royal and RAWSISTAZ, The United Sisters Bookclub (Brooklyn, NY), Judi Belle Raines and the Sugar and Spice Bookclub (Jamaica, NY), OOSA Online Book Club, APOOO Online Bookclub, Michelle Carswell and the Turning Pages Book Club (Upper Marlboro, Maryland), Peace in Pages Bookclub (Upper Marlboro, Maryland), Carolyn Towles and The Buy The Book Club (New Haven, Connecticut) and Adrienne Dortche and the Black Women Who Read Book Club (New Haven, Connect-icut): May God continue to bless you ladies with the continued joy of reading. I am so grateful that so many of you have enjoyed my books. As with all my efforts, this one is from my soul. Hope it touched you. A special shout-out to the amazing DIVERSE DIVAS (Maryland)—You ladies are something else...HOLLA!!!

Knowledge Bookstore (Brampton, Ontario): I hope you enjoy this one as much as the others. Your love from up north means more than you'll ever know. I can't wait to see you again. Sean and Michelle Liburd, know that I love you guys so much! Neil Armstrong: I miss your kind insight more than you'll ever know.

Tracy Grant and Vincent Alexandria: Thank you, guys, for just loving me for me. It means so much. Mrs. Audra Wooten: Did you ever think that you were at the origin of my writing madness? I appreciate you, after all these years.

To Josselyne Herman-Saccio, Mary Icaza and all of my friends at Landmark Associates: Always create new possibilities for yourselves, and recognize the leader in you. Fight off those rackets and balance that with love. Unmessables: Craig Benson, Victoria Torres Bolanos, Anne Flanagan and Melina Somoza: I love you guys.

To Joyce Rosol and the incredible staff at the Henry Ford Rehabilitation Center: Karen, Dorothea, Andy, Lucy, Dr. Diab, Wendy, Debbie, Lisa, Gloria and Rose: Your kindness and stories of love while helping others was a gift from God, as all of you are to me. Thank you so much for everything!!!!

Karen Burd and Steve Nathan: It's such an honor knowing each of you. Every time I need love, you guys call. You're amazing, each of you. Steve, the Giants still suck...(LOL). I love you guys so much! Minister Utrena Johnson: I love you so much and am very proud of the CHANGES God has blessed you with. Keep your eyes to the sky, and it'll get even greater for you. I am humbled by our friendship. Valeeka Peeples-Dyer: You are truly the best. I love you, girl!! James Patterson and Ken Golden: We are gonna do this!!! I can't wait 'til God Blesses us with the completion of the REASON Project. It's going to be amazing, and it's because of you guys. Edwin Mitchell and Luis Barahona: Man, those nights at our Jersey City hang-out spot, drinking those chocolate Patrón shots and jamming on the jukebox really helped me through some grinding times that I never revealed. Your friendships mean so much to me. Having said that, F****** DO IT!!!

TO THE *UNBREAKABLE* PRODUCTION TEAM: To my "Wonder Twins" Lisa Alexander and Lolita Michelle-Cartwright; Kevin Porter, Camille Renee Lamb (aka Jermaine Dupri), Theresa Gonsalves (The Corporation), Theresa Stephens (Gamble/Huff— You are amazing!!!), Jan Forney (Dallas Austin) and Zandra

Denise Barnes (Too real with Yo' Bad Self!!!), Leatha Cross (DJ CRISS-CROSS), Sonya Lee (DJ LEE on the Wheels of Steel), Tiffany Craig and Debra Owsley (DJ OWWW) —Words cannot fully capture the appreciation I own for each of you. Thank you so much for reading the work in progress, offering honest feedback, criticisms, MJ stories and for helping me flesh this thing out. The Beatles say that we get by with a little help from our friends and they were so right. I love each of you so much. Elissa Gabrielle (Quincy Jones): We have yet to meet, but I know you through your giving heart and for showing me what friendship is all about. Thank you so much for being a listening ear, the sisterly encouragement as well as some valuable insight for *UNBREAK-ABLE*. You are a Queen! Nathasha Brooks-Harris: Big Sister, I can't thank you enough for your sisterly love during some grinding times. Se'Quasha Smith (DJ SQUASH)—you are very sweet. Thank you so much for reading this book and keepin' it real with me. Andrea Steward—That night that we hung out and you shared your love for your husband was the catalyst behind this love ballad. From the bottom of my heart, I want to say that I love you.

Orsayor Simmons: You are the best. Those CONVERSATIONS...

Sandra Newsome: in the fourth quarter, the God in you supported me with confidence and love. The end of this book is a tribute to our conversations, what we fleshed out. Thank you so much for all you have done!!!

Gail Diamond: Brooklyn in da house!! You epitomize all that is great when it comes to resiliency, and I'm glad you showed a brother something. God Bless You.

To Dominique Valentin: You are truly a queen. I'll never forget you for what you do for me and my grandmother.

To Janelle (the Dancer) Armstrong: You are the epitome of

strength, and I love you so much for looking after a cornball. You are one bad...

To my secret weapon, Cheryl Faye Smith, (aka Teddy Riley): I needed to run this by you, because since May 18, 2001, I've owned... You know the deal. Good look from the engineering seat—wink. To Lorraine Ross: Thank you so much for catching the last-minute little things.

Allison Hobbs: You are amazing. We're two of the original Strebor posse, and I'm proud of all your accomplishments. Those books you gave me to read... Well, hopefully you see the influence. Donna Hill, Margaret Johnson-Hodge, Gloria Mallette and Bernice L. McFadden: Your support, words and action while my spirit was wavering meant so much. Because of each of you, the laser of focus is narrowed toward the greatness God has in store for us all. I made a promise to you about the REASON project, and I plan to keep it. I love each of you. Brenda Woodbury: Thank you so much for seeing my heart through the madness. God really had to break me down to build me up, and I thank you for being there while I found myself. I treasure our friendship more than you'll ever know. Pastor Timmothy B. McCann: This one would not have been possible without our conversations. As was the case when you wrote those great books that I studied, you mentored me. I only hope I did you, and the old school warriors (Chet "C. Kelly" Robinson, Cole Riley, Marcus Major, Franklin White and Van Whitfield) proud. I even used a one-word title this time—wink.

Robert Fleming: Man... Thank you for reaching a hand down into the abyss and lifting a brother out. Those phone calls helped me more than you can possibly imagine. Hopefully, I can follow the amazing writing examples set by you and our forefathers. Kwame McPherson, Treasure Blue and Alvin L.A. Horn: My Brothers.

Your talents have blown me away and I am honored to be a literary brother. I wish I were as good as each of you; Kwame, that poetic rhythm; Alvin, your jazzy style mixed with social messages and the freak in you. Alvin, remember my words, you're gonna be a great one! Treasure, you are brilliant. Anything you need, I will comply. I love you guys so much! Curtis Bunn: I can't begin to tell you how much you mean to me. You have such a wonderful heart, and I love your work. Thank you so much for an initiative (the National Book Club Conference) that makes a difference in the literary world, and for being a Sports Britannica. I can't wait to just rap with you about sports. God Bless You, man.

To MY BOY, My Dawg, My Big Little Brother Thomas Slater: You know I'm a hafta kick your ass, you crazy mutha… I'm sorry, this is a PG acknowledgment. Man, all these years I searched and hoped for a brother in these waters I could talk to about anything for hours. And lo and behold, He gives me your crazy ass!! Seriously, your talent is so far to the right that greatness is ordained. Stay focused and you'll be fine. Damn, you're the metaphor master!!! I love you so much, you punk, you!!!!

Arsenio Hall: We never met. I've always been a fan, but your struggles and triumph on *Celebrity Apprentice* touched that special, sentimental place in me. I know what it's like to be counted out, and let God help us to rise off the canvas to get the Victory he has in store for all of us. Thank you for being an inspiration, and a warm embrace is in store when we meet. (In Christ, I can do all things, for He strengthens me.)

Michael Jackson—Not a day goes by when I don't think of you. You helped us immensely with your efforts to bring us together under God's sun. God uses all types of people to show His LOVE, and through ALL OF YOU, He let us know how beautiful He is.

Thank you so much for being the creative engine behind my force, and when the day comes where God calls me home, we'll sing the songs and do the video steps. Humbly, I hope I paid tribute to you with this book.

You know, I keep telling myself, "Make it shorter this time, Will..." but as you can see, I can't stop the overflow of love that pours from me. The "songs" for this book? See, what had happened was... Seriously, there comes a time where you must let fear go and reach the destiny God has in store for us all, as fear and faith can't dwell in the same place. And for years, fear has dictated my actions. Fear that I might not be good enough. Fear of what people thought if I let completely loose. Fear caused me to make mistakes in my life and allowed me to let others compartmentalize my gifts in boxes with insults, blatant disrespect and jealousy. The former things have passed away, because through my ups and downs my Father made me UNBREAKABLE.

(Damn, that groove is fire, especially that piano at the end...Oops, there I go again...)

God knows all our hearts, and will bless us accordingly with such. All He asks of us is that we bow down to the source while loving our neighbor as we do ourselves. Once we do this, then we become UNBREAKABLE!!!

Phew...I'm done. If you'd like, hang out with me on Facebook and listen to my Jam sessions: They're from my heart. I have a Twitter account, but as you can see 140 characters aren't enough. The website is coming, I promise.

One more thing before I bounce: whatever you do in life, dare to be great. Be a great person, because doing so gives honor and glory to The Most High. If you're a street sweeper or a dishwasher, be a great one; if you're homeless, be a great homeless person while finding your way. Don't let anyone stop you from God's blessings, and once you claim the victory that comes with being great, accept it with a smile, even more humility, and continue to press forward with LOVE, because it makes the world go round.

LOVE makes us UNBREAKABLE.

LOVE.

There's that word again.

As with everything in life, all you need is LOVE.

A little LOVE is all it takes.

Still.

A little LOVE for each other is all we need.

Still.

When we show LOVE, then we connect with the God that's in all of us.

For God is LOVE, and if we are created in His likeness, we are LOVE as well.

May God be with all of you on your journey through this amazing thing called life.

And may His most precious gift to us all, LOVE, live within you all.

Peace.

"COOP"
areason006@yahoo.com
Unbreakable006@yahoo.com

ABOUT THE AUTHOR

William Fredrick Cooper was born in Brooklyn, reared on Staten Island, and presently resides in Brooklyn, New York. The proud father of a lovely daughter named Maranda, Mr. Cooper is a member of St. Philips Baptist Church in Staten Island, New York, and was the Secretary of Brother 2 Brother Symposium, Inc., a program that encouraged black men and young adults to read fiction literature.

Not only is Mr. Cooper known for his enlightening radio interviews throughout the United States and Canada, he has served as host, executive producer, guest speaker and moderator/facilitator of numerous literary events, of which includes an annual appearance at the University of Maryland, College Park African-American Literary Conference; the 2004 Harlem Book Fair; the 2004 Disilgold Unity Literary Awards Show; the 2004 Bring Your Book to Life Seminar/Music concert in Philadelphia, Pennsylvania; and the 2006 Erotica Lounge and Lingerie show in conjunction with the African American Literary and Media Group Seminar, held in Reno, Nevada.

His first novel, *Six Days In January*, was published in February 2004 by Strebor Books, an imprint of Simon and Schuster. A groundbreaking piece of literature that explores the heart of an African-American man damaged by love, the novel received rave reviews in major periodicals in the United States, Canada, Bermuda and the United Kingdom.

In July 2006, Mr. Cooper appeared in a feature article in the July issue of *Ebony* magazine, "After the Breakup: Get Over it and Get On With Your Life."

His second novel, *There's Always A Reason*, was featured in the March 2007 issue of *Ebony* magazine and was chosen as a Main Selection for the Black Expressions Book Club in April 2007. Positioned on the Black Expressions Book Club best-seller list in August 2007, the *Essence* magazine best-seller in April 2008 and described by many in the African American community as a message-delivering emotional masterpiece, *There's Always A Reason* was nominated for an African American Literary Award in September 2007, appeared on the Master's List for a 2008 NAACP Image Award Nomination in the Outstanding Literary Work Fiction category, and the recipient of four 2008 Infini Literary Awards, including Book of the Year.

Mr. Cooper is a contributing author to several anthologies. "Legal Days, Lonely Nights" appeared in Zane's *Sistergirls.com*; "Watering Cherry's Garden" was written for *Twilight Moods— African American Erotica*; "Snowy Moonlit Evenings" was composed for *Journey to Timbooktu*, a collection of poetry and prose as compiled by Memphis Vaughn; and "More and More" and "Sweet Dreams" were included in *Morning, Noon and Night: Can't Get Enough*, a collection of erotic fiction. "Te Deseo" was a contribution to Zane's *New York Times* bestselling anthology *Caramel Flava*, published by Atria Books/Simon and Schuster in August 2006. "Dear Zane: A Lust Letter From A Fan" appeared as an extra piece in the Zane non-fiction book *Dear G-Spot: Straight Talk about Sex And Love*, released by Atria Books in July 2007.

"No One Has To Know," an erotic duet with Jessica Tilles, appeared in *Erogenous Zone: A Sexual Voyage* in August 2007. "No Regrets," a candid story about Mr. Cooper's literary journey, appears in the African American Literary Award-winning anthology, *The Soul of a Man: Triumph Of My Soul* published by Peace in the Storm Publishing in June 2009.

Mr. Cooper's third effort, *One Season (in Pinstripes)*, was a unique account of the 2009 World Championship season of the New York Yankees; and was published in March 2011 by Strebor Books.

Mr. Cooper can be reached at www.facebook.com/wfcooper, as well as via his email addresses: areason006@yahoo.com and unbreakable006@yahoo.com.